# A Darker Shade of Freedom

## C. James Gilbert

Mechanicsburg, Pennsylvania   USA

Published by Sunbury Press, Inc.
50 West Main Street, Suite A
Mechanicsburg, Pennsylvania 17055

**SUNBURY**
P R E S S

**www.sunburypress.com**

For information about special discounts for bulk purchases, please contact Sunbury Press Orders Dept. at (855) 338-8359 or orders@sunburypress.com.

To request one of our authors for speaking engagements or book signings, please contact Sunbury Press Publicity Dept. at publicity@sunburypress.com.

ISBN: 978-1-62006-385-9 (Trade Paperback)
ISBN: 978-1-62006-386-6 (Mobipocket)
ISBN: 978-1-62006-387-3 (ePub)

FIRST SUNBURY PRESS EDITION: May 2014

*Product of the United States of America*
0  1  1  2  3  5  8  13  21  34  55

Set in Bookman Old Style
Designed by Lawrence Knorr
Cover by Lawrence Knorr
Edited by Jennifer Melendrez

*Continue the Enlightenment!*

This book is dedicated to a pair of very special young ladies, my granddaughters ... Kaylynn & Kinslee

# Acknowledgments

I would like to thank Lawrence Knorr and Sunbury Press for publishing this, my second novel.

I would like to thank my editor, Jennifer Melendrez for another job well done.

I would also like to wish Sunbury Press "continued growth" and "success" in the future.

# ONE

## Terror Comes to Georgia

It was late evening; James was sitting in his office when a rock the size of a cannonball came through the front window of the parlor. A second later he heard his wife, Polly, frantically calling his name. Taking only enough time to reach into the lower desk drawer to locate his .45 caliber revolver, he ran to the parlor to investigate the intrusion. Polly was unhurt but lying on the floor where she'd sought protection from the sudden attack. Shards of glass crunched under his boots as he hunkered down by the broken window and peered outside. On the lawn, just thirty feet from the veranda, were six horses and riders; five of the men held torches. By the light of the flaming flambeaus, James could make out an eerie spectacle: the riders were all wearing something over their heads, possibly masks made of burlap, which completely hid their identities.

At that moment he heard footsteps on the staircase and then his two sisters, Ashton and Kate, appeared in the doorway of the parlor. James held up his left hand and said, "Stay away from the windows."

"We saw them from our bedroom," said Kate, the younger of the sisters. "Who could they be and what could they want, James?"

"I cannot say for sure, but I don't like the way they chose to get our attention." He started to rise but Polly grabbed his arm. "James, you're not going out there?"

"I have to, Polly. It is better than having them come in here. It will be all right." James managed to sound confident but that was for the sake of his wife and sisters. In truth, he had no idea what would happen when he confronted the intimidating display on his front lawn. Deciding not to appear afraid or vulnerable, he opened the front door, revolver in hand, and stepped out on the veranda, closing the door behind him.

1

None of the riders were brandishing weapons and none of them made any sudden moves. In fact, they sat for a few moments as still as fence posts, probably for effect. James was prepared to defend his family but still he prayed that the confrontation would not turn violent. Besides having Polly, Ashton, and Kate in the house, his three-year-old son, James Jr., affectionately known as Jim, was playing in his room upstairs. It was so quiet that he could hear the sound of the torches as the flames labored to consume the resinous cloth.

Then, the rider who held no torch spurred his horse forward a short distance and an ugly gesture ensued. Bringing his right hand up suddenly, he tossed a coil of rope onto the veranda. It landed only inches from James's feet. At the end of the rope was a noose.

"Lieutenant James Langdon," he said with a lisp, pointing a finger menacingly at James. "Lieutenant James Langdon of the Union army, you have been accused of war crimes against the Southern Confederacy. How do you plead?" James was completely taken aback. It was true that he had fought for the Union in the late War Between the States. It was also true that before joining the army, because of his deep hatred for slavery, he had been instrumental in helping slaves escape to Canada. But who were his accusers and how did *they* find out? Even his father, a loyal southerner, had kept his son's secret until he took his own life in April 1865. His father's brothers, his Uncle Stanley and Uncle Joseph knew, but they sold their plantations before the war ended and moved away. And the undertaker in Macon, Mr. Templeton, who had buried James' father, had called him heroic because his family believed that James worked for the Confederate Signal Service during the war and had proudly spread the word. Aside from Polly, the only two people in Georgia who knew his *real* past were his sisters.

"Who are you and how do you know me?"

With his impeded speech and a voice that sounded as if it came from the supernatural world, the man who was apparently the leader provided an answer.

"It is my sworn duty to tell you exactly who we are. In the Province of Sumter County, state of Georgia, we are of

2

the local chapter of the Ku Klux Klan. I am the Exalted Cyclops. Two of these men are Night Hawks, the other three are Ghouls. Riding with us are the spirits of Confederate dead, returned from the battlefield. We are here to see that justice is done and justice is maintained. We will *not* allow you and your nigger minions to defile sacred southern soil or to dishonor our fallen brethren by integrating your inferior genealogy with white purity. We know who you are and what you've done and nothing else matters to us. Now you will plead."

"The war is over," said James. "Hasn't there been enough bloodshed and destruction? If your honored dead could speak would they not agree with me?"

"Agree with a traitor; with a man who sold them out? You are among the lowest swine bred. Our dead *have* spoken and they cry out for vengeance. They demand satisfaction for their needy wives and orphans and they seek retribution on the black hoards like so many belly crawling snakes that are to blame for their pain. The South has risen again; this will be the final struggle to keep our southern way of life and this time ... we will prevail. You have been warned. Get out while you can; you do not belong here." Then he pointed to the noose still lying at James's feet. "Keep that as a reminder. Leave, or we will drive you out."

With that, the leader turned his horse and headed for the road with the others close behind.

James picked up the hanging rope and went into the house. In the parlor, Polly and Kate sat waiting and wide-eyed. Ashton was sitting back in her chair without expression. When Polly saw the rope she nearly fainted. James moved a footstool next to her and sat down.

"Our visitors claimed to be members of the Ku Klux Klan."

"Who are they?" said Kate.

"I have heard rumors of their organization. As near as I can understand, they are a group made up of ex-Confederate soldiers who are dedicated to white supremacy. There are other such groups with different names, but they follow the same doctrine. They are men who did not want the war to end; they do not accept the fact that the Confederacy surrendered and they intend to fight on in spite of the South's defeat. It is their intention to keep the black race from becoming an equal part of southern society and to punish anyone who opposes their cause."

"What were they doing here?" asked Polly

"They know that I fought for the Union. They said that I do not belong here and they said that if I do not leave, they will drive me out." The room was silent as a church. Everyone seemed to be lost in contemplative thought. Then Ashton spoke her mind. "Do you see now, James, what you have brought upon this family? You disgraced us during the war; now, the war is over. But can we go about our business and live in peace? Can we rebuild our lives and put the past behind us? No. Because what you have done will stay with you for the rest of your life and you have made all of us a part of it." Then she rose and went upstairs without another word.

James's relationship with Ashton was strained at best. Unlike his sister, Kate, Ashton had denounced him when she found out that he had joined the Union army. In addition, she had married an Englishman during the war in the hope that he would take her to England, away from the fighting. But he had come to the United States to make his fortune smuggling goods through the Union blockade. He was fired upon and killed by a Union warship and she blamed James for his death. Then, Ashton found herself living alone in a small farmhouse near Winchester, Virginia. James was with General Sherman when he entered Savannah where he found Kate, sent there by their father who thought it to be a safer place. Kate had warned him that reconciliation with Ashton may be impossible. But when the war ended and Kate had returned, they located Ashton, pleaded with her to come home, and she did. In retrospect, James now believed that she agreed simply because she was lonely and had nowhere else to go.

In 1865, after the war, white southerners created the Black Codes. These codes controlled almost all aspects of the lives of the Negroes and left them hardly any of the freedoms that had been won. But in 1866, Black Codes were suspended by Federal officials who deemed them to be too harsh. James believed that the Klan had decided to take matters into their own hands.

Now it was the beginning of May, 1867. The war was just over two years gone. The four of them had spent those two years working to rebuild the plantation and the house that had been ravaged, ironically, by the same army that James had served. The restoration was, in part, a tribute to his late father. But now what would he do? He knew that the visit from the Klan was no idle threat. The Klan's existence could be a prelude to the future. He expected the bitterness of a defeated South to develop into full blown scorn for their liberated property and that a kick or a gouge would be applied whenever possible. And he was sure that discrimination would be the new order. However, he did not anticipate reprisals in the shape of a domination-seeking army dressed in homemade masquerade.

"What are we going to do, James?" asked Kate.

"I need time to think it through. I do know that nothing is worth a member of my family getting hurt. I do know that much."

"Do you really think they mean to do us harm?"

"I think the wise thing would be to assume that they do. The man who did the talking out there did not strike me as someone whom I could reason with. He sounded more like a half-mad fanatic. Why don't you go to bed, Kate. I don't think they will return anymore tonight. We'll all have a long discussion tomorrow."

"Very well, James. I think I'll go up and talk to Ashton. Please try to be patient with her. She doesn't mean any harm."

"I know, Kate. Tell her goodnight for us."

Polly had not spoken a word since James had gone outside to confront the intruders. He knew her well enough to perceive just how shaken she was by what had happened. He sat next to her and pulled her close. He could feel her trembling. "I feel," said James, "that Ashton may be right. There is no one to blame but me for this precarious situation."

5

"You must not think that, James. To do so is to regret all that you've done and to wish that you could undo it. I know that you have no such wish, nor do I."

"You're right of course. But maybe I went too far. I mean maybe I was wrong to decide that we would stay in Georgia. I never intended to, you know. I meant for us to live in Pennsylvania where we made our home during the war. I believed that I had relinquished my right to live here. So tonight, when that Klan leader told me I had no right to be here . . . well, that really hit home."

"Please don't blame yourself. There is no credence in the words of a band of outlaws."

"I agree, Polly, but we must use good judgment at a time like this. I have no fear for myself, but I fear plenty for the safety of my son, my sisters, and for you. Would you consider taking Ashton, Kate, and Jim to Mapletown for a while ... just until I can figure out how to deal with the situation? It will be much easier after I've done everything I can to ensure the safety of my family."

"My dear James," said Polly. "During the war we were separated for many months at a time. You were in almost constant danger and I did my best to live with the loneliness and despair. I even gave birth to our son while you were away. I am sure you remember the promise that we made to each other. When the war ended, we would never allow ourselves to be apart again. I was very serious about that promise and I know that you were, too. We are both Georgians. We were Georgians before the war and we are Georgians now. We have every right to live here or anywhere else that we choose. If we let these people drive us out, then we validate their control and authority here. We encourage them in their attempt to assert themselves. Do not forget about the war itself. It was a struggle for the freedom of all men and the victory was won because right was on the side of the army that achieved that victory. Now, right is on our side and we will prevail because of it."

"Perhaps it is God's will that we stay," said James. "You know me so well, Polly, and you know that I would not want to leave—certainly not this way. It is just that my natural instinct to take care of my family reacts automatically."

"Yes, I know, James, and I will always allow you that because you are a good man and I love you for it. But if it is God's will that we stay then you know that He will be here to keep us safe."

"Of course He will. But if only He would give me piece of mind concerning one more thought that troubles me."

"You think it was Ashton don't you?"

"Ashton?"

"Yes. You think it was Ashton who spread the word about your service in the Union army."

"It hurts very much to say it, but I can think of no other answer. Surely what is done is done, but as our late, great President Lincoln once said, 'A house divided against itself cannot stand.' In these uncertain times, I need to be able to trust her and I don't know if I can."

"I'll admit that she has been very sullen and somewhat distant these past two years," said Polly. "But I do believe that she has good reason. She was not here when your mother passed away or when your father took his life."

"She made her own decisions concerning what she did," said James. "And none of which, I might add, would have been acceptable to Mother or Father. If you ask me, I think her decisions were very selfishly motivated. She *should* have been here for them." Polly gave James a look that told him to think about what he was saying.

"I can read your thoughts, Polly, and I feel ashamed. And I am not offended because I understand your meaning. I did what I felt was right at the time ... but the fact remains that I ran out, too."

"It was a terrible time for all of us, James. We were all afraid of something and there were times when we all wanted to run away. But that is why we are all here now; to restore this plantation, the home of your mother and father. And that is why we must stay, all of us. And we must be a family. Talk to Ashton, James. Talk to your sister and get to know her again. I believe that she needs you."

"I love you, Polly. You are a wonderful wife and wise. I shall talk to her and to Kate as well. I will tell them that we are here to stay. But we must prepare ourselves and guard

7

against being caught unaware. I believe that the Klan means business."

"I believe it, too."

James did what he could to cover the hole in the broken window, made sure that the rest of the doors and windows were secure, and then he and Polly went upstairs to bed. He laid his revolver on the stand where he could find it in a hurry if need be. It was a restless night and sleep was slow in coming. When he did drift off it didn't last, as one little sound or movement from Polly brought him wide awake.

At about 1:00 AM, James was dozing when the sound of horses out on the road activated his reflexes and he sat up shaking as from a bad dream. Polly was snoring slightly; he was grateful that he hadn't startled her. Carefully, he got out of bed, dressed himself, and collected his revolver. Quietly, he made his way downstairs and out the front door to the veranda. All was peaceful but he decided to sit for a while and let his nerves relax. The road was only about two hundred and fifty feet from the front of the house so if anything went by, even at night, James could easily detect it.

After about a half an hour he was beginning to wonder if he had really heard horses going by earlier. The visit from the Klan had put him on edge and he understood how the mind can play tricks. Yawning very widely, he got up and walked to the door and started to open it—then stopped. There was the sound again; it *was* hoof beats. They were coming fast and from more than one animal. Long before they reached his driveway, James could see light from the torches the riders were carrying. My God, he thought, it must be the Klan again. Were they coming back to his house? Suddenly, they came to a stop. They seemed to be milling around like they were searching for something. James could hear a lot of shouting. Then they turned around and headed back down the road at a walk. A single voice called out loud followed by a volley of pistol shots. James heard a scream—the scream of a woman. The riders moved off down the road, first at a trot, and then they picked up speed. Soon their torches were gone from sight. The pitiful wailing of the woman came to James on the night air. He wondered if she'd been shot. He hurried out to the barn, grabbed an oil lamp, and saddled a horse. In just minutes he was on the road and approaching the scene of the shooting. He could hear the woman's cries getting louder and when the light of the moon allowed him to see someone in the middle of the road, he dismounted and lit his oil lamp. He walked up to the woman who was sitting down, cradling the head of a man in her lap. They were Negroes. "It's OK, I'm not going to hurt you," James said as he approached. He hunkered down and set the lamp on the ground. The woman looked up at him and through her sobs she said, "Them Klan men kilt my husband."

"I heard the shooting from my house," he told her. "I was afraid it was the Klan. Why did they kill your husband?"

"We wasn't doin nuthin. We was jes walkin home from my brother's place. We hear the horses comin and we tried to hide in the bushes 'cause we figure they be white men and we didn't want no trouble. But they see us in the bushes and they say that niggers ain't allowed out after dark. My Ezra try to tell them we didn't know but they shoot him anyway and they tell me if I don't get home they gonna come back and shoot me, too."

"I never heard that Negroes cannot be out after dark," said James. "And even if I had I would dispute it. You are free people now."

"Maybe the law says we free but the law don't mean much round here. Anyway, I know why they shoot Ezra."

"Why is that?"

"One of them men was Massa Jeffers. He was our massa afore Mr. Lincoln make us free. Dats why they shoot poor Ezra."

"I understand," James told her. "This was a murder of vengeance. Jeffers made up his mind that his property wasn't just going to go free. I know of Harland Jeffers, but I've never met him. He is another one of these black-guards that the South calls an 'honorable gentleman.' But he's really nothing but a low down, black-hearted son of a—I'm sorry, ma'am. I'm sorry for you and Ezra and I'm sorry I lost my temper. I guess I'll never get used to the hatred one man can have for another because of the color of his skin."

"You be Mr. Langdon ain't you?"

"Yes," said James. "How did you know that?"

"Me and Ezra jes lives a couple miles from here. I know dats your place yonder. And I knows you fit against the federacy in da war. I hear you is a very good man."

James was amazed at how suddenly and rapidly word had spread about his past. He wondered if there was anyone who didn't know he'd fought for the Union.

"What is your name, ma'am?"

"I am Sally Remus."

"Let's get Ezra home, Sally."

Together they put Ezra's bullet-riddled corpse on the back of James's horse and then he helped Sally into the saddle. James led the horse down the road and Sally cried quietly the whole way home.

"Can I help you bury your husband?"

"No, sir, thank you. I'll leave Ezra laid out for his kin to see then we bury him in the yard."

"Somehow, some way, Jeffers will pay for what he did, Sally. I don't know what else to tell you for now but I promise you, he will pay. You know where I live. If you need anything at all, please come and see me."

"You is kinder than I can believe, Mr. Langdon. I never will forget what you done."

"I must go now. I will pray for your husband."

James mounted his horse and headed for home. He thought about what he'd just told Sally about praying for Ezra. What would happen on Sunday when he and his family went to worship? Would they now be shunned there as well? In spite of everything, he still had to give the human race more credit than that, didn't he?

# TWO

# The Trouble Begins

The following morning after breakfast, while everyone was still at the table, James broke the news to his sisters about the decision he and Polly had made the night before. For the time being he kept the shooting of Ezra Remus to himself.

"We intend to stay here and return Father's plantation into a productive business again. That was our intention to start with and we are not going to let a bunch of troublemakers wearing masks drive us out. However, I would be interested in hearing your thoughts on the idea."

"With certain reservations, I would have chosen to do the same," said Kate.

"How about you, Ashton?" James asked. Again, his sister seemed melancholy and slow to speak. When she did answer she simply said, "I will stay ... I have nothing to fear."

What did she mean by that, James wondered. There was that hint of suspicion that James had detected before. If trouble came, wouldn't she be in harm's way the same as the rest of them? Unless she *had* put the dogs on James's trail ... but if so, would she want him to figure it out? There was only one thing he could do. He must talk to her as Polly suggested and see if he could find out what was on her mind. For the moment, he would ignore the situation. He wanted to go over some precautions he thought the family should take and a plan of action should the need arise. James was taking nothing for granted but he suspected that Klan activities would probably occur at night. Broad daylight did not seem to be suitable to their way of doing things. That made them cowards in James's eyes, but even cowards can find courage under the cloak of darkness.

When James felt marginally comfortable leaving the ladies and his son on their own for a while, he hitched a two horse team to the buckboard and headed for Hank Kennedy's store. It was the beginning of the planting season and James needed supplies, including cotton seed.

Starting from scratch and with no labor force, it was not feasible for James to farm all twenty-five hundred acres of the plantation. He hoped someday to hire enough workers to make it possible. In the meantime, he would cultivate and plant what he could. It was also his intention to place a notice in the local newspaper, the *Macon Daily Telegraph*, to find people interested in land to sharecrop.

Kennedy's store was limited in available goods and supplies, but then so was every store in the South. The reconstruction effort was gradually moving food and other necessities into the area, but it would be years before things would be back to normal. In any case, Kennedy's was much closer than Macon and Kennedy tried to supply agricultural needs more than anything else. Of course he also sold whiskey at a small bar in the back of the store, which usually attracted a lot of loafers and shiftless types. Consequently, when James patronized the place he would often have a list from Polly because he did not want her to have to go to the store herself and be subjected to the language or looks from such men.

When James arrived, there were several horses tied up at the hitching rail and two black men were loading supplies into a dilapidated old wagon. Judging from the sounds coming from inside, it seemed that most of the patrons were there for the hard liquor. Hank Kennedy was usually glad to see James because he had something that very few people had in those days just after the war. He had money—and not just money, but gold and federal greenbacks. Because he and Polly had lived in the North during the war they kept their money in a northern bank. When they moved back to Georgia they brought good money with them. Almost everyone else had put their money into Confederate bonds and currency. The value of Confederate money had steadily declined during the war, and afterwards a bale of it wouldn't buy a square meal.

But, as James would soon find out, it was *not* a usual day and Hank Kennedy would not be glad to see him at all.

The minute he walked through the door, James realized he was drawing the attention of every man standing at the bar. But they were not casual glances as at a distracting sound or a minor interruption. They became a gathering of silent stares behind which was meaning and purpose, following James around the room as he chose items from the shelves. It was not easy to ignore the silence he had caused, and with each second that ticked by he became more positive that the tension would soon reach its breaking point.

James heard footsteps come through the front door and then stop about ten feet directly behind him. Kennedy, who had been outside overseeing the loading of the Negroes' wagon, broke the silence with a very unfriendly tone.

"Put them things back, Langdon. Clear out of here and don't come back."

James turned to face Kennedy and said, "I've been doing business here for over a year. Why should you have a problem dealing with me now?"

"I don't think your memory could be that bad, but just in case it is, I heard that you wore a blue uniform during the war. I don't do business with Yankees."

"The war is over, Mr. Kennedy. We need to let the wounds heal, not pick at them."

"Your war might be over, ours has just changed tactics. Now get the hell out of here while you can still do it by yourself."

"But I need supplies."

Time was short for James when he had first walked into the store but now it was gone. The crowd at the bar, eight or ten in all, started towards him and their expressions reflected the violence in their minds. All of them wore some part of a Confederate uniform: a jacket, trousers, or gray kepi. James stood between the front wall and a row of free-standing shelves that ran the whole way to the wall behind him, leaving no possible escape route. When the small army had him blocked in, a heavyset man in front glanced at the storekeeper and said, "You warned him, Kennedy, now we'll make sure he remembers not to come back." Then he put his bearded face nearly up against James's and said, "We're gonna beat you like a nigger, boy." Knowing just how bad the situation was, James decided to make it worth his while.

"It won't compare to the beating we Yankees gave you, fat man," he replied. James drove his right knee into the big man's crotch; the man let out a thunderous yell and dropped to the floor. Someone shouted, "Get him!" and the others rushed forward. James backed up a few quick steps, grabbed the end of a high stand of shelves, and tipped it over in front of them. Pots, pans, lanterns, and more hit the floor with a thundering crash. Two of the attackers tripped and went down. James tried to climb over the wreckage and run out the back but three more men ran around to the far side and cut him off. Swinging hard, he managed to discourage the first man that got close enough but then it was all over. Fist after fist hit his face, ribs, and head. Then two of them held his arms while the others took turns throwing punches.

Finally, the two who were holding James let him drop and he went to his knees. The last thing he remembered seeing through his puffy eyes before they closed was a belt buckle with CSA on it. Through the entire melee, the two Negroes who had come into the store to settle up stood quietly. They watched as James was hauled up from the floor, dragged outside, and thrown into the back of his wagon. He lay there, unconscious, bleeding from his nose, mouth, and eyes. Then one of his attackers walked up behind the team of horses and fired his pistol. Down the road they went raising a cloud of dust while James rolled helplessly from side to side.

The horses ran until they came to a spot in the road that was crossed by a shallow stream. The lure of a cold drink stopped them there and the water flowing under the wagon was the first thing James heard when he regained consciousness. He opened his eyes—that is to say, he tried to raise the lids but they were so swollen that it was very difficult to see through the narrow slits. He was racked with pain from his head to his knees and he feared that he might have a few broken ribs. The sound of the stream offered some comfort because the thought of soaking his face in the cold water was very inviting. With great difficulty, he rolled himself to the back of the wagon and sat up. Slowly he slid down to his feet and was grateful to find that he could stand. Then he dug a handkerchief from his back pocket, squatted over the water, and began cleaning up the dried blood.

James again realized that word of his past had indeed spread far and wide and that the odds were certainly against him staying no matter how reluctant he was to leave. It would be so difficult to admit defeat but he also knew now that physical violence *was* to be expected. For many reasons, life was very rough in the South with all of the destruction the war had wrought. It would take a lot of effort to get a crop of cotton in, which James desperately needed to do. For the moment, his money was holding, but it wouldn't last forever. If they were to make the plantation prosper, productivity was absolutely necessary. How was he to cope with everything and fight a private war at the same time?

Polly was very supportive in spite of the threatening visit from the Ku Klux Klan. She was adamant about staying in Georgia. What would she say when she saw his swollen face? Right was on their side but right was not always there to offer protection against overwhelming odds. He was going home from Kennedy's store empty handed and they still needed supplies for the pantry. It was planting time and he had no seed to put in the ground. And now he was all but stove up from the beating he'd taken. He had to get home.

When James drove up the driveway and passed the house, heading toward the barn, Polly came running out to meet him. He stopped abruptly, afraid there had been trouble while he was away. She was only concerned because James had been gone longer than expected but when she saw him, her concern became hysteria. Her eyes were full of tears as she reached up and tried to grab his hand.

"I knew something was wrong! What happened to you?" Wincing noticeably, James climbed down from the wagon with Polly's help.

"I'm sorry, Polly. Kennedy refused to serve me. There were some troublemakers there and they were full of whiskey. I guess the whole county is against me, maybe the whole state. I don't know how far I'd have to go to be unknown."

"Let me help you into the house. I want to send Kate for a doctor."

"No. I'll be all right."

"You may be seriously hurt."

"I don't think so. I was afraid at first that I might have broken ribs but I think I'm just badly bruised. I will go in and lie down for a while. Everyone here is OK?"

"Yes. Kate is in the parlor with Jim and Ashton is up in her room."

"I want to talk to Ashton. I have to know whose side she is on."

"I understand how you feel, James, but please don't get yourself all worked up. You've been through enough today."

"Don't worry. I just want to talk to her. When we get to the front door, please go in and tell Kate to take Jim out back for a while. I don't want him to see me like this."

When they reached the veranda, Polly did as James asked. Then he went into the parlor, sat down in a comfortable arm chair, and put his head back. Polly went to the kitchen and returned with a cool, wet cloth for his forehead. James was just about to ask her to go upstairs and tell Ashton to come down when his sister appeared in the doorway. When she saw James, the look on her face was of genuine surprise. She walked over to where he was sitting and Polly left the room to give them some privacy.

"What on earth happened to you, James?"

"Hank Kennedy refused to serve me, and when I objected, some of his patrons were kind enough to show me to the door. I got none of the food supplies we need and I got no cotton seed for this year's crop. I'd probably run into the same thing in Macon. I don't know what to do or where to go to get what we need; the Ku Klux Klan have me in their sights and all because word has spread about my having been in the Union army."

"How do you suppose they found out?" asked Ashton.

16

"That's something that has been on my mind since last night. There are very few people who know about that. But whoever it was, it had to be someone that has a personal problem with me."

Ashton had taken a seat and was sitting with her head down, staring at the floor.

"I could handle this if I only had myself to worry about. But I have my family to think of, and of course, there's Kate ..." Ashton's head shot up and she looked at James with an expression of protest.

"Do you think I am to blame?"

"I know that you are deeply upset by my past and because of what happened to your husband."

"My God! You do! You think that I brought all this trouble down on you and everyone else here."

"Ashton—"

"No! Let me finish. What kind of a monster do you think I am? I'll admit that I have been depressed about a lot that's happened. I *did* lose my husband and I *wasn't* here when Mother or Father passed away. Like everyone else, I lived through four terrible years of war and I saw unspeakable things that the Yankees did throughout the South. Yes, for a time, I felt very bitter towards you because you are my big brother and I always believed in you, looked up to you, and felt safe with you. I know you had your own reasons, but it was a blow, James ... an awful blow. You made it easy for me to feel the way I did; but now to be accused of causing such trouble as this. Look at yourself in the mirror. Look at your bruised and swollen face. Am I the kind of person that would be responsible for that? Would I bring that down on you or my sister or my nephew or his mother?"

At that point she broke into tears, got up, and ran for the front door. James called after her but she kept going. He didn't know what to think. Maybe he'd been wrong. It was difficult for him to determine if he felt worse physically or emotionally. Polly came into the room.

"Did I make a terrible mistake?" he asked her.

"I wish I could help you, James, but I can't. You know your sister better than I do and I believe that this is something in which I should not interfere. Somehow we

17

must gain peace in our home before we can hope to find peace with the rest of the world."

"I feel the same way. I never thought I would regret what I did during the war. I felt so sure of myself back then. Now I wonder if I did more harm than good. No matter how badly I want to live in harmony, it seems like an impossible dream. Now I must find a way to resolve my differences with Ashton."

"A day at a time, James. We must take it a day at a time. We must not give up hope. Try to rest. It is time I started fixing dinner."

Polly got up and went to the kitchen. James put his head back and tried to relax. A moment later, the front door opened and Ashton came in and went up the stairs without a word. He thought about trying to talk to her but decided it would be best to wait a while. He was just glad that she was back in the house.

Ashton did not come down for dinner. James asked Kate to take some food up to her. It was getting dark outside and his thoughts were of washing up and getting to bed early. Then he remembered that he had never unhitched the horses and put them in the barn. Ignoring his aches and pains, he made sure he took his revolver, picked up an oil lamp in the kitchen, and went outside. He climbed into the wagon and stirred up the team. It was pitch dark in the barn. James stopped the wagon just inside the door and was about to get down when he heard a noise back near the stalls. He pulled his revolver although he couldn't see a thing. Still, he pointed it into the darkness and struggled with one hand to strike a match and light the lamp.

Without question he was scared and not thinking too clearly because holding a burning lamp made him the perfect target if someone meant to do him harm. But he stood up and held the lamp aloft, illuminating the barn, enabling him to see a dozen men standing beside the horses.

# THREE

# Friends in Need

It was soon obvious to James that there was nothing to fear from the small group of men assembled inside the barn. First of all, there were no burlap masks in the crowd and second, all but three of the men were black. But such a surprise still gave him reason to be wary so he kept the revolver trained on the men as he got down from the wagon.

"What am I to expect from your presence here?" he asked. One of the Negroes, an older man with white hair and beard, stepped to the forefront.

"My name is Hiram Jones, sir. My sister, Sally Remus, told me how you helped her get poor Ezra home after them white men shot him. There are lots of stories going around about you, Mr. Langdon, stories that make black folks happy and most white folks sad. We are all here to try to help you if you want us."

Another black man, younger, and seemingly familiar to James stepped forward. He removed his worn out straw hat and dropped his gaze to the ground.

"My name is Earl Jackson. My partner, Bill, and I," he said pointing to a man standing behind him, "was at Kennedy's store today when them devils gave you a whipping. We feel real bad 'cause we didn't help you in that fight. But we hope you understand, sir, that things are mighty dangerous for a nigger in the South. They might be even worse than before we got this freedom we is supposed to have. When we was slaves, the white man might whip us, but now we ain't his property no more and a nigger's life ain't worth a cent if he be caught out alone, 'specially at night. And it don't matter if we work for wages or work as sharecroppers, we still don't have enough for our families to live on."

19

"That's why we is here," said Hiram Jones. "Maybe we can help each other."

James could see the good sense in their plan right away. The Negroes needed help. James had heard plenty about how they'd been treated since the war ended. The white southern power was determined to keep the black man as a cheap source of labor and deny him the rights he'd been promised by the constitution. James needed help, too. He was already hated for siding with the Negroes and treating them as equals. Why not join forces and stand together against their oppressors? Then James focused on the three white men in the group. Pointing a finger in their direction he said, "You three. What is your stake in this?"

"My name is Jeremy Todd," said a muscular young man with a deep scar across his forehead. He introduced his friends as Chet Rawlins and Aaron Parmalee. "We're here for the same reasons as these Negroes. We all fit in the war, Mr. Langdon. Course we was Rebs, but we don't mind you was a Yankee if you don't mind we was Rebs. All three of us was conscripts anyhow. We couldn't see no sense in the war. Everybody looked at us as poor white trash then and I reckon they look at us the same way now. What little we had before the war was gone when we got home, including my wife and Chet's. The only thing I got to show for my time in the army is this," he said, pointing to the scar on his head. "We got no use for them troublemaking sons a bitches in the spooky costumes. We just want to move on and make some kind of a life for ourselves. All we want is to sharecrop for an honest man."

James was very pleased with all of the men. He liked what he heard and he was impressed by the reassurance that there were still good people in the world; people who could make positive changes for the good of all if they had the power to do it. They were not what they saw themselves as—niggers or white trash—but were just honest men willing to work hard in exchange for a fair wage.

"First of all," said James, "I want to say that I appreciate all of you showing up here tonight even if you did give me a bit of a start. Like you men, I have plenty of reasons for being a bit jumpy. Although you are aware, I want to make it clear that by siding with me, things are not going to get easier for you. The Klan has sworn to drive me out; they have already gotten Hank Kennedy to refuse my business. But I have land, a lot of land—more than enough for all of us and then some—to plant a badly needed crop of cotton. I can set up every man here with as many acres as he thinks he can handle. We'll take our problems as they come and solve them one at a time."

"Well we can help with the first one, Mr. Langdon," said Jeremy. "Maybe Kennedy won't sell you any supplies but me, Chet, and Aaron can get them. Just give us a list of what you want and we'll go fetch it."

"That will be a good start but it will also come to an end if Kennedy finds out that you are involved with me, so you'll have to be careful. All right, it's time to break up this meeting. My wife must be wondering what's keeping me. If all of you can be here in the morning around seven, we'll get started. And one more thing, you can call me James."

They all exchanged pleasantries in parting, and after the men had gone, James unhitched the team and headed for the house. The unexpected visit eased his aches and pains a little. It felt good to know that he was not alone in the struggle against the Klan and all who sympathized with them. James had better ideas other than devising a defense that would amount to taking the law into his own hands. He was hoping that his ties with the Union army might benefit him to compensate for all the damage to his father's plantation. The army was still the authority, having divided the South into five military districts, each with a war veteran general in charge. Each district was supposed to send soldiers out to make sure the blacks were given fair treatment. Maybe having been an officer in the Union cavalry would persuade General Pope, the commander in James's district, to give them some help.

Still, he knew that Pope was under a terrible strain maintaining order in what could still be considered a hostile land considering the bitterness the war had left behind. And no matter how many soldiers patrolled the South, the angry factions would have little trouble going unpunished for many of their unjust and illegal activities. The federal government was trying, but the odds against them were long in the wake of a war and the death of the president who had led the nation through it.

Immediately following the end of the fighting, the southern states had initiated the Black Codes, laws to keep the ex-slaves from voting, serving on juries, getting jobs, owning land, and going to school. So the government started the Freedmen's Bureau to thwart the Black Codes. The bureau supplied food, clothing, medical care, and set up schools.

But it was the sentiments of the people that needed to change. Until black people were accepted as equals, friends, neighbors, and members of society, nothing else would stop the hatred and the violence. Unfortunately, it was easier to drive a herd of pigs than a herd of people and James was well aware of that fact.

Polly was very grateful when he told her about the men who had come to offer their allegiance in the belief that there is strength in numbers.

"At least it is a start," she said.

"Yes it is, and if we succeed, maybe others will join us. If we can utilize the entire plantation, in a few years it will produce as much cotton as it did before the war. Cotton is now more important to the economy than ever. I have read in the papers that the federal government and wealthy northerners are well aware that restoration of cotton production is essential to the financial recovery of the nation. Cotton exports are needed to help reduce the huge federal debt and to stabilize monetary affairs in order to fund economic development, particularly the railroads."

"It sounds wonderful, James. We could ensure a promising future for our children."

James hesitated. "You mean for our child."

"No, my dear husband, I mean our children."

James couldn't believe his ears. He didn't know whether to feel jubilant or scared to death. In the midst of all that was happening, he was going to be a father again? "How long have you known?"

"I've suspected it for a few weeks but I am certain now." Weighing his thoughts and sorting his emotions, James realized that it was indeed jubilation that he was feeling. The news reinforced his constitution and he felt as though no power on earth could stand in the way of accomplishing what he must. "How I love you, Polly, and how happy you have made me with such glad tidings. It is a sign from God that everything is going to be all right. Our family will grow and I pray that someday they will live in a new South; a land where equality is for all people."

"Speaking of family, what will you do about Ashton?"

"I will talk to her again, maybe tomorrow. I feel terrible about our feud but I honestly don't know if she is being truthful with me or not. I have got to reach her in some way. I must endeavor to receive her forgiveness and become her brother again."

"You will, James. I'm sure you will. For now, I think it is time for bed."

"It most certainly is. Tomorrow will be a busy day."

It was a quiet night, but James found it difficult to sleep. He had so much on his mind. It was a mixture of excitement and anxiety that kept him awake. The thought of another child inspired a great deal of happiness in him, but the problems concerning racial tension and the quarrels with his sister diluted the feeling. Still, he looked forward to the following morning because each new day held promise; and now, he had some men who were willing to work with him for mutual benefit.

James was up with the sun and before the morning coffee was ready. The group of men he had met the previous night was assembled at the barn with their wagons, draft animals, and anything else they had that would be of use. James counted heads and was pleased to see that the number had grown. There were now twenty-five in all; enough to work a sizable portion of the plantation. But, scrutinizing their faces, the crowd seemed more somber than high spirited.

"Good morning, gentlemen. It looks as though you are ready to get to work." Quiet replies came from a half dozen mouths; some just stood looking at the ground.

"Morning, James," said Jeremy Todd. "We've all been talking about how anxious we are to get set up and go to planting, but we're wondering if we'll survive long enough to see anything come of it. This morning, Hiram went by a friend's cabin, Isaac Washington—he lived over by Peach

23

Tree Hill. Hiram thought Isaac might be interested in sharecropping with us. When he got there he found Isaac hangin in a tree in the front yard. Even his dog and his old plow horse were dead; their throats were cut. It appears like the damn Klan can do anything they please and the only way we can live is to do whatever it takes to keep from riling them. We know it ain't right, but what can we do?"

James felt a burning anger start at his feet and rise to his head in about ten seconds.

"I can certainly see your point and I am sorry about your friend, Hiram. The plain fact is that this situation is completely out of hand. I am sure that Isaac did nothing to give the Klan reason to kill him. I do not believe that there is any conduct that will ensure your safety. I don't think anything will change until these murderers are brought to justice. Until they are shown that they will be held accountable for their actions, this sort of thing will continue."

"Why don't we go to killin some a dem fellas?" said a Negro whose name James didn't know.

"It would be easy to feel that an eye for an eye is the right thing, but it would only mean that we are no better than they are."

"You mean we can't even be defenden ourselves?

"I didn't say that. If you are attacked, of course you have that right. I was attacked at Kennedy's store and I fought back as best I could. I only mean that we can't go out hunting these men."

"Then what do we do?" asked Hiram Jones.

"I think there are two things that we can do," said James. "The first thing is to unite in a more practical way. How would you men feel about building a camp right here at my house? You can start by using tents for shelter, and later, after our crop is in the ground, we can take some time to build something more permanent. You can bring your families if you have any and we will be unified while we work and while we live. We will be one for all and all for one until law and order are established, no matter how long it takes."

A Darker Shade of Freedom

"It sounds like a good plan." said Jeremy Todd. "I can think of no better. At least no one will be alone if something happens."

"How about the rest of you?" James asked. It appeared as though the Negroes looked to Hiram Jones as leader and spokesperson, and after a few moments of quiet deliberation Hiram said, "We are all in agreement. We'll move our belongings and set up housekeeping here. Can I ask about the second thing you have in mind?"

"Of course. I have been thinking about a trip to Atlanta to see General John Pope. He is in charge of the military district that covers the state of Georgia. I never met the general during the war but I was hoping to explain to him what has been going on here and ask for help. Now I know that I should go without delay. It is certain that the odds are against us because the entire South is in an uproar. I am sure the army has its hands full, but I have to try. Unfortunately, we will have to postpone the beginning of planting season by one day, but that will give all of you time to move your things and Jeremy, Chet, and Aaron can go for supplies. If I can leave for Atlanta by noon, I can be back sometime tonight."

"We will get started moving, James," said Hiram. "It shouldn't take but a couple hours or so. That way we will all be here to watch over things until you can get to Atlanta and back."

"That sounds good," said James. "I will feel a lot better leaving home with all of you here. If you will come over to the house, Jeremy, I'll give you a list of supplies and the money to pay for everything."

After the men left to attend to their business, James sat Polly down and explained the plans that had been made.

"How can you be sure that the general will see you?" Polly asked. "Surely he must be very busy."

"I have no doubt of that, Polly, and I realize that I could be making a long trip for nothing, but I am hoping that my service to the Union will afford me some leverage. I feel that the situation is urgent and I must try to see him. There simply isn't time to send a telegram and wait for a reply."

"I want to go with you, James," she said.

"I don't know, Polly. It is a very long ride. Should you make such a trip in your condition?"

"I think I should take the opportunity to get out a bit while I can. The time will arrive quickly when I will *have* to stay close to home."

He hastily thought it over. "Perhaps you're right. I'll tell Kate and Ashton we'll be leaving."

Kate became alarmed when James told her they were going to Atlanta until he explained the plan to unite with his newfound friends for their mutual protection. Ashton managed a civil attitude and even told James not to worry about anything at home while he was gone. But her words and expression still lacked warmth and sincerity. It remained a mystery that James would have to solve when he returned.

Polly made preparations for the trip such as packing a few sandwiches to eat on the way while James hitched his best horse to the old carriage formerly owned by his father. By eleven o'clock, most of the men were back with their belongings and had begun to set up camp. By eleven-thirty they said goodbye to Ashton, Kate, and to Jim who cried when he realized that his parents were leaving.

With much anticipation, James and Polly began their five hour journey to Atlanta. In spite of all the clutter piled up in the attic of James's mind, he tried hard to focus his attention on the trip and the company of his lovely wife. It would have been much easier if not for all the evidence of the late war that would for some time blight the countryside. As they passed by so many damaged and deserted properties, James could certainly understand the bitterness that had returned in the form of an utterly defeated soldier. He had seen it firsthand in the condition of his childhood home, which was not spared—no matter that he had fought for the Union. But he also acknowledged the fact that it would not have had to come to this except for man's unwillingness to comprise. And he could not help remembering that it *was* the South who fired the first shot. James was so deep in thought that he inadvertently said out loud, "Sadly, it is too late now."

"I'm sorry?" said Polly.

"As am I," James replied. "I didn't mean to speak out loud."

"I'm glad you did. I've been wondering what has taken your attention from me," she teased.

"I didn't mean to drift away. I'm afraid I am becoming preoccupied with too many things that I cannot control. It's just that so much has changed and the changes did not occur over the natural course of time as they should have. They were accelerated by the war. Worst of all, the things that are different are not small and insignificant. I lost my mother and my father in less than two years' time. I cannot help believing they would still be alive if the war hadn't come. My Uncle Joseph and my Uncle Stanley and their families, to whom I was very close, are gone. I don't even know where they are. Thank God I still have my sisters, but I can see that Kate is not the same carefree spirit she once was and Ashton seems to be totally consumed by a combination of grief and hatred. Am I wrong to let all of this affect me so?"

"Of course not, James. Your feelings are perfectly normal. What matters now is how you choose to react to it all. If you accept it as God's will and overcome your anxiety in due course, emerging a stronger, more obedient servant, you will receive God's grace. If you become bitter and vengeful, you have allowed evil to defeat you and all that you hold dear both in your life and in your cherished memories will be lost."

James reined the horse to a stop, turned toward Polly, and cupped her face in his hands. "Am I not the biggest fool that you have ever seen? Will I never realize that for everything God has taken from me, he has given back a hundred fold?"

Polly smiled in a special way that James had come to recognize and understand, then she said, "You are no fool and will never let yourself be. I know that no matter what trials and tribulations life has in store, you *will* overcome."

FOUR

A Hope and a Prayer

When the outskirts of Atlanta came into view, Polly was having a difficult time containing her excitement. This would be her first time in Georgia's largest city since childhood. James's emotions were churning as well but for a completely different reason. It had been less than three years since he had ridden into Atlanta to join General Judson Kilpatrick's cavalry; less than three years since he had seen the sky over the great city filled with smoke.

"I wish you could have seen Atlanta before the war, Polly. It was beautiful. I am sure that the people who live here have made great strides in rebuilding what used to be the rail hub of the South, but there will still be a lot of evidence of the Union occupation."

"I am sure that is true," said Polly. "But tell me about the city, James. I know you remember when she was the star of the South. Tell me as much as you know of how she used to be."

"Well, let me see. Before the war, Atlanta was a very important rail and commercial center and yet it was a relatively small city. It actually ranked ninety-ninth in the United States in size, with a population of about ninety-five hundred."

"That *is* rather small," said Polly. "Please go on."

"It had several major railroads," James continued, "such as the Western & Atlantic, which connected Atlanta to Chattanooga, Tennessee, one hundred and thirty-eight miles to the north. A series of roads connected the city in all directions to neighboring towns and states."

"My mother brought me here once but I was only three at the time," said Polly. "I wish I could remember the way it was then. Tell me about the heart of the city, James. Was it busy?"

"Indeed it was. In the center of the city was State Square. The original Atlanta Union Depot stood right in the middle. The square was bound by Marietta Street on the northeast, Pryor Street on the northwest, Loyd Street on the southeast, and Alabama Street on the south. Around the square were many retail stores and warehouses. There were some fine hotels in Atlanta before the war, like the Atlanta Hotel, also known as Thompson's Hotel on the northwest side of State Square. It was run by Dr. Joseph Thompson. I stayed there several times with my family when I was young. Then there was the Trout House, located next to the Masonic Hall on Decatur Street. It was built in 1849 by John F. Trout. The Washington Hall Hotel was built in 1846 and operated by James Loyd. Sadly, all three were burned along with much of the city by General Sherman's men."

"Is it difficult for you James? Coming to Atlanta?"

"I suppose it is, somewhat. All of Georgia is special to me but I have some very fond memories of this city."

"I can understand how important Atlanta was to the Confederacy. I am sure she did all she could," said Polly.

"I have heard that, during the war, the Rolling Mill expanded their operation and provided a major source of armor plating for Confederate Navy ironclads, including the *C.S.S. Virginia*. There were also a few prominent newspapers that flourished here such as the *Atlanta Southern Confederacy* and the *Daily Intelligencer*, which actually moved to Macon during the Union occupation in 1864.

"It was a beautiful place, Polly. Throughout the whole city the streets were lined with oak and magnolia trees. It is difficult to believe that anyone would lay waste to such an appealing setting—even in war time. I'm glad that I had no hand in her destruction."

"You speak so eloquently about Atlanta, James. You help me to imagine how it must have been. I can picture the city with its streets filled with horses pulling fine carriages, the sidewalks busy with happy citizens, the hustle and bustle of the stores and shops, and all of it bathed in graceful civility."

"I expect it will be again someday," he said. "But this is today and we should find a place to leave our horse and carriage and hurry along with our business. We have a long ride back and I'll feel better when we get home."

"As will I, James. I'm glad I came, but you're right. We shouldn't tarry."

As they drove down Peachtree Street, they scanned the area, looking for a stable where they could leave their rig. Spying a respectable looking older gentleman coming out of a barber shop, James pulled the carriage to the curb and hailed the man as he walked toward them. "Good day, sir. Could you tell me where my wife and I might find a stable?" Before speaking, the man surveyed them very inquisitively, reached up, and rubbed the back of his neck. Then he said, "Going to the barber is a rather enjoyable time, especially if the conversation in the shop is lively, but I do hate those infernal hairs that fall down the back of my neck, you know what I mean young fella?"

"Yes, sir, I do," said James with a smile. "I usually don't feel comfortable until I take a bath and wash them away."

"My thought exactly, young man. Now then, you say you're looking for a stable?

"Yes, sir. I once knew Atlanta well but that was a long time ago. We have business in town and we need care for our horse and somewhere to leave the carriage."

"Makes sense, young man, makes sense. The best places are gone—the war you know. Damn Yankees burned nearly everything. There are a few new places of course; folks have need of a livery barn now and then."

"Yes, sir, they sure do."

"I know just the place. Over on the corner of Whitehall and Alabama Streets is the City Livery, right up the street from Redwine & Fox drugstore. They just put in the first soda fountain that Atlanta has ever had. I'll wager that it's the most popular place in town. You can stop by and get your wife some ice cream after you drop off your horse and carriage. Now how does that sound?"

"That sounds like just the place for us. Neither my wife or I have ever seen a soda fountain," said James in an attempt to humor him.

"You'll enjoy it, young fella. You too ma'am," he said, smiling at Polly. James was noting the time but enjoying the conversation with the old gentleman. He was very friendly and a bit comical, James thought.

"Could you also tell me, sir, where I might find General John Pope's office?"

The man raised his eyebrows and said, "General Pope's office?"

"Yes, sir," James replied.

"You have business with General Pope, young fella?"

"Yes, sir, I do."

In a tone much less congenial he said, "It's over near City Hall somewhere." Then he started down the street and James could hear him muttering to himself, "Wasting my time talking to a fella who has business with that blue coat General Pope."

James was very sorry that he had riled the old man. To Polly he said, "Another example of the bitterness the war left behind, I suppose."

"Don't take it to heart, James," she said as she squeezed his hand. "Let us go and visit the soda fountain."

After a quick but pleasant meal, the couple drove to State Square to find General Pope's office. They soon found out that it was located in the big brick building right next to City Hall. But, for all their trouble, they were very disappointed to find that the general wasn't in. A clerk in a corporal's uniform told them that General Pope would be back in about an hour.

"I'm sorry, Polly," said James. We haven't much choice but to wait, are you feeling up to it?"

"Yes, James, I don't mind waiting a while."

"Where do you think you would be the most comfortable? Would you rather sit inside or wait in the carriage?"

"I am quite comfortable in the carriage. I may take a nap though."

"That's fine," said James. Polly settled herself in the back seat of the carriage; James checked the time. It was 4:30 PM.

In spite of his anxiety, James also dozed off and awoke at 6:45. Upset with himself, he carefully climbed out of the carriage without disturbing Polly, who was still asleep. He hurried into the building and asked the clerk if the general had returned.

"Yes, sir, the general is in now. What is your name, sir?"

"James Langdon." The clerk took some papers from his desk, looked them over carefully and said, "I can't find your name anywhere, Mr. Langdon. Do you have an appointment to see the general?"

"No, Corporal, I don't."

"I am sorry, sir, but General Pope doesn't usually see anyone without prior arrangements."

"I was afraid that might be the case, Corporal, but this is a very urgent matter and there wasn't time to make any arrangements. My wife and I have traveled all the way from Macon and I would greatly appreciate it if you would try to get me in to see him." Luckily for James, the clerk was a considerate soul and agreed to see what he could do. But in just a minute he was back to tell James in a very apologetic tone that the general would not see him. The news was devastating. The entire effort to come to Atlanta in the hope that the army could provide some protection against attacks by the Klan may have been presumptuous. Still, to have come all that way and fail to see the one man who might be able to help was totally unacceptable.

"I understand your position, Corporal, and I don't want to put you at risk, but would you please try again? Tell the general that I was a lieutenant in the Union cavalry during the war, which has a lot to do with why I need to see him."

The corporal reluctantly got up from his chair and said, "I doubt that it will do any good, Mr. Langdon, but I will try once more." This time, James could hear shouting coming from General Pope's office. He could not make out what was being said, but he knew it wasn't pleasant.

Suddenly, the door of the office was jerked open and the large frame of the bombastic General John Pope filled the doorway. He glared at James, nearly causing him to get up and leave the building.

"Are you Mr. Langdon?"

"Yes, General, I've come the whole way from Macon to see—"

"You were in the Union cavalry?"

"Yes, sir, I was."

"Under whose command may I ask?"

"General George Stoneman in the beginning, then I was with General Buford at Gettysburg. After that I served under General Judson Kilpatrick during the march to the sea." General Pope stared at James as if he didn't believe a word of what he was hearing.

"Come into my office, Mr. Langdon, and have a seat." James wished that he had a moment to check on Polly and tell her that he had gained an audience with the general, but he was afraid if he hesitated he would lose his opportunity forever. Instead, he hurried into the office and sat in a chair facing the desk. General Pope closed the door, took his seat, and said, "Tell me, Mr. Langdon, why did you enlist in the Union army?"

"I enlisted after President Lincoln issued the Emancipation Proclamation. I wanted to see slavery outlawed, and when Mr. Lincoln expressed the same interest I joined to help accomplish that purpose."

"I see. Now tell me what you are doing here today."

"We are having a very bad time in my part of the state, sir. No doubt you are familiar with the Ku Klux Klan. They are terrorizing the area with no restraint whatsoever; there are frequent murders of black citizens. And there is something else, General. Somehow, the word has spread that I fought for the Union during the war. I had a visit from the Klan myself. I am not concerned for my person, but I am worried about my family. A number of my black and white neighbors are joining with me to sharecrop my land, but associating with me makes things harder on them. I came here today to ask you to send some of your soldiers in the hope that we can maintain some semblance of order. If the violence goes unchecked, it will only get worse."

General Pope gave the matter some quiet thought. Then he said, "First of all, Mr. Langdon, you must appreciate my situation here. I am in charge of the Third Military District. This district is comprised of Georgia, Florida, and Alabama. That is quite a bit of territory to patrol. You must also understand that yours is not the only such complaint.

Indeed I am familiar with the Klan; in fact, one of our old adversaries is responsible for starting that organization, Nathan Bedford Forrest. I have learned that he is the Grand Wizard, whatever the hell that is. Lastly, I would need a hundred times as many soldiers as I have to effectively govern an area this size. The number of soldiers that I have fluctuates constantly. Sometimes I might have as many as fifteen thousand. Sometimes I might have less than a thousand. Even my men are harassed by the Klan. There have been a number of confrontations over the last two years."

James was disappointed with what he was hearing, not to mention a bit surprised. It was obvious that he had no idea just how big the problem was; he also had no idea that the number of soldiers sent to uphold the law in the district was so small.

"Can you offer any suggestions, General?"

"I hesitate to say arm yourselves and fight back because we could end up with enough skirmishes to add up to another war. But you certainly have the right to defend yourself and your property and that is what I think you should be prepared to do."

"I thank you for your time and for making me aware of the magnitude of the situation, sir." James got up and held out his hand to the general. Pope took it in a firm grip and then he said, "I will do what I can, Mr. Langdon. You say that you live near Macon?"

"Yes sir; about twenty miles south."

"Don't expect too much, but I will try to get a cavalry unit to your area; at least for a little while. If we can curtail the violence, maybe we can discourage the Klan a bit. Good luck to you, Mr. Langdon, and have a safe journey home."

Due to a long standing reflex, James raised his right hand to salute the general and he smiled when he realized it wasn't necessary. But General Pope returned the salute and said, "I'll bet you were a good soldier."

"I tried, General, I really tried." James left the office, thanked the corporal for his help, and then hurried out to the carriage. Polly was awake but occupied with watching the goings on in the busy city.

"Am I correct in assuming that you saw the general, James?"

"I did, dear, and I found him to be a very agreeable man in spite of everything I've heard about him. But it is debatable concerning how much he'll be able to help. He said he would try to send some soldiers to patrol our area for a while."

"It sounds like our trip was a success," said Polly.

"We will certainly keep a good thought. For now though, we must get started for home. It will be way past dark until we get there."

An hour later, the city of Atlanta was far behind them. By the time darkness had set in, James could tell that Polly was getting tired. The trip had gone well to that point but he still worried that a carriage ride of the distance they had to cover was a little too much considering her condition. Just about a mile ahead of them was a fork in the road; to the right would take them to Macon, to the left would take them home. Just after making the left turn, James caught sight of a light as from a lantern or a torch by the side of the road. As they got closer he discovered that there were several men on horseback, a few of them holding torches. When they were close enough to see that the men were wearing masks, James panicked.

In an instant he grabbed the whip and brought it down sharply on the horse's back. She was a good young horse; able to pick up speed quickly. Still, a horse pulling a carriage was no match for good riding stock carrying a single man. Careening down the rutted road they went with the Klan no more than fifty yards behind them. James's heart was pounding and Polly was clinging to the seat, white knuckled and terrified. He tried desperately to think of a way to lose their pursuers before they were overtaken. Then he heard the sound of gunfire. With one hand he held the reins and with the other he pulled Polly close to him in a feeble attempt to shield her.

"They are right behind us, Polly!" James yelled. More gunfire mixed with loud shouts came from the masked riders. The carriage was taking a beating, which it could not stand for long. It was not in the perfect condition as when James's father had owned it. A bullet tore through the back of the carriage and whistled past James's head. The frenzy reached its peak; something had to give and it did. One of the trace chains broke from the harness and the carriage went out of line with the horse. The vehicle headed off the right side of the road, snapping the other chain. Polly screamed as they plummeted down a long embankment, bounced over top of a rotting log, and flipped end over end, coming to rest upside down at the bottom. Both of them were thrown from the carriage into the tall grass that grew on the embankment. Having had the wind knocked out of him, James lay face down in the grass, unable to cry out for Polly. He raised his head and looked up toward the road. By the light of the torches he could see the men sitting on their horses; James felt like wounded prey within striking distance of a predator. But instead of finishing the job, several of the riders fired their pistols into the air to punctuate the point of intimidation then they turned away and headed down the road. James could hear the sound of their galloping horses fading into the distance.

As soon as was humanly possible, James got to his feet and, ignoring the sharp pain up and down his right side, started frantically searching in the dark for Polly. He called her name but there was no reply. He was crying and struggling to maintain self-control. Finally he found her lying on her back not far from the overturned carriage; he was praying incessantly that it had not rolled over her. She was breathing but she was unconscious. James was afraid to move her but he could not leave her and go for help. They were miles from Macon and even farther from home. And there were no houses close by; at least none that were inhabited. With the tears nearly blinding him, James looked to the heavens and cried out, "Dear God, don't let her die."

# FIVE

# Defining James Langdon

James crawled to the wrecked carriage to look for anything useful in the storage box in front of the rear seat. As the carriage was upside down, the contents of the box spilled out when he opened the lid. Among the items he found was a canteen of water, an old oil lamp, and his revolver, all of which he was grateful for. The globe on the oil lamp was cracked but the lamp worked and that was all that mattered. Glad for the light but horrified by what it revealed, it hurt James very deeply to see Polly's face streaked with blood that trickled from a cut on her forehead. He removed his shirt, tore it into three pieces, wet one piece, and gently mopped the blood from his wife's face. Polly stirred a little and let out a quiet moan.

"Polly, can you hear me?" By the light of the lamp James could see acknowledgement in her expression. Then she opened her eyes and melted his heart when she tried to smile.

"I can hear you, James."

"Can you tell me where you hurt?"

"My head hurts and my right leg is throbbing, too. Are you hurt, James?"

"I'm fine, my dear. I want you to lie still and relax. I will find a way to get you to a doctor. Please, just lie still."

"I will, James."

James was overwhelmed by her responses and so thankful to God, but he knew he had no time to waste in getting help. Besides the other things he found in the carriage, there was a heavy blanket. He retrieved it quickly and covered Polly. As he was seeing to her comfort, he heard a sound like something or someone wading through the tall grass not far away. James grabbed his revolver, cocked it, and took a crouching position in front of Polly. Whatever was out there seemed to be moving very slowly and was not trying to hide its presence. Then James heard a sound that he recognized. It was the quiet nicker of a horse. He held the lamp aloft and the animal walked up to the wrecked carriage and stopped. What a welcome sight, thought James; quite possibly their salvation. James turned to Polly and said, "God be praised, dear, our horse has wandered back to our rescue. I can fashion a crude travois and I'll get you to a doctor."

James set to work and within about thirty minutes he had everything ready. First he led the horse up to the road and then he went back down the embankment, carefully lifted Polly, carried her to the top, and laid her on the travois. Then he turned the horse around; they headed back to the fork to take the road to Macon.

As they approached the fork, James was once again alarmed by hoof beats coming down the road. He decided to take the offensive this time, lighting the oil lamp, holding it high, and stepping into the middle of the road with his revolver cocked and ready. There were two riders moving at a trot. When James raised the lamp they slowed to a walk, coming to a stop close enough for him to make out their faces. It was a great relief when he recognized Aaron Parmalee and Chet Rawlins.

"I can't tell you how good it is to see you fellas," said James. "We've had an accident; Polly needs a doctor right away."

"We were afraid something happened, James," said Aaron. "It got late and Jeremy said we better come out and find you. How can we help?"

"I need you to go to Macon and get a doctor. I'll get Polly home as fast as I can. You can travel much faster than us so by the time we get home, you and the doctor shouldn't be that far behind. Go now and get him, please, go now."

"We'll hurry," said Aaron. With that, the two men spurred their horses and headed toward Macon at a dead run. James turned his horse around once more. He checked to see how Polly was doing. Her breathing seemed perfectly normal but she did not respond when he talked to her. He could not tell if she was asleep or unconscious. Panic began to well up in him; he took the horse by the halter and led her down the road as fast as he could.

Hour after hour they plodded along the desolate road, which stretched so far that at times it seemed that it was leading them in circles. James kept his revolver handy but all was quiet except for the clip clop of the horse's hooves and the sound of the travois poles dragging in the dirt. At regular intervals he stopped to check on Polly and tried to get her to take some water.

By 2:00 AM, James was exhausted both mentally and physically. His right leg was hurting badly and the pain in his side had increased but he could think of nothing except Polly's condition and what the extent of her injuries might be. To add to his mental burden, he blamed himself for what happened. From the moment she told James she wanted to go along he had an uneasy feeling about her decision. James was not one to exercise preponderance over other people, least of all his wife. But now he wished just once that he had been firm and dissuaded her from going.

It was just after 3:00 AM when, finally, he could see light from the house in the distance. They were almost there. As James led the weary horse up the driveway, several of the men who were now camping in the yard, including Hiram Jones and Jeremy Todd, came running over to see what had happened. "We were worried, James," said Jeremy. "I sent Aaron and Chet out to look for you and Polly. Did they find you?"

James did not utter a word. He lifted Polly from the travois and limped toward the house with her cradled in his arms as Hiram and Jeremy stared after him. Before he could climb the steps to the veranda, Kate was at the door, her pretty face etched with worry. "The doctor is on his way," James said to her. "Let me know the instant he arrives." Then he carried Polly up to the bedroom, barely noticing Ashton, who was standing at the bottom of the stairs.

He carefully laid his beloved wife down on the bed and then he knelt down beside her and held her hand. He bowed his head and began to pray in silence; tears dampening the sheet beneath him. As he begged the Almighty Father for divine intervention, his concentration was interrupted by Polly's sudden grip on his hand. James

39

raised his head and saw that her eyes were open and a brave smile was on her face.

"Polly, my dear, Polly," he said. "How are you feeling?"

"I'm not sure," she said in a feeble whisper. "I feel a bit sleepy and I have a pain in my head; I'm worried about the baby."

"As am I," he assured her. "Just rest and lie still. We've had a bad accident. Do you remember?"

"Yes. I remember going down the hill in the carriage and I seem to remember a terrible crash at the bottom, but after that I can't say what happened."

"It isn't important now, Polly. We're home and the doctor should be here any minute. You're going to be fine, just fine." James wished he could take comfort in his own words but he knew that Polly was in much more pain than she was admitting to.

There was a knock on the bedroom door. James got up, wincing from the pain in his side, and went over to answer it. Standing in the doorway were Kate and a young man in a black suit holding a small brown leather bag. "This is Dr. Ward Bartholomew, James. He has taken over Dr. Mead's practice." Kate turned away and James stepped back and motioned for the doctor to enter.

"I'm told that you and your wife were in a bad accident," said Dr. Bartholomew. "I can see that you are in a great deal of pain, Mr. Langdon."

"We can discuss that later, Doctor. Please look to my wife."

"Yes, of course. It might be better if you waited outside, Mr. Langdon." James didn't want to leave the room but he didn't argue. Maybe the doctor thought the examination would go better without an emotional husband standing by. Out in the hallway he leaned against the wall and tried to collect his thoughts. There seemed to be so much to ponder: the trouble surrounding him, the meeting with General Pope, the men outside, and all the work that needed to get done. But for James, nothing could take as much as a step forward until he knew that Polly was going to be all right. Someone laid a hand on his shoulder. He hadn't even noticed that Kate had come up beside him.

"Coffee?" she said, holding out a steaming cup. James took the cup and sipped the hot brew. The heat, the aroma, and the strong flavor seemed to have a calming effect.

"What happened out there?" Kate asked.

"We ran into the Klan again," he replied. "They chased us until the carriage broke loose from the harness. We plummeted over the side of a steep embankment; we were thrown from the carriage."

"My God! Whatever shall we do?"

"I don't know," said James with an uncharacteristic hint of warning in his eyes. "But I do know that if Polly is seriously hurt ..."

He did not finish his thought but it was not necessary for Kate. She could see the state her brother was in and it frightened her almost as much as everything that was happening.

"We were terribly worried, James."

"We?"

"Why, yes, Ashton and I."

"Yes," James replied. "Ashton."

Before Kate could say anything else, the bedroom door opened and Dr. Bartholomew came out into the hallway. The doctor looked at Kate and said, "Would you excuse us, miss?"

"Certainly," she said as she took the coffee cup from James and turned toward the stairs.

"I have thoroughly examined your wife, Mr. Langdon. My conclusions are that she has suffered a mild concussion and she has sustained minor cuts, contusions, and probably a hairline fracture of the left arm. She will have to remain in bed for at least six weeks and I have supplied her with something for the pain, but she will make a full recovery from these injuries."

"I am eternally grateful, Doctor. I will see to it that she gets all the rest and attention she needs and ..." James felt a wave of fear wash over him. It originated in the demoralized look on the doctor's face. Then suddenly he wondered why Polly would have to stay in bed for six weeks? There was something else; something else the doctor had to tell him.

"What's wrong, Doctor? There is something more isn't there?"

Dr. Bartholomew shifted his feet. "I'm afraid so, Mr. Langdon. Your wife ... has lost the child she was carrying and ... she will not be able to have any more children. I am sorry."

"But how could you know that, Doctor?"

"Your wife is also suffering from trauma to the pelvic region; quite possibly a fracture. I have to tell you that the chance of a future pregnancy is extremely remote."

James stood as still and inanimate as a fencepost, but in his mind there raged a fury the likes of which the war had never seen. All he could think about was his innocent wife and all of her goodness, her inability to hurt another living soul, and the murderers who killed their child and took away the happy anticipation of future children because of their loyalty to hell and its dreaded master. It seemed that all of his life he had been destined to abhor violence and the mistreatment of others, caring so much for God and His teachings that he turned against his own father rather than turning a blind eye to the sin of slavery. But now *he* wanted violence. Now *he* had been slighted in a manner so deeply felt that he longed for the destruction of those who would grind humanity under their evil jackboots while somehow managing to believe that it was right and just.

Through the paralyzing trance came the voice of Dr. Bartholomew, bringing James back to the moment. "Mr. Langdon, I would like to examine you now."

"Have you told my wife she can't have any more children?"

"No, sir, I haven't. I thought that you should choose the right time and tell her yourself."

"I thank you for your wisdom, Doctor. You may examine me now."

When the doctor was finished, he found that James had a cracked rib and many nasty bruises. He wrapped James's rib cage and told him to also take it very easy for a few days.

"If your wife's pain becomes too severe, send for me immediately," said the doctor.

"I certainly will. Thank you for coming."

Then Dr. Bartholomew left with the promise that he would be back in a day or two to check on Polly.

During the following few weeks, most everything around Langdon Plantation seemed to be progressing. The biggest example of improvement was that with his new work force, James was able to get more than a thousand acres of the plantation planted in cotton. The most wonderful improvement was that Polly was well on her way to recovery and seemed like herself again ... almost. James had waited three days after the accident to tell her that she would likely have no more children. For days she was under a deep depression; something that James had never seen her undergo before. God would see them through, she finally told James, and he agreed. But secretly he struggled with the reality of it along with the vengeful notion that had taken hold of him after the accident and had not let go. He did not speak of it to Polly because he knew that she would heal him with truth, and for once in his life, he did not want that.

James was also keenly aware of the turn that his relationship with Ashton had taken. He had never really gotten the chance to have that long talk with her and he now had himself convinced that he had no desire to speak to her. They soon grew accustomed to ignoring or avoiding each other and James took comfort in that. No matter how hard he tried to deny it, he *did* believe that Ashton had something to do with the Klan's personal hatred for him and he blamed her for what happened to Polly. James even went so far as to believe that she was comfortable with their shattered relationship because she held James responsible for the death of her husband and now that score was even. Above all, James felt a deep disappointment in himself because he knew that God had put him into a situation that would truly define his character and he was in danger of failing. Polly could see the bitterness in him, put there on the night of the accident, and she did everything she could to help him regain his true nature. But eventually she realized that it would take time for James to unload this particular burden.

He had grown very restless due to his unsettled issues and often he would get out of bed very early in the morning and quietly roam around outside almost as a sentry on duty. On one such early morning rise, he sat on the veranda and stared into the dark sky. It was peaceful and quiet; a combination that James was craving more and more. He found himself thinking about Mapletown and the little house that he and Polly shared during the war. He thought about Reverend Pyle and the other friends they had left behind. What would their lives be like if they had stayed? There was no way of knowing, but James was inclined to believe that they would be better off. What, he wondered, had happened to the South? What had so misguided the motivation of the southern people? Why had they clung to the practice of slavery for so long until finally they turned this beautiful region into a barren wasteland tormented by violence and controlled by men of low moral character? Were they not now piling a disaster on top of a catastrophe? Why were they acting as if stupidity were a virtue? James wondered if things would ever change. He wondered if there would ever be harmony between North and South, between black and white. But he had realized before the war had ended that if the slaves gained their freedom it would be a very long time before the word would hold any true meaning. For the moment, it was a darker shade of freedom.

At length, he broke away from his train of thought and got up to stretch his legs. The sharecropper's camp was sound asleep as James walked by; good rest for good men, he thought. When he reached the barn he stopped again, letting his nostrils fill with the sweet smell of the haystacks inside. Suddenly he heard a sound that he soon identified as that of a horse scratching the ground with its hoof. He quietly moved forward a few steps and could see the animal tied to the corral fence a few yards from the barn. Instinctively, he reached for his revolver and slowly walked around the barn, searching for the horse's owner. When nothing turned up, he crept to the side door, cautiously opened it enough to pass through, and stepped inside. He inched his way down through the barn until he heard sounds coming from an empty stall about twenty feet away. From where he stood he could see a faint light as from a lantern that was turned very low. Inside the stall, a very busy man was raking a pile of straw to the middle of the floor with a pitchfork. It did not take much reasoning for James to understand what the man intended to do. He was about to burn the barn to the ground. To leave no doubt, James waited until the scoundrel had finished his preparation and picked up the lantern before he said, "If you drop that lantern, you will be the next thing to fall." Startled by James's appearance, the man jumped back a step and his free hand dropped toward the holster on his hip. But when James pulled back the hammer of his revolver, the man froze. "All right, friend," he said. "I guess you're giving the orders."

"You're right about that, mister, and you'd better not misunderstand me. Put your empty hand on top of your head and come out of that stall." The man complied without hesitation. James walked up to the intruder, put his revolver right in the man's face, and reached down and disarmed him. Then he grabbed the lantern, turned up the flame to better illuminate the dark interior of the barn, and then hung the lantern on a nail. Although James did not expect a satisfactory answer he said, "Who are you, mister?"

"I reckon we don't need to get that friendly," he replied. "I know who you are and that's what matters to me."

"How do you know me?"

"Everybody knows who you are, nigger lover."

James could feel the heat rising up through his body. He needed no one to tell him that he was face to face with a member of the Ku Klux Klan. He also knew that the attempt to destroy his barn was another effort intended to drive him out. James had still not gotten over the accident that had forever taken Polly's ability to have children. Now he had caught a member of the diabolical Klan trying to do him more harm.

"You Klansmen claim to be the born again Confederacy but you are nothing more than a cowardly disgrace. Your

General Lee was an aristocratic gentleman; how do you think he'd feel about your cowardly tactics?"

"Leave General Lee out of it and go to hell, nigger lover."

"I don't like that word, mister," said James, as he pulled a little tighter on the trigger of his revolver.

"I don't give a damn what you don't like. We woulda killed you that night out on the Macon road if the Grand Cyclops would have let us."

"Macon road?"

"Yeah, you remember when you took that buggy ride down over the hill?" Then he grinned at James with such evil mockery in his expression and such taunting in his voice.

James extended his arm toward the miscreant as if to get the muzzle of his revolver as close to the man as he could.

"I should kill you now, you no good bushwhacker," said James. Then he elevated the muzzle to a point right between the man's eyes. But as he did so he prayed to God, asking to have his self-control restored before it was too late. Then he heard a voice from somewhere behind him; a soft and gentle voice. He stepped to the side so that he could look around and still keep an eye on the Klansman. There stood Polly, flanked by Hiram Jones, Jeremy Todd, and some of the others.

"James?" said Polly. "I awoke and you were gone. I had a feeling that I should come and find you." She walked up to him and took his left hand in hers. "We'll be all right, James. You know that we will always be all right." James felt ashamed for wanting so badly to justify killing one of the men responsible for the devastating accident. He had wanted closure so much that he nearly destroyed something more precious than what he had lost.

"Forgive me, Polly. And I thank you for being the answer to my prayer." Then he motioned for Jeremy Todd to come closer, handed Jeremy the Klansman's gun, and said, "Tie this man securely and lock him in the stall. No one will feed him or give him water. Tomorrow morning we will take him to the sheriff's office in Macon." Then he put his arm around Polly, nodded his thanks to the other men, and walked his wife back to the house.

As they were preparing for bed that evening, James said to Polly, "As much as I believed that I wanted to, I could not harm that man in the barn this morning; even when he admitted that he was one of the men who chased us on the Macon road the night of the accident."

"It was a defining moment for you, James, and you simply proved once again who you really are. God did not send me out there this morning to save you from yourself. We both knew that you would do the right thing." James fell asleep that night feeling strangely at peace with himself. He was finally able to put the accident behind him and he was ready to face a new day.

# SIX

# Local Law

After breakfast the following morning, James, accompanied by Jeremy Todd and Aaron Parmalee, took the captured Klansman to the sheriff's office in Macon. James did not know Sheriff Harper Ketchum, except for what little information Jeremy and Aaron were able to provide. Ketchum was from Tennessee and it was believed that he had ridden with Nathan Bedford Forrest during the war. No one seemed to know why he showed up in Macon, but in the midst of the turmoil following the late conflict, Ketchum managed to secure his position when the aging Sheriff Tanner retired.

The sheriff was at his desk when James, Jeremy, and Aaron, marched their prisoner into his office. Ketchum surveyed the party for a quiet moment with no telltale expression on his face, and then he smiled at James and assumed a businesslike manner. "Can I help you gentlemen?" he said.

"My name is James Langdon, Sheriff. I own Langdon Plantation, about twenty miles south of here." James paid particular attention when he stated his name to see if there was any noticeable reaction from Ketchum but there was none.

He held his expression steady, even when he said, "Yes, Mr. Langdon, I've heard of you. What is the trouble here?"

"I caught this man on my property yesterday morning. He was about to set fire to my barn. I can prove my charge against him."

Ketchum raised an eyebrow at the prisoner and said to James, "Why do you think he wanted to burn your barn, Mr. Langdon?"

James knew perfectly well why, but he had certain reservations about going too deep into the story of the trouble that began with the first visit from the Ku Klux

48

Klan. He knew better than to place too much trust in people he didn't know, and besides that, he knew he couldn't *really* prove anything except what he'd seen in the barn with his own eyes. And even if he could confirm that the intruder was one of several men who were responsible for the accident on the Macon road, would the law side with him?

"I don't really know, Sheriff. I can only tell you that he was about to drop a lantern into a pile of straw when I stopped him."

"What's your name, mister?" Ketchum said to the prisoner.

"Boggs. Milliard Boggs."

"How do you reply to the charge, Mr. Boggs?"

"I figure it's his word against mine."

"Mr. Langdon says he can prove it."

"Let him, if he's got time to waste," said Boggs.

The sheriff opened his desk drawer, extracted a piece of paper, and slid it across the desk to James. "Here is a complaint form, Mr. Langdon. Sign it, I will fill in the details, and you will be notified when Mr. Boggs is to be tried for trespassing and attempted arson." Then the sheriff got up, showed Boggs to an open cell, and locked him inside. James signed the form and handed it to Ketchum. "I appreciate your help, Sheriff."

"It is my pleasure, Mr. Langdon. If you have any more trouble, well you just let me know."

When they were back out on the boardwalk, James turned to his two companions and said, "What do you fellas think?"

"I think it all went a little too easy," said Jeremy

"I agree," said Aaron. "That there Boggs character seemed awful calm to me. It was like he knew he didn't have anything to worry about."

"I cannot disagree; I didn't have a good feeling myself," said James. "Still, can a man in the sheriff's position keep his job if he doesn't carry out the duties of his office? I would like to believe that the law is still respected and the men who enforce it, respectable. We'll have to wait and see. Before we leave town, how would you fellas like to go across the street to Folmer's Tavern for a beer? I'll buy."

They crossed the street, entered the tavern and took seats at a table near the door. James couldn't help feeling that there were eyes all over him. It was very difficult to live in an area where you are not welcome, he thought, especially when it happens to be your home. He knew that time would weaken memories and ease the tension but it could very well take a great deal of time. When they'd finished the beer the men got up right away and headed for the door. Jeremy was the first to step through the doorway but then he stopped so suddenly that James, who was second in line, bumped right into him. "Look, James, look across the street. Look who just came out of the sheriff's office." James followed Jeremy's direction and to his complete disappointment, he watched as Milliard Boggs stepped off of the boardwalk, casually mounted his horse, and rode out of town.

"It really hurts to see that man just ride away from this," said James. "Not to mention how upsetting it is to see the kind of law we have around here."

"Maybe he made bail," said Aaron, attempting to lighten the load of the moment.

"In twenty minutes?" said James. "Let's go home."

With the spring planting complete, James and his men turned their attention to other things. When their alliance was first established, part of the plan was to build a permanent structure to house the sharecroppers and their families. Of the twenty-five men in the group, fifteen of them had wives, and of the fifteen couples, twelve had children totaling twenty-nine little ones in all. It was decided that a two-story building with five thousand square feet of living space per floor would be constructed. Interior walls would be built to allow each family and area of five hundred square feet and the single men would be allowed two hundred and fifty square feet each.

The women were kept equally busy. Some of the younger ones worked with the men to build the new quarters and the older women made sure everyone had plenty to eat by doing the cooking and baking. The older children, some of whom were all of twelve or thirteen, minded the younger ones. Polly and Kate set up some roughly constructed tables and benches in the back yard and took on the responsibility of educating all of the children who were old enough to learn. At four and a half years old, Jim also attended school. Ashton, still locked in her cocoon of isolation, volunteered to keep the house in order.

James noted that they had established a content little community of people wishing only to be left to their own devices and their own pursuits of happiness. They were united, committed, and they possessed genuine concern for one another, but the constant threat hanging over them worked a hardship on their collective spirit. The Klan remained very active in the area and stories of their terrorism and wicked deeds were frequent news. In the event that supplies were needed, James always sent at least a half dozen men to fetch them and they always went armed; strictly for protection. It was also necessary to send Jeremy, Aaron, or Chester along because the Negroes were not allowed in town unless accompanied by a white man.

To complete their need to be self-sufficient, James suggested that the temporary school be used as a place of worship on Sunday. Before the war, Aaron Parmalee had studied for the ministry. The war interrupted his plans and he never finished what he'd started. But his knowledge of the bible was extensive and James deemed him more than capable of teaching the word of God. Even Aaron's appearance seemed to mirror the images James had seen of the apostles: his hair hung below his shoulders and his beard reached to his belt.

Still, the denizens of Langdon Plantation knew that things could not remain as they were forever. They all knew it was not right to let any man or group of men restrict their freedom. But, having survived the war to see the aftermath, they figuratively wept for the future when they thought of a showdown with the Klan.

After two weeks of hard work, the new building was beginning to take shape. The framework was complete except for the roof, and some of the exterior boards had been nailed fast. Usually James and his family took their meals in the house while the sharecroppers dined in the camp. But since the beginning of the construction project, the work continued until the evening meal was ready and James always had an open invitation to eat with his neighbors.

It was a Friday in the latter part of July; a day that saw very good progress on the job and very high spirits among the people. Even James allowed himself to be more at ease than he had been since before the Klan had showed up on his property.

At about six PM the big bell in the smokehouse cupola began to ring and the grateful laborers laid down their tools and headed for the well pump to wash up. On the way to the house, James met Polly and Kate coming out the door, each carrying two large pitchers of lemonade. "We're all dining together this evening," Polly told her husband. "Come join us after you've had a turn at the wash basin."

"I will be right out," he replied.

Everyone waited, mouths watering, until James came out and sat down beside Polly. Aaron Parmalee led the gathering as they recited grace, then the hungry people passed the bowls and platters. The women had really outdone themselves, to the delight of everyone, as they filled their plates with roasted beef, potatoes, peas, sweet corn, and fresh baked cornbread with molasses. When the ample repast had been devoured, the cleaning chore was unusually ignored as lively conversation sprang up all along the tables. So pleasant was the gaiety that it nearly lasted until the sun had gone down.

At length, the attention of all was turned to clearing the tables. James got up and walked toward the barn. One of the men had mentioned shortages of some of the building materials and he wanted to take inventory before retiring for the evening. Just as he was reaching for the door handle, he turned his attention toward the road and noticed a shimmering glow against the darkening sky. James walked over to the rail fence; climbed up, rested his knees on the top rail, and stared out across the meadow. After close observation, he estimated that the illumination stretched out over a distance of a hundred yards and that it was slowly moving down the road; it was coming closer. James felt his muscles tense and his heart beat faster.

"Torch light!" he said out loud. Under the circumstances, there was no such thing as jumping to conclusions. He leaped from the fence and ran toward the house as fast as he could go, screaming a warning as he drew near.

"Klan! Klan!" he shouted. "Polly! Where are you, Polly?" From somewhere in the crowd he heard a reply. "Here I am, James."

"Polly, the Klan is headed this way!"

"Are you certain, James?"

"I am. Gather all the women and children to the house and get them into the cellar. Where is Jim?"

"He is in the house with Ashton."

"Thank God. All right, gather the women and hurry. We only have a few minutes. Find Kate. Have her help you." Polly ran off, shouting for Kate.

By that time the men were crowding around James in a state of panic. A few had grabbed lanterns. James reached for the closest light and jumped up on one of the tables.

"Listen to me, men! Get your weapons and extra ammunition if you have it. There is a small army coming down the road. I believe they mean to attack. Where is Jeremy Todd?"

"Here I am," said Jeremy as he pushed through the crowd.

"Take fifteen men and spread them out from the camp to the barn. Make sure they find some good cover. Any man Jeremy doesn't take will come with me and we'll take up positions around the house. Get to your places now and put those lanterns out as soon as you're ready. No one fires until I do."

Jeremy counted out fifteen men and the rest retrieved their firearms and met James at the house. When the men were deployed, James went into the house to make sure the women and children were secure in the cellar. He told Polly to lead the other women in prayer and to stay in the cellar no matter what happened. Then he went out through the front door and crouched behind one of the columns that supported the roof over the veranda. From his position he could see as far as the road and it was indeed a sobering sight when the lead riders carrying torches stopped at the edge of his front lawn. Immediately, the

53

Klansmen began to dismount and form lines three deep along the road. As James and his men quietly watched from cover, the first rank, about thirty or forty former Rebels, began walking slowly toward the concealed defenders. When they were only about twenty-five yards from the line held by James and his men, they stopped suddenly, and pushed the ends of their torches, which they had shaved to a point, into the ground, creating a row of light. Then they turned and hurried back to the road and reformed in front of the second rank.

James realized that the Klan was lighting the battlefield. He also realized that he and his men could have rubbed out quite a few of the masked racists; such perfect targets they made of themselves. But James had told his men not to shoot until he did and it was not in him to fire unless fired upon.

When the moment of truth arrived, all three ranks, about two hundred men in all, started forward. During the war, the weapons had been much further advanced than the tactics. The commanders believed that in order to take a fortified position, you massed your men and attacked, but battle after battle, the attackers were cut to pieces. The generals couldn't see what a mistake this was when the war began and they still hadn't figured it out by the time the war ended. They never understood that it was the main reason for the high casualty rate. James and his men were outnumbered four to one but if the Klansmen were going to march into the teeth of the monster, the odds would be considerably more even.

Slowly and formidably they marched across the lawn; a man in the center of the first rank carried a Confederate battle flag. They stopped at the edge of the light provided by the torches and the first two ranks knelt down. The third rank raised their rifles and fired a volley straight ahead into the darkness. Then they knelt down to reload and the second rank stood and fired. When the second rank knelt and the first rank stood up, James aimed low and hit the flag bearer in the leg. The shot was a signal for his men to follow suit and after three more Klansmen fell, the others scattered and took cover wherever they could find it.

In spite of himself, James had to admire the courage displayed by the Klan. They had deliberately sacrificed a few of their own men to force their enemies to reveal their positions. Once the Klansmen located the muzzle flashes of James and his men, they knew where to direct their fire and the battle was on.

For almost an hour the shooting continued. Bullets were flying all around James, thudding into the big column, the front wall of the house and smashing through the window behind him. Men were screaming on both sides; James feared for the lives of his men, and he could not keep from thinking that he was to blame. The Klan promised to drive him out; he had explained that to everyone in the beginning, but still he felt responsible. Then he thought about Ashton. His feud with her had never been resolved; it had simply become a permanent stalemate. But now the question entered his head and burned through his mind like a branding iron. Was it his own sister who had spread the word about his service to the Union during the war?

The thought was suddenly pushed away. In the midst of death whistling through the air, the Klansmen were forming up again. If they charged in earnest they would likely overrun James and his men. Then he heard something in the distance that was still as familiar as if he'd heard it the day before. It was the sound of a bugle and it was blowing the command to charge. Was it Klan reinforcements? No, James thought; it couldn't be because the Klansmen heard it, too, and they were pulling back to the road. Some of them were running for their horses and others were helping their wounded or trying to carry off the dead.

The shooting ceased and James could see some of his men moving slowly into the light. Down on the road it was pandemonium. Horses were rearing, men were cursing, and the sound of the bugle drew nearer. Pistol shots rang out as the Klan beat a hasty retreat up the road. Then James heard someone shouting but he couldn't make out the words; three mounted soldiers came up the driveway and a large number of others passed by, chasing after the Klansmen.

James descended the steps from the veranda and walked toward the soldiers in blue who were dismounting their horses. He was intercepted by Jeremy Todd.

"We were pretty lucky, James," said Jeremy. "We only have three wounded but one looks pretty bad—a chest wound."

"Get the wounded to the house, Jeremy. Tell Polly to bring the women and children up from the cellar then tell her to see what she can do for the injured; we'll send for a doctor."

Before Jeremy could walk away, one of the soldiers approached and said, "I heard you say you have wounded."

"Yes, sir," said James. "We have three wounded. One is pretty serious."

"I am a doctor, Captain Kenneth Spencer, at your service."

"We'd be most grateful, Captain. This is Jeremy Todd. He can lead the way."

"Jeremy," said the captain.

"Captain Spencer. This way, please."

James turned his attention to the other two soldiers who were standing next to two dead Klansmen. The soldiers turned toward James as he approached and to his very great surprise, a familiar voice said, "Hello, James."

"Alvin?" James replied. James had served with Lieutenant Alvin Mitchell under General Sherman during the war. James had saved Alvin's life when their cavalry troop attacked Joe Wheeler's command at Macon and Alvin had returned the favor at Ebenezer Creek. But now Alvin wore the gold oak leaves of a major.

"Major Mitchell," said James. "It has a nice ring to it. How on earth did you wind up here?"

"I was assigned to General Pope's headquarters a few months ago. I heard about your visit and your request for help. I'll tell you, James, it is nearly impossible to keep order in a territory covering three states. The killing of Negroes is rampant; fighting the Ku Klux Klan is like fighting another war. I sometimes wonder if the Negroes were not better off when they were slaves. I understand that the Klan has a personal vendetta against you."

"They do, indeed. They know about my service to the Union."

"How did they find out?"

"I only wish I knew," said James, without mentioning Ashton.

"What will you do, James?"

"I will stay and hope that tenacity can win the day."

"I wish you all the luck ..."

Mitch's troopers returned without taking any prisoners. His second in command, Captain Smith, reported that the Klan had scattered into the fields and wooded areas and he felt it best not to follow.

"That's fine, Captain. No sense getting some of our boys killed for nothing." To James, Mitch said, "I wish I could do more for you, James. It was just a stroke of luck that we showed up here tonight. The general sent us to Macon to pick up a string of horses that had been stolen by two men from Macon from a Federal Supply Depot. I requested permission to detour to your plantation for a look-see. The general acquiesced right away—he said he agreed to do what he could for you."

"Yes, he did, and he certainly turned the tide for us by sending you and your men."

"Well we'll have to be heading back to Atlanta. But maybe we threw a scare into them; let them know that we are around and might show up when they least expect it."

"I can't tell you how much I appreciate what you did, Mitch. Your timing was perfect. I don't know how much longer we could have held them off. And seeing you again has been a wonderful surprise." The two old friends exchanged a cordial handshake. They turned their attention to the two dead Klansmen.

"We'll take care of these bodies for you, James," Mitch said. "We'll drop them off in Macon. These Rebels can bury their own dead."

James bent over one of the bodies and pulled off the mask. He did not recognize the man. Then he removed the second man's disguise and the familiarity of the face spoke volumes about the severity of the predicament in which James was mired. It was Sheriff Harper Ketchum. James looked up at Mitch; his old friend noticed the bewildered expression.

"Do you know this one, James?"

"Local law," James replied.

# SEVEN

# The Assessment

When the sun rose the following morning, its brilliance was so uninhibited, which only served to prove that it was not influenced by any circumstance on earth. But beneath the golden rays, James, along with the rest of the occupants of Langdon Plantation were assessing their situation based on events that had occurred the night before. The Klan's threat to drive him out had been brandished once again, this time, with a lethal result. Two of the men wounded in the battle would recover but the man who was hit in the chest had died during the night. And the only thing that made his passing any easier was the fact that he had no wife or children. Routinely, when breakfast was finished, work would have resumed on the sharecroppers' quarters. Instead, when the morning meal had been eaten, everyone gathered for the funeral of the first martyr to their cause. Aaron presided over the ceremony and, Jess, as he was known, was buried in the Langdon family cemetery.

At the conclusion, several of the men helped to fill in the new grave and then without prompting or direction, the entire crowd gathered around the tables at the sharecroppers' camp, all except Ashton. James took the opportunity to speak to the gathering.

"It is a sad day, my friends; we have lost one of our own. I never got to know Jess very well in a personal way, but I was certainly aware of his hard work and his willing spirit. He was pulling equally with the rest of us to make a better life. We find it difficult to understand why he deserved such a fate but we bow to Almighty God and give Him the right of way. But, as we move on from this we must continue our struggle against the forces of evil; for ourselves, and for Jess, so that his death was not in vain. But the door is open to any man, at any time, who feels that his future lies elsewhere."

James picked up his son and gave Polly a nod toward the house. But Hiram Jones stood up and said, "Wait, Mr. Langdon, uh, James. We all want you to know that there is not one among us who would ever think of leaving this place. We all agree that what happened last night is hard to just let go like it was nothing, but we also feel that it has made us stronger because we did not go through it alone. You pulled us all together here and treated us in a way like nobody ever done before. You given us a sense of respect for ourselves and for each other, and that is the best thing that any man, woman, or child can get from this life. Listening to your words this morning, we see more than ever that your heart is made of truth and your promises are made of iron. And our future lies here and nowhere else."

"I thank you, my friends. Let us begin the Sabbath early; rest today, and tomorrow we will take our petitions before the Lord."

James, Polly, Jim, and Kate headed for the house. By the time they reached the veranda, Jeremy Todd had caught up with them. "Can I talk to you, James?"

"Certainly." He handed Jim over to Polly and invited Jeremy to take a seat.

"I guess I sort of wanted to tell you my own personal thank you, James."

"You're a good man, Jeremy. But I feel that we are all in each other's debt. No one here stands in a higher place than anyone else."

"Well, that's what I'm a thankin you for. You've done more for me than to just treat me fairly. You've taught me a lot about right and wrong. I told you that I fought for the Confederacy, maybe not by choice, but I fought for it. But I never did think about the Negroes and how they figured in to the whole mess. I didn't hate them, didn't really think of myself as better than they were; I guess I just looked right through them. Maybe it's because I was called white trash and the only difference betwixt me and the slaves was that I was free. But workin here with you; workin side by side with the Negroes gave me the chance to really get to know them as people. It gave me the chance to see that they are just like me. It gave me the chance to see just how wrong it was to call them property and sell them at auction along with the cattle and the horses and the swine. And you've taught me about shame and it hurts to know I fought for the wrong side in the war, conscripted or not. That's what I'm a thankin you for."

James put his arm across Jeremy's shoulders. "The trouble with this world, Jeremy, is that God doesn't get enough credit and the Devil doesn't get enough blame. You are not white trash and you never were. God never created such and those who hang that kind of label do the Devil's bidding. Everything you've just told me is simply a re-wording of a passage in the bible; put your faith in God, not man."

"Holy smoke!" said Jeremy. "And I never even read the bible, but you can bet that I will. I don't read so well but I'll ask Aaron for help. He's a good reader."

"I am sure that you will find it to be very interesting. There are many stories of God's power and how he gave that power to oppressed people so that they could defeat the forces of evil."

"You mean like he did for us last night?"

"Yes, rather like that. But the bible also says that God helps those who help themselves and we must continue to do just that."

"Will we win in the end, James?"

"We will, Jeremy, but I'm afraid that it will not be without sacrifice. We've already learned that."

"Yes, we have. Do you think the Klan will ever leave us be?"

"I can't answer that exactly but I must admit that I find it difficult to be optimistic. I really believe that Major Mitchell and his soldiers were a real blessing showing up the way they did. Not only did they save us last night but it will certainly give the Klan something to think about. It may back them off for a while because we finally have something on our side that poses a threat to them. Of course, they must know that the Union occupation forces are spread very thin and that the soldiers are not at our beck and call. Still, the sudden opposition in force will make them the slightest bit wary."

"One thing for sure," said Jeremy. "We know we can't count on the law around here."

"No, we certainly cannot. The law and the Klan are one and the same. And we don't even know how many white men in the whole county or in the state aren't members of the Klan. It is hard to trust anyone. I learned a hard lesson that day at Kennedy's store. Every time I go into Macon I know that I am passing men on the street that would just as soon see me hanging from a tree. If nothing else, we are painfully aware of the odds against us."

"Well, James, I think I'll go see Aaron and ask him if I can borrow his bible."

James went into the house to look for Polly. He found her in the kitchen, hard at work scrubbing down the cupboards. Taking a seat at the kitchen table, he sat in quiet reflection; wondering if he was doing all he could for the people who depended on him. Over the course of recorded history; all the way back to ancient times, the world and the people who lived in it were described as being civilized. But it was perhaps the only word in the English language James had trouble understanding. To be civilized meant possessing the ability to read and write; having virtues such as modesty, morality, intelligence, and compassion. But to James it meant something in addition to that. It meant being non-violent, non-aggressive, and without barbarism. It also meant a world where people had respect for themselves and respect for others; a completely harmonious setting that was totally without fear. He now realized that what he was imagining was a place called heaven and that civilization was at the bottom of the evolutionary chain; perhaps not even resting on the outermost fringes of heaven.

He felt a sense of helplessness growing within himself; a self-inflicted feeling of failure, guilt of epic proportions. He knew and understood that he was not chosen to be the savior of the world, nor did he believe that his friends and family expected it of him. And yet, so deep was his desire to deliver them from the surrounding evil that he feared he might self-destruct if he did not come to terms with his limitations.

"James? James?" said Polly as she massaged the back of his neck. He looked up, immediately recognizing the concern on her face.

"Polly."

"I was so busy that I didn't realize you were here, James. Then I spoke to you but you looked as though you were a million miles away."

"I guess I nearly was. I don't know where I was going, but I know that I wasn't here."

"Share your thoughts with me."

"Concern, Polly, simple concern. The Klan raised the ante last night and I don't know if I can cover the bet. There was a time during the war when I thought that nothing could be as bad as what was going on around me. I was convinced that when it was over, people would be so tired of violence and destruction that they would embrace a peaceful existence and never let it go. Now I cannot believe how wrong I was."

"I remember, my dear James. I remember how it was during the war. You were so brave and you were so selfless; you took it as your sacred duty to join the slaves in their struggle to be free and you never quit, not even after so nearly being killed in battle. I remember every time I see the scars you will carry for the rest of your life. And I remember how we talked about the opportunity given to our generation; the chance to defeat an evil that had plagued our country from the beginning. Now I ask you to take heart, my darling; rejoice in the Lord because He gave us the strength to accomplish our task and the strength to endure until the task was complete. Take heart, James, and carry the thought always in your mind that for good and for all time, slavery has ceased to exist. When a task is finished, what are we to do but go on to the next? We both knew that securing freedom for our black brothers and sisters was only the beginning. We knew that there would be much more to do before they were completely in freedom's care. But we must have been willing to walk these extra miles; otherwise we wouldn't have taken the first step. I understand your suffering, my husband, and it is all right to grow weary of the fight. We are, after all, only human; we are equally prepared to laugh or to cry."

James got up from the table, wrapped his arms tightly around his good wife, and said, "I will speak with God before I go to sleep tonight and I will thank Him again for the day that I met you." Then he kissed Polly and headed for the hallway.

"Where are you going, James?"

"I'm going to find Ashton."

James knew that if Ashton was not about she would be in her room, and that was where he found her. When she opened the door there was no telltale expression on her face. He did not know if she had any desire to speak to him or if she would rather that he walked away.

"May I speak to you, Ashton?"

"If you wish," she said. James walked into the room and sat down on the cushion-topped window seat, and Ashton sat on the edge of the bed.

"I wish very much to make peace with you, Ashton, not only because it's the right thing to do but because you are my sister and family should be everyone's first concern."

"Are you sure that you do not wish to rephrase your statement?"

"If you could find it in your heart to forgive me, I wouldn't have to. I understand your meaning, you know. You are referring to my actions during the war. If I could only make you understand how difficult it was to live with the choice I made. Not a single day went by that I did not tire under the burden of guilt, which became a parasitic feeder; an all-consuming cancer that could not even be removed by cutting it away. So heavy was my heart, weighted down by concern not only for the safety of my family but for the risk of destroying the relationships I had with them. And if you should ask me why then did I not fight for my family I would say because I could not bring myself to do something even worse."

"Something even worse, James?"

"Yes, fight to protect slavery." There was a brief silence, a very uncomfortable moment when neither of them spoke. Then Ashton broke the silence.

"I admit, James, that I am confused and have been for a long time. I am sure I needn't tell you that war can have damaging, sometimes irreparable effects on people. It left me in an utter state of despair. I don't know how to feel about things ... I don't know how to put so many things that have happened behind me. Maybe that's why I decided to blame you. Maybe I didn't really believe it was entirely your fault, but I blamed you because it helped me to tie all the painful memories into one tidy bundle, making it easier to focus on a cure for my broken heart. I am ashamed to say it but maybe I have even been to the point at which I thought destroying you would end my nightmares and give me a completely new start. But if you've come to ask me again if I am the one who spread the word about your past, the answer is no."

"I want to believe that, Ashton, and I will try, I really will try."

"So where does that leave us?" she asked.

"I guess that's up to the two of us. If we both want to put the past behind us, we can both have a new start. What do you say?"

"I don't know. Sometimes I feel uncomfortable around the Negroes."

"Why?"

"I'm not sure. Maybe it's because I never had to share my home with them before. Maybe, no matter how they act, I get the feeling that they have an inner hatred for me because of my white skin."

"Is there any other reason?"

"No. You forget, James, that I believe in God, too. I have given it a great deal of thought and I have come to the conclusion that it was God's will that the South should lose the war because slavery was such a terrible sin. Now I have to forget the Old South, the old ways, and the old beliefs, and learn to treat the Negroes as equals. It won't be easy, but maybe you can help me."

"Of course I will, Ashton. So will Polly. I know that when you really get to know these people you will see them in a new way. Just give them a chance."

"I'll try, James. I promise to try."

"I wouldn't ask for more." James got up and walked over to where Ashton was sitting. He bent down and kissed her on the forehead. He wanted to say more to her but was afraid too many words would somehow ruin the healing that had begun between them. And he hated himself for thinking it, but if Ashton was not being honest, she did a beautiful job of pretending. Then he walked out of the room feeling as though a tremendous weight had been lifted from his shoulders and his heart.

# EIGHT

# The Infiltrator

In spite of the traumatic clashes with the Ku Klux Klan, the remainder of 1867 passed without another incident. But it did not by any means indicate that the Klan was any less active or resolute. News had spread that the Klan had met in Nashville, Tennessee to form an organization they called the Invisible Empire of the South—the premise being that the emancipated slaves, carpetbaggers, and others were forming a faction that must be fought. It was also reported that the Democrats of Tennessee were backing the Klan to gain support in upcoming elections. Still, James's optimism was lifted by several positive results before year's end. More Negroes from the surrounding area came, anxious to become sharecroppers on his plantation; their number totaled almost one hundred by the end of 1867. Secondly, the cotton yield was very high considering the number of acres they had been able to cultivate, which would increase in the future with the growing work force. And best of all was the peace that had taken root between James and his sister, Ashton.

Surely life was not perfect by any estimation. James had had trouble finding transportation to the mills for the cotton crop and it was still difficult to secure supplies of any kind if the merchant suspected they were for Langdon Plantation. All too often, stories would reach their ears of another random killing, undoubtedly at the hands of the Klan. All over the South, the white supremacists were burning black churches and schools. But James and his people were managing and moving forward while keeping a constant watch for trouble. That was all they could do for the time being. James also did his best to keep up with the latest local, state, and national news. His special interest was the progression for the betterment of the lives of the Negroes; more changes in the laws and more guarantees

67

that their rights would be protected. Of course, laws in the South meant very little when they were being broken by those whose business it was to enforce them. In the wake of the war, even the government in Washington was being pulled in several different directions by several different factions. Like the uninspired, do-nothing administration of President Buchanan *before* Lincoln, the difficult administration of President Johnson, who was a victim of his own beliefs, lost control of Reconstruction to the Radical Republicans *after* Lincoln. The Radical Republicans, however, were the faction most compatible with James's wishes for the Negroes and their future, but how long could they retain any power in the government when they were opposed by every other political group in Washington? All the facts added up to one despairing conclusion; until things gelled in the capital, the progress James was hoping for would move at a snail's pace.

Consequently, when the Fourteenth Amendment, the Reconstruction Amendment, was ratified on July 28, 1868, James did not see it as a major victory for the former slaves. The Fourteenth Amendment forbade any state to deny any person life, liberty, or property without due process of law, or deny any person in its jurisdiction equal protection of the laws. But President Johnson's plans for reconstruction tipped the scales in favor of the Southern whites in power, and as long as those racist state governments were in place, nothing was going to change. When Pennsylvania's Thaddeus Stevens, leader of the Radical Republicans, died on August 11, 1868, his constituents lost much of their enthusiasm for punishing the Confederacy.

For most of that spring and summer; after the new crop of cotton had been planted, James kept everyone busy with the construction of more housing for the new sharecroppers and their families. The project took them to harvest time in October and resumed as soon as the last bale of cotton was shipped.

Then the month of November brought a memorable day, when the news that former General U.S. Grant was elected the eighteenth president reached Langdon Plantation. The former Union commander defeated Horatio

Seymour, the former governor of New York. James was glad to hear the news, Grant being his choice for the position. But it did not ease the irritation that dogged him because he had not cast a vote. James had considered going to Macon with every man that wanted to go. But he knew that it would only cause trouble, which further irritated him for allowing inalienable rights to be stripped from himself and his men. According to the United States Congress, freed black men were now permitted to vote. As a white man and a land owner, James had always enjoyed the privilege. But he was all too aware of popular sentiment in Georgia and how unwelcome he and his black friends would have been. He had heard that, in Savannah, a pitched battle had broken out between Klansmen and former slaves when the blacks tried to vote. So where was he to turn for help? Even the Freedman's Bureau had been disbanded by President Johnson because he had no desire to help the former slaves. More and more, the word "justice" seemed to be a word with no clear understanding.

Aside from the election, something else occurred that day; another man came looking for a chance to sharecrop on Langdon Plantation. James was on the roof of the new building when he cast an eye down toward the main road. He could see a lone figure plodding along on a mule, heading in their direction. When the man turned his mule into the driveway, James climbed down from the roof and walked out to meet him. The visitor was a black man, maybe thirty years old, dressed in moth-eaten work clothes and a straw hat that looked as though his mule had been nibbling on it. He wore no shoes and from the look of his calloused feet, he seldom did.

"Step down, friend," said James.

"Thank ya, suh," he replied. The man climbed down, started to speak, then stopped abruptly and removed his hat as if he'd made a mistake by forgetting to do so. He seemed nervous and fidgety but James was not at all surprised by the stranger's manner. He was accustomed to seeing that kind of behavior from Negroes. After years of slavery, and considering that life had not improved much since gaining their freedom, they knew that it was still necessary to tiptoe around most white folks. James understood but hated that attitude and he did his best to erase it from the minds of those who worked on Langdon Plantation. More than anything he wanted them to know equality in their lives.

"What can I do for you?"

"You is Mr. Langdon?"

"That's right."

"My name is Buford Bell. I was wantin to know ifn you could use another hand."

"Welcome, Buford. I can always use another good man. Do you have a family?" Buford hesitated before answering, and then he dropped his head and said, "No." Judging from the man's reaction to the question, James thought he may have had a family and lost them. He was not about to make matters worse by questioning Buford any further.

"We are making more living space, but until it is finished, I'm sure you can bunk with one of the single men. You can move your belongings over whenever you want to."

"Alls I own is on my ole mule, suh. I is much obliged for the job workin for you."

"Well, Buford, you'll be working for yourself as much as you will for me. When the crop is harvested, I pay my workers forty percent of the crop produced from the land they farmed and I pay twenty percent in product and twenty percent in cash money. That way you have money in your pocket right away and twice as much when the cotton is sold." Buford perked up considerably when James explained the terms.

"You is a mighty fair man, suh. There ain't no place else in Georgia where a black man can git treated that good. Everybody else I knows gots nothin left after da harvest when da bills is done paid. I finds it mighty hard to believe."

"Well, Buford, I just want to make a living, not a killing. I will do all right the way things are and I want the men and women here to be rewarded for the hard work they do. Well then, unless you have questions, I will introduce you to the man who is unofficially in charge of the camp and he will get you settled in."

James took Buford to see Hiram Jones. Hiram had no problem finding a volunteer to share his space until the new quarters were finished. Then James told Hiram, "Let me know from time to time how Buford is doing. He seemed a little bit distant to me, as if he had a big load on his mind. I just want to be sure that he feels at home here."

"Surely I will keep an eye on him, James; he'll be fine."

One evening a week later, Hiram found an opportunity to speak to James in private.

"I see what you mean about Buford. He seems more than willing to work and he doesn't cause any trouble, but like you said, he seems distant. It's like he don't want to get to know anyone real well and he don't want anyone to get to know him. I tried talking to him a couple times but he always has a way of getting around the subject. He has something on his mind all right."

"Well, we'll just have to be patient with him, Hiram. It takes some people longer than others to adjust. As long as he is trying to get along, we'll give him all the help we can."

A couple days later the new building was finished and everyone including Buford had their own living quarters. James was very happy with the way he was progressing with the plantation and he hoped that his father, God rest his soul, would be happy, too. That night, when it was time for bed, he told Polly that he was feeling very relaxed and he was looking forward to a peaceful night's sleep.

At about three o'clock in the morning, he was gone to the world when his deep sleep was interrupted by Polly, vigorously shaking his shoulder. He awoke with a start and sat up trying to rub the sleep from his eyes. "What is it, Polly?"

"Listen," she said in a whisper. "Do you hear it?"

James sat still for a moment and then, even though the window was closed, he could hear a disturbance coming from the sharecroppers' camp. It sounded like angry voices somewhere outside their quarters. Another minute passed and more voices were added making the ruckus grow louder. James didn't wait to hear more. He got up and dressed as fast as he could. "Stay here, Polly. There must be something wrong."

71

Quickly, he went downstairs and out through the kitchen door. The sound of the argument was much louder outside. James could see light coming from behind the new building and more lights were flaring up from candles being lit throughout the quarters. The whole community was coming alive. Just as he reached the new building, Jeremy Todd came out to meet him.

"We got trouble, James."

"Is it an intruder?"

"Not exactly; it's more like a troublemaker who was here all the time."

"I don't understand."

"Come with me."

James followed Jeremy to the crowd of men who had gathered by the well behind the sharecroppers' quarters. They had formed a circle around the well, and when James elbowed his way to the center, there was Buford Bell sitting on the ground with a terrified expression on his face.

"What's going on here? Buford, what happened?" When there was no reply from Buford, Jeremy gave James an explanation. "I came outside a little while ago to have a smoke. I reckon Buford didn't know anyone was out here. I saw him head off in the direction of the barn, then I lost sight of him in the darkness. After a few minutes I saw him come back with what looked like a bucket in his hand. He was also carrying a lantern, but it was burning low and not givin off much light. I wasn't too curious about it until I saw him headin back to the well pump. I followed along and when I was close enough to see what was goin on I could make out that he was tryin to pry up one of the boards that covers the top of the well. I called out his name and that spooked him pretty bad. He tripped and fell and ended up where you see him sittin right now. James, that there bucket is full of lye."

"Lye? Do you mean you think he was going to ...?"

"Yes," said Jeremy. "He was gonna poison the well."

James couldn't believe what he was hearing. It didn't make sense. He knew that something was bothering Buford but he never thought that he posed any threat to anyone. He bent down in front of the frightened man and

72

said, "Buford, you must have a pretty good reason for trying something like this. What is it?"

Buford looked up at James with the most pitiful look in his eyes.

"I never did want to, suh," he said. "You gots to believe I never did want to."

"If you want me to believe you then you'll tell me the perfect truth about why you tried."

"My wife, suh, my wife and my two little ones. They is gonna be kilt ifn I don't do this."

James was even more confused. Buford had told him that he didn't have a family.

"I want you to start from the beginning. Tell me what led up to this."

"I was workin a piece a land near bouts ten miles from here. It was give to me a couple years ago by ole Massa Bell who give me my name, too. My wife and me and da little ones were his property. He was a ole man and when da war done ended and he say I was a good worker and he give me da land jes fore he died. One night I hears a sound outside, I looks out the window, and I see some burnin torches in the yard. I see maybe ten men on hosses wearin these scary masks coverin they faces. I knowed it was them Kluxes and I was afeared. But I goes outside to ax dem what they is wantin wit me. One man say they ain't gonna hurt me and my family long as I do what they tell me. I ax him what he wants me ta do and he say go to Langdon Plantation and hire on wit the Yankee. Then he say I gots ta find where you keeps da lye and dump a bucket full down da well. Then I can git my wife and little ones. He say ifn I don't do it he gwine to kill dem."

Buford began sobbing and the mob of men around him, knowing the pain he was suffering, began offering their sympathies. James was immediately consumed by anger. He should have known the Klan was behind it all like he should have known that the lull in harassment was no reason for getting his hopes up. They were just devising a new plan of attack. This time they had sent a Trojan horse. The Klan swore they would drive James out and there was no denying that they were a very resourceful lot. The remaining problem was how to find Buford's family and rescue them from the Klan.

"Do you know where they are holding your family, Buford?"

"No, suh. They wouldn't let me go back in da house dat night. They say jes you go right now boy and git on your mule or you never gonna see dat family a yourn again."

"I see. Well, the first thing is to find out where they are and then we'll find a way to get them out. Did they tell you how much time you have to get your job done?"

"No, suh."

"I'm sure they won't wait forever and you've been here almost two weeks. On the other hand, I know that it's pretty important to them that you accomplish your mission and considering they have your family, they will be pretty confident that you will do what you are told. Let us hope that time is on our side."

"I is mighty grateful, suh. I knows I don't deserve no help."

"You're wrong, Buford. What you don't deserve is having your family kidnapped like this. Why don't you go in and try to get some rest." Then to the whole group James said, "Why don't you all go back to bed." Then to Jeremy he said, "Would you get Aaron and Chet and come over to the house?"

"You bet," Jeremy replied.

James took the men into the kitchen, started a pot of coffee, and everyone took seats at the table.

"I sure am open to suggestions if you men have any. This may prove to be an extremely difficult situation." Each man sat silently, working the problem over and over in his mind. Aaron was the first man to offer an idea. "I think maybe we should take a page from the Klan's book."

"How do you mean, Aaron?" said Jeremy.

"Well, I mean send someone into their camp with a good story and an interest in joining their band. Maybe then we can find out where Buford's family is being held and maybe even devise a plan to free them from inside their own lines."

"Do you have someone in mind?" James asked.

"Yes," said Aaron. "Me."

"I admire your willing spirit, Aaron," said James. "But I wonder if you realize the risks involved. First and foremost, how can you be sure that none of the men you meet will know that you come from Langdon Plantation? And if that does not prove to be a problem, can you be convincing enough to gain their trust? It won't be easy to deal with people who have such a wary nature—and if you are found out, nothing will save you."

"I appreciate your concern, James, but I do understand the dangers and I believe I can do this. In fact, I may be the only one who can."

"What makes you so sure?" said Chet. "You've even been to Macon with the three of us. James is right, you could be recognized."

"I don't reckon so," said Aaron as he stroked his long beard for effect. "If I shave myself clean and cut my hair short, I'll look like a different person."

James thought about it for a moment and then said, "Aaron, you just might have an idea there. But are you sure you want to make the sacrifice? I mean, I know that you've left your beard and your hair uncut for a long time. It must mean a great deal to you."

"It does, James. But it means very little compared to what Buford's family means to him. I must do what I can to help." James was deeply moved as were Chet and Jeremy.

"Very well, Aaron," said James. "Let us discuss the rest of the details."

The four men sat until dawn, finalizing a plan that they hoped would result in the rescue of Buford's family—if possible without anyone getting hurt. It was decided that very early the following morning, Aaron would be completely shaved and shorn then he would sneak away under the cover of darkness and attempt to join up with the local Klan. Then he would try to find out the location of the hostages, form a plan for their rescue, and sneak back to the plantation in the middle of the night with the information.

"You must not allow yourself to become impatient," said James. "There is no telling how long it might take to get answers, assuming that you'll be able to at all. But you cannot get them by asking questions. Questions raise suspicion. All you can do is act your part and keep your ears open."

"Try not to worry, James, and tell Buford not to worry either."

The next morning at about two o'clock, Aaron was ready to leave. James could not get over the difference in his appearance. Even he could not believe that it was the same man.

"You're all set, Aaron," said James. "Above all else, be careful and never be caught off guard. As you are doing God's work, I would like to pray with you before you leave."

So the two men bowed their heads and sought the Lord's protection and guidance. When they were finished, Aaron mounted his horse and quietly rode off into the darkness.

# NINE

## Midnight at Culpepper Plantation

Two days after Aaron left, Thanksgiving arrived; a special time to pay homage to God, and always in the presence of family and friends. But for Buford Bell, the revelry was stifled by the absence of his family; for everyone else it was the absence of Aaron Parmalee. Aaron was not only the little community's preacher but also a very dear friend. James looked for as many things possible to occupy his mind, but every night, after Polly was asleep, he prayed for Aaron's safe return.

Still, as always, there was much to be thankful for. It truly seemed as though James's relationship with Ashton was finally harmonious. Sometimes in the evening he would sit by the fireplace with his oldest sister and they would reminisce about the old days and talk about prospects for the future. She even revealed personal goals to him; her hopes of one day marrying again, for example. Now and then Kate would join the conversations as well as Polly and Jim.

Jim was now six years of age and totally engaged in an unspoken worship of his father. He followed James everywhere the elder Langdon would allow, and when he couldn't follow it was rarely without protest. It often reminded James of his youth; growing up with his father, but with some very definite distinctions. Primarily, James meant for his son to grow up understanding that all people were the same inside and that outward appearance was simply God's way of telling who was who.

When three weeks had passed since Aaron's departure, a nervous tension was beginning to show in some of the men. James was having second thoughts about the plan himself but it was worse for Jeremy and Chet. They had both known Aaron for most of their lives and it was becoming increasingly difficult to find the words to pacify

77

them. The waiting was also taking a huge toll on Buford. His fears had so overtaken him that he not only believed that Aaron was dead but that his family was dead as well. It was, in fact, the same day Buford told James he could wait no longer that the Klan made its first ever daylight visit.

James was on his way to the house one morning after somehow talking Buford out of leaving when he saw a lone rider sitting on his horse near the hitching post at the edge of the front lawn. The man wore no mask but he was Klan just the same. His facial expression was stern and steady like the grim reaper on collection day and he held a staff with a white flag attached in his right hand. James was unarmed but he knew he would have no need of a weapon. The man was there for a parlay and not even the Klan's distorted sense of honor would allow violence in view of a flag of truce. Nevertheless, James walked toward the visitor with measured dread as if he were heading to a showdown.

"What is it you want here?" James asked the stranger.

"Got a message for you, Yank. Your man, Parmalee, is found out. He had us fooled real good for a while but he got to talkin one day about somethin that happened at Shiloh during the war and I put it together just who he was. I guess both our spies failed to get the job done, huh, Yank?"

"Is Aaron all right?"

"He ain't all right but he's alive."

"So what are you doing here?"

"Like I said, I got a message. We woulda killed your friend—"

"How would you have justified killing Aaron?" James interrupted. "He was a Rebel soldier. He fought for the South."

"He *was* a Rebel soldier. Now he's a traitor; too bad. But we didn't kill him ... there's somethin we want more. We want the nigger, Buford. We're willin to make a trade, Parmalee for the nigger. We'll even throw in the nigger's woman and kids so you're gettin a deal, four for one."

"If we did agree to the trade, how would we make the exchange?"

"About five miles from here is what's left of the Culpepper Plantation."

"I know where it is," James replied.

"Then you know there ain't nothin left except the barn. We'll be at the barn tonight come midnight. We'll have Parmalee, the woman, and her kids with us. You bring the nigger and we'll make the swap. If you ain't there by midnight, we'll hang Parmalee and shoot the kids, then the woman."

"How do I know you'll keep the agreement? How do I know you won't try to kill us all?"

"The Grand Cyclops has instructed me to give his word as a loyal southerner and if *you* were a loyal southerner you would know that a southerner's word can't ever be broke."

"I will give your proposal some serious thought."

"Think all you want but remember, we'll have a noose hangin from the center beam of that barn tonight. It's up to you whose neck we put in it."

With that, the Klansman turned his horse and rode off. James turned around and there stood Jeremy and Chet just out of earshot. They hurried over to where James stood, idly straightening the brim of his hat.

"What did he say, James?" Jeremy asked.

"Aaron has been discovered."

"Is he all right?" asked Chet.

"They beat him but he's still alive. They want Buford. They want to trade Aaron for Buford at the old Culpepper Plantation tonight at midnight. They say we can have Buford's woman and children, too. If we don't show up they'll hang Aaron and shoot the woman and the children."

"What are we going to do?" said Jeremy.

"I wish to God in heaven that I knew. Don't say anything to Buford. I need some time to think. I'll be out in a little while." James headed for the house leaving Jeremy and Chet standing there with looks of bewilderment on their faces.

Once inside the house James found Polly in the parlor, busy with her mending chores. She had only to look at James to know that something was very wrong. He sat down next to his wife and told her about the unwelcome visitor. When he was finished, Polly put down her mending and took him by the hand.

"I won't ask what you are going to do because it would only add to your frustration. How could there be an easy answer to that question? It would seem that those people finally have us in a situation that renders us completely helpless."

"I don't see how I can save them all, Polly. I can't let them hang Aaron and I can't sentence Buford to death; and what about Buford's family? If Buford *doesn't* surrender to them, he'll lose his family and we'll lose Aaron. If we attempt a rescue by force, there is no telling how many might be killed."

"I wonder, James, should you talk to Buford and let him decide what should be done?"

"I have considered that, Polly, but I cannot think of a more difficult position to put a man into. I believe that he would sacrifice himself for his family, but I'm not ready to let that happen yet. We still have some time. There must be a way."

James rose abruptly and left the house without another word. As he descended the veranda steps and headed for the camp, Jeremy came running toward him at high speed.

"James! Buford's gone!

"Gone? What do you mean he's gone?"

"He overheard me and Chet talking about the meeting tonight at Culpepper Plantation and he got on his mule and lit out. We would a had to shoot him to stop him. I'm sorry, James."

"That fool," said James. "I know how he feels but he's going to make a bigger mess of this whole thing. If he's caught by the Klan they'll hang him straight away and who knows where that will leave Aaron and Buford's family. And if they don't get him and we can't find him we'll have nothing to bargain with tonight. All right, you and Chet saddle three horses quickly and grab your pistols. I'll be with you in a minute."

"OK, James."

James hurried back to the house, entered through the kitchen, and retrieved his own weapon. He was grateful that he didn't see Polly or his sisters. He had no time to explain. Then he left the house and sought out Hiram Jones. He told Hiram to keep an eye on things and then ran to the barn. Jeremy and Chet were ready to go. James leaped into the saddle.

"Which way we headed?" Jeremy asked.

"Culpepper Plantation," James replied.

The three men galloped out to the main road and turned right. A few miles later, James pulled his horse to a skidding halt and stood up in the stirrups. He searched the surrounding area but Buford was nowhere in sight. "Where could he be?" said James. "He couldn't have gotten far on that old mule."

"He didn't have more than a five minute head start," said Chet.

"Well, he either headed in another direction or he heard us coming and found a spot to hide."

"Why would he do that?" asked Jeremy.

"I guess he figures we'd try to stop him and he's got it in his head to handle this his way. We'll ride a bit farther and if we don't find him we'll have to play this without him."

The three men ended up riding the whole way to the deserted plantation without finding a trace of Buford. They approached the barn cautiously but there wasn't anyone around.

"I was planning to ride out here anyway to take a look at this old barn," James told the others. "I wanted to see the layout hoping it might give me some ideas. Stay out here and keep a watchful eye, Chet. Jeremy, you come with me."

James and Jeremy dismounted and walked over to the dilapidated structure. In the front end there were two large doors that met in the middle and swung, one to each side. A stout wooden bolt slid through an iron handle on each door to keep them closed. James slid the bolt back and opened one of the doors just enough so the two of them could enter. Inside, the barn was wide open down the middle with stalls on the right side and more stalls and a tack room on the left. Each side had a mow floor about twelve feet high running the whole length of the barn. Running across the center from one floor to the other was

a large hewn beam. James remembered the Klansman
mentioning that beam. That, he had said, was where the
noose would hang tonight.

"Any ideas?" asked Jeremy.

"One or two; let's get back."

As they made their way home, the three men searched
the countryside, but no Buford. An hour after returning, a
heavy cloud cover rolled in and the wind began to pick up.
By eight o'clock that evening it was raining. James was in
the parlor with Polly and Kate; Ashton was keeping Jim
occupied upstairs.

Polly brought coffee for everyone, and then they talked
about the meeting at Culpepper.

"It would be useless to deny that I am afraid, James,"
said Polly. "I have the most terrible feeling and I can't get
rid of it."

"I feel the same way," said Kate. This is so much more
than any of us bargained for. When the Klan attacked us I
was sure that I had seen the worst and you and the men at
least had the advantage of fighting on your own ground.
This time you will be out in the open, meeting the Klan at a
place chosen by them. Many of you could be killed."

"Not many, Kate. Only Jeremy, Chet, and one volunteer
from the single black men will go with me."

"What?" Polly said. "You mean you're not taking a
formidable show of force?"

"I can't do that, Polly. Right now the Klan claims that
they only want one black man, Buford. If I show up with
fifty black men, they may not want to stop at that. It will
only add fuel to the fire, I'm sure of it. I believe we'll be
much safer if we do this according to what was agreed
upon. The Klansman gave his word."

"And what is that worth?" said Kate. "We've all had an
intense lesson on the behavior of the Klan by now. Have
you forgotten how despicable those people can be?"

"No, Kate. I haven't forgotten, nor will I ever. But I have
no choice."

"But you don't even have Buford," said Polly. "What will
happen when they find out? God knows I do not wish for
anyone to be hurt, but even if you have a plan only Buford
can help to make it work."

"I am hoping that a miracle happens before they find out. I'm scared, too, Polly. I feel the same as I did when I started helping slaves escape during the war. I had no idea how I was going to accomplish my mission. I just took things as they came and God was right beside me. The only thing I can do tonight and every day of my life after that is to pray that He *stays* beside me. We decided together in the beginning that we would stay in Georgia. We placed our trust in the Almighty and we stayed."

"Yes, James, we did. I will ask God, as I constantly do, to keep you safe along with the others and to forgive me for my human frailties. The girls and I will all pray until you are home safe again."

It was after 10 o'clock and there were final preparations to make. James hugged his wife, kissed her, and told her he would be back. Then he kissed Kate on the forehead and headed out to the barn. On the way, he stopped and asked Hiram to send all of the single black men to the barn as well. Of the thirty-one men in the group, every one of them volunteered to make the trip posing as Buford. James settled on Marshal because he was a strong young man about the same age and he had a mule that could have been a twin to Buford's. By 11 o'clock they were ready to leave. It was pouring rain and James hoped that somehow the foul weather would give them an edge. Jeremy would drive an old covered carriage, hopefully to transport Buford's family. James and Chet would ride their horses and Marshal would ride his mule.

The thing that worried James the most was the fact that he did not know the whereabouts of Buford. If the Klan already had him they might not be at the barn; or they might show up regardless, breaking their word by setting a trap for James. If the Klan didn't have him then James would have to take fast action before they had a good look at Marshal. Their success was almost completely based on a hasty judgment call after assessing the situation at Culpepper.

Because of the heavy rain, they all wore slickers and slouch hats. Hopefully, Marshal could keep his identity hidden a little longer under his rain gear. About a mile from the plantation, Chet stopped on the road to prepare another helpful measure while the rest of them moved on.

As they approached their destination, it was easy to see that the two large barn doors were standing open and the inside was brightly illuminated by lanterns and torches. Getting closer, they could see a fair number of horses tied to a couple remaining sections of rail fence. James would need to see more but he was already processing all information as it presented itself. Owing to the rain, the Klansmen were in the barn, contained to some extent, with less room to maneuver than if they were outside. But when they started up the driveway, James again became distracted by one thought ... where on earth was Buford?

Only one hundred feet separated them from the open barn doors. James and Marshal rode abreast, with Jeremy behind them in the carriage. Closer and closer they moved at a painfully slow walk until the three of them stopped about twenty feet from the doorway. In spite of his preoccupation, James noticed that, very wisely, Jeremy turned the carriage around so that he would already be pointing towards the road. "Stay put," James whispered to Marshal then he nudged his horse until he was just inside the barn. Now the entire scene was in front of him and a quick survey showed promise. The Klansmen, dressed in their disguises, lined the edge of the loft floor on both sides. Their number totaled at least fifty. Down on the ground under that center beam stood Aaron's horse; Aaron was in the saddle with a noose around his neck. One Klansman held the horse's bridle to keep him still. The pounding rain against the tin roof was almost deafening. James scanned the inside of the barn, looking for a black woman and two black children but he didn't see them and it made him nervous. Then the first man in line on the right loft floor, whose speech was impeded by a very noticeable lisp, spoke in a voice loud enough to be heard above the rain.

"Where is the nigger?" he demanded. Without looking back, James motioned to Marshal, who brought his mule forward then stopped just behind him. Satisfied, the Klansman said, "We stand here tonight looking down on you and your nigger dog, Yankee. It is for us to show you the meaning of Southern loyalty and brotherhood and for that reason alone we have come to keep our solemn word. We shall give you back your unclean friend, the black bitch, and her dog pups. You have brought us the seed of the evil propagation and it is with him that we will take our revenge." James needed to stall to give Chet time to approach the barn from the rear and carefully untie the Klan's horses without spooking them. Then, if they managed to get everyone they came for, the horses would stampede on the way out. Chet would be waiting for them a mile down the road, ready to throw a rope barricade across it to slow down pursuit. First, James had to try to get Buford's family out of the barn before the exchange was made. Shouting to be heard over the pouring rain, James said, "I do not see the Negro woman and her children. Bring them out, let them go, and we will make the trade you have demanded."

"No! Before they leave they will watch the execution of their nigger sire and partner so they might understand that the power in this land was, is, and ever shall be white!"

With that, the situation had become hopeless. There was no way to get Aaron and Buford's family out of that barn before trouble started, and even if there was, it would take a miracle to get everyone home. He could think of no plan because he had no idea where the woman and her children were. He could only guess that they were being held in one of the stalls; all cloaked in darkness beneath the loft floors. The only advantage James could see was that all but the man holding Aaron's horse, the Klansmen would have to come down a ladder single file to get to the ground. Still they could use their weapons from where they were. The time had come; the Klan was getting restless.

"Send the nigger in to take that white traitor's place."

James reached under his slicker and placed his hand on the butt of his revolver. Buford's absence had spoiled any chance of ruining the Klan's evening. The main concern now was to try to save Aaron. He had risked his life to help Buford and he deserved better than to be hanged for it. James hoped that by a surprise move he could race into the barn, get the noose off Aaron, and then shoot over the Klansmen's heads to force them to seek cover. It was madness, but with no time to plan James had to do the first thing that came to his mind. He said a quick and silent prayer and poised himself to act ...

Before he could spur his horse, Marshal kicked up his mule and moved past James, heading for the center of the barn. "Marshal, no!" James cried in a low voice, but the mule kept moving. James was shocked. What would the Klan do when they found out it wasn't Buford? The mule stopped right beside Aaron's horse. The Klansman stepped up on a wooden box so he could remove the noose from around Aaron's neck. Then he cut the rope that bound his hands. Aaron touched a toe to his horse's side and the animal moved toward the open barn doors. Then, very slowly, the mule started to turn until its rider was under the noose. But when the black man on the mule removed his hat, James could not believe his eyes. It was Buford! Where did he come from? When did he trade places with Marshal?

Aaron was nearing the doorway. The following thirty seconds passed so quickly that James would never remember the sequence of events. The Klansman lifted the noose up to place it around Buford's neck. Buford lifted his right leg and kicked the man in the face, toppling him off the wooden box. He kicked his mule and rode toward the barn doors raising his right hand that was balled in a fist and shouting, "Niggers is free! Niggers is free!"

The audacity of the move was so unexpected that for several moments everyone was transfixed in disbelief. But when Buford cleared the doorway and James whirled his horse around behind him, the Klansmen began yelling obscenities and clamoring down the wooden ladders. James fired his revolver attempting to scatter the Klan's horses while Jeremy sped out of the driveway with Buford and Aaron right behind him. As James followed after, the scene at the barn was utter chaos as the Klansmen poured out of the open doors and tried to mount their frantic horses.

As he headed up the main road, James could hear gunfire behind him. Although he was out of range, he knew the Klan was sending the message that they were in pursuit. A mile from the barn James raced past Chet, who was waiting to deploy the barricade. The rain was coming down harder than ever and the road was slick with mud. Not until reaching the driveway to Langdon Plantation did James slow down. He continued on to the dry confines of the barn, and there he found Jeremy, Buford, Aaron, and Marshal.

"Is Chet on his way?" asked Jeremy.

"I'm sure that he is," James excitedly replied. "I passed him on the road. He should be here soon. Aaron are you all right?"

"I'll be fine," Aaron said.

The adrenaline was still coursing through James's body. His feet were on the ground but his heart was still in his throat. With more zeal than he intended he walked over to Buford and said, "Where did you disappear to and what in the hell happened back there? What about your family?" Buford was overwhelmed and more than a little scared. He could see that James was upset and he tried to speak but the words wouldn't come. Jeremy stepped in to try to calm the situation. He put his hand on James's shoulder and said, "Easy, James. Take yourself a deep breath and I'll explain.

"When Buford left here he went over to his place to see if the Klan was holding his family there. That's why we couldn't find him when we went lookin. He lives in the woods so he could easily tie his mule some distance away and sneak up close to the house. His place was deserted so he stayed there until dark and then he went to Culpepper Plantation. He got there hours ahead of the Klan and hid his mule out behind the barn. Then he waited for the Klan to show up. When they came, he watched through a crack in the wall and saw two of them bring his family in and put them in the tack room, tie them up, and gag them. Then Buford kept watch; he saw a couple more of them show up with Aaron. The Klansmen lit the barn up, but as you saw, everything under the loft floors was dark. The tack room was the only place in the barn that had a door leading outside. After those people climbed up to the loft, Buford sneaked into the tack room and got his family out of there. The rain made so much noise that the Klan didn't hear nothin. He took his family out back, put them on his mule and sent them out across the fields to the main road. Then they came here. When we showed up he waited until you had the Klan's attention, then he eased his way over to Marshal and traded places with him. When you waved him forward, you were waving to Buford. Marshal got into the carriage with me and then all we could do was to wait and see what happened."

"I am sorry for my anger, Buford. I know you were afraid for your family. In your place, I would have done the same thing."

"Dats alright, suh, I knows I made things hard. I can't never say thanks enough for what you all done."

"Well," said James. "I guess for the moment, everything turned out fine."

"Almost," said Aaron.

"What do you mean?"

"Chet still isn't back."

Aaron's remark was a sober reminder. Chet wasn't back and he certainly should have been by that time.

"Should we go look for him?" said Jeremy.

"I wish we could, but it's too dangerous. The Klan is out there somewhere and their mood will be more hostile than ever. If Chet isn't back by first light, we'll look for him."

"It might be too late by then," Jeremy replied. James thought it over for a moment. He was weary and concerned about Polly. He knew she would be awake and worrying. But he knew that Jeremy was right. "Very well, Jeremy, you and I will go. Marshal, wake Hiram Jones and tell him to have some of the men stand sentry duty until morning. Aaron, please go and tell Polly I'm all right and I'll be home soon. Let's go, Jeremy."

The two men mounted their horses and rode back out into the dismal night. They took their time and moved carefully down the soggy road. The rain was finally slowing down. By the time they were within a couple hundred yards of the rope barricade, the clouds had parted and the moon provided enough light to cast shadows on the ground. Just short of the barricade, James noticed something in the road. He dismounted his horse and Jeremy did likewise. Upon closer inspection they could tell that a horse had fallen in the mud then apparently had struggled to get to its feet again. There were many hoof prints around the area. Then they continued on until they reached the barricade and there a gruesome sight presented itself. The ropes had been ripped away by the obvious collision; the road was torn up something fierce, and three dead horses were lying in a heap. To add to the ugly spectacle, the horses had been shot, undoubtedly because they had broken their necks or a leg in the accident. The night had taken on an eerie silence; the air was thick with a sense of foreboding. They walked off the edge of the road to bypass the equine carnage and then got back into their saddles.

With silent trepidation, James and Jeremy covered the last mile to the scene of the night's previous calamity. When they started up the driveway they could see a horse wearing a saddle, peacefully grazing not far from the barn. Their worst fears were confirmed as a closer view revealed that the animal belonged to Chet. The big barn doors still stood open almost as a challenge to the stout of heart to enter. Clouds were still moving overhead, intermittently blocking the moonlight. The inside of the barn darkened as a puffy mass went by. The two men rode through the doorway, then a bit farther, and then they reined to a stop. Once again the night breeze brushed the clouds from the face of the moon and there was Chet's body, hanging from the rope attached to that center beam. Pinned to his shirt was a note that read: "Traitors Be Ye Warned."

Without a word, Chet's two bereaved friends cut him down, laid him across his saddle, and took him home.

# TEN

## Nothing Less Than Justice

Chester A. Rawlins, having no immediate family, was buried in the Langdon family cemetery. It seemed fitting at least to have him near his closest friends, Jeremy and Aaron. When the funeral was over, everyone went about their business. It was almost Christmas, but the spirit that hung over Langdon Plantation was not an especially festive one. It was understandable; not only because of Chet's death, but moreover because his demise was no accident. Their faithful friend had been murdered and it seemed that the guilty persons would once again go unpunished. The one consolation was the overwhelming gratitude shown by Buford not only toward the men who helped to rescue his family but to everyone else in the sharecroppers' camp. He was a good man who wanted what every normal man wanted: a chance to make a life for his family.

James figured that, for the moment, the Klan was satisfied that they had evened the score. They did not get Buford but Chet was payment enough because to them the only thing worse than a nigger was a nigger lover. But walking away from the cemetery that morning, an irritating mental parasite crawled into James's brain and began to prod his subconscious. He knew it was a demand that he take action against the Klan but he couldn't help thinking that it could prove to be an exercise in futility. He wanted desperately to see the Klan punished by the law but the odds against it were long.

James needed to rejuvenate his obstinate will and support his cause to the end as he had done during the war. He knew that Polly, Jeremy, and Aaron would agree with him.

Suddenly, he felt a little better about himself and the annoying parasite moved on. First, he located Jeremy and told him to come to the house and bring Aaron along. Then he asked Polly to make a fresh pot of coffee and when the men arrived they all went into the parlor and made themselves comfortable.

"I know Chet's death has hit everyone pretty hard; no one as hard as you, Jeremy, and you, Aaron. I know that you fellows were very good friends and so I know that you will agree with what I have to say. Someone has got to answer for this crime. Surely we will never see every Klansman at Culpepper last night held accountable, but if enough pressure is brought to bear, maybe the name or names of those most responsible will come to the surface. We must challenge that sacred brotherhood of theirs and see how well it holds together when they stand in judgment before a higher authority."

"I reckon we don't have to tell you how much respect we have for you, James," said Aaron. "We have never known a better man, not even during the war when we lived or died depending on the kind of man that was next to us in a fight. We know because we have seen that there is no better man to be next to than you. Jeremy and I are ready to do anything that you see fit to bring Chet's killer or killers to justice."

"We are behind you all the way," said Jeremy.

"You know how I feel," said Polly.

"Very well then. We will need to get word to Georgia's governor, Rufus Bullock. He is a very strong supporter of African American equality. Because of the black vote, he defeated ex-Confederate General John B. Gordon in the gubernatorial election this year. He has many enemies among the Klan. I believe that he would take a personal interest in what happened last night."

"I am surprised by the governor's point of view," said Polly. "He isn't your usual southern politician."

"That's because he isn't southern, Polly. He was born in New York and he moved to Augusta later in life. If we can get anyone to act on this, I believe that he is the man."

"Where do we find the governor?" asked Jeremy.

"I reckon I can answer that," Aaron replied. "Strange as it seems, that is one thing I learned from the Klan when I was among them. They said that the state capitol just moved this year to Atlanta. It used to be in Milledgeville, you know. The governor lives in a three story house on East Peachtree Street between Ellis and Baker Street."

"Thank you, Aaron," said James. "That information is very helpful. Now we just have to find a way to communicate with him. I'm afraid that we can't send a wire or even a letter, not from Macon anyway."

"A communication may have to be delivered in person," said Polly. James felt a chill go down his back after hearing Polly's suggestion. He couldn't help remembering what happened the last time the two of them traveled to Atlanta.

"We may have to think of something else, dear," he said.

"I'm sorry, James; I didn't mean to raise a bad memory."

"Its fine, Polly; we'll find a way to send word."

"I will go to Atlanta, James," said Jeremy

"I will go, too," Aaron echoed.

"I appreciate your offer, my friends, but are you sure you want to make the trip? We've all been through a lot in the last year or so."

"It's been no worse for us than for anyone else," Aaron replied. "Chet was a friend to all of us but I reckon Jeremy and I knew him best. We think it's our place to do this for him, and maybe do something for all of us. If there is any way to see that the Klan answers to the law, it could help a whole lot to quiet things down around here."

"You're right, of course, Aaron. Sooner or later the violence in the South has got to be brought under control. The people who govern this country, whether they are local, state, or federal, have to realize that nothing will improve or progress as long as crime operates unabated. I will write a very carefully worded letter for you to deliver to Governor Bullock. Somehow you must see that he reads it and then bring back an answer from him. I will tell the governor that the welfare of the state hangs in the balance; that he must act and that we will accept nothing less than justice. Can you men be ready to leave this afternoon?"

"We'll be ready when the letter is finished, James," said Jeremy. "We'll ride by day so as to give us every advantage. If we are lucky, we should be back tomorrow with news."

Together, James and Polly composed a letter that they hoped would move Governor Bullock to action. If there was even the smallest chance that the governor didn't realize it, they wanted to make it clear to him that for the good of his political future he must act immediately to bring the situation under control. They also reminded the governor that the first step, after years of suffering, had finally been achieved: the slaves were freed. It was now time for the southern people to accept the fact that blacks were equal and the time would come when they would be accepted and afforded the same rights and opportunities as anyone else. Why go through years of violence, torture, and bloodshed before showing the racists that they could no longer take the law into their own hands? In short, why go through another war?

James remembered something his father had told him years before, something that he had totally disagreed with. His father said, "Examples have to be made." But he was talking about a slave he had whipped for trying to escape. Now, James was thinking the same about the Klan members; examples had to be made. When the letter was finished, Jeremy and Aaron left on their mission of hope, the same as James and Polly had a couple years earlier. James anticipated their return the following day, and more than that, he anticipated Governor Bullock's support of their endeavor to plant the seed of justice in Georgia.

James went out to the veranda just to sit; to ruminate about the past and contemplate the future. It seemed that many times since the end of the war and the decision to stay in Georgia he had searched his soul, wondering if he had done the right thing. Considering all that had happened in the past three years, it was so very easy to assume that life would have been much easier if he had kept his family in Pennsylvania. Had he been right, by the end of the war, to believe that he had relinquished his ancestral citizenship? Was it hard to dispute the fact that he would have been more welcome in Pennsylvania because of his service during the conflict? Roads not taken were all he could think about. Maybe that was the rationalization that kept him going. James could never be sure things would be different had he gone the other way.

93

He could only go on the outcome that was made possible by his choice.

Still, there was that one thing that nagged him on a regular basis; how did the word leak out about his Union service? James was no coward, nor was he the kind of man who would not take responsibilities for his actions. However, he was also not a fool and understood that to live in Georgia his past was better left in the past.

Even though it was painful to accept, James had a logical reason to believe that Ashton was responsible. He knew, of course, that even taking into consideration all she had been through, it was a pretty harsh thing to do. On the other hand, James had seen for himself the effects that war could have on human emotions; at times, even his own.

But since their heartfelt conversation, things had changed between them and he did not wish to upset her again. She had denied any involvement and James wanted desperately to believe her; that was the end of it.

The front door opened, and Jim came out to the veranda looking for his father. He probably would have liked to climb into his father's lap but he had recently proclaimed himself a big boy and sitting on his father's lap was something that big boys simply did not do. But he did sit very close to James, placing his small hand on his elder's shoulder.

"Mother says you are sad and I came out to make you happy again," he said.

"Well if anyone could raise my spirits, it would certainly be you, son," his father replied. "Why does your mother say that I am sad?"

"I think it's because there are some bad men that won't leave us alone."

"I see. So you know about the bad men do you?"

"Yes, Father. I know that some men do bad things because Mr. Aaron tells us stories about that in Sunday school. He says that not everyone does what God tells them to do and it makes God sad. I think that's why you are sad and Mother is sad."

James was touched by his son's reasoning. Suddenly he felt the need to unburden himself; he thought that teaching his young son something about life was just the way to do it.

"Even though you are very young, Jim, there is something I want to tell you that I hope you will understand. This is something that I want you to remember your whole life. When the good Lord made the world, he made a great many living things. He made trees and flowers, birds and fish, animals and people; just to name some of them. When he made all these wonderful things, he did not make only one kind of each, he made many different kinds. Let's think about the trees the Lord made. There are oak trees, maple trees, cypress trees, pine trees, and lots more. Among the animals there are deer, bears, foxes, raccoons, and many others. More importantly, when the Lord made people, he made those of us with white skin, the Negroes with black skin, Indians with reddish skin, and lots of others whose skin may be the same color but they are different because they come from different countries and speak different languages and have different ways of life. But the thing you have to remember is that no matter where they come from or how they speak or what color their skin is—they are still people. They need the same things like food, water, clothing, a home; and they have the same feelings like happiness, sadness, love, and anger. Do you understand what I am trying to tell you?"

The small boy thought for a moment and then, to James's astonishment, he said, "People are different but they are the same?"

James was overwhelmed; he pulled the boy onto his lap, hugged him close, and many months of anxiety completely disappeared.

"You make me so happy, son," he said, with a tear in his eye. "You must always remember that the Lord loves all people and we must love all people, too, and the only sad part is that not everyone feels this way."

"Do you mean those bad men, Father?"

"I'm afraid so, son."

"I will never be a bad man, Father ... I promise."

"I know you won't, Jim. Now, young man, go in to your mother and tell her that your father is happy again."

"I'll go right now, Father." With that, he hopped off his seat and ran into the house.

The following afternoon, Jeremy and Aaron returned from their trip to Atlanta. Judging from their excitement, it was obvious that the journey had been worthwhile. James took them into the kitchen so that Polly could hear the news while she worked with Kate to clean the cupboards and line the shelves with paper.

"You wouldn't believe what we had to do to get the governor to read your letter, James," said Jeremy. "We come pretty close to gettin arrested for even tryin to see ole Bullock and when we did get into the building we had to bribe an uppity clerk to take the letter to him. The clerk said the governor was busy tryin to get a couple last minute things done becuz he was leavin for New York to spend Christmas. But the governor is a good ole boy and once he read your letter he asked me and Aaron to come in to his office and we sat there with him while he wrote an answer. I hope it's a good one." Then he pulled the sealed envelope from his pocket and handed it to James, who tore it open and quickly read it to himself. When he finished, it was difficult to tell from the look on his face if it was a positive response or not.

"Well, I was right about one thing; the governor is very concerned about the state of things in Georgia, in particular, the activities of the Ku Klux Klan. He says that there are still not many people in the South who would raise a hand against the Klan no matter how many Negroes they kill but the fact that Chet was white would give him a lot more support in prosecuting the guilty person or persons. But I am afraid that the good news ends there."

"What do you mean, James?" asked Polly.

"The governor goes on to express the difficulties in identifying Klan members because many people are in favor of their work and they protect them. In many cases, the local authorities are either Klan members or Klan sympathizers. He says it can be nearly impossible to get enough real evidence to get them to trial and even more difficult to get a conviction."

"I reckon we know somethin about that," said Jeremy.

"You're right," James replied. "The governor also says that if we can identify the men who hanged Chet ourselves, and if we can get the proof, he will take up our cause personally."

"It sounds like he is asking you to take the law into your own hands," said Polly.

"In a manner of speaking, he is. But how on earth are we supposed to find out who was directly responsible much less get irrefutable proof? We would need Alan Pinkerton for that and we could never persuade him to drop what he's doing and come to Georgia to hunt Chet's killers."

"I might be able to help us a little," said Aaron. "I know who a few of the local members are."

"I almost forgot about that, Aaron. I guess you met some of them when you posed as a new recruit."

"I can even tell you how to find a couple of them, but I don't know how much it will help. They keep a lot of things secret. I tried to make them believe that I wanted to join up with them but they don't trust you all at once. It takes a while, and they told me I would have to be initiated before I would be a member."

"Well, at least we are on the right trail," said James. "We might be able to use this information to our advantage. But we will still need to find proof before we can go back to the governor."

"Where does that leave us?" Aaron asked.

James thought in silence for several minutes and the other three watched as a very determined look spread over his face. At length he said, "How would you fellas like to go for a ride?"

"Where to?" they said in unison.

"Culpepper Plantation."

"What for?" said Jeremy.

"To look for evidence; I know of no other place to start. We know that everyone involved in Chet's death was there that night."

"I wonder if your search shouldn't be narrowed down," said Polly.

"What are you getting at, dear?" James asked her.

97

"I realize that everyone present when Chet was hanged is guilty of being an accessory to the crime, but I know that you understand the impossibility of bringing all of them to justice. Who is really the guilty one?"

"I think I understand, Polly. You're talking about the leader; the man who gave the order."

"Yes, James. He would be the one most responsible and if it was possible to prosecute him, maybe it would be the best example for the rest of them."

"I remember the first night they came here. The man who did the talking identified himself as the Exalted Cyclops. I also remember that he had a very distinct speech impediment, a lisp. The Klansman who did the talking that night at Culpepper Plantation spoke the same way. I don't think I will ever forget his voice. I guess he would be the man we're looking for."

"I reckon so," said Aaron. "And the Exalted Cyclops *is* the leader of the local chapter. The Grand Dragon is the leader of all chapters in the state. I don't believe he would have been at Culpepper. The Exalted Cyclops would be the man we are after."

"This all sounds so promising in theory but it pales in comparison to the reality of it. We all know how rough the Klan can be. Two men have been lost already and each time it happens it becomes more difficult to live with."

"On earth as it is in heaven, James," said Aaron.

"Believing that is the only thing that helps," James replied. "Finding out who the Exalted Cyclops is will not be easy, but it will be many times harder to prove that he had Chet hanged. Are you ready to take that ride to Culpepper Plantation?"

"What can you hope to find?" asked Polly.

"Perhaps nothing, dear, but it might be worth a try. Just knowing that the man we're after was there seems reason enough to take a look around."

"Maybe you're right, James. I suppose anything is worth a try."

With that, the three men left the house and headed for the barn to saddle their horses. They rode towards the ruins of the plantation in silence, each man lost in his own thoughts about that fateful night. However, when they were within sight of their destination, James pulled his horse to a sudden stop and pointed in the direction of the tragic scene. "We're too late," he said. Aaron and Jeremy sat with their jaws hanging open as they surveyed the site of the old barn, which someone had burned to the ground.

"It kind of makes you think doesn't it?" said Aaron.

"About what?" Jeremy asked.

"About what we might have found."

"It makes me think, too," said James, "that maybe the Klan is feeling more of a need to destroy any evidence linking them to an unlawful act. Is there any chance that they could be feeling the tolerance for their activities running out?"

# ELEVEN

## A Chink in the Armor

For a brief time, the challenge to prosecute the man responsible for Chet's death was put on hold. The holidays were upon them and James knew how important it was for everyone at Langdon Plantation to enjoy the revelry of the season. It was not healthy for hearts and souls to be too long under a cloud of gloom and despair and he did everything possible to bring the spirit of Christmas to his family and to the sharecroppers, whom he considered his friends.

However, when 1869 had been properly ushered in, he believed the time was right to move ahead with the attempt to bring down the Klan. It was his hope that the incident at Culpepper Plantation was fading in the memories of the guilty, giving them reason to think that they had nothing to fear. James admitted only to himself that he still thought the odds were long against any real success, but he found reason to be more optimistic when he sat down once again to discuss the situation with Jeremy and Aaron. Aaron told James what he could about the few men he met while he was trying to infiltrate the ranks of the Klan in the hope of locating Buford's family. But nothing gave James any ideas until Aaron said, "There was one other fella that I met once at one of the liveries in Macon; he worked there. Let me think on it a minute and see if I can remember his name ... his first name was Lewis, I believe, and the last name was, uh ... now I remember, Lewis Prichard."

"Lewis Prichard? I know him; in fact, I used to know him quite well," said James. "My father had many business dealings with his father, Solomon, in the old days. Solomon had a plantation just east of Macon. Sometimes he would come here and now and then he would bring Lewis along. We would go fishing in the pond out behind the barn. It sure seems like a long time ago. I lost track of Lewis when I started school in New York. If I remember correctly, he went to school in North Carolina. But the thing that surprises me is that he would be involved with the Ku Klux Klan."

"What surprises you so?" said Jeremy.

"It's just that I am thinking about the kind of boy he was. I don't believe there was a mean bone in his whole body. Once, he caught a small catfish and decided to throw it back, but the hook was pretty deep and the fish died. Lewis felt so bad that we quit fishing and went home. I tried to talk to him about it but it was no use. I realize that it was a long time ago, and I guess my memory of him is molded around the boy he was then, but still—it doesn't seem that a person that gentle would grow up to become a member of a group like the Klan."

"No tellin what the war did to him," said Jeremy. James thought about Ashton and the changes the war had made in her. He also remembered how old and debilitated his father had looked after the war.

"You're right of course, Jeremy," said James. But I want to try ... I want to create an opportunity to talk to him and see what I can do. Which stable does he work at, Aaron?"

"Washburn's Livery over on Magnolia Street."

"I'd rather not go there to see him. I wouldn't want to start any trouble. I can't be sure how he would react to seeing me. I'll have to try watching for him to leave and then follow him."

"I know the place closes at six o'clock except for a man who has a room in the back and stays all night in case somebody needs help real bad," said Aaron. "I reckon Lewis leaves around six."

"Thanks for the information, Aaron. I'll be there tomorrow just before six to see if I can catch him leaving work. I'll depend on you and Jeremy to watch over things while I'm gone."

"We'll do that," they assured him.

The following day at five-thirty, James was across the street from the livery. After tying his horse to the hitching rail he pretended to have a minor problem with the saddle, checking the cinch, making adjustments, while casually casting glances toward the stable. He was not certain that he would recognize Lewis easily. It had been more than ten years since James had seen him and a person's looks can change a lot in that length of time—especially from a child to an adult.

Shortly before six, a young man emerged from the livery barn leading a big gray horse; James took a long hard look at him. The sun was on its way down so he was not positive that it was Lewis, but he decided to find out. Mounting his horse, he hesitated a bit until the subject of his attention could get astride and head of out of town. Then he followed at a distance, which decreased as it grew darker. The man on the gray horse was riding easy as if he was in no hurry to get to where he was going. He was heading east, building James's confidence that he was following the right man. Solomon Prichard's plantation was east of Macon; maybe Lewis still occupied the property, and maybe Solomon was still there as well.

James was lost in thought as he plodded along behind his quarry. The moon provided some light and his eyes had also adjusted, but perhaps he had become too complacent about his purpose. He was moving into a long, sweeping bend in the road when a shot rang out, shattering the quiet evening and causing James's horse to rear. He lost his grip on the reins and slid out of the saddle and down the horse's back, landed on his feet, stumbled backwards, and fell down. His horse did not bolt, but by the time James could gather his senses and get up, the rider he'd been following was looking down at him with a gun in his hand.

"Would you like to tell me why you were dogging my tracks, mister?" he said.

"I am looking for Lewis Prichard ... I thought you might be him."

"Who are you and what do you want with me?"

"I'm James Langdon." There was a short uncomfortable silence and then Lewis spoke.

"I didn't recognize you in the faint light. Don't keep me waiting too long because I can't possibly guess why you were looking for me."

"I'd like to talk to you, if you don't mind."

"That's difficult to answer, Langdon. I might have an answer if I'd had time to think about it, but under the circumstances I don't know if I want to talk to you or not. We were friends once, but you know as well as I do how long ago that was. You also know that a great deal has happened to change things since then."

"I understand completely, Lewis, but if we could just put our differences aside for a little while I would be happy to explain." Again there was silence while James's boyhood companion made up his mind. Finally he said, "I guess I could spare a little time. What's on your mind?"

"Is there somewhere else we could talk?" James asked.

"I was just going home. It's just a mile or so up the road. We can go there."

"Thank you, Lewis."

"I wouldn't be thanking me yet if I were you."

James remounted his horse, appreciating the fact that his former friend had put away his pistol. They headed up the road in silence; James, wondering what Lewis was thinking, concluding that the other man was wondering about James's thoughts. He knew that the Prichard plantation was a mile or two up the road and so figured that Lewis did in fact still live there. But as he rode up the driveway, even in the light of the half-moon he could see that another proud southern estate had met an untimely death. The main house was completely caved in; the top of the once graceful staircase jutted out into the starry sky, looking as if you could climb it to Heaven. All of the outbuildings were wrecked save for one small structure, and in front of it was where Lewis stopped his horse.

"This used to be a slave cabin," he said. "Now it's my home." He dismounted and tied the reins to a porch post; James did the same. When they walked up to the front door, Lewis took a lantern from a peg in the wall, lighted it, and then opened the door. In spite of its outward appearance, the little two room cabin was furnished surprisingly well. The lovely rugs and the beautiful pieces of fine furniture were no doubt salvaged from the ruined mansion. Lewis set the lantern in the middle of a lovely oak dining table and told James to take a seat.

"I don't know why, but you've got your opportunity, Langdon, so start talking."

"I need your help, Lewis."

"You're blunt, I'll give you that. What would possibly make you think that you could come to me for help?"

"I guess because I knew you once; because I knew you as a friend."

"Meaning what?"

"Meaning that when you know someone you learn a lot about them, and I learned a lot about you in the old days. You were a good person, honest, compassionate ... you knew right from wrong and you had respect for the former. You grew up educated and you are an intelligent man."

"I suppose I should say that it's kind of you to come out here and list all my credits but it's getting us nowhere and I'm getting impatient," Lewis said in a sarcastic tone.

"All right," said James. "I would like to know what changed you."

"What changed me? Oh boy, you really are looking for trouble."

"No, Lewis, I am not looking for trouble." Then James sat in silence. He could see that a fire was smoldering inside the other man and threatened to burst into flames at any minute, but James held his ground. He believed that if there truly was good in a person it was there forever, and he somehow felt that he could bring out the good in Lewis Prichard. Then Lewis did something that James didn't expect. He got up from the table, went over to a liquor cabinet, and retrieved a bottle and two glasses. Returning to the table, he set the glasses down and poured whiskey into both. Then he took his seat and pushed one glass toward James. Lewis took a healthy sip and then said, "Why do *you* say I've changed?"

"I know that you are a member of the Ku Klux Klan and I say that the boy I knew would never have joined such a group."

Lewis looked at him with an inscrutable smile on his face. It was almost an evil smile ... or perhaps it meant all right, you asked for it.

"Maybe I have changed and what of it? You saw what happened to this plantation. I'm sure you've seen what has happened to many others. The South is my home; it was your home, too, until you left it to join the side that caused all this. Is what you did any better than joining the Klan?

104

For four long years I fought for my country: watching my friends die, seeing the cities and towns destroyed by the Yankees." Lewis refilled his whiskey glass, emptied it, and continued.

"My father, whom I am sure you remember, was shot to death trying to defend his land and his property, and my mother lives in a permanent state of shock at my Aunt Margret's home in Atlanta. My younger brother, Seth, died at Gettysburg, and Sarah Barlow, the girl I was to marry is now living in Chicago with her husband. Am I bitter? You're goddamn right I'm bitter!"

Lewis filled his glass again and swallowed the contents. James knew the alcohol was a bad influence, only worsening the emotions that were churning inside the young man. He needed to calm the situation or there would be no hope of accomplishing anything. James also began to have mixed feelings concerning his purpose. Lewis had been a childhood friend; a representative of an enjoyable time in life that could only be revisited in memories. Although the two had drifted far apart, James understood his former friend's loss and he felt a genuine sense of sympathy for him. He needed Lewis's help but he would only accept it if he could get him to understand and to agree that James was right.

"I am truly sorry for the way things turned out, Lewis, not just for you and me but for every victim that the war produced. I lost my parents, too. My mother died while I was away and my father committed suicide before my very eyes. I have spent years rebuilding their plantation, which was also devastated by the Union army."

"And you don't regret taking their side?"

"No, no I don't. A man can never cope with life until he can first learn to be honest with himself. I guess that is what enabled me to take the direction I did when the war broke out. Slavery was wrong, Lewis, and the South was wrong to practice it. Oh, I understand the economic reasons behind it, but to use the Negroes because they were an essential part of profitability made it even worse. They are people, Lewis. They are just like you and me and they did not deserve to be treated like animals."

"You might be right and you might not," Lewis replied. "But I wasn't raised that way."

"I know that you were not; more's the pity. Nothing could be more sinful than prejudice except teaching it. That is why a man must think for himself. Put your trust in God, not man."

"I guess I have to give you credit for having the nerve to go against your father; I never would have. But I can't apologize for being loyal to mine either. I guess that's why I joined the Klan. I have to be loyal to my countrymen; it's all I have left."

"But can't you see that they are not justified in their actions? It is just a continuation of slavery. If they can't own the Negroes then they will forcibly and illegally keep them subjugated; not allowing them to exercise their rights. And if that isn't enough, they are committing murder, indiscriminate killings of a people who never asked to be brought to this country in the first place. Where is the honor in that? As for your own life, belonging to a group of masked outlaws is not all you have left. You can rebuild this plantation as I am doing with mine and get your life moving forward in a positive direction again."

James suddenly realized that his own emotions had risen in defiance; antagonizing the situation in spite of the fact that it was the last thing he wanted to do. It became very clear to him that he had pushed his argument too far when Lewis responded to his last comment by saying, "This elegant shack we're sitting in is the only part of this former plantation that I own. The rest is owned by a goddamn carpetbagger who bought the land for the back taxes!"

James did not know what to say. He knew he had weakened the credibility of his petition and Lewis was now too far under the influence of the whiskey. The only thing he could do was to back down, go home, and try again another time. He got up to leave, but Lewis raised a hand and in a slow inebriated voice said, "Wait a minute, Langdon. You said you needed my help."

"I think we should talk about it another time, Lewis."

"Why? Because I'm a little bit drunk? Whiskey don't muddle me none. I do this every night."

"I'm sorry to hear that, but I still think we should wait. If you're willing, we'll talk again."

"But I don't want to wait. In fact, I insist." At that point, Lewis pulled out his revolver and leveled the barrel at James. The situation had gone from a little uncomfortable to very dangerous. James realized that he did not know this man anymore and that he could not make any predictions about what he might do.

"Put the gun down, Lewis. I came here in peace and I intend to leave the same way."

"Sit down, and I will lower my weapon."

James sat back down and was quite relieved when Lewis lowered the weapon and laid it on the table.

"Now then, what do you want from me?"

"Very well ... were you at the Culpepper Plantation just before Christmas when Chet Rawlins was hanged in the barn?"

Lewis eyed him wistfully, going through quite an array of facial expressions as if he were painstakingly trying to read James's mind. Finally, he spoke slowly, measuring his words, attempting to anticipate their effect. Even in his condition he was seemingly apprehensive about making an incriminating statement.

"Yes, I *was* there that night."

"What I want, Lewis, is the name of the man or men who gave the order to hang Chet. And I want you to testify to it in court. I do not mean to see you in trouble over this. I just want anyone who was in a position of authority, ordering or carrying out the order for the murder of Chet Rawlins."

Lewis sat back in his chair as if he were struck by a blow to the jaw. He blinked his eyes rapidly; trying to focus his bloodshot optics. Then his face took on a sheepish grin; then he began to chuckle; and then he began to laugh. It began as a normal reaction to a joke or an amusing sight and then it escalated into a howling, uncontrollable seizure like that of a man who had gone completely mad. James got up again but Lewis paid him no mind. The only emotion that was awake in James's entire body was pity; an almost overwhelming grief for another victim claimed by the hatefulness of war. James left the small dwelling and

went out to his horse. He could still hear the awful raving
as he rode away.

It was after eight o'clock in the evening when he
reached home. It was very disappointing to report that,
although he did manage to have a talk with Lewis Prichard,
the chances were not at all promising that anything
positive would come from it.

Later that evening, James sat in the parlor with Polly,
Ashton, and Kate. The women worked at their sewing
chores while he tried to relax and settle some issues in his
mind. He was beginning to believe that, due to their
tenacity—not to mention a lot of help from God—they had,
in a sense, beaten the Klan. They had not allowed
themselves to be intimidated to the point of abandoning
the plantation and everything they hoped to accomplish.
The plantation was up to about seventy-five percent of its
previous production and another year or two would see it
at full potential. It was gratifying to have reached one of
the most important goals James had set for himself when
he first decided to rebuild after the war. It meant that his
father's legacy would live on for future generations.

But, despite their small sense of victory, the
lawlessness of the Klan was still a threat, the random
killing of Negro citizens was frequent, and churches and
schools were still being destroyed. And closer to home, the
murderer, or murderers, of Chet Rawlins had not been
identified and held accountable. James could not help
feeling that a successful prosecution of the case would be
the best course to establish law and order.

Polly could see how deep in thought he was and as
usual she expressed her concern.

"Is there anything I can do, James?"

"I guess I'm just upset with myself, really."

"How do you mean?"

"I mean that I should be counting my blessings instead
of being sad because I can't change the world. I have so
much to be grateful for and I want to do something for
those people who are less fortunate than I am. I wish I
could do more to help the Negroes enjoy the rights they
have earned and are entitled to as citizens of this country."

"Do you have something in mind?"

"Sadly, no. That is where the part about wishing I could change the world comes in. The only thing I do know is that I would need to find other people who feel as I do. If you want to make changes, you need lots of support. The more people you have pushing in a given direction, the better the chances of getting something done. That is how the destruction of slavery came about. The abolitionist movement; thousands of people joining together in the same interest was what got the job done. Even the Emancipation Proclamation wouldn't have been worth the paper it was written on if not for the support of a lot of good people."

"I think," said Polly, "that you should consider running for public office. That would be one way of getting your ideas in front of a lot of people."

"You are exactly right, Polly," said Kate. "Maybe that would give you the power you're looking for to change the world."

"I agree with them," said Ashton. "Running for public office would measure your popularity with the people. If you are elected, you know that people are willing to follow you. And if they are behind you then you have the power to get things done."

"I thank you for your suggestion, ladies, and I think that you have a good point. But I never saw myself as a politician. And even if I did, I think I can already measure my popularity with the people. Are you forgetting that some of those people want to drive me out of the state?"

"None of us are overlooking what has happened the last couple of years, James," said Polly. "We also realize the magnitude of being targeted by the Ku Klux Klan. We have practically been made prisoners in our own home because it has been too dangerous for anyone to go very far from here alone. The situation has kept all of us preoccupied, to say the least. But do we know that every white man in this state besides you, Jeremy, and Aaron are members of the Klan? Do we know that we are the only people for miles around who support equal rights for Negroes?"

"Polly has a good point, James," said Kate.

"She does," echoed Ashton.

James let the conversation sink in for several minutes. In spite of his longtime desire to see things change, never had he entertained the notion of seeking public office. But even if he could somehow get elected, would he be the right man for the job?

"I have to admit, the idea opens up a lot of possibilities," he said. "However, there is one piece of unfinished business that I need to attend to first. I must try again to talk to Lewis Prichard; I must make another appeal. I know that I have the support of Governor Bullock if I can only find evidence to convict the guilty person. I have got to win this battle before I can engage the enemy in the next."

James went to bed that night with a contentment he had not known in quite some time. Perhaps it meant that there were good things ahead; good things for all people. He spent longer than usual saying his prayers before drifting off into a deep sleep.

Two days later, the good feeling James had experienced made a real effort to become more realistic. He was working in his office after breakfast when Polly knocked on the door and said, "There is someone here to see you. He didn't want to come in; he is waiting on the veranda."

When James opened the front door he was astonished to see Lewis Prichard sitting on the swing. Lewis stood up and said, "If you don't mind, I'd like to talk to you."

"Of course I don't mind. Won't you come in the house?"

"If it's all the same to you, this swing is good enough for me."

"OK, let's sit down."

The two men took a seat and then Lewis began explaining what was on his mind.

"I don't want any trouble. I mean, I have to have your assurance that no matter what happens, I walk away."

"I don't know what you want to tell me, Lewis, but I promise that if I can't guarantee you immunity then I won't let you get involved."

"I guess I can't ask for more than that. OK, I'll trust you. I have done a lot of thinking since you came to see me. I've done a lot of soul searching; somehow, you stirred up a lot of issues for me. I am fairly ashamed of the impression I gave you the other night; my drinking and all. I just hope you can understand. I've been through a lot since before the war—none of it good. I came home to find that my whole future was gone and I was angry, resentful, and vulnerable. I suppose that I was in need of something that I could relate to, something familiar. When I was approached by a few of the boys I served with, when they told me they did not intend to concede defeat to the Union and their idea of how we should live, I fell like a house of cards. My old compatriots were all I had left, and at the time, I needed what they had to offer."

He stopped talking and looked at James with a helpless expression on his face. James sensed that he needed a little encouragement to finish his story. He was obviously at the mercy of something that was eating at him from deep inside. He so reminded James of the boy he fished with long ago.

"Lewis, you would have every reason to believe that, given the situation, I might say anything I think you want to hear to get your help. It isn't true. I have fond memories of our relationship when we both had reason to believe that we lived in a never-ending paradise. It would be a privilege of inestimable value to go back there for just one day. I'll admit that when I left your house the other evening I was sure that the Lewis Prichard I knew was gone for good. I am glad to see that I was wrong. I have seen more than once the terrible effects the late war has had on people; I have seen it in my own family. I want you to know that I understand perfectly how and why you became involved with the Klan."

"That means a lot, James; I thank you for that. I, too, remember better days. But I have to be honest with you; for the Negroes I have no love or hatred. They have no meaning to me anymore. Before the war I saw them as the laborers who worked the fields and brought the harvest in. I don't think I ever considered their lives and what it must be like to be a slave. Maybe that sounds terrible to you but that's how it was for me. I know they were sometimes whipped if they caused trouble but I always felt that if they didn't want to be punished then they should do what they were told. I was punished when I got out of line, too; I realize now that it wasn't really the same thing."

"No, Lewis, not the same thing at all. But the days of slavery are over and going back to that serves no purpose. It is the present that we should be concerned about."

"Very well," he replied. "I have seen a lot of things, James, a lot of ruthless, brutal things that are not really acceptable to my nature. In other words, if I can help you, I would be doing it simply because I want to bring about an end to the rampant violence. After fighting a war I would like to live in peace for a change. It amazes me that some of the boys never get enough fighting. Not long ago I found out that Nathan Forrest resigned as the Grand Wizard because the Klan had gotten too violent even for him. It really impacted me when I heard that. He was such a fearless cavalry leader and I thought that if *he* felt that way, then what was I doing in the Klan? And I have seen things get much worse since I joined them. At first we rode around at night just trying to intimidate people; trying to scare them into submission. Then it began to get more violent, more destructive, until cold blooded murder was a regular occurrence. When they hanged Chet Rawlins I got real scared; I knew they had gone too far. You've been very lucky, James. The Klan has a personal grievance against you. The funny thing though is that they want to run you out of Georgia but they've been warned not to harm you or your family. It's as if someone higher up is holding them back. I don't really understand what it's all about."

"I have another concern, Lewis. This is a very serious business; it may end up sending someone to the gallows. If you do what I ask, I fear you will be letting yourself in for a lot of trouble with the Klan. They may even hate you more than they do me."

"I've considered that, James, and you make a very good point. But it took a lot of guts to follow your conscience as you have done. Let me have the chance to do the same."

"Very well, then I need to know who was directly responsible for Chet's death. I also need you to testify in court against him. I have been in touch with the governor of Georgia. The governor will support this effort if I can discover the guilty person and provide evidence that will hold up in a court of law."

"I was there the night Chet was hanged. I won't describe the entire evening because you were there for most of what happened, too. When you and your friends escaped, not to mention the Negro Buford Bell slipping through our fingers, our leader, the Exalted Cyclops, was outraged. We chased after you but that barricade Chet put across the road really did the trick. The front riders slammed into it full force and ended up in a twisted pile of men and horses. A couple of the horses broke their necks and one or two others broke a leg; they had to be shot."

"Yes, we saw them when we went back to look for Chet that night."

"A few of the boys were pretty banged up, too. Some of us in the back rode around the pileup and continued the chase. If you remember, it was raining hard that night."

"I remember the rain."

"Well, the road was awful muddy and not too far from the barricade, Chet had the misfortune of having his horse go out from underneath him. His horse scrambled to its feet and took off and in no time we had Chet surrounded. We took him back to the barn and held what I prefer to call a mock trial. Of course he was found guilty and the Exalted Cyclops, well, Harland Jeffers, ordered us to hang him. I guess that makes us all responsible though, doesn't it? I mean, anyone who was there is to blame."

Yes, Lewis, that's the way the law, sees it. But under the circumstances I think if we can get the leader convicted it may suffice. The Klan is an elusive group and they are well protected by local people who are in favor of their actions. I'm sure it is very difficult to make arrests let alone get convictions. That is just the point; if the governor can prosecute the leader, if he can cut off the head of the monster, it might just send a message that will have the Klan feeling a bit uneasy for a change. I think he will be willing to settle for that."

"I sure hope you're right."

"I promise you, Lewis, that I will not give the governor your name unless he is willing to trade your freedom for your testimony."

"OK, how do we begin?"

"I will contact Governor Bullock right away and inform him of the situation. I will withhold your name until I find out if he is willing to accept our terms. If he does, we'll tell him who is responsible for Chet's death and that you are ready to testify in court. If he won't agree, maybe we can find another way. Now that I know who the murderer is, I won't rest until he pays for his crime. I happen to know that Chet's death is not the only one for which he is responsible. That being said, I will include in my letter to the governor a list of people who should be subpoenaed and why; I will also ask you to give me a list of your own containing names of other Klan members, for example."

"I hope it's over soon," said Lewis. "In the meantime I have to work on disassociating myself with other Klan members. It won't be easy; they take a dim view of anyone who wants to quit. But I can't participate in their activities anymore."

"I am very happy with your decision, Lewis; if only you could influence more men to do the same. Unfortunately, I know that is not possible. You must be very careful. I don't need to tell you how rough they can get if provoked."

"I'll be careful, James. Just let me know the minute you hear from the governor."

"You can be sure I will."

Lewis got up from the swing, offered his hand to James, and then he left. James went back to his office, sat down, and began composing another letter to the governor. His spirits were high and he was very optimistic about the chances of bringing Chet's murderer to justice now that he had help on the inside. He was, however, very concerned for Lewis because it did not take a genius to know what would happen to him if he were found out. James believed that he could trust Governor Bullock and he was sure that the governor would be satisfied to have the Exalted Cyclops in his clutches. Still, if all were in agreement, the time would come when Lewis would go before the public and let it be known that he was responsible for the Klan leader's arrest. That would be another mountain to climb.

# TWELVE

# The Governor's Reply

After four very difficult years since the war had ended, James could finally sense a more relaxed state of affairs concerning his presence in Georgia. Perhaps it was because he had stood his ground against the Klan and made it clear that he meant to stay. Or maybe it was because things were changing in and around Macon. People came and people went; old businesses were changing hands and new businesses were being established whose owners knew nothing of old feuds. All James knew was that there was a different feel to his occasional visits into town. Making money, especially in a poor southern economy, seemed to take priority over everything else and most of the merchants were more than willing to do business with him.

It was just as obvious, however, that nothing much was budging in favor of the black skinned race; white supremacy was very much alive. But along with maintaining the growing success of the plantation, James was cognizant of the need for much more equality between the races, and his thoughts were geared toward a new plan of action as soon as the matter of Chet Rawlins's death was concluded.

Almost two weeks had passed since he'd sent his all-important letter to Governor Bullock. Time was moving along quickly as time always does; already, the men were busy preparing for the upcoming planting season. James was hoping the whole ugly business would be behind him by the time the season began.

It was a clear, bright Sunday morning in February; church services had just concluded and everyone was heading in to breakfast after listening to another inspiring sermon delivered by Aaron Parmalee. James, Polly, Ashton, Kate, and Jim were walking to the house when an unexpected visitor turned his horse into the driveway and rode slowly toward them. Even from a distance, the rider's appearance seemed suspect; James immediately put his guard up.

"Jim, take the ladies into the house," he said. "I won't be long."

Jim escorted his mother and aunts up to the veranda, disappearing through the front door. The newcomer brought his horse to a stop. James turned to extend a greeting, but after a closer look, words seemed to fail him. The stranger was dressed entirely in black, from the hat on his head to the boots on his feet. His horse was a tall, coal black stallion and the look on the man's chiseled face would have made the grim reaper seem like an amiable character. A voice as cold and deep as the lower regions completed his sinister aura.

"Lookin for James Langdon."

"I am James Langdon. Would you step down?"

"More comfortable where I am. Got a bad leg. I'm Roland T. Ramsey, Deputy Marshal out of Atlanta here on orders from the governor. Word is you know a man who can identify some of the members of the Klan in this area. I've come for that man."

James had been anxiously waiting for word from the governor but he felt that something was very wrong with this callous creature who was claiming to represent the governor's interest. But James's communication with the governor was in confidence, so who else could have sent this dark emissary?

"I'm afraid I don't quite understand the meaning of your request, Mr. Ramsey. I *do* know a man who can identify the Klan members but as I explained to the governor—"

"Well, don't explain it to me, Mr. Langdon," Ramsey interrupted. "I have come for the murderer who wants to save his neck by hangin his friends. That's about what I would expect from a bunch of rubbish like these masked cowards."

"The man who is willing to help the law is not a coward, Mr. Ramsey. It takes a lot of guts to do what he is prepared to do. His heart was never really in it; all he wants now is to see the violence stop and—"

"I thought you were a law abiding citizen who wanted to see the Klan get what's coming to em," he replied, cutting James off again. "Sounds to me like you don't know which side you're on. The governor wants to clean up this goddamn gang of troublemakers and your gutsy friend can point the finger at them sons a bitches. I'll start with the leader, and then I'll deal with the rest of em."

"I don't believe that the man I know is guilty of murder."

"They're all guilty, Mr. Langdon, and if you ain't willin to cooperate, then you're guilty, too. Now, I got a job to do and it's to clean out this nest of Rebels. And you can bet that I won't stop until I see every last one of them hanged."

James was astonished. This just couldn't be happening. He refused to believe that he had so misjudged the governor. Even if Bullock insisted on rounding up every Klan member in the area, he wouldn't send a half mad fanatic like Ramsey to represent the law, would he?

"I'm not sure you know which side you are on either, Mr. Ramsey. Are you here for justice or are you here for revenge?"

"Don't you talk to me like that you son of a bitch! If you're gonna stand there and defend these southern scum then you and I are likely gonna end up goin at it, boy!"

"Not all southerners are scum."

"I'll allow you that becuz I hear you fought for the Union. But I know what these damn Rebels are capable of. I spent almost two years in Libby Prison during the war. I left a leg there and I'll be walkin on a tree stump for the rest of my days. What would that do to *your* sympathies?"

"I spent almost six months in Andersonville. I was captured not far from Savannah after General Sherman pulled out."

Ramsey sat back in his saddle, tried to reply, but kept his silence. His mouth had run out from under his brain; he could no longer feel that he had bested James. Finally he said, "Are you gonna give me that name?"

"Not until I speak to the governor myself."

For a minute, James thought Ramsey might pull his pistol. It was obvious that his refusal had touched the deepest nerve in the bitter man's body. Instead, in a

117

surprisingly steady voice he said, "I'll give you forty-eight hours, Mr. Langdon. Then I'll be back to arrest your witness ... or you."

With that, the frustrated lawman turned his tall black horse and galloped down the driveway. James hurried into the house; Polly and his sisters were waiting.

"Who was that man?" Polly asked.

"Roland T. Ramsey. He says he's a deputy marshal sent by the governor."

"You sound skeptical," said Kate.

"I am, very skeptical. This man has a score to settle with the South and I don't believe that due process of law holds any importance for him."

"Why would the governor send such a man?" said Ashton.

"I have no way of proving it but I am not too sure that he did. I guess if he is in fact a lawman, it could be possible that he found out about the situation and he's taking the opportunity to exact a pound of flesh. He was in Libby Prison during the war, and as I said, he has an axe to grind with former Rebels. If my hunch is correct, in forty-eight hours we'll have a very angry man coming here to arrest me because I have no intention of giving him Lewis's name. However, it will be far worse if I have misjudged the governor and he really did send Ramsey to handle this. Then it could mean serious trouble with the law if I do not comply."

"But if the governor sent Ramsey, wouldn't he have sent a posse? One man cannot go up against the Klan," said Polly.

"You are quite right, Polly. That is just one more reason to make me think that Ramsey is acting on his own authority."

"So what will you do?" asked Ashton.

"There is only one thing I can do. I have forty-eight hours to talk to the governor and verify or discredit Ramsey's story. After that, maybe I can sort things out."

"When will you leave, James?"

"I'll have to leave first thing in the morning, dear. I'll take Aaron with me and I will have Jeremy look after things while I'm gone."

After breakfast, James had a talk with Jeremy and Aaron.

"I have to agree with you about the governor, James," said Jeremy. "Aaron and I met Governor Bullock in person and he seemed like a regular sort of fella to us. I don't figure he would send a man like the one you described, do you, Aaron?"

"No, I don't. I reckon this Ramsey isn't willin to put the war behind him either."

"Well," said James. "We will have to find out fast. We'll leave at sunup tomorrow Aaron."

"I'll be ready."

The following morning the two men took the road to Atlanta. After two hours of hard riding, James slowed his horse to a walk; Aaron did likewise.

"We'd better pace them a bit Aaron. It's a long ride to Atlanta and I don't want to wear the horses down so much that we have to spend the night. The more I think about the conversation with Ramsey the more wary of him I become."

"I reckon you can't be too careful with a man like that. I saw some boys pretty near completely lose themselves during the war. Their bodies came home but their spirits were left at Gettysburg or Cold Harbor or some awful place. It's even worse for those who spent time in a prisoner of war camp. North or South, those places were hell on earth."

"They certainly were," James replied. A sudden flashback reminded him of Corporal Tim Fallon; a young soldier from New York. James had shared a canvas covered hole in the ground with him at Andersonville and he watched him die there. It was easy to understand how a man could lose his mind in a place like that; James came close himself.

"Look up ahead, James," said Aaron. James followed the direction of his friend's gesture and saw a group of men on horseback heading towards them.

"I think I see a flag ... yes, and another man is carrying a guidon. They must be soldiers."

The two men reined in their horses and waited for the approaching patrol to reach them. The blue clad officer in

119

front raised a hand and the horse soldiers came to a stop. James immediately recognized his wartime friend, Major Alvin Mitchell.

"Hello, Mitch. Happily we meet again."

"Greetings to you, James. It's good to see you. Where are you heading?"

"Atlanta. Hopefully we will be able to see Governor Bullock."

"The hell you say; we have been sent here by the governor to see you."

"Is that a fact?"

"Yes. The governor has detailed my men and me to execute the plan you initiated to arrest and prosecute for murder the leader of the local Klan. If we are able to take into custody any other members, such as any man holding a designated position in the klavern, the governor would consider that a bonus. But in his opinion, orders and the responsibility of those orders come from the leader, and that is the man he wants."

"What about the ex-member who is willing to identify this man?" James asked.

"The governor will personally give your witness amnesty for his help in this matter. Of course, you will be called upon to testify as well."

"Yes," James replied. "I assured the governor that I would. I can describe everything that happened that night. Jeremy Todd and I were the ones who found Chet's body. I also believe that I can identify the leader by his speech impediment. Will Jeremy and Aaron be asked to testify?"

"I will let you know about that," said Mitch. "For now, the governor just wants you and your witness who, again, will not be prosecuted; he will be released."

"I have to be sure of that, Mitch. I gave my word to this man that he could walk away when this is over."

Mitch nudged his horse a little closer to James. He pulled a piece of paper from his coat pocket and handed it to him.

"Here is a letter from the governor, James. You can read the conditions for yourself."

James read the letter and then handed it back to Major Mitchell. All was satisfactory except for one thing.

"There is one new wrinkle in the plan, Mitch."

"Oh? What might that be?"

"A man by the name of Roland T. Ramsey."

Mitch raised his eyebrows as if he had just heard that his home was directly in the path of a cyclone.

"How do you know Ramsey?"

"I didn't know him until yesterday morning. He came to see me; he said he was sent by the governor. Our conversation was not a pleasant one, especially when I refused to give him the name of my witness. He has given me until tomorrow morning. If I don't comply with his request, he intends to arrest me. He is one very intimidating sort of man."

"Was he dressed like an undertaker and riding a black horse?" Mitch asked.

"That's him. I gathered that he is on his own personal vendetta and I believe that he will do what he threatens."

"You're right about that, my friend. He is not to be taken lightly."

"What do you know about him Mitch?"

"The best way to describe him is to say that he is a hired killer and he works for the Klan."

"The Klan?"

"Yes. I know he probably led you to believe just the opposite, but he is a professional killer, paid by the Klan to assassinate Klan enemies. He is as cunning as he is ruthless and he is very adept at committing the deed and then making a clean getaway. Twice I was ready to close in on him and twice he slipped through my fingers. He is wanted for several murders in Atlanta, and along with my other duties, I follow up any leads on Ramsey that I can get. He is high priority and I will let anything else drop in an instant if his trail becomes hot. Ramsey doesn't ride around at night shooting defenseless Negroes. He is assigned to take out difficult targets, such as politicians bringing heat down on the Klan. It is no secret that he is gunning for the governor. He has made one attempt already. Governor Bullock is a staunch opponent of the Klan, as you probably know."

"I guess he never spent time in Libby Prison like he told me."

"On the contrary, James. He spent time there all right, but not as a prisoner. He was the assistant commandant under Major Thomas P. Turner. He and the jailor, Richard Turner, no relation to the commandant, were on Secretary of War Edwin Stanton's list of men to be tried for war crimes after the war for their terrible abuse of prisoners. But after President Johnson fired Stanton, charges were never brought. In February of 1864, one hundred and nine inmates escaped through a tunnel that took them seventeen days to dig. They managed to break through to a fifty foot vacant lot on the eastern side of the prison and re-surfaced beneath a tobacco shed inside the grounds of the nearby Kerr's Warehouse. When the last three men were ready to start down the tunnel, they heard a noise behind them, which they thought were rats at first. It turned out to be Ramsey; standing there with a pistol pointed at them. Out of desperation, the three men jumped Ramsey, took his pistol, and one of the men stuck in Ramsey's leg a knife he had been digging with. They left the assistant commandant lying on the ground, writhing in pain, and made good their escape. Fifty-nine of the men made it back to Union lines, two of them drowned in the James River, and forty-eight were re-captured. As for Ramsey; I guess that knife had a lot of dirt and bacteria on it because he developed gangrene in that leg and it had to be taken off by the prison surgeon, a man by the name of A.W. Thomson. As mean a man as Ramsey was, the loss of his leg made him even worse."

"How do you suppose he ended up at my place and what is his real purpose?"

"I think I can make a pretty accurate guess. We've known for some time that there are eyes and ears in our department that belong to the Klan; another puzzle we are trying to solve. No doubt the word has spread about your communications with the governor and that there is a man in your county willing to expose the leader of the Klan and have him arrested for murder. Sure as hell, Ramsey was sent to find out who that man is and kill him before he can testify."

"It certainly adds up, Mitch," said James. "I'm relieved to learn that I have not misjudged the governor, but the intervention of Mr. Ramsey changes things a bit."

"It does, indeed, but it might have changed things for the better."

"You're thinking about setting a trap for Ramsey?"

"You catch on fast, my friend. But we have to set the trap well. As I said, he is cunning."

"Do you have any ideas, Mitch?"

"Not exactly, but for now, I think it would be a good idea if you went home. I know he said he would be back in forty-eight hours, but who knows if he will wait that long. You head home and my men and I will find a spot to set up camp a few miles away. Then we'll come to your place tonight under the cover of darkness. That will give me time to decide how I want to handle this. There is one more thing, James. I think you'd better give me the name of your witness. I think it's time I know all the pertinent facts."

"I think you're right, Mitch. His name is Lewis Prichard. You will pass his father's old plantation on the way to mine; about ten miles from here on the left. He lives in an old slave cabin near the remains of the main house."

"That's fine," said Mitch. "You will still go and get him when the time comes. He may think you've double crossed him if we show up. But just in case anything should happen ..."

"I understand; we'll get moving. I'll be looking for you to arrive sometime after dark."

With that, James and Aaron turned their horses and galloped off toward home. Major Mitchell and his men stayed put to give them time to get a good distance out ahead. It seemed to be taking forever to reach the plantation. The more James thought about the man in black, the more he urged his horse to pick up speed. He knew that Jeremy was more than capable of overseeing things when James was away and he had plenty of help if he should need it. Still, James wanted to be there if Ramsey returned. He wondered what Mitch might come up with to lure the killer into a trap; it was of the utmost importance to catch him before James could take Lewis to

Mitch and his men. Otherwise, it would be too dangerous and the arrest of the Klan leader would have to be delayed.

Finally, the big barn at the plantation came into view. James and Aaron galloped up the driveway and their eyes fell upon a scene that instantly terrified them. About thirty Negroes had formed a circle and their attention was focused on something lying on the ground. As James approached, he saw Roland T. Ramsey's black horse tied at the hitching rail. He jumped to the ground and pushed his way to the center of the circle. Hiram Jones was bent down over the body of Jeremy Todd. Jeremy was conscious but blood was seeping from the bullet hole in his right shoulder.

"What happened here, Hiram?" James yelled.

"We ain't quite sure, James. We heard a shot and we come a runnin; Jeremy was on the ground and a man all in black clothes was walkin toward the house."

"My God! Do you mean he's in the house?"

"Yes, sir, he is."

"Aaron, Hiram, look after Jeremy!"

James made his way through the onlookers and ran for the veranda. When he got to the front door he hesitated for just a second and then he opened the front door slowly and went inside. There was an eerie silence, which alarmed James more than if he'd heard screaming. He took a few steps up the hallway and then he heard a voice he was already able to recognize.

"We're waiting for you in here, Langdon."

James walked to the doorway of the parlor; there he saw his whole family, Polly, Jim, Ashton, and Kate, sitting on the floor. All of them, even his seven-year-old son, were gagged and bound at the wrists. James could see the terror in their eyes; Jim sat quietly as if he were in shock.

"I'm glad you hurried home, Langdon. I get impatient real quick, and when I get impatient I often do things that people don't like very much."

James was at a complete loss. He knew the situation had to be handled very carefully and somehow he would have to keep the volcano inside him from boiling over.

"I thought you said forty-eight hours, Ramsey."

"Mr. Ramsey, if you don't mind."

"Yes, Mr. Ramsey." James humored him.

"You may learn that I am a bit of a liar; I find that having the advantage in any situation is always helpful. I might say forty-eight hours and then come back in twenty-four just to catch people off guard. If they don't really know when to expect me, sometimes they give themselves away, just like you did."

"Like I did?" said James.

"'Like I did,' *what*?"

"Like I did, Mr. Ramsey?"

"You'll get it eventually. Yes, like you did. I saw you and your friend riding out early this morning and I tagged along. It paid off. I saw you having a powwow with them blue bellies. I have a feeling that you were tryin to pull something on me, Langdon. Naturally, I had to get back here before you so I could make sure that this thing is gonna turn out like I want it to."

In spite of the hatred that James felt growing inside himself for this smug killer, he grudgingly had to admit that Mitch was right: this was a cunning individual. The self-confidence was coming out of every pore in his body; he was relaxed and insulting with the way he called James by his last name while insisting that James call him Mr. Ramsey. But worst of all, he was sitting across from the people that James loved most in the world with a pistol cradled in his lap.

"What are your intentions, Mr. Ramsey?" James asked.

"Owing you nothing I might still spare you the details, Langdon. I want the name of the traitor who intends to identify the Klan leader and there is nothing I won't do to get it. Are you still curious about my intentions?"

"No, Mr. Ramsey, I think I understand."

James could see his entire world coming to an end. The moment could not be direr. He could not stall and he could not think of any way to get his family into a safe position. Mitch and his soldiers were just a few miles away but it was of no help to him; by the time darkness fell it would be too late. But even if he were willing to give Ramsey the name he wanted, would he be satisfied and leave without further incident or would he take a member of James's family with him as a guarantee?

"Your time is up, Langdon. I want that name. I don't intend to wait around until your soldier friends show up."

"I am not a fool, Mr. Ramsey. I recognize the futility of my position. My only concern is for my family and I only want to know how I can ensure their safety."

"There is only one way to do that and that is to give me what I want. Deliver it."

"Deliver, Mr. Ramsey?"

"How long will it take to go find this man and bring him here?"

"Maybe a couple of hours," said James.

"Then send somebody to go get him. Just tell your messenger to say that you need to see him. When they get here I'll take the traitor and go."

"Very well, I'll get a man started."

"And, Langdon, tell him to hurry; my impatient nature, you know."

James hurried out the door without a reply. Outside, most of the sharecroppers and their families waited silently for news. When James approached the crowd, Hiram Jones walked over to meet him.

"Is everybody all right, James?"

"Yes, for now. How is Jeremy?"

"Aaron says he will be OK. The bullet went straight through his shoulder and he lost some blood, but with proper care he'll be fine."

"Hiram, go and get Aaron for me and please hurry." A few minutes later Aaron came on the run; James explained the situation very quickly.

"I have no choice but to ask you to ride into Macon, find Lewis Prichard, and tell him I need to see him right away. Try to remain calm and reveal no sense of urgency. I am agonizing over the thought of it but what else can I do? Ramsey has my whole family and my only chance of rescuing them is to hand over Lewis Prichard. Maybe I can think of something before you return; maybe everything will turn out all right somehow; I will pray that it does. Now go, and hurry."

Aaron climbed onto his horse and took off like a shot. James went back into the house to sit with his family and wait. Ramsey seemed satisfied that all was going well.

Fortunately, he was all business and did not try to make small talk. James was in no mood for any more of his irritating comments. He looked at Polly, his sisters, and his son and tried to put a reassuring smile on his face. He also kept a close eye on Ramsey, who was in turn keeping a close eye on all of them.

The time went by painfully slow; it seemed like eternity until the sound of horses coming up the driveway brought everyone to attention. Another minute passed and then there was a knock at the door.

"Let our friend in, Langdon," said Ramsey.

James got up and went to the door, opened it, and was nearly bowled over to see Major Alvin Mitchell standing there in civilian clothes. Mitch could see the confusion in James's eyes and he quickly took charge of the situation.

"Hello, James, I understand you wanted to see me."

"Yes, uh, Lewis, I have news. Come in."

James stepped over to the parlor doorway and Mitch followed. Ramsey got up and pointed his pistol at Mitch. Mitch played his part very well. He looked at James as if he was completely surprised and then he said, "What's going on here, James?"

"Lewis, this is Roland T. Ramsey," said James.

"Thanks for the introduction, Langdon, and who are you?" Ramsey said to Mitch.

"I'm Lewis Prichard. What do you want with me? Why the gun?"

"You and I are gonna take a ride, Prichard. Your fellow Klan members are real upset with you."

Mitch, still playing his part, looked at James and said, "Is this a setup, James? You're turning me over to him?"

James prayed that Mitch knew what he was doing and he played along with the attempt to fool Ramsey.

"I'm sorry, Lewis. I had no choice; I had to save my family."

"And you did, Langdon," said Ramsey. "I'll be taking this rat with me and you can untie your frightened but otherwise healthy family."

Ramsey advanced slowly toward Mitch, gun in hand and James could see for the first time how the killer struggled to walk on his wooden leg. Ramsey motioned with his weapon for Mitch to go to the front door. Mitch shot an irate look at James, opened the door, and walked out ahead of Ramsey.

James hurried into the parlor and freed Polly and then he told her to help Jim and the girls. Then he went to the window and watched as Mitch started down the steps of the veranda. Ramsey descended the steps in an awkward fashion. All of a sudden Mitch dove to the ground; one second, two seconds ... a shot rang out. Ramsey pitched forward and rolled down the last two steps. James ran to the front door and out onto the veranda. Mitch was already on his feet; he grabbed Ramsey's arm and wrestled the pistol out of his hand. From over near the sharecroppers' quarters, Aaron and Mitch's soldiers came running to the scene. Ramsey had been hit in his good leg but he didn't seem to feel physical pain any more than he felt sympathy or compassion. Mitch wrapped a kerchief around Ramsey's wound and then he explained what had happened.

"I saw your friend, Aaron, racing down the road and I knew something was wrong. We stopped him and he told us what was going on. We rode over to Lewis Prichard's place, explained the whole story to him, and he fixed me up with these clothes. Then we came over, sneaked in behind your barn, and I put my men into position. This is Sergeant Jonesy Fitzsimmons," Mitch said, pointing to one of his men. "He was in the U.S. Sharpshooters during the war and I would match his expertise with a rifle against anyone. I told him to wait until I created a separation between me and Ramsey and then to put a ball in Ramsey, but not a killing shot."

"I'd say he did an excellent job," said James.

"He certainly did. Ramsey will live long enough to go to the gallows. I am very happy to finally get this man in custody. The governor will be happy, too. We will keep Ramsey in isolation, being very careful to make sure his arrest is kept secret. We will even leak out a rumor that Ramsey was successful; Jeffers and his defense attorney will be completely unnerved when Lewis appears."

James realized that he had temporarily forgotten about the governor, Lewis Prichard, and the whole reason for

Mitch to be there in the first place. The interference of Roland T. Ramsey had completely intimidated him.

"So you talked to Lewis then?" said James. "Where is he?"

Mitch put two fingers to his lips and whistled loudly. Lewis came out from behind the house and walked over to the group of men.

"Hello, Lewis. I would introduce you to everyone but I guess you have already been brought up to date," said James.

"Yes, I have. I'm glad you and your family are all right, thanks to Major Mitchell here."

"He's a good man; it looks like he saved us all," James told him.

"That's true. It is a bit unsettling to find out that there was a killer on my trail."

"I hope it doesn't change your mind about testifying," said James.

"On the contrary; I want to testify more than ever. It has been another lesson on just how dangerous the Klan can be and how important it is to do anything possible to slow them down."

"I am going to send Ramsey back to Atlanta with two of my men," said Mitch. "You will go with them, Lewis, and be placed in protective custody until you testify; then you will be free to leave. We'll take good care of you; you'll be comfortable. If you don't mind I would also like you armed so that I'll have another good man to keep an eye on Ramsey during the trip."

"I'd be happy to help guard the man who was sent to kill me," said Lewis.

"Fine, fine." To Sergeant Fitzsimmons, Mitch said, "Take Ramsey into Macon and get his leg looked at by a doctor, and then get him to Atlanta as soon as possible. The rest of us will pick up the Klan leader, Harland Jeffers, and then we'll be along."

James expressed his gratitude once more to Lewis and assured him that he would see him at the trial when the time came. Then he said goodbye to Mitch and thanked him again as well. As for Roland T. Ramsey, the coldblooded killer had not uttered a word since before he was wounded. Maybe he was too busy planning an escape or maybe he had resigned himself to the fact that a wanted man's luck has to run out sooner or later. James would never forget what the man had put his family through and he could not resist a few parting words to make his feelings clear. He walked over to where the man in black sat on his horse and said, "Goodbye *Ramsey.*"

To James's complete amazement Ramsey replied, "Goodbye, Mr. Langdon."

The soldiers moved out with their charges and James went into the house to comfort his family.

# THIRTEEN

## The Trial of Harland Jeffers

On April 26, 1869, the men at Langdon Plantation began planting the new crop of cotton; two days earlier, James had received word that the trial of the local Klan leader was set for April the thirtieth. It had been decided by the prosecuting attorney that only James and Aaron would need to appear in court.

By now, the workforce of sharecroppers totaled a full complement and the entire twenty-five hundred acres of the plantation was being cultivated and seeded. James no longer worked in the fields side by side with his men but found a full-time job in just running the business.

So, when the time came to leave for Atlanta, he knew he could go without a worry concerning the management of the plantation. James had designated Jeremy Todd and Hiram Jones as the foremen in charge of the field operations and everything ran smoothly under their experience and guidance.

After arriving in Atlanta, James rented rooms for Aaron and himself in a boarding house on Peach Tree Street; the trial was set to begin at 10 AM. After breakfast, he picked up a copy of the *Atlanta Constitution* and scanned the headlines for a story about the proceedings. The man who would be presiding over the case was a Supreme Court justice by the name of Henry Kent McCay of Northumberland County, Pennsylvania. McCay had been appointed by Governor Bullock in 1868. Reading further in the story, James learned that McCay received an A.B. from Princeton in 1839 and read law in 1842. After that he was in private practice in Americus, Georgia from 1843 until 1861. He then served as assistant quartermaster of the 12th Georgia Regiment during the war. James wondered what McCay's feelings were toward the Ku Klux Klan but he decided that there was little to worry about considering he had been chosen by Governor Bullock. The Federal District Attorney was a Unionist by the name of Amherst W. Stone.

The courtroom was packed; no doubt this was a high profile case, stimulating a lot of interest. Like the rest of the Deep South, the Klan was very strong in Georgia. In James's opinion, this case could well set a precedent for future trials to follow; that was one of the points that made winning it so important. James knew that if you want to let daylight into a cave, you have to start with one small hole. If a conviction could be gotten against Harland Jeffers, the effect could be monumental for curtailing the worst of the Klan activities: indiscriminate murder.

Still, as James always understood, it would be a long hard road to travel for the blacks before equality would be realized. He had hoped that the new president, a solid Unionist, would take a firmer stand against groups like the Klan, seeing them as resentful rebels unwilling to conform to the doctrine of the victorious North. Grant was a decent man, albeit a naïve one, who, from what James could gather, seemed to let those around him go their own way. By reading every line in the paper concerning the conflicts of the healing nation, it was obvious that the president did not sympathize with the anti-black element, nor did he support the punitive approach of the radical Republicans. The result of Grant's moderation was the reestablishment of power in the hands of white Southerners; which undoubtedly meant the denial of rights to blacks.

Shortly before 10 AM, Harland Jeffers entered the courtroom escorted by two deputy sheriffs. No one can read another person's mind but if James were to guess he would say that Jeffers looked as though he hadn't a care in the world; very confident for a man being tried for murder.

At 10 AM the bailiff silenced the crowd and called for everyone to rise while the judge entered the courtroom and took his esteemed chair behind the bench. The prosecution began with its opening remarks; the defense followed. Jeffers's attorney was a man by the name of Augustus E. Johnson from Athens, Georgia. He was a tall, thin man, probably mid-forties, dressed in a fine suit that gave him a very dapper appearance. His attention to personal detail was marred only by a most ridiculous looking hairpiece, perfunctorily situated and the wrong color. But the occasional tittering ceased after the man's powerful voice and domineering presence were exhibited. However, Amherst W. Stone was not a man who was easily intimidated and as the stage was set to begin calling witnesses, the crowd was prepared for a hard fought legal contest.

The first several witnesses produced little toward the overall opinion of guilt or innocence. They were called mostly to establish the character of the defendant, touching on the subject of the Ku Klux Klan and whether or not Jeffers was a member; a point that was not entirely settled. After that, a number of former slaves, owned by Jeffers, were called, and that was when the brutal side of the man became apparent. The problem was, the ignorant Negroes were no match on any level for Augustus E. Johnson and he shredded their testimony into confetti. He very easily twisted their words and got them so confused that they ended up looking foolish, discrediting themselves. Then the prosecution gained some ground when Mr. Stone called Sally Remus to the stand. Sally was sworn in, settled herself in the witness chair, and covered her face with a most resolute expression.

"State your name, please," said Mr. Stone.

"My name be Sally Remus."

"Do you know the defendant, Mr. Harland Jeffers?"

"Yes suh, I knows him."

"What was your relationship to the defendant, Ms. Remus?"

"Me and my husbin, Ezra, was his slaves."

"How long did you live and work on Mr. Jeffers's plantation?"

"Years and years. I met my husbin Ezra dare afta Massa Jeffers done bought him down in Atlanta."

"Were you ever mistreated by Mr. Jeffers? Were you ever beaten or punished in some way?"

"No suh, not me or Ezra, but we never did give him no reason. But we seen plenty who was whipped."

"Ms. Remus, tell us where your husband is today."

"Objection," said Mr. Johnson. "I fail to see what the location of her husband has to do with this case."

"If I may be allowed to proceed, Your Honor, my question has a great deal to do with this case."

"Overruled," said McCay.

"Now then, once again, Ms. Remus, tell us where your husband is today."

In a shaking voice and with a tear in her eye, Sally replied, "My Ezra is with the Lord, suh."

"I am sorry to hear that Ms. Remus. What happened to your husband?"

Sally looked directly at Harland Jeffers and replied, "Massa Jeffers kilt him."

A strong undertone of whispering ran through the courtroom. After a few minutes Judge McCay tapped his gavel.

"Again, I am sorry, Ms. Remus. Could you explain to the court exactly what happened?"

In minute detail, Sally regaled the court with the story of what happened the night her husband was killed. She did not hesitate, stammer, or stop at any point to search her memory. She told the story as if it had just occurred the night before. When she finished, the defense was given the opportunity to cross examine.

"Now, Ms. Remus, you said that this incident happened late at night. How well were you able to see out there along the road at night?"

"I could see good. Massa Jeffers had mens with him and they had torches burnin"

"You said that you and your husband had worked for Mr. Jeffers, is that correct?"

"We was his slaves, yes suh."

"At the time when you and your husband were Mr. Jeffers's slaves, what were your personal feelings toward him?"

"Personal feelins?"

"Yes, did you like him, did you hate him, did you fear him?"

"Me and Ezra jes tried to do what we was told. We never wanted trouble."

"But you haven't answered the question, Ms. Remus," Johnson insisted. "What were your feelings toward Mr. Jeffers?"

"I reckon I feel the same as you would ifn you had a massa that owned you like a animal."

"I think the picture is becoming clearer, Ms. Remus. I think that what we have here is a simple desire for revenge."

"I don't know dem words, suh."

"What that means, Ms. Remus," said Johnson in a loud accusing voice, "is that you and your husband were once Mr. Jeffers slaves. You obviously have hard feelings toward him, your husband got himself killed, quite possibly due to some fault of his own, and now you want this court to believe that Mr. Jeffers is responsible in order to get even with him!"

The crowd erupted again, much louder this time. The judged banged his gavel and issued a strong warning to anyone who disrupted his court. Sally was clearly flustered, which was the result Johnson was hoping for. Johnson continued his attack.

"Now, Ms. Remus, I will give you a chance to tell us the truth by asking you again ... what really happened to your husband?"

Sally was crying now and she was so injured by Johnson's accusations that she had lost her composure.

"I is telling the truth. Massa Jeffers kilt Ezra," she cried.

"What other proof do you have that it was Mr. Jeffers that killed your husband out on the road on a dark night by the light of a few torches?"

"Becuz I will never forget his voice as long as I lives."

Having done the best he could to discredit the poor woman, Johnson said, "No further questions, Your Honor."

The next witness called by Mr. Stone was James. He was sworn in and then he took his seat. The prosecutor asked James to tell in his own words what happened the night Ezra Remus was killed. Again, in great detail, James told the court what he heard and what he saw, making certain that everyone understood how adamant Sally was about who killed her husband. When Mr. Stone was finished, he reserved the right to recall James at a later time and then Mr. Johnson stood up looking like a hungry wolf licking his chops.

"Mr. Langdon, you served in the Union Army during the war, did you not?"

"Objection," said Mr. Stone. "The war is over, Your Honor. I fail to see the relevance."

"I am merely trying to establish an abolitionist's opinion of a former slave owner, Your Honor."

"Abolitionist?" said the judge.

"Yes, sir, it is widely known that Mr. Langdon was involved in helping slaves escape before joining the army."

A hushed but audible ahhh went through the crowd and James could feel the angry stares from some of the people. He was surprised to note that he was no longer concerned in any way about his past or having it revealed.

"Objection overruled," said the judge.

"Now then," said Johnson, feeling a little victorious. "You served in the Union Army during the war, correct?"

"Quite," James replied.

"Naturally you have no love for anyone who bought and sold Negroes, correct?"

"Not exactly," James answered, willing to do anything to derail the smug attorney. "My father bought and sold Negroes and I loved him very much; it is just that I did not agree with it."

"But as for someone else like Mr. Jeffers, you more than likely feel contempt, correct?"

"I would have contempt for those who have no respect for the *new* law of the land; the new law that says that the Negroes are free people like everyone else. Furthermore, I have no respect or tolerance for someone who would gun down an innocent man just because that man was finally able to walk away from a life so beneath what he deserved that it is an abomination before Almighty God."

"You are well educated, aren't you, Mr. Langdon?"

"Yes, thank you."

"Then how is it that you are not intelligent enough to understand the danger you are in by accusing an innocent man of murder?"

"I have done no such thing, Mr. Johnson."

"What makes you so sure?"

"Because I was there that night. I arrived on the scene just minutes after Ezra Remus was killed. I comforted his grieving widow and there is no chance that she is mistaken about the identity of the man who killed him; as she said, his voice and impeded speech are unmistakable."

James had struck hard with his testimony and the defense attorney was reeling just a bit.

"No further questions," said Mr. Johnson.

The atmosphere in the courtroom had gotten quite thick and it was time to let things cool for a bit. The judge dismissed the participants for a noon break, imparting to the crowd that court would reconvene at 1PM. James and Aaron left the courthouse and walked up the street to a small café.

"You did a good job, James," said Aaron. "You really over ran that damn Johnson."

"I wish I could share your optimism, my friend. I would like to think that I gave him some grief but I am more concerned about the effect I had on the jury. And I hope the best is yet to come. I still think that Lewis will be the most important witness. I believe that he can tie it all together."

At 1PM the trial resumed and the first witness called was Aaron. He turned out to be an excellent orator; thanks to his preaching experience he did a fine job telling the story about his attempt to infiltrate the Klan, what happened when he was discovered, and what happened the night that Chet was hanged. Even more impressive was how he handled himself under the cross examination of Augustus E. Johnson. When it was over, the judge dismissed him from the trial. At 3PM, court was adjourned until 10AM the following morning.

"There is no need for you to stay in Atlanta," James said. "Why don't you head for home in the morning?"

"Are you sure you won't need me?"

"I'm sure. You can bring everyone at home up to date. Tell Polly that I am fine and I'll be home as soon as it's over."

After breakfast the following morning, Aaron left Atlanta and James walked down to the courthouse to wait for the trial to continue. Most of the morning was filled with more character witnesses, and at noon, Judge McCay called a recess until 1PM.

Shortly after the trial resumed, James heard the door open in the back of the courtroom. He turned to look back and saw Lewis Prichard come through the doorway. Lewis stood with his back against the wall and five minutes later he was called to take the stand. James made a point of watching for a reaction from Jeffers when Lewis's name was called; he was not disappointed. Jeffers turned in his chair and watched Lewis as he made his way to the witness chair. As soon as he took his seat, Jeffers turned to his attorney, put his arm around Johnson's shoulder to further shield their conference, and fell deep into conversation. After a few minutes of shaking heads and hand gestures, Johnson turned around, fixed his gaze on a man seated in the second row and motioned him forward. The middle aged man dressed in a plain brown suit, got up, walked to the end of the row of seats and made his way toward the waiting attorney. Bending down between the two men; more hand gestures and head nodding ensued. Then the man, obviously having received instructions, turned and hurried out of the courtroom. Then Jeffers and his attorney turned their undivided attention to Amherst Stone as he began to question the key witness.

"Mr. Prichard, are you acquainted with the defendant?"

"Yes, sir, I am."

"What is your relationship to Mr. Jeffers?"

"Specifically, I was a member of an organization that he belongs to."

"Would you tell us the name of the organization?"

Lewis hesitated for a moment as if he was about to walk through a doorway to a place from which there was no hope of returning. He glanced around the courtroom, probably looking for familiar faces; unfriendly ones. Then Mr. Stone pressed for a reply.

"Should I repeat the question, Mr. Prichard?"

"No, sir," said Lewis. "I heard the question. They call themselves the Ku Klux Klan."

Another audible murmur circulated through the crowd, offering no clear evidence as to whether it was approval or disapproval. Jeffers sat perfectly still; James sensed that the defendant was drilling a hole through Lewis with his eyes.

"Where were you on the night of November 27th, 1868, Mr. Prichard?"

"I was at the old Culpepper Plantation south of Macon."

"Who else was there?"

"Most of the members of the local Klan klavern, a man named Aaron Parmalee, and a Negro woman named Sadie and her children."

"That sounds like a curious group," said Mr. Stone. "Now Mr. Prichard, would you tell us in your own words just exactly what happened that night?"

Slowly, and in very great detail, Lewis mesmerized the crowded courtroom with the entire story of everything that happened at Culpepper Plantation. The room was silent as a church while he described the events as they unfolded in the old barn. As Lewis reached the part about capturing Chet on the road that night and taking him back to the barn, the man in the brown suit returned, went up to Jeffers and his attorney, and knelt down between them. James could see a heated discussion going on and then the man in the brown suit stood up abruptly and returned to his original seat. It was clear that things were running amuck at the defense counsel's table, and when Lewis told the court that Harland Jeffers instructed his followers to hang Chet Rawlins for crimes against the Confederacy, Augustus E. Johnson jumped up and said, "Your Honor, I object!"

"On what grounds, Mr. Johnson?"

"Your Honor, I have it on good authority that Mr. Prichard has been coerced into delivering this preposterous testimony."

"By whom?" said Judge McCay.

"I uh, I, am not at liberty to say at this time, Your Honor," Johnson stammered.

"Well, you had better say, Mr. Johnson, or else withdraw your objection."

Mr. Johnson looked around as if he were waiting for someone to help him out of the corner he'd painted himself into. Apparently something had happened that tore the guts out of the defense attorney's case and he stood there as awkward as a bastard at a family reunion. The irritation on the judge's face left the defense attorney no options.

"I withdraw my objection," said Johnson.

The situation had deteriorated to such a degree that when the time came for cross examination, Mr. Johnson amazed everyone by saying, "No questions, Your Honor."

On the other side of the courtroom Mr. Stone informed the judge, "The prosecution rests."

"Do you wish to call any more witnesses?" the judge asked Mr. Johnson. But Mr. Johnson wasn't listening. He was far too preoccupied with an intense conversation with his client. At regular intervals, the attorney would shake his head no in a dramatic fashion. Finally the judge grew tired of being ignored and he punctuated that fact with his gavel.

"Mr. Johnson! Do you wish to call any more witnesses?" With a great deal of reluctance in his voice Johnson said, "Yes, Your Honor, I would like to call Mr. Harland Jeffers to the stand."

"Have you informed your client that he is under no obligation to testify?"

"Emphatically, Your Honor," the attorney replied.

"Very well. Mr. Jeffers, would you take the stand, please?"

Jeffers got up and made his way to the witness chair, was sworn in, then sat and immediately began to fidget in his seat.

"Would you please state your full name?" said his attorney.

"My name is Harland Henry Jeffers."

"I believe that it is your wish to address this court."

"Yes, Mr. Stone."

"Then you may proceed."

Jeffers put an artificial smile on his face and began to speak slowly, obviously choosing his words very carefully. Everyone in the courtroom experienced his lisp.

"Gentlemen of the jury, ladies and gentlemen in the courtroom today, please give me your undivided attention. I want to apologize for the misuse of your time today because there is no need for any of us to be here. We are

140

all good loyal southerners and we all know to what extent the people of the South stand by one another. We proved that in the late war and we are proving it still. Our gallant armies, after doing all they could, may have been forced to surrender, but the true human spirit, the true southern spirit can never be subdued. We are still looking out for our own and we always will. There was no murder at Culpepper Plantation on the night in question, my friends. The only thing that occurred that night was the rebirth of patriotism, the steadfast protection of our God given right to our way of life. Hear me, friends: I am not a murderer, I am but one of many saviors of the people; the men called upon and willing to shoulder the task handed down by our forefathers, whose vision of this land and of southern society must be preserved."

As Jeffers droned on and on, James sat and listened in disbelief. And from the moment he started speaking, his attorney, Mr. Johnson, sat with his head in his hands, evidence that his client was putting the finishing touches on a complete disaster. The man was doing his best to justify the murder of Chet Rawlins by convincing the jury that serving what he believed was the southern cause constituted no crime. But in so doing, he was admitting to have done the crime for which he was charged. Consequently, the jury, regardless of their personal feelings, would have no recourse other than to find him guilty.

After only three hours of deliberation, the jury did just that. James deduced that Lewis Prichard's testimony was indeed the prosecution's best weapon, and when he appeared in court, the defense knew it was not prepared to counter it. Keeping the arrest of Roland T. Ramsey quiet had been a brilliant move. Thinking that he had done his job had lulled Jeffers and his attorney into a false sense of security. James would never know if Mr. Stone had anything at all up his sleeve to control the damage but it was certain that he never wanted his client to take the stand, knowing that he would burn the case to the ground. Apparently Jeffers thought that his best chance was to rely on southern loyalty. He believed he had nothing to fear in a southern court; exactly the kind of attitude that James wanted to see change.

Judge McCay, upon receiving the jury's verdict sentenced Harland Henry Jeffers to be hanged on the first of May. James had mixed feelings. He was glad that justice had been served and he was glad that the Klan had been held accountable for Chet's death, proving that their hostile activities were not unquestionably sanctioned by the southern people. But he was sure that the only reason Jeffers was convicted was because Chet was a white man.

Before James left the courtroom, he spotted Sally Remus preparing to leave. When she saw him she came over to thank him again for being so kind to her.

"I reckon you was right, Mr. Langdon. You said someday Massa Jeffers would pay for killin my Ezra and you was right. But it don't bring my Ezra back do it?"

"No, Sally. Sadly, it doesn't."

"Ya know, Mr. Langdon, now that it's over I feels sorry for Massa Jeffers. How do that figure, suh?"

"You're a good soul, Sally. You know that killing is wrong and that it does nothing to ease the pain. I wish more people felt the way you do."

"Well I is gonna say a prayer for Massa Jeffers. Somehow I feels like that will ease my pain."

"May God bless you, Sally. Good luck to you," said James.

"The same to you, suh."

James walked out of the courthouse and stood on the steps, hoping to run into Lewis. As he was waiting, someone came up from behind and tapped him on the shoulder. It was Major Alvin Mitchell.

"How are you feeling about the outcome, James?"

"I wanted justice, Mitch; I hope that is what I got."

"I take it you didn't want to see Jeffers hang."

"I understand that it's the way we do things, but I must admit—it bothers me a little."

"You're a good Christian, James. Do you have any idea how many people in this world would take a life and never give it a thought?"

"No, but I learned during the war that there are quite a few."

"Yes, unfortunately, that is why we need such harsh measures to keep it in check."

"I guess you're right, Mitch."

As James stood there talking with his friend, he suddenly noticed the man in the brown suit walking down the sidewalk across the street; the man who had been called from his seat by Jeffers's attorney.

"Mitch, do you know that man over there?" he said, pointing his finger. "The man in the brown suit." Before Mitch could answer, two soldiers stopped the man, put a set of manacles on him, and led him away.

"That," said Mitch, "is Daniel Ebersole. Do you remember I told you I was sure that the Klan had eyes inside the governor's office?"

"Yes, I remember," James replied.

"Well, Mr. Ebersole is the man we suspected and today we were able to get proof. I had a man in plain clothes watching him and when he was called to the defense table and then suddenly left the courtroom, my operative followed him. Sure enough, Ebersole went into the governor's office. The operative was able to signal the clerk, who then fed our suspect a helping of false information. The clerk told him that Roland T. Ramsey had broken down and confessed that Jeffers had hired him to kill your friend, Lewis. The clerk also told him that Ramsey would be willing to testify for certain considerations. All of this, if it were true, would be highly confidential; information that Ebersole would have been bound to keep secret. When he immediately ran back to the courtroom and spoke to Jeffers and Stone, we knew he was spilling the beans. That gave us the grounds we needed to arrest him. From what I've heard, it is also what prompted Jeffers to demand that he be able to take the stand. Of course his attorney knew he was committing suicide."

"I guess it's finally settled," said James. "I'd like to think that we can enjoy a little peace, for a while anyway."

"That would not upset me," Mitch quipped.

Just then, James caught sight of Lewis and called out to him. "I have to be going, Mitch. Again, it was good to see you, and I thank you for everything; you and your men were a great help, not to mention the governor's assistance. Please give him my regards when you see him."

"I will, James. I hope we meet again someday."

"As do I, Mitch, but I hope it will be under happier circumstances."

James shook hands with his old friend and then he hurried down the front steps to catch up with Lewis.

"I wanted to thank you for your very great help," said James.

"It is I who owes you, James. I wish I'd have had better sense than to get mixed up with the Klan. It just carried over from the war, I guess. It was a crazy time."

"That it was, Lewis; a time we will never forget. But all I want from it now is a better future."

"So do I, but I don't know what my chances are in Georgia. I was thinking I might get away for a while, let things calm down."

"Funny you should say that, Lewis. Have you ever been to Pennsylvania?"

"No, I never have."

"During the war my wife and I lived in Mapletown for a couple years. We met some wonderful people there and made some good friends. It is just a dozen miles north of Morgantown in western Virginia—excuse me, West Virginia. I worked in the bank there for a while." James pulled an envelope from his coat pocket and handed it to Lewis.

"This is a letter of recommendation from me to the manager of the bank in Mapletown. His name is Henry Jarvis and he is a good man to work for. I know you would be a perfect fit and there is no better future than the banking business. I think you could find happiness in Mapletown. Why don't you give it a try?"

"It sounds real nice, James. I appreciate your confidence in me."

"It is something that I would bank on," said James with a smile. "I will be sad to see you leave Georgia though."

"Georgia is my home, James. I will be back someday. But for now, I want to get my life on track. I'll head home, put my affairs in order, and strike out for Mapletown."

James and Lewis rode together until they reached the remnants of the plantation where the old South was about to become part of Lewis's past forever. The two boyhood friends shook hands cordially and James said, "Goodbye, Lewis. I would be happy if you kept in touch."

"I promise to do that. I'll let you know when I decide to come back, but don't expect it too soon. Of course, that doesn't mean I won't come back from time to time for a visit."

"That sounds good," said James.

Then Lewis jarred James's nostalgic heart when he said, "Maybe we'll go fishing."

# FOURTEEN

# The Political Path

By the year 1870, it suddenly appeared as though the Ku Klux Klan had scattered to the four corners of the earth. James knew that the fire of the Klan had not died out but was only smoldering. Still, news of Klan violence had dropped off to some extent, creating an illusion of peace. He realized that equal rights were still two words that no one ever used together in the same sentence. However, the recession of the masked terrorists left behind a promise of more progress in the future.

Life on Langdon Plantation was a bit more pleasant for all who lived and worked there, and that was something the inhabitants hadn't enjoyed for a long time. After years of adversity and overcoming one obstacle after another, James at long last found himself able to focus more on his family and spending quality time with them. Jim was going on eight years old and under his father's watchful eye was becoming quite a horseman. The two went riding every chance they got, which always resulted in a stop somewhere along the way for a long father-son conversation. James was very proud of his boy, who was wise beyond his years.

Polly, since the day she first came home to the plantation, had worked tirelessly at restoring their home to its former glory with astonishing results. The inside was immaculate and well arranged and the lawn, with its lovely flower gardens, resembled the exuberance of the time when Martha MacGruder, the stern Irish woman, took care of them for James's mother. James knew that his parents would be pleased with the way everything looked and it gave him a great deal of satisfaction.

Kate was twenty-three now and, aside from helping Polly with the housework, was spending most of her time practicing the piano and learning to speak French. She had studied both subjects before the war and was now able to resume, thanks in part to James having hired a part-time instructor. Social events had also been a large part of Southern life that had endured a serious interruption due to the conflict. But slowly, people were making an attempt to pick up those particular pieces of their lives and Kate was especially fond of the interaction.

Perhaps the most significant new development was something that James more or less found out about by accident. It seemed that Ashton and Jeremy Todd had discovered an attraction to one another and were actually keeping company in a very subtle way. James was happy about the news and quite approving of future possibilities. Jeremy was a good man; the kind that would make a good husband and prove to be a good provider. Maybe he was just the man to help Ashton put her past completely behind her. Of course, James was not taking anything for granted; time would tell.

It was also time for James to resume his involvement in what had long since become his lifelong mission: equality for the black skinned race. He believed that God called upon all people to serve in one capacity or another and he further believed that this cause was his discipleship. The Thirteenth Amendment to end slavery had been realized in 1865. The Fourteenth Amendment to protect the rights of freed slaves had been gained in 1868. But there was much more to be done before the darker shade of freedom could evolve into equal status with the white folks.

The idea of political involvement had been discussed by James and his family and Congress was the level upon which he had his eye, however, the country was still mired in a period of reconstruction, and in 1867, the eighth congressional district had been eliminated. In addition, Georgia had still not been re-admitted to the Union. Until things changed, he would have to find another way.

Fate suggested a way one day while James was in Macon on business. The *Macon Telegraph* carried the story of Mayor George S. Obear's brief illness and subsequent death. A special committee had been appointed to hold an election to fill the position. James quickly decided that he would throw his hat into the ring. In a town with a population of almost 11,000 people, the position of mayor could give him some practical experience as a politician and as an administrator. He could work to influence his constituents towards acceptance of the freed slaves as useful, productive citizens ... and if he could change the sentiment of Macon, why not the state of Georgia? By the time James had finished reading the story, his hopes were soaring a mile high at least. Then he let his feet settle firmly back upon the earth and told himself that he was absolutely and positively dreaming. He knew what he would find if he surveyed the general attitude of the people, but he so believed that the more worthwhile the result, the greater the challenge—and long odds had always stiffened his resolve.

The committee chairperson was a man by the name of Alfred Crenshaw. Crenshaw was a prominent citizen and served as the town treasurer. He also owned a tannery located on the outskirts of Macon. James did not know the man or whether or not he was from the area. He did know that the tannery was opened shortly after the war. Mr. Crenshaw was in his office when James arrived. Sporting his most congenial smile, James walked into the office, offered his hand and said, "Good Morning, Mr. Crenshaw, my name is James Langdon."

Crenshaw looked up from his ledger, lowered his wire rimmed spectacles, and said, "Ah, that's better."

"I beg your pardon?" said James.

"I don't need my specs except when I'm reading and writing. I can see you much better without them." Crenshaw took James's hand and gave it a firm shake.

"What can I do for you, Mr. Langdon?"

James held up the paper, pointed to the story about Mayor Obear, and said, "I'd like to make a bid for the position of town mayor of Macon."

"I see, well, what do you offer as qualifications? I'm just curious ... the decision isn't up to me, but I can tell you if you stand a fair chance."

"Well, sir, I am a native of Bibb County. I am a businessman, I own and operate Langdon Plantation located about twenty miles south of Macon, and I was educated in New York before the war."

"I see, yes, it sounds to me as though you should be able to handle the responsibilities connected with the job. You should probably get the word out as best you can so that people know you intend to run. You can post notices in all public places, put something in the local paper, and you can make arrangements to give a speech at the town hall if you like. Unfortunately, time is short. The position must be filled as soon as possible and the election will be on March the 15$^{th}$, which is just two weeks away. There are a lot of other details but nothing you need to know unless you are elected. Whoever is chosen will undergo a period of orientation to bring him up to date."

"I really appreciate your help in this, Mr. Crenshaw. I will get started immediately on my campaign."

"Good luck to you, son. If you're elected, we'll be working together, part-time."

James left the tannery feeling pretty good about the conversation with Mr. Crenshaw. He understood that he would not be as well received by everyone as he was with the tannery owner and he had no idea how many others would vie for the position, but he was feeling optimistic nonetheless and he couldn't wait to tell Polly.

That evening, a comprehensive campaign was born in the Langdon home, and the following day James began actively running for mayor. He learned that there were two others seeking the office: one of them, a man by the name of Barnabas Tyler was somehow related to John Tyler, the tenth president of the United States and a native of Virginia. Mr. Tyler had proposed a public debate with his two opponents, and James agreed to the challenge.

Two days before the election, James, Polly, and Kate traveled to Macon to listen to the debate. Ashton stayed behind to take care of Jim, who was suffering from a sore throat and a stuffy nose. Many of the plantation workers also made the trip to support their candidate. Before the debate, each man was given ten or fifteen minutes for an introduction and a short speech outlining his goals for the town.

The first man to speak was Mr. Tyler, who was clearly hoping to influence the voters by his political heritage. His personal qualifications were not too impressive other than

149

the fact that he was an attorney from a school that
evidently no one had ever heard of. But his rhetoric was
loud and boisterous; when he was finished he strutted
back to his seat with all the pomp and circumstance of a
peacock.

The second speaker was a newcomer to the South; a
carpetbagger from New York City. His name was Richard
Newhouse and he did not seem to be intimidated by the
undertone of jeers and accusations of political interests for
personal gains. When he was finished there was no
applause; only a murmuring of disapproval accentuated by
a few boos.

When James took the podium, he delivered his speech,
which was well prepared and very specific concerning his
ideas for improvements necessary to allow the community
to move forward, to grow, and to recover from the wartime
recession. In a bold gesture to avoid future insinuations of
false pretenses, James began to speak about his real
motivation for the community.

"My friends, in case you have not already heard, the
state of Mississippi and the state of Virginia were recently
readmitted to the Union. This was accomplished simply by
ratifying the Fifteenth Amendment to our Constitution."

James paused for a moment for effect and to scan the
crowd for any signs of a discordant attitude toward his
remark. Contrary to his expectation, everyone's attention
seemed to have been captured by it.

"My interests in the success of our town are equal to
my interest in the success of our state. Georgia must
become part of the Union so that we might once again have
representatives in Washington who will look to our needs
and our wellbeing. We must let it be known that the good
people of Macon support the ratification of the Fifteenth
Amendment, which just last month became the law of the
land. But we must be pure of heart in our support,
meaning that we support the amendment because it is just
and not simply to be readmitted so that we can thumb our
noses at its purpose and do as we please. The Fifteenth
Amendment is the law of the land, but in practice, freed
blacks are still denied the right to vote in increasing
numbers. Free public education for all children has now

been established throughout the South through the efforts of Federal laws, but black children are not afforded the same opportunities for education as white children".

As James moved deeper into his speech with more and more passion, a few people started drifting away. He realized that by going all in too quickly he could destroy his future chances to instill the idea of equal rights. As smoothly as possible he wrapped up his speech and returned to his seat amidst a surprising round of applause.

The debate that followed was not really a debate at all; at least, it followed no recognizable format. It was, in truth, a political gambit contrived and engineered by Barnabas Tyler for the purpose of destroying the reputations of his rivals. Tyler took it upon himself to orchestrate the proceeding, which was a complete breech of protocol to begin with. Once gaining the attention of the crowd he commenced throwing questions at his opponents; not about their views on subjects of interest to the town, but rather, personal questions about their past; a political witch hunt. Although the whole fiasco was entirely out of line, James refrained from dismissing himself and going home. He decided that maybe some good might come of Tyler's desperate attempt to steal an election by giving James the chance to show that there was nothing he wished to keep hidden. In the end, judging from the comments coming from the crowd as it dispersed, Tyler had done himself more harm than good. But James knew it was never prudent to be presumptuous and that only the outcome of the election would designate the winner.

The following two days were passed in silence concerning the election. No one admitted to superstitious beliefs but rather that they did not think it wise to get one's hopes up to high. However, the calm was shattered on the morning of the election when Jeremy raced up the driveway on horseback shouting for James. Jeremy had gone to Macon earlier that morning with over three hundred black workers who intended to cast their ballots. James got up from his desk and hurried outside to see what was wrong.

"They won't let us vote, James!"

"What are you saying, Jeremy?"

151

"There's a bunch a roughnecks hangin around the town hall and they won't allow the black men to vote."

"Have they hurt anyone?"

"No, but I guarantee they will if the men try to force their way in."

"Did you tell the men to stand fast?"

"I did. I told them not to start anything. I told them to wait until you and I got there."

"Very good, Jeremy, you did the right thing. Give me a minute to saddle my horse; saddle a fresh mount for yourself. I will appeal to these people to obey the law."

Almost an hour later, James and Jeremy arrived in Macon. When they reached the town hall, the scene was a confrontational one. A large crowd of black men filled the street in front of the town hall for fifty yards in each direction. In front of the building, a much smaller group of white men stood in two rows lining the walkway to the entrance. Occasionally a nervous white citizen showed up to walk between the two rows of vigilantes, went inside, voted, and then hurried out and away from the area. But if a black man got too close, the defenders would spread out and issue a verbal warning to keep away. As James guessed before he even arrived, the black men stood in the street with empty hands but the troublemakers were heavily armed. It was something he had gotten used to but something he would not change. James would make every effort to see his friends exercise their right to vote, but he would take them home having been denied the right if the choice was that or bloodshed.

"Stand with the men," James told Jeremy. "Keep them calm and I will see if reasoning with these men will do any good." Then he rode his horse to the hitching rail in front of the town hall and dismounted. He approached the first two men in line and said, "Who is in charge of this group of protestors?"

"Protestors?" said a tall thin man dressed in a plaid shirt and faded gray trousers.

"Yes. You men are obviously protesting the right of these black citizens to vote."

"Did ya hear that?" he said to the man next to him. "Black citizens." Then to James he said, "They ain't black citizens. They is niggers and niggers ain't got no rights, not in Georgia anyhow."

"You're wrong, my friends," said James. "The Constitution of the United States says that these men have been given the right to vote."

At this, the angry group of bigots broke their lines and started to close in around James. Another man, an older, rather soft spoken person said, "We all know who you are, Mr. Langdon, and we know what you've been up against the last five years and we know why. But out of respect for your father and your family name we are ready to let that part of the past alone. No matter how this looks, we really don't want any trouble. But we have all had too much forced down our throats since before the war and we are not willing to be told what we have to put up with in our own town. You use the word friend, but if you are a friend to them then you can't be a friend to us."

"But I consider myself a friend to all men," James replied. "If any of you were being denied your rights, I would be just as concerned."

"That statement would not be considered popular, Mr. Langdon, because you are as much as saying that blacks and whites are equal and we just don't see it that way."

"Your name is Gerald Branson is it not?" James asked.

"That's right, I'm Branson."

"I thought I recognized you, sir. You knew my father well, didn't you?"

"Yes, I did. I had quite a few business dealings with your father in the old days. That is why I am trying to control the attitude of these men. They have given me their word that there will be no trouble as long as these blacks don't try to force their way inside. If they do, I won't be responsible for what happens. So it's really up to you if there is trouble here today, Mr. Langdon."

"Progress is inevitable, Mr. Branson. Times change and people change; it is part of life. The day will come in this country when blacks and whites *are* considered equal. Someday the law will be enforced."

"That may be so, Mr. Langdon, but it won't be today, and if I'm lucky, it won't be in my lifetime. We aren't breaking any laws or Sheriff Renner would be here to take action against us. Now the last word has been said. Take your workers home or face the consequences."

James felt it burn a little when Mr. Branson said he and his friends weren't breaking any laws and that the sheriff would be taking action if they were. He doubted that very much. He remembered an incident just a few years earlier concerning the sheriff of Macon, Sheriff Ketchum, killed on James's property fighting on the side of the Ku Klux Klan. The statement also reminded him about a conversation he'd had with his father before the war concerning slavery. 'It was the law of the land,' his father had said. 'We are not outlaws down here,' he had proclaimed. It stings as much today as it did then, James thought.

In any case, he had lost the argument. The black men of Macon and Bibb County would not be voting that day. It would be a later time when James might see things go the other way. For now, all he could do was to ask his black friends to go home and he thanked them profusely for making the trip because he knew they had come to support him in the election.

"We're leaving, Mr. Branson. Violence takes a holiday and I am grateful for that at least."

"As am I, Mr. Langdon, as am I."

In the interest of unity and sincerity toward their bond with the black men, neither James nor Jeremy went into the town hall to vote.

The following morning, James was completely caught by surprise when a messenger was sent from Macon to inform him that he was, in fact, the new town mayor. The messenger was a middle aged man by the name of Edwin Forbes, a staff member to the late Mayor Obear. James was not acquainted with Edwin and found it difficult at first to read the man's disposition.

"I must admit, I am quite surprised by the message you are here to deliver," James said upon receiving the news.

"Yes, I can understand that, Mr. Langdon, all things considered."

"All things?"

"Yes, sir, I mean the confrontation at the town hall yesterday and everything."

"You seem to have a problem completing your thoughts verbally, Mr. Forbes. I assure you there is nothing to fear from expressing yourself and I would much prefer it."

"If you insist, Mr. Langdon, I will express my thoughts. Personally, I have nothing against you. I am well aware of your loyalties and still I feel no ill will toward you in spite of the fact that I served the Confederacy during the war. Nine out of ten people in this world have proven themselves to be narrow minded, but I happen to be in the ten percent group. I believe that a man should do what he feels is right because that constitutes a true definition of the word freedom. Most people think you should do what you think is right but only if it is agreeable to them; otherwise the principal of freedom suddenly changes."

"I like the way you think, Mr. Forbes, please go on."

"As you wish, sir. I have to tell you that the reason you were elected is because you are, in this case, the lesser of three evils. Richard Newhouse never had a chance of winning. The last thing Macon needs is an opportunist from New York looking to dictate policy in a southern town. Tyler started out to be the front runner by virtue of his lineage but destroyed his credibility with that sham of a debate he staged two weeks ago. He's lucky he wasn't tarred and feathered. That leaves you. Most of the voters felt that you have the intelligence to do this job and that you will not fail to act in the best interests of your hometown. Yesterday was a good example of that fact. It may surprise you further to know that after you ended that standoff peacefully and sent your Negroes home, most of those men went into the town hall and voted for you."

"I see, well, I am surprised by that information, Mr. Forbes, and may I say that their confidence is well placed. I *will* be steadfast in my dedication to Macon and to the citizens thereof, but be it known: at the same time I shall never falter in my dedication to my fellow man. If there is any way that I can begin a revolution in Macon towards the establishment of equal rights, I will do it. We are all humans alike, color notwithstanding, and the world needs the concerted effort of everyone to make it a world that God will shower with His blessings."

"I have heard, Mr. Langdon, but now I see for myself. It's no wonder that the Klan couldn't drive you out or make you quit. You are a man who commands respect and I can assure you of mine. As mayor, you will be given the opportunity to pick your own staff if you are not satisfied with me, Cyrus Pike, or Felix Gray, the current members. I won't speak for the others but if you keep me on I will pledge my total support."

"I am proud to have you on my staff, Mr. Forbes, and I look forward to meeting the others. I do not anticipate making any personnel changes and hope that it would never come to that."

"Thank you, sir. There will be a meeting in the town hall this afternoon at 2 PM. You will be sworn in as mayor and given the opportunity to address the town council and the other civic leaders." Then Mr. Forbes extended his hand and said, "Congratulations on the election, and please, call me Edwin."

"Thank you, Edwin. I know we will work well together. I'll see you at two."

James stood watching as Edwin rode down the driveway and out of sight. He sensed a real accomplishment having won the election regardless of the circumstances. Maybe he was the best of the worst but he was chosen in spite of his reputation and that was something very solid to build on.

James went to the house to tell his family the good news. Polly was very proud of her husband; Ashton and Kate were excited; Jim believed that his father was the most important man in the world. Everyone wanted to attend the ceremony and James couldn't have been more pleased.

At exactly 2 PM, James was sworn in as the mayor of Macon by Judge Walter B. Fenton, president judge of Bibb County, Georgia. After the ceremony, Judge Fenton spoke to the gathering, reminding the people as well as outlining for James, the duties of a town mayor.

"The mayor is always considered the head of the town, running the business and day to day administration of the town. The mayor also sets the tone for the culture and future of the town's operations, and acts as the chief spokesman for town activities and legislation."

Then, speaking directly to James, the judge said, "As mayor you will work with the town council and other town entities to enact legislation such as the town's taxes, liquor laws, or others. You will be the presiding officer at all meetings and will sign all official documents.

"Additionally, you will appoint many positions such as those for advisory committees and executive positions such as town clerk, town treasurer, fire chief, and sheriff.

"You should ensure that the town is kept clean for citizens to experience a good quality of life and enjoy good health.

"As the executive officer in charge of budgeting you will encourage and attract new business to the town. This action helps to build the town's tax base and creates jobs for citizens. As mayor you should be open minded, listening to the citizens, staff, business, and department heads to receive input about changes or potential changes to legislation. As mayor you should make goodwill and public appearances at business openings, school functions, and community functions.

"Finally, as mayor you will work with administrators and town officials to reach a budget that falls within the given parameters of the town's income. You will present and adopt that budget as well as ensure the funds are distributed in a proper and equitable manner. Each year you should also oversee the re-budgeting process to ensure funds have been appropriated and utilized correctly."

As James listened to and absorbed the judge's words, he understood that running a progressive and successful town was much the same as running a progressive and successful business—only with more help to do it. Beyond that, what stuck in his mind the most were the powers and duties that, to James, would allow him to influence the people to develop not just the town's dominant culture but rather the multi-culture. He knew he had a hand in everything now and he believed that the opportunity had come. But he also understood that what would be most required was an infinite supply of patience. He had first to test the waters, measure the resistance to his ideas, and see who he could count on for the most support. Maybe if he could capture the gratitude and respect of the people, they would in turn be more tolerant of his concern for the black population.

James addressed his constituents briefly but poignantly, and then he was escorted to the mayor's office by his staff, Judge Fenton, and Sheriff Renner. He expressed his gratitude to the judge for officiating, set a meeting for the following morning with his staff, and then he asked Sheriff Renner to stay for a few minutes. When the others closed the door behind them, James offered the sheriff a seat.

"I especially wanted to speak to you, Sheriff, because I feel that you have such an important responsibility, which is of course, keeping law and order in Macon."

"It is one that I take very seriously, Mr. Mayor."

"I am certainly glad to hear that, Sheriff. It is my hope that we can see eye to eye on the letter of the law because it is the very core of a safe and secure environment."

"If I may take the liberty, Mr. Mayor—"

"Feel free, Sheriff Renner."

"I believe I can see where this is going ... you are wondering why I did not intervene when the Negroes were prohibited from voting."

"I appreciate your candor, Sheriff. Yes, that is my question."

"I was born in Macon, Mr. Mayor. I have lived here all of my life. My family was dirt farmers; we never owned a single slave. My father was a proud man whose biggest obstacle in life was to live down the label 'white trash.' He was honest and hardworking and he raised me to believe that I was as good as any other man and that the lack of riches did nothing to change that. Still, he broke his back to make sure that I was educated because he wanted for me something that he deserved but never had: respect. My father hated slavery because he believed that the only accomplishments a man could be proud of were his own. He always said that it was easy to get rich from the deprivations of others and for His own reasons, the good Lord did not intend for life to be easy. When the war broke out, he didn't want me to fight. He could see that the

Confederacy was wrought by the rich man to protect his own selfish interests. He did not want me to be one of the thousands of young men who were sacrificed for something of no moral value to them."

"What on earth did you do?" James asked in fascination.

"I refused to go," the sheriff replied. "I just kept telling everyone that I had to stay home to help work the farm. Finally, one day a conscription detail came by the farm, threw me into a prison wagon, and transported me to the front lines. I ended up in Petersburg, Virginia, just before the siege. I was there when the Yankees exploded the tunnel under our earth works. I was struck by a large shard of flying wood. It almost went clean through me and I spent the next ten months at Chimborazo Hospital in Richmond. I owe my life to the chief surgeon, James B. McCaw. In May of 1865, the Yankees took over all the hospitals in Richmond and they literally shipped me home. My father had died of pneumonia ... my mother died the following year of a broken heart."

"It's a very touching story, Sheriff. I admire you for the way you've come through it. Many men would have let it destroy them."

"It came close, very close. But I decided that my father's struggle would not be in vain. I believe that he would be proud of me; he had a great deal of respect for the law."

"So where do you stand now as a symbol of the law?"

"Truthfully, I find myself in a very difficult situation. If I had used force on Election Day, it would have come to bloodshed. As I said, I've lived here all my life so I know just about everyone. I was so grateful when I heard that you ended the standoff peacefully. On the other hand, I support you in your endeavors for equal rights because my father hated slavery. So where *does* that leave me? I fear that I may be useless to you; a lawman who can't enforce the law."

"I disagree, Sheriff. I think you are just the kind of man this town needs. You have integrity and that will take you a long way. We have a lot in common, you and I, and from now on you will not be alone. We will overcome the evils of bigotry together and we'll do it without violence or brute force. I just needed to know your point of view and I couldn't be more pleased by what I've heard."

"I must say, Mr. Mayor, that you are a man who instills confidence and I believe that you can actually make this happen."

"*We* can make it happen."

James stood up and offered Sheriff Renner his hand. Renner shook it cordially and said, "By the way, my name is Jude, Mr. Mayor."

"I'm glad to know you, Jude, and when it doesn't have to be Mr. Mayor, call me James."

The sheriff left the office and James sat down again and took a long look at his surroundings. Anticipation overwhelmed him as he ruminated about the future. He was lining up his ducks and soon, he thought, they would be in a row. Then he got up and left the office to collect his family and head for home. On the way the talk was lively and he couldn't wait for the next morning to begin his first full day as the mayor of Macon.

# FIFTEEN

# Shocking Discovery

In the days that followed, James quickly realized that his position as mayor was not a full-time job. This was a good thing, however, because he still had a business to run at home. It was decided that he would spend three days a week on average at his desk in town, altering his schedule when the need arose. When he was not in Macon, matters were left in the very capable hands of his staff. Edwin Forbes proved to be consummate aid—able to handle much of the daily routine with the skill and diplomacy of a seasoned veteran. Cyrus Pike, a man in his late twenties, held an accounting degree from the University of North Carolina at Chapel Hill. An impressive and likable young man, it was rumored that Cyrus was compiling some practical experience before moving on to Washington where he hoped to someday work for the Commissioner of Internal Revenue. Felix Gray was a bookish, whiney little man with wire rimmed spectacles and hair the color of his last name. A hypochondriac by nature, he was never without a bottle of what he referred to as his wonder drug, which was a concoction of bark, bethroot, and water boiled together then strained before adding sugar. It was rumored that he fed the same cure all to his cat because he believed the animal thrived on it, but he was a genius at organization and James depended on Felix to keep a detailed schedule for him.

While James worked to change the complexion of Macon, the Federal Government worked to change the complexion of the nation. In May, Congress passed a Ku Klux Klan Act, specifically aimed at the Klan's efforts to thwart the blacks' right to vote. The bill carried heavy penalties for anyone disrupting a citizen's right to vote under the Fifteenth Amendment.

161

In July, Georgia finally ratified the Fifteenth Amendment and was readmitted to the Union. It was the last of the Confederate states to do so. Consequently, when the third session of the 41$^{st}$ Congress convened in December of 1870, it was the first time since 1860 that representatives from all the states were present.

By the following year, James and his staff had transformed Macon into a smooth running model of efficiency. It was evident that he was a popular mayor among the people due to his care of the town, but his personal views on equal rights went unappreciated. It became painfully obvious that the white citizens would support him on any issue except integration. Frustration became the norm; day after day James forced himself to do his job, keep the people happy, and hope that things would eventually change. The only success that his limited power would allow was to make sure that the blacks' segregated lifestyle was bearable by ensuring that their schools, churches, and personal property were protected under his jurisdiction. To that end, Sheriff Jude Renner was a great help, creating a deep friendship between the two of them. If not for friends like Jude, Jeremy, Aaron, and if not for an understanding, caring wife like Polly, James would have resigned his position as mayor. His anxiety in conjunction with the distinct feeling of being used by the white population in Macon was beginning to get the better of him.

One evening near the end of April, Jude stopped by the plantation to visit James and Polly. When James answered the door, Jude handed him a copy of the *Macon Telegraph*.

"I know you weren't in your office today and I thought you might like to see this."

James took the paper and invited his friend to sit in the parlor. Polly came in and, seeing the visitor said, "It's nice to see you, Jude. I'll get some coffee." Polly left the room, the two men seated themselves, and James scanned the front page of the paper. Another Ku Klux Klan Act had been passed. This time the law declared that any act by armed groups such as the Klan could be treated as rebellion and put down by military force. The article further stated that the president was also empowered to suspend the writ of habeas corpus in enforcing the Fifteenth Amendment. When James finished reading, he handed the paper back to Jude and said, "This is good news to be sure, but unfortunately it amounts to nothing more than another superficial act by the Federal Government. Washington is so heavily laden with problems that any real help for black people is so far off the agenda that it will take another hundred years before anything is done. The Grant administration is becoming increasingly tarnished with scandals and the politicians, especially the Republicans, are quite disillusioned by Grant's lack of leadership. I cannot see a chance for him to be re-elected next year, and I for one am not sorry."

"I guess you're right, James. The Klan gets some attention because they are the most visible proponent of segregation and black subjugation."

"Exactly," said James. "The Federal Government is the adhesive that keeps the Union together, but the infrastructure is weak on behalf of the blacks. Until we get action at state and local levels, nothing will ever change. I've tried and gotten nowhere. Every proposal I make is cut down before I get a chance to speak in public to support it."

Polly appeared carrying a tray of coffee and homemade cookies. After serving James and Jude, she poured a cup for herself and then sat down next to James.

"I hope you gentlemen won't mind a bit of female company," she said, hoping to ease the tension.

"Not at all," said James.

"I second that, Polly, and thank you for the refreshments," said Jude.

"We were just discussing the futility of my efforts as the mayor of Macon," James told her.

"It does trouble me that you feel that way, James," she replied. "In fact, I would debate that statement if I didn't know what you were actually referring to."

"I don't wish to trouble you, Polly. I just wish there was some way I could reinforce my patience; I just need a little encouragement, I suppose."

At that moment Jim came tearing into the parlor with two young black boys right on his heels. They were laughing and yelling, deeply involved in a game of tag. When Jim was within Polly's reach, she grabbed him by the collar and said, "Hold on there a minute, young man. What is the meaning of this disregard for rules about romping in the house?"

"I'm sorry, Mother. Jeb and Bodie and I are playing tag. They were chasing me and I guess I just forgot."

"I see, well, what is a fitting punishment for three energetic young scalawags, Father?" she said to James.

"I believe that I would refuse to let them have any of your fresh homemade cookies until they promise to eat them while they are playing outside," James said with a smile.

"Very well then, what do you say, boys? Does playing outside while eating cookies sound good?"

"Yesum!" was the unanimous reply.

"Have I your promise on it?"

"We promise," they answered.

"All right then, go to the kitchen and see your Aunt Kate. Tell her to pass out the cookies and make sure Jeb and Bodie get their share."

Jeb and Bodie headed for the door; this time, with Jim chasing them. But as Jim reached the doorway of the parlor he suddenly turned and said, "Mother, can Jeb and Bodie spend the night in my room?"

"I'm afraid if I say yes you boys will do more skylarking than sleeping."

"No, Mother, I promise we'll sleep after we talk for a bit."

"Father, your opinion?"

"Have a good night, son, and talk quietly."

"Yes, sir," the boy replied as he raced off to catch up with his friends.

After a few moments of silence, James noticed that Polly and Jude were grinning at each other and once they were sure they had James's attention they turned their grins in his direction.

"Did I miss something?" he asked.

"I should say you did," Polly scolded.

"What were you saying about a little encouragement?" Jude asked him.

"I really did miss something," said James. "It was wonderful and sad at the same time. Wonderful because when my son looks at those two boys all he sees is his friends. He doesn't notice anything different about them. But it's sad because the whole world could get along just as well if only they would realize that we are all alike."

"Maybe this shows us something, James," said Polly. "Maybe another generation will make a big difference."

"Yes," Jude agreed. "Could it be that your son and his friends are seeds for the future?"

"I would like to think so, but bigotry is not inherent it is taught, and the wrong kind of teaching is what produces a bitter crop."

The conversation was interrupted by a knock at the front door; James got up to answer it. He was surprised to find Jeremy standing on the veranda looking like he was coming down with the chilblains although the temperature had to be eighty degrees.

"Is something wrong, Jeremy?"

"No, sir, I mean no, James, that is, can I talk to you?"

"Of course, Jeremy, any time at all. Would you like to come in?"

"No I'd like to talk to you in private."

"Very well, have a seat."

Jeremy sat down on the swing and James accompanied him. It appeared as though Jeremy needed a minute to summon the courage to speak his mind. When he was ready he blurted out his thoughts.

"I want to marry your sister, Ashton."

James was quite taken aback by the unexpected statement, so much so that he had trouble getting his tongue untied, which only added to Jeremy's nervous condition.

Feeling an enormous amount of pressure, Jeremy said, "Did I say something to upset you, James?"

Then a smile on James's face started to grow and spread wider and wider until his cheeks began to ache. He thought a great deal of Jeremy and his declaration was twice as pleasing as when Polly had first told James about the quiet romance between Jeremy and Ashton.

"Jeremy, may I say that you have just presented me with my second pleasant surprise of the evening. It would make me very happy to have you as part of my family. Have you asked her yet?"

"No I haven't. I was kinda waitin until I asked you first. I mean, she knows how I feel and she has as much as told me that she would have me but I just wanted to be sure of how you felt first."

"Well, I am sorry that I have done such a poor job of showing how I feel about you, Jeremy. I count you among my very best friends and now we will be related. Would you like to come in now?"

"I sure feel a lot better getting that out. I'm still shakin a little but I reckon I'll calm down directly. But I won't come in jes yet. Ashton said she would wait for me back by the garden. I'll go ask her, and if she hasn't changed her mind, maybe we'll both come in after bit."

"I look forward to that," said James. Then he shook the future groom's hand, slapped him on the back, and said, "All the best my friend, all the very best."

"Thank you, for everything, James."

While Jeremy headed for the garden, James went back inside and sat back down next to Polly.

"Who was it, James, and why do you look so happy?"

"It was Jeremy ... he had something to ask me." Polly did not question further and James was glad. He did not want to say more and risk spoiling the couple's chance to make the announcement. About fifteen minutes later he heard the kitchen door open and close. Footsteps sounded in the hallway and then stopped at the doorway to the parlor.

"We didn't know you had company, James," said Ashton when she noticed Jude. James made the necessary introductions and then Ashton said, "We are going to be married."

James, Jude, and Polly got up, executed a round of applause, and then handshakes and hugs were distributed with equal enthusiasm.

"Have you decided on a date?" asked Polly.

"No," said Ashton. "We have a lot of planning to do before we can pick a day. We also have to decide where we are going to live, which is something that I will leave up to Jeremy."

"I would like to offer a suggestion in regards to a home," said James "Why not stake off a piece of land here and build your house?"

"Do you mean it, James?" asked Ashton.

"Indeed I do. I'm sure you can find a site that will please you both."

"What do you think, Jeremy?" said Ashton.

"I think that your brother is a very generous man."

"Don't be so sure, Jeremy," James replied "I'm just making sure one of my top foremen is close by when I need him," he said with a chuckle.

"Ashton, you must allow Kate and me to help with your wedding. We'll make it an event to remember."

"I would be very grateful for your help, Polly."

"I'm so excited—we'll start tomorrow," said Polly.

"It is getting late and I should be riding for Macon," said Jude. "But I want to once again offer my congratulations and best wishes to the future bride and groom and I will be looking for an invitation."

"I will see to it," said Jeremy.

"Please, Jude," said Polly. "Wait for a few minutes; I will pack some of my cookies for you to take home."

"I feel guilty taking advantage of your hospitality, Polly, but homemade cookies are pretty hard to turn down by an unmarried man."

"I will go to the barn and saddle your horse, Jude," said James. "Take your time and come out when you're ready. Ashton, Jeremy, your wedding will be a joyous occasion. I will talk to you later."

James walked out and headed to the barn; he was feeling like a huge weight had been lifted from his shoulders. Earlier he was mired in a mild depression but after the comic antics of Jim and his friends and the wonderful news from the intended couple, he was ready to face the world again with newfound energy.

James lowered and lit the large lantern that was suspended by a rope and pulley near the center of the barn. Then he raised the lantern about fifteen feet in the air, which spread the light, illuminating the barn almost as well as daytime. Jude's horse was a sleek black gelding that reminded James of a horse named Tar that he had ridden during the war. He led the gelding from the stall and then walked over to the tack room to fetch Jude's saddle. As he placed the blanket and bent over to pick up the saddle, footsteps on the gravel outside fell upon his ear. Expecting it to be Jude, he stayed focused on his task until the footsteps stopped outside the big door and no sound immediately followed.

James turned slowly toward the doorway and the sight upon which his eyes fell took his breath away. There before him stood a lone figure dressed in dark clothing and the burlap mask of a Klansman. It had been quite some time since he had seen the intimidating costume and he was in utter disbelief at seeing it now. At first the man stood as still as a stone and when he did make a move it was to raise the revolver he was clutching with his right hand. Then the ghostly figure took a half dozen steps toward him; stopping perhaps eight or ten feet away.

"Mayor James Langdon," he said in a deep monotone.

"I am he," James replied. "What do you want with me?"

"I should think that is plain enough."

"But why?"

"Maybe you will understand if I do this." Reaching up with his left hand the Klansman suddenly grabbed the mask and jerked if off his head. Nothing on earth could have prepared James for the instant when recognition set in.

"My God! Uncle Stanley!" It was indeed one of his father's brothers, who had owned a plantation before the war but had sold out and left before General Sherman got into Georgia. The youngest brother, James's Uncle Joseph, had done likewise. They had tried to persuade James's father to do the same but his father stayed only to see his plantation ruined, leading to his abrupt but successful attempt at suicide rendering James an unwilling witness.

"I'm glad you remember me, boy, because I want you to know who is responsible for sending you to hell so you can tell the Devil to be expecting Stanley Langdon."

"Your presence here unlocks a mystery that I have been trying to solve for years—how the Klan became informed about my past."

"That's right, boy, it was me. It seems very ironic now, but if it wasn't for me you would have been dead a long time ago. My band of brothers wanted to kill you when you first decided to rebuild your father's plantation. But I said no. I told them to do anything it took to drive you out but not to kill you or harm your family. We tried to dislodge you but you stuck like a tick on a hound dog; you had your chances. But the worst of it is you weren't satisfied to work this land, make a living, and let us pursue a victory from a rebirth of the Confederacy. You pushed and pushed and rubbed our faces in shame the way you took care of these goddamn niggers."

"I was only doing what I believed to be right, Uncle Stanley. I explained the same thing to my father before he died."

"Before you killed him you mean!" shouted his uncle. "You destroyed his will to live along with the fact that you worried your mother into an early grave. Don't try to fool me, boy; I know what you are. You killed your father, your mother, a number of my brother Klansmen, and now you're the mayor of Macon, and why? So you can try to help them low down niggers have the right to call themselves equal to a white man."

James's situation was desperate; the insanity was plainly represented in his uncle's eyes. If he didn't think of something, his uncle would shoot him dead, of that he was sure.

"I am sorry for the way things turned out, Uncle Stanley. I may have followed my own conscience but I did not intentionally hurt anyone. You and your brethren on the other hand have hurt quite a few people."

"They're not people! They're niggers!" His uncle took another step forward. "Will you honestly tell me before I blow your head off that these niggers are as important as my boys, Clark and Jessie? Do you know about my boys?"

"Yes, I know about them and it pains me as it does you. I loved Clark and Jessie."

169

Then Uncle Stanley started to cry. His obvious pain was almost more than James could bear but there was nothing he could do for the irrational man.

"My boys died as loyal soldiers to their country. My Martha is a mute. She has not uttered a word since we buried our boys. And Joseph's son Jefferson came home with a hole in his guts after seeing you in a Yankee uniform at Gettysburg. I lost everything and now you're gonna lose everything, too."

Stanley raised his revolver a little higher so that it was leveled at James's face. He cocked the hammer and James said a quick prayer and closed his eyes. An unbelievably loud gunshot rang out, but astonishingly he felt no impact. He opened his eyes; his uncle lay on the ground facing the barn door and just outside the door lay the body of Jude Renner. James checked his uncle for a pulse but found nothing. He hurried over to the door and bent down by Jude's side. There was a bullet hole just above the heart and the wound was bleeding profusely.

"I'll get you to the house, Jude. I'll send for the doctor."

"No," he gasped. "He hit me hard. I thought I had the drop on him but I took one too many steps and he heard me. He turned and we fired at the same time." Jude fell silent; his breathing was extremely shallow.

"Oh, Jude, please don't let me lose another good friend. Dear God, please don't take Jude away."

Jude exhaled one last time and was gone. James cried the likes of which had no equal. When he was once again aware of his surroundings he saw that a crowd had formed in front of the barn door. He saw, Polly, Ashton, Jeremy, and many of the black workers. No one attempted to speak comfort to him and he was grateful for that because for the moment, his entire body was insensate. When he could speak he asked some of the men to take the bodies to the root cellar and cover them for the night. Then he walked back to the house alone.

# SIXTEEN

# A Time of Reckoning

The ensuing pall that hung over Langdon Plantation on the morning of the last day in May was indescribable. To climb a ladder with a boulder on one's back would have been effortless compared to taking the bodies of Uncle Stanley and Sheriff Jude Renner to the undertakers; James performed the task alone. During the trip to Macon, he tried with all his concentration to make some sense of everything that had happened since the end of the war. It was all so reminiscent of the trials and tribulations he had endured during the four years of the conflict. It was difficult to understand the overwhelming guilt he lived with back then considering that he was convinced he was doing the right thing. Worst of all, in spite of the fact that he had no harmful intentions, people that he cared deeply about and people he didn't even know ended up hurt or dead.

James was beginning to think that he had unknowingly started something that had inevitably followed a destructive pattern and now it could not be altered. It was as if he had tampered with some unknown force thereby unleashing a curse, dormant for a thousand years—except that he did not believe in curses. So what then was he to make of it and what was he to do next? Then, as he drove along in the wagon, listening to the clip clop of the horse's hooves on the road, which spoke to him in a language that reminded him of where he was going and why, he had his answer. 'Stay the course,' said the voice inside his head. Immediately he knew the voice was right because to do anything less would be to abandon his principals; he would cease to be James Langdon.

By the time he reached the Templeton Funeral Parlor, the shock of the previous evening had subsided to a bearable level. He knew that his grieving had only just begun but that was at least a natural experience. It would

171

take time for closure to arrive; James would put forth a diligent effort to move it along.

Henry Templeton was a longtime acquaintance of James's father, John; in fact, Henry had buried him. Now, Henry and John were together again and Henry's son, Harvey, operated the family business.

Jude Renner had no wife, no children, and no family at all that James was aware of. It would have been no problem to have him interred in the town cemetery, but James would never have considered it. To him, a close and true friend was the same as family and he intended to lay Jude to rest within the little wrought iron fence at Langdon Plantation. As for Uncle Stanley, James was sadly the closest family left to care for him. His sons had perished in the war; his wife, James's Aunt Martha, was an invalid. James had no idea where his Uncle Joseph might be or what was left of his family. The only thing to do was to bury him next to his brother, John, on Langdon Plantation and James felt honored to have him there. His heart was full of sympathy for his late uncle and he would have no trouble replacing the terrible memory of the tragedy in the barn with a thousand memories of a good man and a once-loving uncle.

After making the arrangements to have the bodies prepared for burial and brought to the plantation two days hence, James drove to the *Macon Telegraph* to notify the paper of the news. He told the editor to mention that anyone interested in the position of town sheriff should notify the mayor's office in writing and they would be considered. Then he went into the town hall to ask his staff to handle matters for a period not to exceed a week.

When he returned home, Polly was waiting to comfort him and as he was ready to properly mourn for a good friend and a good uncle, James accepted her compassion with grace, dignity, and gratitude. The two of them took a long quiet walk to a peaceful spot near the edge of the meadow behind the barn, and when they felt as though they were alone in the world, the need for conversation was indulged.

"I know how difficult the death of a friend or family member is for you, James, and I know that it becomes more difficult each time."

"As always, Polly, your gift for healing has an immediate effect because you know me so well. You know just where I hurt and how best to ease the pain. But you're right ... it becomes more difficult each time. I would not dare to begin listing the tragedies we've seen and the friends and family we've lost for fear that I might well self-destruct."

"I do not believe that you are the self-destructive type, my dear husband."

"Until last night I might have agreed with you; today I am not so sure. I am afraid, Polly. Afraid that if I continue my work I am inviting more tragedy into our lives. That might seem like an irrational statement but it has been the pattern for the last ten years. I fear that I could be on the verge of a mental breakdown. On the way to town this morning I pleaded with my mental capabilities to render a decision on what I should do and the answer came: stay the course or compromise your principals. I was in complete agreement until perhaps an hour ago. Now, all I want is to resign as mayor, run this plantation, and live my life."

"It is so very true that a great deal has happened in the last ten years; no one could dispute it. But somehow you have convinced yourself that you are directly responsible. I am sure that deep inside you know it isn't true, but you are such a conscientious man that you are extremely acceptant of guilt. According to the dictionary, conscientious means governed by or conforming to the dictates of conscience. Whenever tragedy occurs in your life, it so overwhelms your metaphorical heart that you feel obligated to punish yourself by taking the blame for it. I love you for that, James. It is the foundation for your compassion, your decency, and your gentle personality. My only sorrow is that we will never be able to pass it on to more children."

Polly went silent for a moment as a tear ran down her cheek. James kissed the tear from her pretty face and said,

"I am sorry, my dear wife, I didn't mean to cause you sorrow."

Then Polly smiled at him; it was a true emotion that had produced the tear but the smile said, "Do you see what I mean?"

Then she said, "We are living our lives in turbulent times, James. We can't escape it. Everyone who ever lived became involved in the events occurring in their lifetime, especially if they lived through a war. Sadly, that happened to us. We believe and we pray but we cannot prevent tragedy nor should we blame ourselves for it. It is all right to grieve—we wouldn't be human otherwise—but if there is blame to place, the Lord will see to that."

"Your perception of life staggers the imagination, Polly; your understanding is exceeded only by your wisdom. I think that I should bring my own outlook more into focus."

"Perhaps you could benefit from an example, a real life instance that you can hold on to," she said. "You once met President Lincoln, didn't you?"

"I had that privilege, yes."

"It must have been intoxicating to be in his presence."

"I will never forget it."

"You and Mr. Lincoln shared many of the same qualities. He embarked on a very important mission when the war came, just as you did. He was faced with reuniting a torn country. It is hard to imagine the weight of the responsibility that must have rested upon his shoulders; harder still to imagine living with the decisions that he had to make. It was his job to send thousands of young men to defend the Union, knowing without doubt that many of them would never return. How it must have torn at him to read the accounts and receive the reports time and time again of another battle that had claimed the lives of many soldiers. As painful as it must have been, I am sure that Mr. Lincoln did not personally blame himself for every individual loss of life or his own life would have come to madness. He mourned the heavy losses but he understood the circumstances and he knew that death was a significant part of what needed to be done. Mr. Lincoln possessed the courage to stand his ground and I know that you do also. Yes, my dear husband, mourn your losses as is your human right, but allow them to make you stronger. In the end, men like you and Abraham Lincoln will triumph."

James tried to think of the right words to tell Polly how much she had eased his anxiety but he was unable to express himself. But it was fine; the relationship they shared was never demanding and they could sense things in one another when mere words would not suffice. Hand in hand they started back to the house; each of them revitalized by the magic that was their perfect compatibility.

Two days later, Jude Renner and Stanley Langdon were buried in the little family cemetery at Langdon Plantation. Aaron Parmalee performed the service and James delivered the eulogy, moving the gathering of mourners with his words and silently vowing to himself to stay the course.

The day after, at James's insistence, Polly, Ashton, and Kate began planning Ashton's wedding. Jeremy had chosen a site to build a home for his bride and himself and James was the first to volunteer his help with the construction. Less than a week after the funeral he was back at his office in the town hall and the members of his staff couldn't help but notice the new burst of energy with which he performed his duties. The first order of business was to select and appoint a new sheriff from the stack of resumes that had been submitted.

After intense scrutiny of the candidates and some background investigations conducted by Edwin Forbes, James chose a man named Simon Strickler to succeed his late friend Jude Renner. Contrary to the reasons James cited for his choice, secretly he had made his selection based primarily on geographic origin. Simon was a northern transplant from Pennsylvania; he had served under his brother Lieutenant Alexander Strickler in Company E of the 87th Pennsylvania Volunteers during the war. It remained important to James for Macon to have a sheriff whose point of view concerning black rights was in sync with his own. Initially, there was no proof of that; James was simply hedging his bet by taking advantage of having an applicant from the North.

However, when he invited the new sheriff to his office for some unofficial conversation he soon realized that he would have to cut his losses. Simon was not as congenial as Jude had been, not that he was difficult or argumentative; he simply was not endowed with the same friendly nature. At times James found his attitude impossible to read. On the subject of his feelings toward the blacks; he appeared to be neither hot nor cold.

"I was surprised to hear that you were in the Union army, Mr. Mayor. You are from near Macon aren't you?"

"That's correct; I own and operate my late father's plantation. I surprised a lot of my fellow soldiers during the war, too."

"Does it upset you when someone asks about it?"

"Not especially, no. Their curiosity is usually satisfied when I tell them that I did not believe in slavery."

"I guess that does explain it," Simon replied.

"Would I be too presumptuous to think that you were not fond of the practice?" said James.

"Forgive me, Mr. Mayor, but that sounds like a leading question. I fought for the North because I am a northerner, and unlike you, I could find no reason not to fight for my native land. When the president decided to free the Negroes, some of the boys complained like hell and it got a lot worse later in the war when the prisoner exchanged stopped on account of the Rebs refused to treat the Negro soldiers the same as the whites. Personally I chose to ignore the whole issue and I kept telling myself that I was fighting for the same reasons as when I joined the army in the first place. In my outfit there was a few contraband Negroes that latched onto us somewhere near Winchester, Virginia after they escaped from a tobacco farm. One of them, a buck named George, claimed he was a house worker and did all the cookin for his owner's family. One night we let him cook up something that he called wilderness stew. It turned out to be the best thing we ever tasted; the captain turned the company cook into a rifleman and George kept the job until the end of the war. The other two Negroes were good workers, too; helpin with the horses and some of our equipment."

"Did that alter your thinking about Mr. Lincoln's new purpose for winning the war?"

"No, sir, it didn't. I have no interest in the Negroes and no concern over them being slaves or being freemen. I treated the Negroes in camp the same way I would any new recruit that I didn't have anything in common with."

"Except that you would have fought to defend the new recruit?"

"When I was in battle, Mayor, I was fighting to defend everyone behind my lines. And the only men I killed during the war were white."

"I appreciate your honesty, Sheriff, and I see no reason why we wouldn't be able to work together. My main expectations of you are that you respect and uphold the law."

"I will work with you to that end, Mayor, and I hope you were not offended by anything I said; I meant no offense."

"No offense taken, Sheriff. Thank you for your time."

Sheriff Strickler took his leave and James sat back in his chair to let the outcome of the meeting settle over him. He decided that he would have to see the sheriff in the performance of his duties before he could make a proper assessment of his choice.

Ashton and Jeremy's wedding plans were complete and the date had been set for July 15, 1871. When the happy day arrived, the occasion proved to be instrumental in so much more than marking the beginning of a loving couple's dreams. The affair, attended by most of the ranking socialites from Macon and surrounding Bibb County, resembled the carefree days before the war—staged in elegance and performed in grandeur. The Langdon house was in bloom with lavish flower arrangements, the food and refreshments were suitable for royalty, and the orchestra playing sweet strains out on the lawn had come all the way from Atlanta.

The festivities worked on James like a tonic, filling him with joy, entertaining him with laughter, and rejuvenating his weary soul with its peaceful setting of utter civility. Perfection was achieved for James that day, if only temporarily, as the black workers attended the wedding mingled with the other guests without a hint of indignation or a single telltale glance. James concluded that it was a gift from the people of Macon for all he'd done that they checked their prejudice, no doubt compromising because the wedding was held at James's home and was no reflection on them. He did not care; he was enjoying it.

When evening came, the only thing left was to give the happy couple a proper sendoff. Jeremy and Ashton had decided to spend a week in Atlanta for a honeymoon. Their new home was complete and waiting for them thanks to the concerted efforts of every man who worked on Langdon Plantation. If James could not see interracial unity anywhere else, he could always see it in the little world he had transformed simply by allowing people to be equal.

All the guests crowded the front lawn as Mr. and Mrs. Jeremy Todd prepared to climb into their flower covered carriage and take the road to Atlanta. Before Jeremy could help Ashton inside, James took his sister's hand and led her a few steps away.

"Before you leave I must tell you that I wish for you all the happiness in the world. More importantly, I must pour from my heart a most sincere apology. I am sorry that I ever believed that it was you who informed the Klan about my past. I should have trusted you especially after you told me you weren't responsible. I know you better than that; I am sorry."

"I think we should share the blame for something that was no more than a misunderstanding, James. I gave you reason to feel the way you did; I realize that, and I am sorry, too. I feel nothing for you other than a deep sisterly love, the same as I did on the day of your eighteenth birthday. Do you remember?"

"I remember, I will always remember. Go now and be filled with joy."

James returned his sister to her waiting husband; he shook Jeremy's hand and offered his heartfelt congratulations. The couple drove off as an almost deafening cheer let loose and then the celebration was over.

It was late when the last guest departed but James did not feel tired. Polly found him sitting on the swing and joined him.

"Could anything have made it a better day?" she asked.

"Nothing that I can think of," he replied. "Did you see it, Polly? Did you see for a brief time how wonderful life is when people forget their differences? It was like Jim at play with Jeb and Bodie."

"I saw it, James. I am very glad I saw it. No matter how bad things look at times, God never fails to provide a little hope just when we need it most."

"He certainly does," James replied. I think that the lift he gave me today will sustain me for quite a while."

The following week, James was in his office in the town hall when a frantic knock was laid upon his door. The door opened and Felix Gray stuck his head into the room. "Mr. Mayor, come quick, there is an altercation taking place out in the street."

"Get the sheriff," said James as he jumped up from his chair. Felix took off as fast as his bow legs could carry him and James was only two steps behind. Out in front of the town hall was a public watering trough used by passersby to refresh their animals. As James approached he could see a horse, a mule, and a rather large white man who had a grip on the back collar of a local black man and was shoving his head beneath the water.

"Let that man up," James shouted at the ruffian.

"Who the hell are you?" the miscreant shouted back.

"I am the town mayor and I am telling you to release that man."

By this time Sheriff Strickler had arrived on the scene with one of his deputies, Ned Barnes.

"What's going on here?" the sheriff demanded. The burly stranger jerked the black man's head up out of the water, the victim gasping for breath.

"I was jes learnin this nigger to make way when he sees a white man comin. He was waterin his mangy mule at this here trough and when I come up with my hoss he just kept waterin his mangy mule. You needn't have troubled yourself, Sheriff. I'm learnin him."

179

"Release that man, get on your horse, and head out of town," said Strickler.

"Am I hearin you right, Sheriff? You takin the side a this nigger?"

"If he was there first, you should have waited your turn," Strickler replied.

"I must a made a wrong turn somewhere and ended up north somehow. What kinda town you runnin here, Sheriff?"

"The kind that demands law and order."

"Well dunkin an uppity nigger's head in a hoss trough *is* law and I got no respect for a nigger lovin sheriff or his mayor who don't know that."

Sheriff Strickler's blood was up and he had grown tired of talking to the disrespectful trouble maker. Without another word he grabbed the man by the arm and swung him around in a circle, landing him in the middle of the trough. "Go on home, Jessup," he said to the black man.

Jessup took his mule by the halter and led him off. With a mouth full of threats mixed with unbelievable profanity, the stranger pushed himself up to a standing position. With a blood curdling yell he grabbed a large knife from his belt and stomped out of the trough toward the sheriff. But Strickler was fast on his feet; sidestepping and tripping the man, who ended up on his face in the street. The sheriff grabbed his wrists and held him steady until Ned Barnes could restrain him with a set of manacles. Pulling the ill-tempered brute to his feet, Strickler said, "Take this fool down to the jail, Ned, and lock him up. I'll be there in a little bit to set charges against him."

James could not believe what he'd just witnessed. It was true that the stranger had made a mistake by attacking the sheriff with a knife but James had his own perception of the incident. In his mind's eye, the town sheriff had sided with a black man over a white man and the significance of it was monumental as well as unprecedented. The sheriff tipped his hat to James and then started down the street after his deputy.

"Sheriff Strickler," James called out. The sheriff stopped and turned around. "So that contraband Negro in your company was a pretty good cook, was he?"

Strickler showed a little smile and said, "Yes, sir, he was."

For James, the ledger had been balanced and he set his sights on the future with great anticipation.

# SEVENTEEN

## Old Friends and New Enemies

For six years, James remained the mayor of Macon, Georgia. He had come to believe that he could have remained as such for the rest of his life had he so chosen. Although he had come to enjoy the position in spite of the permanent opposition to his dreams of racial equality, by 1876 he knew it was time to move on and to cast his net for bigger fish. From the beginning he felt that in order to exact real change in laws and possibly constitutional amendments he needed to serve on no less than the congressional level. However, representatives from Georgia had ceased to exist in 1867 until re-establishment of the eighth congressional district in December of 1873. But as difficult as it was for James to believe, Ulysses S. Grant was re-elected as president in 1872 so when the opportunity to try for a congressional seat came the following year, James passed it by. He always told himself that the only sad thing about the end of the war was that it took away from Grant one of the only two things he was good at in life; the other thing being marriage.

James decided that he would wait until Grant was out of office knowing that the two of them would never have gotten along. Irrefutable proof of that came in March of 1875 when Congress adopted a Civil Rights Act that guaranteed all citizens, regardless of race, equal enjoyment of public facilities such as transport, restaurants, and hotels. It also stated that no one may be excluded from jury service on the basis of race. In the course of debating the bill, another old Union general, Benjamin Butler, one of the last of the Radical Republicans, proposed an amendment that would compel the racial integration of all schools in the South, but President Grant had the amendment removed. James was furious when he read the story in the *Macon Telegraph*.

In June, another Civil War veteran of the Union, Rutherford B. Hayes, Governor of Ohio, received the presidential nomination by the Republican Party; the Democrats nominated Samuel J. Tilden, Governor of New York. In order to give more time and attention to gaining a congressional seat, James resigned his position as mayor and appointed Edwin Forbes to be his successor.

After filing the necessary paperwork and paying the fee, James's name was added to the Republican ballot. Larger aspirations require larger efforts and he knew that sitting around Macon would not get him elected to congress. When James resigned as mayor, Felix Gray expressed an interest in working for him as his campaign manager. James was delighted. He knew that Felix would be an irreplaceable cog in his political machine. The first order of business was to plan a statewide tour to meet the voters, shake some hands, and find out what was uppermost in the minds of the people of Georgia. Felix set to work immediately and soon had a schedule for a trip that would last for two months and include stops in Atlanta, Albany, Augusta, Columbus, and Savannah.

Polly would accompany him and, as school was closed for the summer, Jim would go as well. Hopes were high as the trip began; everyone was anxious to reach the first stop: Columbus. But the Langdons soon found out what life was truly like in the public eye; one day it could be thrilling and the next it could be frightening. The crowds they encountered numbered in the thousands and the comments that could be heard over the din were usually a mixture of approval and disapproval. James had included as members of his staff, three security guards whose presence was of great comfort to him and his little family.

It was difficult to measure success as the tour progressed from city to city save for the feedback from the pollster. Based on this unofficial information, James believed he had reason to be optimistic but his feeling was sorely challenged when they reached their last stop on the tour: Atlanta. One evening after a fundraising dinner at the Statehouse in Southwest Atlanta, James was delivering a speech when a shot rang out, throwing the crowd into a panic. Two of his security guards pushed and shoved their way through the screaming mob in pursuit of the gunman while the third grabbed James and used his large body to make a path to a carriage waiting outside. Polly and Jim had stayed behind at the hotel, for which James was grateful—that and the fact that no one was hit by the bullet he believed was meant for him.

The following morning James received a report on the incident. The shooter had been arrested; a man named Clement Potts. Potts claimed to be an unofficial spokesman for the people of Atlanta and said that he was only trying to intimidate a candidate who would never represent the best interests of Georgia. But Potts had a criminal history of violence, especially against blacks and their white supporters and he was believed to be a member of the Klan.

James was not surprised. Having seen how deeply hatred can be rooted in the human species, he sadly speculated that the Klan in some form or another may have become a permanent part of American society. He had endured a number of confrontations with the Klan in the past and had every reason to believe that he would again find himself pitted against those white supremacists that he now referred to sarcastically as, "My old friends."

For James, Polly, and Jim it was good to return home after a very exhausting two months and they were satisfied that there was nothing left to do except to wait for the results of the upcoming election. James put the whole affair out of his mind, keeping a good thought and never obsessing about his desire to see inside the legislative body of the Federal Government.

If it is true that all good things come to those who wait, it is also true that the waiting time is usually negotiable. Sometimes a good thing is received on the first try; sometimes it takes more than one attempt. When Election Day came that year, James was closely beaten by his opponent and his plans to battle the forces of racism from Washington would have to be put on hold. His party's presidential candidate had nearly as much trouble, as Samuel J. Tilden won the popular vote by a margin of 250,000 votes. But there were disputes over the voting of Florida, Louisiana, South Carolina, and Oregon.

Consequently, neither candidate was able to claim a clear victory. It was necessary for Congress to set up an Electoral Commission to rectify the presidential deadlock. On March 2, 1877, Hayes was declared the winner and President Grant allowed him to take the oath the next day to forestall any further challenge by the Democrats.

As much as the sting of defeat unsettled James for a short time, he was properly grateful to his staff, especially Felix Gray. The job he performed was top notch; in fact, James had largely underestimated Felix's expertise and his influence in all things political. It turned out that James had actually given as good an account of himself as he did due to Felix's connections in Washington; a secret the wily little man had seen no reason to reveal.

Weeks after the election, Felix visited James at home and gave him some information that changed his opinion of Rutherford B. Hayes entirely. According to underground sources at the capitol, Hayes had managed to secure the presidency by garnering favors from Democratic leaders in exchange for a Republican promise that the president would withdraw the Federal garrison under the Reconstruction Acts and generally ignore the enforcement of the Fourteenth Amendment that guaranteed the civil rights of the blacks. Appointing a Southerner to his cabinet was an agreement that Hayes also made. In April, Hayes withdrew Federal troops from South Carolina and then from Louisiana, the last of the former Confederate states to be governed with Northern support. And so it was that Hayes won the White House by a single electoral vote, in large part because of his conciliatory gestures toward the South. Reconstruction was officially over and the Civil War was officially ended.

But however he had gotten there, Rutherford B. Hayes was the president and James was very pleased. He knew that the new president was an amiable man who had many worthwhile ideas for government and country. Included on his agenda were plans to reform the system of civil service appointments, which was based on the spoils system established under former President Andrew Jackson. Hayes also wanted to restore popular faith in the presidency and to reverse the deterioration of executive power that had set in after Lincoln's death. He intended to deal with corruption in the postal service. But the goal of the new president for which James was most grateful was Hayes's desire to convince the South to accept the idea of racial equality.

Having lost the congressional election, James would return to life without politics, wait for his next opportunity, and watch the progress of the new administration in Washington. Perhaps it was a good thing that he did not make the leap from local politician to the level of the Federal Government too quickly. Maybe, he thought, someone wiser than he was suggesting that a rest was in order. Still, politics had gotten into James's blood, but not because he had succumbed to the attraction of power. It was because he had seen what could be accomplished by a body of people working together for a common goal. It was in that same vein that his "Old Friends," the Ku Klux Klan, had been opposed to the result of decreasing numbers and diminished activity.

It was not long, however, before the "Old Friends," were replaced by "New Enemies." Late in 1877, James became aware of a new cloud on the horizon; a very dark one. With the old guard of white southerners back in power, the ex-Confederate states had quickly taken measures to put the black man in his place and keep him there. State laws were established to completely segregate the former slaves; these laws became known as "Jim Crow."

James learned that the term originated around 1830 when a white minstrel performer, Thomas "Daddy" Rice blackened his face with charcoal paste or burnt cork and danced an absurd jig while singing the lyrics to the song, "Jump Jim Crow." The story went on to say that Rice created the character while traveling in the South where he saw a young black boy dancing and singing a song ending with the chorus words:

"Weel about and turnabout and do jis so,
Eb'ry time I weel about I jump Jim Crow."

Some people believe that a Mr. Crow owned the slave who inspired Rice's act—thus the reason for the term in the lyrics.

In spite of all that James had seen in his lifetime, he still found it incomprehensible that such a wedge could be driven between two peoples because of the color of their skin. He could not understand what most people saw that he did not see. But as time went by, he *did* realize that Jim Crow was not just a series of rigid anti-black laws; it was a way of life. Under Jim Crow, blacks were reduced to the status of second class citizens. Jim Crow was the legitimization of anti-black racism. Many Christian ministers and theologians preached that whites were the Chosen people, blacks were cursed to be servants, and God supported racial segregation.

At every educational level, it was the belief that blacks were innately intellectually and culturally inferior to whites. Pro-segregation politicians gave inspiring speeches on the great dangers of integration: the mongrelization of the white race, which would lead to the destruction of America. Newspaper and magazine writers regularly referred to blacks as, niggers, coons, and darkies; and even worse, their articles reinforced the dominant culture's perspective of black stereotypes. Even children's games portrayed blacks as inferior beings. Most major societal institutions reflected and supported the oppression of blacks. It was decided that, if necessary, violence must be used to keep blacks at the bottom of the racial hierarchy.

Jim Crow laws affected all aspects of everyday life; James often wondered how the blacks were able to learn the dos and don'ts before they were deemed in violation of some nonsensical law, rule, or regulation. A black man could not shake hands with a white man because it implied social equality. A black man could not offer his hand to a white woman because he risked being accused of rape. Blacks could not eat with whites and if they did the whites were served first and some sort of partition had to be between them. Blacks were not allowed to show affection toward one another in public, especially kissing, because it offended whites. Blacks were introduced to whites; never whites to blacks. Blacks could not assert or even intimate that a white person was lying. They could not lay claim to or overly demonstrate superior knowledge or intelligence. Blacks could not curse a white person,

187

laugh derisively at a white person, or comment on the appearance of a white woman, and this was only the beginning.

The Jim Crow laws and system of etiquette were undergirded by violence both real and threatened. Whites could physically beat blacks with impunity. Blacks who violated Jim Crow laws risked losing their homes, jobs, even their lives. Blacks had very little legal recourse because the Jim Crow criminal justice system was all white. Violence was instrumental for Jim Crow; it was a method of social control.

One afternoon James told Polly that he was going into Macon to see how Mayor Forbes was getting along, but that was only part of the reason for his visit. He was in the mood to vent his frustration and his intention was to drop in on Sheriff Strickler. He knew that there was nothing he could do to interfere with the changes that had come about but he was looking for any insight as to just how strictly the Jim Crow laws were being enforced in Macon. There was no one in the sheriff's office when he arrived so he decided to take a seat and wait. As he walked past the door that led back to the cell block, he stopped for a moment to look through the small opening near the top of the door. He could see all five cells through the opening and he could also see that three of them were occupied. Each of three cells held an adult black man; all were stretched out on the crude cots, their only comfort. James was still standing at the door when Sheriff Strickler walked in.

"Mr. Langdon?" said the sheriff with surprise in his voice. "What can I do for you?"

"Nothing really, Sheriff, I just came in to see how you're doing."

The sheriff's face took on a skeptical expression and he said, "I see, well I appreciate your concern. I'm doing fine. I don't mean to be offensive, Mr. Langdon, but what are you really doing here?"

"I'm not offended; you ask a fair question. I wanted to know if you are enforcing these new laws I've been reading about."

"I'm the sheriff ... that's my job."

"Do you agree with the restrictions to these people's lives?"

"I have nothing to say about it. If I had a problem with the new laws I would find something else to do for a living. I know how *you* feel, Mr. Langdon, but to me, they are laws."

"You know as well as I do that they are unfair and humiliating. It is the Old South returning to power. Those laws are designed to keep the black man in his place and nothing more. They were better off as slaves; they've gained nothing by the Thirteenth Amendment."

"I can't argue with you and I won't," said the sheriff. "Now, if there isn't anything else, I have other business to attend to."

"There is one other thing," said James. "I see you have three black men locked up; what have they done?"

A moment earlier Sheriff Strickler had held his irritation in check; now he let his feelings go.

"I'm afraid that's none of your business. You are not the mayor anymore and if you go any further with this, you will be interfering with the performance of my office."

"What I really want to know is who will be defending them in court?"

"I doubt that anyone will."

"But everyone is entitled to legal counsel; it says so in the constitution."

"It also says that you can't force someone to do something they don't want to do and nobody is going to defend those black men and not a single person is going to blame them for not wanting to. Right or wrong, that's just the way it is."

"Then I will defend them," said James.

"Have you been to law school?"

"No, I haven't, but in this case I don't think it would matter. At least they would have someone who will try to get at the truth."

"It wouldn't do any good. The truth is that they are black and even if you could prove their innocence in a dozen different ways, they will still be found guilty. Go home, Mr. Langdon. There is nothing you can do."

189

Without another word, James stomped out of the sheriff's office and slammed the door. At that moment, for the very first time, he truly regretted his decision to stay in Georgia when the war ended. He headed home shrouded in defeat and disappointment. He was ashamed to call himself a Georgian and a Southerner. It was difficult to believe that the black man had been brought to America in chains against his will. He toiled as a slave for over two hundred years and watched his family do the same. He did not ask for any of it. Then when he finally got his freedom, the whites used him as kindling in their fire of bitter revenge. Hell, thought James, I am ashamed of being white.

# EIGHTEEN

# The Repetition of History

By the fall of 1878, many things were changing while, unfortunately, many others stayed the same. Cotton was still being harvested on Langdon Plantation and the dual society of the South was still very much in place. But James had become an uncle by the birth of Jeremy and Aston's daughter, Madeline; Kate was engaged to a railroad engineer from Columbus; and Jim would soon be turning sixteen.

It was time for young Jim to leave home as his father had done; time to familiarize himself with higher education. After a lot of conversation and consideration, it was decided that the University of Georgia would be the college he would attend. It was a very different feeling, James thought, to be on the other side of the separation; he could remember well when he had left home for school in New York. It was roughly ninety miles from Macon to Athens where the school was located, but James felt like his son would be a world away. Jim would come home for holidays and other scheduled breaks but he would live in one of the dorms the rest of the time.

All James could think about the day Jim departed was how quickly the moment had arrived. Surely his own parents must have felt the same way when he left for school. James wanted to take his son to the train station in Macon to see him off but Polly wished to say goodbye to him at home. She said the distance between them would seem so much greater if she had to watch him board a train. Her motherly instincts brought a smile to James's face and he graciously complied with her wishes.

Polly seemed quiet and reserved for a week or so after Jim left. James knew that she was feeling a sense of emptiness and he did his best to comfort her; actually they comforted each other as he was feeling a loss himself. Now

191

and then he would see Polly sitting out behind the house, talking with Jim's best friends, Jeb and Bodie; they missed Jim, too.

As time eases most anxiety, James and Polly eventually got used to the change and life seemed routine again. Still, they looked forward to the holidays and their first visit from their budding young college student.

Then one afternoon in early November about a week before Jim's birthday, a courier came by the house with a telegram. Receiving the communication, James put it into his shirt pocket without opening it as he was preoccupied with something else. It was not until that evening while sitting in the parlor with Polly that he remembered it. He handed the telegram to Polly and said, "I forgot all about this, Polly. Would you like to see who it is from?"

She took the telegram, opened it, and then let out an audible gasp. James looked up from his newspaper and immediately noticed that his wife had been completely unnerved by the telegram.

"Polly? Is something wrong?"

"Our son is in jail," she said in disbelief.

"What? I don't believe it. Let me see that." James took the paper from Polly's shaky hand and read the contents himself. The telegram was from the City Marshal's Office of Athens, Georgia. Jim was being held on assault charges and the City Marshal was requesting that the parents of James J. Langdon Jr. come to the marshal's office at once.

"There must be some mistake, Polly. I don't believe a word of this. Our son would never assault anyone. Please go and start packing and I will find someone to drive us to the train station."

Polly got up without a word and headed for the stairs. When they were ready to leave, Hiram Jones brought the carriage to the front of the house; they loaded their bags and started for Macon. It was 10 PM by the time they got to the station and the next train would not leave until 11 o'clock. Anxiety was high but there was nothing to do but wait.

"What on earth could have happened, James?" said Polly.

"I have been searching my mind for an answer to that but for the life of me I cannot imagine what this is all about. I only know that Jim is not prone to violence and if he was involved in a physical altercation he must have had a very good reason. Please try not to worry, Polly, and I will try to take my own advice. I know how difficult it is, especially sitting here waiting for this blessed train."

When the train arrived, the two of them boarded for what turned out to be a silent trip. The train pulled into the station in Athens at 1 AM; they immediately hired a man who was waiting around the station to charge a fare to transport anyone needing a ride. His buckboard did not provide a pleasant trip but neither James nor Polly complained; getting to the marshal's office was all that mattered. At 1:30 AM they walked through the door only to find a deputy who was half asleep at the front desk. James let the door close with a bang and the startled deputy abruptly got to his feet.

"What can I do for you folks?" he inquired.

"To start with you can let us see our son, James Langdon Jr." said James. "Then you can tell us about this preposterous charge of assault."

"Oh, I'm afraid the charge isn't preposterous," said the deputy as if he wasn't familiar with the word. "He did assault two other men, Mr. Langdon."

"Can we see him?" James asked.

"Well, we do have regular visiting hours but it looks like you and the boy's mother traveled some to get here, and considering the circumstances I guess I can let you see him."

"I thank you for that, Deputy. Please lead the way."

The deputy came from behind the desk and took them through a heavy wooden door back to the cell block. They followed to the end of the row and in the last cell on the right, Jim was lying face down on the cot; his hair in an unkempt state and his clothes somewhat in tatters.

"Come on out when you're through but don't take too long ... I'm kinda breakin the rules, you know." The deputy walked away, leaving them to their visit. None of the cells close by were occupied, adding to their privacy.

"Son," said James in a whisper. "Mother and Father are here."

Jim rolled to his side and then he sat up and rubbed his eyes. When he got to his feet and walked over to the bars, James and Polly were horrified. The boy's face was a mass of bruises and one eye was swollen and nearly closed. His lower lip had been split and there was dried blood on his forehead. Polly started to cry, reaching through the bars in an attempt to hug her son.

"My dear God!" said James. "What has happened to you, son?"

"I am so ashamed that you and Mother had to come here, Father. It hurts me more than my cuts and bruises."

"Never mind that, James, just tell us what happened."

"Well, I was coming out of a little café over on Prince Avenue and I saw two rough looking gentlemen accosting a young black girl. She was no older than I am and they would not let her go on her way. They were abusing her verbally and they were grabbing her in a most inappropriate manner. I politely asked them to stop bothering the girl and I asked them to please let her go about her business. They asked me what business is was of mine and they called me a nigger lover. I told them the girl was an Afro American, not a nigger, and then they shoved me to the ground and continued to harass this defenseless young girl. I got up and told them if they did not leave her alone I would notify the authorities. They started laughing ... now I know why. One of the men said that I could notify the authorities if I had time to waste and then he said he would give me an even better reason to run to the sheriff. That's when he hit me in the mouth and I fell back, cracking my eye on the corner of the café entrance. Then the two of them went back to picking on the girl. I got up and tried to pull one of the men away and then both of them began to give me the beating that put me in this state of appearance. I tried to defend myself but it was useless against two men as big as they were. Finally a policeman came by or I guess they would be beating me still. I give the hooligans credit for one thing—they told the policeman exactly what happened. At that point I was sure that they would be arrested. Instead, the officer secured my hands

194

behind my back and marched me down here, locked me in this cell, and I have been here since then. I told the marshal that I couldn't miss my classes but he said that it wasn't his concern. I'm very grateful to one of the deputies, Mr. Smith, for sending the telegram for me."

"Do you mean that the other two men were not arrested?"

"No, Father, they were not."

While James listened to his son's story, his anger boiled over, understanding all too well what happens when you challenge those narrow minded, self-appointed members of the chosen race. He was surprised he hadn't guessed the circumstances when he got the telegram.

"I am split in two, son, by feeling so sorry this happened to you and feeling so proud of you at the same time. Have you had any medical attention?"

"Yes, Father, they brought a doctor in to examine me but he didn't say much, stay long, or do anything for me."

"I can't say I'm surprised. We are here now and your mother and I are going to get you out of this cell and we are going to get this travesty of justice straightened out. Polly, wait here with Jim while I go speak to this deputy."

James headed for the cell block door with only a few seconds to harness his anger. He knew that he would be of little help if he couldn't control his emotions. The most important thing, he thought, was to get Jim out of that cell and take him to a doctor. After that, the battle to preserve his son's innocence would begin.

The deputy was dozing again when James walked up to the desk and his disposition was less than affable when he opened his eyes and saw James glaring at him.

"Your visit is terminated," he said. "You and your wife will have to leave."

"I want my son released, right now, tonight."

"I'm afraid that isn't possible. The marshal has to handle that and he won't be here until eight o'clock tomorrow morning."

"My son needs medical attention and some decent food. I want him out of there and I want him out right now."

"Now you look here," said the irate deputy. "Your son has been looked at by a doctor and he had his supper. You

195

can come back in the morning and talk to the marshal, or if you'd rather, I can fix it so you can spend the night in the cell next to your son. You have five minutes to get your wife and leave or your son won't be the only one in trouble."

James wanted desperately to lock the deputy in one of his own cells, take Jim, and go. He knew that his son was being unlawfully charged and unlawfully jailed but there was no way he was going to accomplish anything by further agitating the witless deputy. He had to hold his insides in until eight o'clock in the morning and maybe then something could be done. Without a word he went back to the cell block to get Polly and to tell Jim that they would be back at the stroke of eight.

James and Polly took a room at the closest hotel they could find but they did not even try to sleep. They spent the next five and a half hours talking and contemplating the future.

"Have they set bail, James?" asked Polly.

"The deputy didn't say and I didn't ask, but I sincerely doubt it. I think they just threw him in that cell without any proper procedure whatsoever. It's been a hard lesson for us, Polly, but we have certainly learned that standing in support of the black race is the most unpopular thing you can do in this country. And how can we effectively support them anyway? The law means nothing to these defiant oafs down here. They despise the liberated slave and nothing is going to change their ignorant, pigheaded, narrow-minded attitudes. I feel like I am at the end of my rope. What do I tell my son? Do I tell him, next time let the bullies have their fun abusing the young black girl and don't get involved? Do I tell him to respect the policemen and the law even though they are making a mockery of justice and deserve no respect? No, I say no. I cannot tell my son that. That would be like telling him that slavery was right and it should not have been destroyed. It would be like telling him that my principles, the guiding light I have followed all my life, was leading me astray. I cannot tell him that, and not because I think he should honor his father by living by the same doctrine, but because in the eyes of God Almighty it is the right thing."

"It is the repetition of history," said Polly. "I remember what it was like during the war; how you took to your cause and risked life and limb for what you believed to be right. I remember how you were chased, chastised, and wounded for your cause, and even though I supported you with all my heart, I remember how I suffered to see the hurt the evildoers inflicted on you. And as difficult as it was, it would have been even more so to tell you to abandon your fight and leave the task to someone else. Here we are again ... our son has embarked on his mission. Although he doesn't yet fully comprehend it, he is standing up for what he believes is right: coming to the rescue of someone who needed his help. Now we share the pain, James; feel the aching in your heart, tearing at you inside after seeing your only son bruised and battered. But no matter how much we might want to tell him to give up the fight, we know the world would be the worse for it."

"We will do what we've always done, Polly—we will pray and when need be we will pray harder. We must make it through with God's help or not make it at all. I know our son would not have it otherwise. It is nearly 7 AM. Let's go get some breakfast and then go rescue our son."

At eight o'clock sharp, James and Polly entered the city marshal's office. Fortunately, the marshal, a man by the name of Zebulon Howard, was already in his chair. When they stepped up to the desk, the marshal looked up from his paperwork.

"You must be Mr. and Mrs. James Langdon Senior," he said in an exceptionally unfriendly tone of voice. "My deputy filled me in on your visit earlier this morning. I gather that you are here to get your boy?"

"That is correct," James replied. "I think you should know, Marshal—"

"There is nothing I need to know from you, Mr. Langdon. But let me give you a nickel's worth of free advice. We don't need or want troublemakers like your son in our town. The best thing you can do for everyone concerned is to take him home until he learns how to act in decent society."

"You are accusing my son of being the troublemaker in this case?"

'What would you call starting a fight in public?"

"My son did not start that fight. He was attacked by two grown men and nearly beaten to death with little or no chance of defending himself."

"And I say it was his fault," said the marshal with fire in his eyes.

"I see," said James. "Yes, it is all very clear to me now. My son took the side of a young black girl who was being harassed by two uncouth louts and that is why he is in jail while the real perpetrators are probably at this very minute out on the street abusing some other defenseless child."

"You know something, Langdon? The dislike I first felt for you is developing into a great hate. I won't pull any punches here. In this town, and in this state, niggers have their place in society. I expect them to know their place and stay in it. And I don't like any colorblind fool to show partiality to any nigger—and if they do, I hope they get what your boy got. I'm going to look the other way every time. Furthermore, there isn't one thing you can do about it because it's the law. Now, if you want that boy of yours out of jail you can post a two hundred dollar bond and I'll gladly release him."

James knew that the marshal was baiting him but he was past caring. He also knew that what he was about to do would not help the situation one bit. He could take criticism, verbal abuse, and threats all day long, provided they were directed at him. But as soon as the marshal spoke the first derogatory syllable about his son, he had unknowingly awakened the sleeping giant in James.

Polly had stood silent throughout the boiling of tempers, but she knew her husband and she knew that his restraint was on the verge of collapse. As composed as a pastor in church and as skillful as an artisan mediator, she saw that it was time to intervene.

"James, dear, I have something to say to the marshal."

James looked at her in surprise but in an instant he understood what she was doing and he wisely gave her the right of way. In a voice that closely resembled charming, Polly stepped in front of James and said, "Now, Marshal Howard, I have been standing here quietly listening to your unadulterated claptrap, your abusive characterization of my son, and your racist comments. Our son has told us the entire story and we know that every word of it is pure truth. I will not waste my time passing any judgments on you—you are responsible for your own spiritual welfare. Furthermore, our son is innocent and he will not suffer any repercussions from a criminal history. He will not appear at any bogus trial and he will not be subjected to further criticism from you. You will release our son this minute or my husband and I shall hire the finest lawyer that money can buy and you, your deputies, and your office will undergo the most intensive investigation that you can imagine. Because you see, we have rights, even if we are nigger lovers."

Upon issuance of her final word, she displayed a smile so sweet that only the daggers in her eyes gave credence to the warning she'd leveled at Marshal Howard. With gritted teeth, he picked up a set of keys, tossed them to one of his deputies, and said, "Let him out."

Five minutes later, out on the street, James kissed Polly and said, "Thank you, dear, I was about to fight a battle I couldn't win but you turned the tide."

"I thought that a woman might be able to get away with a little more than a man but I do apologize for stealing your thunder. I love and admire you for standing up for our son and I realize that sometimes physical involvement is the only way to reach a settlement. But I know we can agree that we have our son and that is all that matters."

"We can agree," said James. "Let's find a doctor."

A thorough examination attested to the fact that, although bruised and a bit swollen in a few places, Jim was fine. There was one more mountain to climb and that was to take him back to school and see if a few days absent carried any penalties.

"We should speak with the president of the university," said Jim. "I want to be sure that everything is straightened out, but President Butler is a very busy man and very difficult to gain an audience with."

"We'll do our best," James told him. "If your mother and I have to stay for a day or two we will."

The president was in his office when they arrived and to everyone's surprise, when his secretary told him the

Langdons requested a meeting, he told her to send them right in. However, as James entered the office a sense of foreboding came over him and the first justification for his feeling came when President Butler did not rise to his feet to greet them. He waved them to the chairs in front of his desk, laced his fingers together, and waited until the three of them sat down.

"I will do you the courtesy of not prolonging this uncomfortable situation by telling you very candidly that I think it would be in the best interest of everyone concerned if your son would simply withdraw from this university."

Prepared and yet totally unprepared for such a shock, James and Polly sat for a moment; stunned while President Butler's words settled into their ears. When he was able to reply James said, "Sir, did I understand you to say that our son is not welcome at this institution?"

"I apologize for my indelicate candor, Mr. Langdon, but take a look at your son. His appearance is a complete contradiction to our standards and I simply must maintain the integrity of this school."

This time it was Polly who seemed poised to traverse the desk and apply a brisk slap to Butler's face, but James intervened.

"Do you realize, sir, that my son is not only guiltless of any wrongdoing but was in fact trying to help a young girl in need when he was attacked by two of your local barbarians?"

"I am completely aware of the facts, Mr. Langdon. I received a complete report from Marshal Howard."

Marshal Howard again, thought James. How faithful the racists were to one another. He couldn't believe it; even at an institution of higher education it was the same. They had no goodwill for black skin or for anyone who treated those with black skin as equals. James was nothing less than astonished. It was over in Athens and the University of Georgia and that was all there was to it. James didn't care anymore; he would not have his son in a bigot-ridden school no matter how esteemed its so-called reputation was supposed to be. When Polly said, "President Butler, is there any other alternative to withdrawing?"

Butler replied, "I could expel him."

"No," said James. "That will not be necessary in the least. There are two different points of view here, Mr. Butler. You would not have our son sully your campus of white supremacy and I would not allow your misguided values to influence my son. Good day to you, sir, and if you should ever have need of absolution, I am sure that you won't have any trouble finding a confessional marked whites only."

With that, the Langdons got up and headed for the door. It had been a trying day but James and his family did not feel as bad as they might have expected. Jim would choose another school, perhaps having learned something from his experience. They boarded the train for the trip back to Macon and soon left their bad day behind. Even though James did not intend to let his son's official indoctrination to the world get the better of him, in the back of his mind he renewed his pledge to resume the struggle for equal rights for his subjugated fellow man. He thought about the day when people, both white and black, would attend the same schools, churches, and work together to create a better world for all. But it would never come about unless there were people who were willing to accept the dauntless task of bringing about change—and he was committed.

"You know, Polly, I have been thinking. I have decided to abandon my interest in a congressional seat. I think that the state legislature is where I need to be."

# NINETEEN

## The Governor's Picnic

The incident concerning Jim had a profound effect on James, but, not wanting to upset Polly further, he chose to leave the subject closed. When their son was accepted to George Washington University in New York, the same school James had attended, they felt that a solution to a serious problem had been found. Jim's education was a high priority and if he settled into the northern setting and succeeded in his studies, it would come as a great relief to his parents.

James was beginning to give a lot of careful thought to running for the Georgia State Legislature. More to the point, he was planning a campaign schedule because his mind was made up about doing his best to get elected. He had plenty of time, however, because it was early spring in 1879 and he would have to wait until 1880 before he could run for office. Every two years, the voters of Georgia elected members to the General Assembly and it was always in the even numbered years. The Senate and the House of Representatives made up the General Assembly. Both houses held the responsibility of judging the election and the qualifications of their members. James was looking to be elected as a state senator, and to qualify, a candidate had to be twenty-five years old, a citizen of Georgia for at least two years, and a resident of the district in which he was running for at least one year. The General Assembly had 236 members, 180 representatives, and 56 senators.

The legislature made the laws for the state and James hoped to attack the Jim Crow laws from within. But he knew that he would have to look for support from his fellow members, should he get elected, and he was pretty sure that it would take more than a little effort. He could imagine no other way to push for changes, and without changes, the separate societies in the South would last until the end of time.

In May of that year, Kate married her railroad engineer, a Mr. Bradford Stanton from Columbus, and moved to that city where her new husband had a beautiful house in one of the most prestigious neighborhoods in the city. It was now only James and Polly in the house, which was quite a change after years of living with their son and James's two sisters. But they understood that time goes on and with the passing of time come life's alterations both large and small. The peace and quiet was pleasant and they were happy that their loved ones were settling in to very promising futures.

Then one day while James and Polly were in Macon to do some shopping, they chanced to see a notice posted on the community events board hanging outside the town hall. There was to be a big celebration in Macon for the 4th of July and the governor of Georgia, Governor Alfred Holt Colquitt, would be present as the guest of honor. A grand picnic would be held in the grove by Kelsey's Creek on the Lester Jessup farm just east of town. Tables would be provided and set up by the town of Macon and two steers, provided by Lester Jessup, would be barbecued to feed the crowd. Individuals, couples, and families could bring their own side dishes, deserts, and liquid refreshments.

"This sounds like fun, James," said Polly after reading the notice. "We should plan to attend."

"I couldn't agree more," he replied. "We can send word to Kate and Bradford. I'm sure that Jeremy and Ashton will come, and Jim will be home from school by then. I will also spread the word to the sharecroppers and their families; the more the merrier I say."

"I am quite impressed by the governor's impending visit," Polly said. "He will be the most dignified guest Macon has ever had."

"That he will ... I almost wish I was still the mayor. Then I would be assured an opportunity to speak with him."

"Maybe you will get the chance anyway, James. If he is a personable man I would think he will speak to as many of the citizens as he has time for."

In the weeks that followed, Polly intermittently spent time making plans for the picnic. Many of the sharecroppers and their families expressed an interest in going and some of the women joined forces with Polly to decide what they would prepare and to estimate how much of everything it would take to feed everyone. As the event drew near, excitement reached its peak. The picnic was the perfect distraction especially for James; it would do him good to relax and enjoy the festivities.

On the morning of July 4th, several wagons were loaded with food, covers for the tables, plenty of lemonade, and parents with their children. Altogether there were fifty-two adults and twenty-nine children in their group. When Jim came home from school he surprised his parents by bringing with him a young lady; a classmate whom he had been spending time with. Her name was Elizabeth Shaw and she was from Boston, Massachusetts. She was, in fact, a cousin of the late Robert Gould Shaw, the young colonel who had led the 54th Massachusetts, a regiment of black soldiers, to victory during the war until he was killed in an assault on Fort Wagner on the coast of South Carolina. Jim had invited Elizabeth to spend a couple weeks with his family before going home to Boston. James and Polly were very happy to have her as their guest; her family had been very active in the abolitionist movement before the war.

The four of them would ride together in the carriage leading the small caravan into town. Ashton, Jeremy, Kate, and Bradford would join everyone at the picnic. Conversation was lively and anticipation was high. The miles to Macon were passed in no time at all.

When they arrived at the picnic grove there was already quite a crowd gathered along the bank of Kelsey's Creek. The governor's visit was quite an occasion and no one wanted to be left out. Many of the tables were occupied, but with the large turnout that was expected, there were plenty of vacancies available. All of the men helped to unhitch the wagons and take care of the horses and mules. The women and children unloaded the wagons and began setting the tables.

A committee formed by the mayor planned games for the children, such as marbles, blind man's bluff, jump rope, and drop the handkerchief. The adults enjoyed pitching horseshoes, fishing, playing cards, and just visiting with friends and neighbors. Of course, there were sections of the grove designated for white guests and other areas designated for blacks. This was according to the law and according to social ranking but James, his family, and his friends were not paying any attention.

The governor was due at 1 PM, after which the picnic would begin. At 12:45, the sounds of the official town band could be heard coming down the road toward the picnic grove, leading the procession that included the governor and the mayor, riding in a carriage led by two white horses. A platform and steps leading to it had been constructed to provide a proper place for the governor to impart his words of wisdom. When the procession came to a stop, the band finished playing, "Hail to the Chief," and then Governor Colquitt was escorted to the platform by Mayor Forbes and his staff. Everyone gathered around when the governor took the podium; after a vigorous round of applause, he began to speak.

As James listened to the remarks from the leader of the state he couldn't help having mixed feelings. The words were good words—progress, moving forward, bright future—but the governor was obviously speaking to the white people gathered there and not the black. For them, the future would be pretty much like the past: segregation, subjugation, and very few choices. James wondered how any state, country, or civilization could move forward when half the people were not included in the planning or the final result.

When the governor was through, another deafening applause was rendered by the white folks, and a few of the blacks, and then it was time to eat. The main course was roasted and ready; trays were carried up and filled to overflowing with hot beef—white section first. James and his people had six long tables sitting end to end, situated in an open space between the white tables and the section designated for the black crowd. James and Jeremy took the trays up for meat and then without a second thought, the Langdon family sat down, not as a group, but rather in amongst their black friends as they had done many times at home.

Beginning at the end of the row of tables they passed the meat and the bread and the vegetable dishes from black to white and white to black. It was a family style setting and they sat, served, and ate like family.

About halfway through the meal, James got the strangest feeling, almost as if someone was standing behind him, watching his every move. As inconspicuously as possible, he glanced from side to side and realized that his group had suddenly become the center of attention. Then he looked closer at the expressions on the other people's faces and noticed that the black people sat with mouths open wide in fear while the white people's eyes were wide open with anger. It was not until that moment that he realized that his family and their black friends were probably in violation of about twenty different laws. Tension began to grow and he wondered how many others in his group were feeling as uncomfortable as he was. James was unsure of what to do; even worse because he didn't feel he should have to do anything. He could not bring himself to change the way they dined, and even if he did, he doubted it would make any difference at that point. He decided to pretend not to notice the angry stares and hope that everyone could finish their meal. But given the sad circumstances in which the world found itself, there was unfortunately no way that some troublemaker was not going to open his big mouth.

"Are we gonna just sit by while these law breakers and their niggers disgrace the governor's picnic?" shouted a man two tables over.

James recognized him; it was Abner Hardy, one of the men who had kept black men from voting when James was running for mayor. His comment was loud enough to be heard by everyone there, including the governor, and for a moment the entire gathering was frozen in silence. Then all at once a verbal barrage broke loose and it seemed like every white person there except for James and his family was shouting their disapproval, which quickly turned to profane racial slurs and insults.

The ruckus got so bad that Sheriff Simon Strickler finally went up to the governor's platform where Governor Colquitt sat with his interrupted meal. The sheriff pulled out his revolver and fired it into the air to get the crowd's attention. After the sound of the gunshot died away there was complete silence. Then the sheriff holstered his weapon, walked down from the platform, and headed directly over to James.

"Mr. Langdon, I see you are marching to your own tune."

"I mean no disrespect, Sheriff, and I'm certainly not trying to start a riot. We are simply breaking bread the way we do at home. I don't think it is the concern of anyone else; it's our usual way of doing things."

"It is when you do it in public at a public gathering. What you do at home is your business, but you are not at home and as you can plainly see there are a lot of concerned people here today. I would also like to point out that you put me in a very difficult situation, especially with the governor being here today."

"What would you have me do, Sheriff?" said James.

"I'm afraid that you will either have to segregate your table or you will all have to pack up and leave."

"Otherwise you will arrest us?"

"The laws pertain to your Negro friends; I will arrest them if I have to."

"But who would bring the charges? I certainly would not press them," said James.

Sheriff Strickler let out a big sigh and stood quietly for a minute. James knew that he was being very obstinate and he was not pleased with himself. He had nothing against Sheriff Strickler and did not wish to put him on the spot. On the other hand, the rancor in his heart had been building for so long and he was tired of keeping it in check. Finally, Hiram Jones, who was seated next to James said, "We'll move to another table, Sheriff. We don't want any trouble."

Hiram got up and nodded to the others; they took their plates and went over to an empty table in the black section. James as well as the rest of his family watched, dejected by the sight.

207

"Sorry, Mr. Langdon," said the sheriff. "I would tell you
to adjust and conform to the times but I understand how
difficult that can be. Enjoy the rest of the day."

James would not enjoy the rest of the day; he had lost
his appetite and he could not escape the irritation of the
smug expressions on the faces of the white crowd. In spite
of everything, he was at least grateful to Hiram Jones for
being the one to suggest the move. It was the only way to
avoid trouble, something that James ordinarily would do,
though somehow he could not bring himself to do it that
day.

After all hunger had disappeared, most of the people
went back to their recreational activities, but James's
family and friends began packing the wagons to leave. He
was just about to climb into the carriage when he heard
someone call his name. He turned around to see Sheriff
Strickler walking toward him.

"Are you in a hurry, Mr. Langdon?"

"We seemed to have worn out our welcome and I believe
everyone's enthusiasm for this picnic has faded away."

"I can't say that I blame them and I am sorry, but as I
told you before, I just have to do my job. It isn't always
pleasant, but it's still my job. Anyway, the governor would
like to see you before you leave."

"The governor wants to see me?"

"Yes, I don't know what's on his mind ... I don't know if
he was impressed or angered by the disturbance, but he
asked me to bring you over."

"I guess my curiosity is up. Just let me get the others
started for home."

Polly wanted to wait for James and so did Jim and his
lady friend. Everyone else exchanged goodbyes and left the
grove. James accompanied the sheriff over to the
governor's table; Strickler made the introductions and
walked away.

"Sit down, Mr. Langdon," said the governor. James took
a seat. "That was quite a little uproar. Would you mind
telling me what it was all about?"

"I apologize for the disturbance, sir; the Negroes who
sharecrop on my plantation are friends of mine and my
family. We make no distinctions about the color of one's

skin at home. We often eat together and never considered the fact that we would have to do any different anywhere else."

"I see. I'm glad to know that you are not generally a lawbreaker and I suppose this little fracas today can be overlooked. But I cannot say that I agree with your feeling concerning the equality of the races. It is the consensus that on every level blacks are simply not equal to whites. I wonder if you can appreciate that the way we handle the liberation of the slaves here in the South is best for everyone. We do not put the Negros down because of scorn or hatred nor do we design a place for him because we lost a war and the right to keep him enslaved. It is simply to give him a place where he is comfortable; he can function to capacity in his own environment and therefore flourish to the point of maximizing his own potential."

The governor stopped talking to let his words sink in; the silence was calculated for effect. Indeed, his words had an effect, but not the one he was hoping for. Inside of James's mind, a whole different reception of his little speech was taking place. The governor's argument sickened him and made him want to depart from the bigot with no respect intended. It reminded him of the day that his own father tried to justify slavery. The twisted logic; the ridiculous reasoning was more than he could bear; and now he was listening to the same kind of claptrap from another self-proclaimed genius.

But James had an idea who he was dealing with before the governor had even opened his mouth. He knew that Colquitt was a staunch defender of Southern state's rights and the expansion of slavery in the West. When the war broke out he joined the Confederacy as a captain of infantry and quickly rose through the ranks to Major General. After the war, he returned to his plantation in Baker County; one of the largest plantations in postbellum Georgia. Colquitt stridently opposed congressional Reconstruction policies; he was a true representative of the Old South.

"I suppose, Governor, that we will have to agree to disagree. I follow a much different belief than you and I am not concerned with a person's education, intellect, or culture. In the eyes of Almighty God, who created us, all people are equal and it is not for anyone to alter God's intentions or take it upon himself to decide superiority or inferiority. I would like to suggest, sir, that we each play our own game and see how it comes out."

James felt much better about what had happened that afternoon. Another battle was fought and lost to the overwhelming numbers of the racist army but he had been given the opportunity, ironically at the governor's own request, to politely tell the leader of the state just what he thought.

As he excused himself and got up to leave, Sheriff Strickler came back to the platform. James made his way down the steps and while he was still within earshot he heard the governor tell the sheriff, "I will remember the name James Langdon."

# TWENTY

# His Father's Son

On January 1st in the year 1880, the building of the Panama Canal began. On March 31st, Wabash, Indiana became the first town to be completely illuminated by electric light. On October 4th, the University of California was founded in Los Angeles, and early in November, James was anticipating the election of the Georgia General Assembly. He had spent most of the year campaigning for a senate seat and within days he would be notified about the results.

As hopeful as he was about the election and about the opportunity to propose change, he knew once again how long the odds were against him. But it had never been in his character to give up when a cause was as important and as deeply rooted as the issue of equal rights. James had called in every favor he could to gain support; now it was up to the voters.

When the telegram came from Atlanta, the urge to open it was just slightly stronger than the fear that it carried bad news. But to moderate the strain on his nerves, James handed the communication to Polly and asked her to read it. Even before she said anything, the smile on her face served as confirmation that he had secured a seat in the Georgia State Senate.

"Only your modesty prevents me from planning a celebration, Senator Langdon," she said. "You will take the oath of office next year on January 5th, 1881."

"This is wonderful news, and thank you for understanding that a celebration isn't necessary, Polly. It is far more important that I familiarize myself with the expectations of a senator and to spend some time writing a few bills I want to introduce to change existing laws. The General Assembly meets in regular session on the second Monday in January for no longer than forty legislative rather than calendar days each year. I will want to leave for Atlanta soon after the holidays."

"You will need to find an office in the city that you can lease or rent."

"Yes," said James. "I will need a place to work when I am not at the capitol. I will also have to find living quarters to use during my stays."

"Your time has finally come, James. You will have the chance to make a difference. Will it not be wonderful?"

"I love your encouragement, Polly, but I certainly have my work cut out for me. Making and changing laws is all about majority ruling; I will need people who agree with me on certain issues and I don't know how many I can find. I have one other reason to worry—Governor Colquitt."

"Governor Colquitt?"

"Yes, I never told you, Polly, but when I was walking away from his table the day of the picnic I heard him tell Sheriff Strickler that he would remember my name; but it will not be in a positive way. Our conversation was not an agreeable one; he has the attitude of all those who support white power. He was in favor of the expansion of slavery in the West and he was the perfect example of a Confederate officer."

"Maybe he has changed since the war."

"No, Polly, he hasn't changed; if you had heard the conversation, you would understand."

"But he doesn't have all the power in the state."

"That's true, but he can veto any bill that is introduced and if he does it would take two thirds of the members of each house to override it. He can make things pretty difficult for me and I have every reason to expect him to do just that."

"Yes, I see what you mean. But let's not worry about the governor right now, James. Go into your job with a positive outlook; failure and success will balance. I am sure that there are triumphs ahead."

"Of course there will be, Polly. We must believe."

The Christmas season was particularly enjoyable for James and his family that year. Jim was home for the holidays; his young lady friend Elizabeth Shaw was with him, partly because her parents were in Europe and partly

because Jim promised her a special surprise for
Christmas. As it turned out, the surprise was also for
James and Polly because they had no idea that their son
was planning to propose to Elizabeth. It was a happy
occasion made even happier when the newly betrothed
couple assured James and Polly that there would be no
wedding until their educations were complete and they had
time to prepare for a promising future.

That evening after the announcement, James and his
son went out to the veranda, and in spite of a temperature
of about forty-five degrees, the two of them sat down to
talk.

"Are you happy, Father, about our plans, Elizabeth's
and mine?"

"I could not be happier, son, and I know that your
mother feels the same way. Elizabeth is a wonderful young
woman and I truly believe that you were made for each
other."

"I must agree, Father. I know that it is important to find
a mate with whom you are compatible; not about
everything, for surely there will be minor differences of
opinion in any relationship. But I mean compatible on
issues that really matter such as how children should be
raised and how to live a life that the good Lord would
approve of. I am fortunate to have parents like you and
Mother and I know that I need only follow your example
and I will be on the right path."

"You compliment us perhaps more than we deserve,
son. It is not easy to see yourself the way others see you;
something that might make the world a better place if we
could. I only know that I follow what I believe and I live my
life accordingly; praying constantly for the Lord to keep his
beacon out before me."

"Your advice sounds reliable to me, Father, and I will
always do the same. In keeping with that, there is
something else on my mind. I wish to find a way, as you
have, to get involved in the struggle for fair and equal
treatment for our black friends. Elizabeth feels the same
way, which is another reason that I fell so deeply in love
with her. Due to the outcome of the war, she is satisfied
that her cousin, Robert, did not die in vain. Now, as a way

to honor him, she wishes to see black people enjoy the freedom that her cousin and so many others died to bring about."

"I am touched by your desire and Elizabeth's to take up the fight against this terrible injustice. I have seen enough in my lifetime to believe that things will change someday, but it would be impossible to know how long it will take. But the more the banner is raised and the more people there are who are willing to raise it, the sooner it might happen."

"It can't happen soon enough, Father. The situation is so bad for black people in this country. There is no law enforcement that is willing to protect them; you could kill a black person any time for any reason with impunity."

"That is why the laws have to be changed. I must find support in the state government to get them changed."

"How can Elizabeth and I help, Father?"

"I will need a staff to help me in Atlanta, but you and Elizabeth must finish your educations."

"We will be finished in just a few months," said Jim. "Can you make do without us until then?"

"I will make do, son. It will be a pleasure working with you and Elizabeth; together we will challenge the system."

As father and son sat in pleasant conversation, they were interrupted by the sound of someone coming up the driveway. They got up and walked down the steps of the veranda to greet their visitor. A horse and wagon came to a stop in the light of the lantern that was mounted on a post near the driveway. To their surprise, it was Sheriff Strickler from town; they wondered why he should be traveling in a wagon.

"Good evening, Sheriff," said James. "What brings you this far from town at this hour?"

"Bad news, I'm afraid," Strickler replied. "Several hours ago I was in my office when Marcus Poe came by to report some trouble about five miles outside town. Poe is a local Negro; he works for the blacksmith, Gerald Fitz. He led me out to the place where he came upon the altercation and we found the body of an elderly Negro man hanging from a tree; he was lynched."

It was then that James noticed the blanket-covered form in the sheriff's wagon; a form that was unmistakably a body.

"I am fearful of asking this question, Sheriff, but why did you bring this unfortunate soul all the way out here?"

Strickler hesitated for a moment and then he said, "To ask you to positively identify the body."

James and his son Jim were horrified. The sheriff's comment could mean only one thing: the dead man was a friend of theirs. The two of them had just been discussing the rampant, terribly unlawful treatment of blacks and now one of their friends had fallen victim to murder. Reluctantly, James and his son walked to the side of the wagon. James pulled back the blanket, viewed the corpse, and hung his head. It was Hiram Jones. Sadness, anger, and disbelief welled up inside him all at once. He looked at Jim and saw tears streaming down his face. Hiram had been one of the family's closest friends; he had been there since the beginning. It was Hiram who had brought the first group of men to James's plantation and suggested that they stand together against the Klan. It was Hiram whose sister Sally's husband died at the hands of the Klan. He was an old man and he was fallen upon by ruffians and killed like an old deer to a wolf pack. The difference was that wolves killed for survival and Hiram's killers did it out of hatred.

How long, James wondered, would God allow these senseless killings, these terrible transgressions until he would strike mankind down and punish him for his evil nature?

"What happened, Sheriff?" James asked.

"I wish I could answer that, Mr. Langdon, but I can't. Poe said he didn't recognize any of the men involved. There were two of them; they were white, of course, but he didn't stay around too long because he was afraid he might be seen. I'm sure those men would have killed him, too."

"So you are telling me that it ends here and nothing will ever be done about it?" said James.

"I guess that's about right. I am sorry. I know it doesn't help, but I am sorry. I don't like this any more than you do, Mr. Langdon. I have no hatred for anyone that I know of and I have never made any distinctions among people because of their color. But the hard truth is that even if I could arrest the men who did this they would probably never be held accountable."

"I am sure you're right," James answered. "I feel sympathy for you, Sheriff. I believe that you are a good man and it must be difficult to be so hampered in regards to your job. It must confuse you as to the definition of justice."

"I must admit, I have had my fill of the southern way of life—no offense. I have decided to move back to Pennsylvania. I submitted my resignation a week ago. Next week a new sheriff will be sworn in."

"I wish you well, Sheriff; Pennsylvania is a fine place to live. I thank you for coming out here tonight. If you will take Hiram's body to Templeton's Funeral Parlor I will be grateful. Tell Mr. Templeton that I will come by in the morning."

"It is the least I can do. I guess this is goodbye, Mr. Langdon. Like you, I hope the world changes for the better someday. I will remember you as one of the men who worked so hard to try to change it."

"Thank you, Simon. Goodbye."

The sheriff got back in the wagon and headed for town. James put his arm around his son's shoulder and they walked back to the veranda and sat down again. Young Jim was in deep emotional distress. Hiram had been almost like a grandfather to him, many times taking him fishing along with his two best friends, Jeb and Bodie. It was like living in a world inside a world; on the plantation everyone lived in perfect harmony. But outside the boundaries lived the darker side of humanity. If only the plantation could be an isolated, self-contained existence there would be no reason to leave. But man was not designed to live in one tiny corner of his world, even if it was the closest thing to heaven on earth. James tried in vain to console his son but he believed he failed because of his own need for consolation.

"He was just an old man, Father. It makes no sense at all to kill a defenseless old man. Where does that kind of hatred come from?"

216

"I guess it comes from generations of ignorance and has manifested itself into a belief. When preachers tell people that God has ordained the discrimination of blacks, they need no justification at all to despise and mistreat them."

"Then how will things ever change?"

"I sometimes wonder if they ever will, son. The thing we must realize is that evil has its place in the world the same as good. The Lord allows this out of necessity so that he can see which we will choose to follow. That is why I am so intent on making changes in the laws. You cannot change the way a person thinks nor can you make them accept what they outright reject. So we make laws in an attempt to control human behavior so that we might create a peaceful society."

"So we have to force people to get along?"

"In a manner of speaking, yes; it is not a perfect solution but if it ensures the safety and welfare of everyone then it is *also* a necessary evil."

"It isn't an easy world to live in, is it, Father?"

"No, son, it isn't, but there is always hope, and that is what keeps us going."

"I feel the need to be alone, Father. Would you please extend my apologies to Mother and Elizabeth? I want to go quietly to bed."

"Good night, son."

James watched as the distraught young man went into the house and shut the door. Another period of mourning was at hand; it had visited all too often in the past several years. Hiram would be sorely missed by everyone. James sat by himself for a few more minutes and then he reluctantly went inside to tell Polly and Elizabeth the sad news.

Two days later, Hiram was buried in the Langdon family cemetery near Chet Rawlins. Everyone on the plantation was considered family and James insisted that all deceased members rest together, provided they had no other family plot of their own. During the service, which was performed as always by Aaron Parmalee, James found himself glancing around at the large group of mourners and realized that his son was not among them. Even Elizabeth was there to pay her respects to a man whom she hadn't known except from descriptions and stories she'd been told, but no Jim.

When the funeral was over, James went to find him. After a search of the house and the grounds, he finally found his son in the barn, sitting up on the seat of the spring wagon.

"Jim, I was worried about you. I noticed that you were not at the funeral."

"I'm sorry, Father, but I can't believe that Hiram is gone. I couldn't go to the service because I couldn't face the stark reality of it. I came in here to sit because I feel closer to him in here."

"How so, Jim?"

"Do you remember when you first met Hiram?"

"Why yes, it was here in the barn. I was putting this wagon away."

"Yes, Father, you were putting this wagon away and found Hiram and a group of men waiting for you."

"That's right ... Chet, Jeremy, and Aaron were among them."

"I was drawn to this spot somehow and this is where I chose to say goodbye to Hiram. He is not the first friend we have buried and I know he will not be the last. It is fitting and proper that we take care of our friends even unto death; people die, of course they do. But I can no longer accept losing a friend who should still be with us. If we could do something before someone else is taken from us, maybe we wouldn't have to attend so many funerals."

"I understand completely, Jim, and I feel your pain."

"I know you do, Father, I guess that's why I'm telling you all this—because it helps me to talk to someone who understands. But now I've got to do more. I know that you are leaving for Atlanta soon; I want to go with you.

James was taken by complete surprise. He knew immediately what his son was saying; somehow he had to change his mind.

"Jim, your education ... you're so close to finishing."

"I know that, Father, but I think that going with you is more important. "

"You must think of your future and Elizabeth's. You are upset, Jim, and rightly so, but I beg you to reconsider. I promise you that your place in Atlanta is secure just as soon as your graduation is over. I ask you to sleep on it and let me know tomorrow, please."

"Very well, Father. I will think it over. I'll let you know tomorrow. Right now I just need to be alone."

"Of course, son. Stay here as long as you like."

That evening after supper James noticed that Jim and Elizabeth were on the veranda, oblivious to everything except their conversation. When Polly went in search of her husband after the dishes were neatly put away, she found him in the parlor pacing the floor.

"Come and sit with me, James," she said. James sat down beside her; they joined hands and he began to relax a little. When Polly had his full attention she said, "You needn't worry so. Jim will finish school."

"I sure hope you're right, Polly. Hiram's death has been very unsettling for him—for us all."

"It certainly has," she agreed. "But Jim will do the right thing, and if you'd like, I can tell you how I know."

"Please do," said James.

"It is because he is just like you."

James put his arm around her and pulled her close. He kissed her and whispered a soft and sincere "thank you" into her ear. He was convinced that no man anywhere had a wife with more kindness, love, and wisdom. As if she actually had the ability to predict the future, the following morning James and Polly bid farewell to Jim and Elizabeth, who were on their way back to school.

# TWENTY-ONE

# The Lion's Den

On January 2nd, James arrived in Atlanta and secured temporary lodging until more permanent quarters could be found. In three days he was to be sworn in as a state senator representing the district of Macon. He wished that Polly could be there but the separation and those in the future would have to become part of his new endeavor. It was so much like the war years; leaving home to fulfill his duty to his fellow man and his maker.

When the first senate meeting was scheduled, James arrived early hoping to meet some of his colleagues and get a feel for the atmosphere in the state government. Most of the people he met welcomed him to his new position but he soon found out that people in government were like people everywhere else. They were full of gossip pertaining to other members, their shortcomings and their attitudes. Unwillingly, James listened and nodded his head but he was left wondering how people who seemed to pull in opposite directions ever got anything accomplished.

The meeting itself, much to James's dismay, was long and drawn out due to the inability of the members to agree on even the simplest point. It was as if most of them were reluctant to go along with any idea that they did not themselves initiate. Maybe it was a massive power struggle, each man believing that since he was a senator he should therefore make the decisions, all the while overlooking the fact that the next man had the same level of authority.

Still, he endured the sleep-inducing period and stayed focused on his own reasons for being there. In the end, the meeting did actually produce results; a vote was taken that settled the issue of how tall the street lamps in every major city in Georgia should actually be.

After a month of such meetings, James decided to introduce a bill that he had been working on tirelessly for weeks. He knew that it would not be wise to be too overzealous with his push for black equality; he would try to peck away at the Jim Crow laws little by little. His first legislative bill proposed that public schools should be integrated in the interest of saving taxpayer dollars, which were being wasted by maintaining two different school systems.

On a Monday morning in mid-February, James went to the Office of Legislative Council to speak to an attorney about his proposal. A homely young secretary led him to a conference room with a long table, each side having ten chairs. She invited him to sit down and then left the room to summon the attorney with whom James would be speaking. Five minutes later, a man in his thirties with a weak chin, receding hairline, and sleeves rolled up to the elbows entered the room. He closed the door, offered his hand to James, and said, "Mr. Langdon, I am Matthew Sharp. I understand that you are one of our newest members."

"Yes, Mr. Sharp," said James while shaking the attorney's hand. "I've been here just a little over a month."

"Oh," said Sharp. "And you've already got a suggestion on how to make Georgia a better place to live?" James could not tell if the attorney's remark was sarcastic or congenial.

"I would like to introduce a piece of legislation that I believe would be good for the taxpayers of the state."

"Indeed, well, show me what you've got."

James extracted paper work from his briefcase and handed it to Sharp. While the attorney read over the papers, James waited for a reaction. After a few minutes, he received that for which he waited but it was not quite what he was expecting. When Sharp finished reading, he looked across the table at one of Georgia's newest senators and smiled a huge smile; then he started to laugh, and then he sat back in his chair and nearly lost all control of himself to his comic emotion.

James waited for several minutes for Sharp's insulting behavior to subside and then the attorney said unconvincingly, "I'm sorry, Mr. Langdon, but this is a joke, isn't it?"

"It isn't a joke at all," said James in a tone that bore his irritation. "This is a legitimate piece of legislation and I have every intention of representing it."

"I see," said Sharp as his humor faded. "And how far do you expect to get with it?"

"What do you mean?"

"I mean that a bill can be shot down at any stage of the process and I doubt that this nonsense will ever even be formally introduced."

James was past insulted at that point and he did not restrain himself from letting Sharp know it. "I will thank you not to refer to this bill as nonsense, sir. It is my job to produce such ideas to better my community and state. It is only your job to inform me of any legal issues."

"You want the legal issues? Very well, I can tell you that the Supreme Court has handed down a series of decisions that virtually nullified the work of Congress during Reconstruction. What you have to understand is that to most people, nig—" Sharp thought better of his word selection and then continued. "Black people are considered second class citizens and they will remain as such forever. Just because they are as free as white people, that does not make them equal to white people."

"And *are* they as free as white people, Mr. Sharp? Would you consider yourself as free if the law didn't respect and protect your property or your life? Would you consider yourself free if there were a million simple things that others could do but you could not? This has nothing to do with freedom. This has to do with narrow-minded jackasses who take it upon themselves to play God and dictate policy concerning the rights of human beings. Well, let me assure you, sir, that no one, no one, has the power to say that this man doesn't belong here or that man is not as good as another. God have mercy on the bigots and racists in the world because, come Judgment Day, they will serve as kindling for Hell's fire!" With that, James grabbed his papers and hurried out the door. He did not calm down until he reached his domicile and there he collapsed in frustration. It reminded him of the time he spent in Washington D.C. when he was waiting for his first assignment as an officer in the Union cavalry. The bits and pieces of conversation he overheard in the hotels, the dining rooms, and on the street made him feel that he'd made a mistake by joining the army. Black people were not treated much better in the North than they were in the South and yet President Lincoln said that the war had come to be about freedom for all people. He was as confused now as he was then when in a moment of weakness he almost deserted and went home.

Fatigue and depression having taken their toll, James fell asleep where he sat and he remained there until late afternoon. At five o'clock he awakened but kept his seat still thinking about the meeting with Mr. Sharp.

A loud knock at the front door jerked him upright in surprised because he knew of no one in the city who had his address. When he opened the front door, a tall dark haired man in a very nice suit was looking up the street and then down as if he feared someone he knew might see him standing there.

"Can I help you, sir?" James asked.

"Are you Senator Langdon?"

"I am. Can I help you?" he repeated.

"May I come in, Senator? I'd like to speak to you."

"Certainly, come in."

James led the way to a small sitting room in the back of the house and offered the stranger a chair. Without an introductory handshake the newcomer said, "My name is Reginald Marston; I am a senator from the Taylor district, right next to your Macon district."

"What can I do for you, Senator?"

"It might become a bit redundant with the senator, senator exchange. Why don't you call me Reggie?"

"Very well, Reggie, you may call me James."

"I'm here, James, because I heard all about your meeting with Matthew Sharp."

James was about to protest when Reggie said, "Don't be upset, James. It's something you'd better get used to. Nothing in the General Assembly is kept secret for very long. Maybe you are already learning that."

"I'm beginning to," James answered.

"I could tell you every man who has a mistress and give you her first name. I could tell you which members are the most likely to take a bribe from some businessman who wants certain legislation passed. You could be as clean as a whistle, but if you are not careful the dirt will rub off. You have to make friends if you want to succeed as a senator—oh not the kind of friends you would invite to your house for dinner, but men who are willing to trade favors by voting on your behalf if you will reciprocate."

"It all sounds quite disconcerting to me," said James.

"Indeed it does. You are in the lion's den now; be careful you don't get eaten alive."

"Did you track me down just to warn me or are you recruiting new friends?"

"Maybe a little bit of both. I wanted to let you know that you may already have a partisan group that you can count on."

"I'm afraid I don't quite follow you."

"I will go out on a limb and assume that you are an advocate of the equal rights movement in this country."

"Since there are no secrets in the General Assembly I suppose I would be foolish not to admit it," James replied.

"That is correct, and by the way, I like your sarcasm. You'll make a great senator. Anyway, I probably don't have to tell you that you are treading a difficult path, much like the abolitionists of old. Your cause is as appealing now as theirs was then."

"Granted," said James.

"Good, now listen. There are other members that feel the way you do except that it might be for different reasons."

"Go on."

"Over the last couple of years, there have been others who considered legislation such as yours but they never bothered writing a bill because they knew it was useless. When we heard about your meeting with Sharp today we thought perhaps the time had come; maybe we had an unofficial leader with guts. But before you begin to have faith in your fellow man, let me explain further. This group of which I speak believes that a civilization has to grow and move forward. If it doesn't move forward, it dies. There was a time when no one would have believed that the slaves would one day be free, but it happened. It took an entire war, but it happened nonetheless. That being said, we believe now that the day will come when the Negroes will have the same rights as whites; hell we might have a black president someday," Reggie said with a chuckle. "If Negroes had equal rights, instead of turmoil we would have harmony. We could turn the United States into a world power. There must be close to six and a half million Negroes in this country. Why not give them their rights and turn them into useful, productive citizens? It could only make life better for all of us. I mean, we don't have to start marrying them, do we? The racial lines could still remain pure."

Suddenly James was again feeling the depression he'd brought home with him from the meeting with Attorney Sharp. He didn't know whether he should consort with Reggie Marston or throw him out on his ear. The man did not have the slightest concern for the blacks; he was only willing to do something for them if it was sure to pay off big for him. Still, the thought of a group of members who might immediately be willing to help him push through the legislation he so desperately wanted passed was a temptation that was hard to resist. Was Reggie's prophesying already coming true? Was the dirt beginning to rub off? James decided to listen a while longer.

"There is one other thing to consider in this matter, James: votes. Our future, yours and mine, is dependent upon votes. As it stands, the Negroes have the right to vote, but as you know it is not being upheld. If we can pass an equal rights bill there will be more voters, grateful ones. Even the Negroes are smart enough to know who makes the laws. If we push this through we can keep our jobs forever."

"And what about the white voters, Reggie? Aren't you afraid that they will run for the hills if you get such a bill passed?"

"My dear James, politicians have been controlling the minds of voters for years. Simple psychology will carry the day for us. I told you earlier that equal rights are inevitable and it's true. If we make the white voters think it is their idea, acceptance will be so much easier. Anything is easier to accept if it isn't forced on you. Most of the bitterness

directed at the Negroes in the South today comes from
losing a war and losing dominion over their slave property.
The result of that has been an eruption of violence and
bloodshed. But if whites approve the idea themselves then
they can feel good about it because it was their decision
and they are in control. Sure we may lose some votes;
those of the non-conformists. But the Negro votes we gain
will more than make up for it."

James was in awe, not because of the perverse genius
of Reggie Marston, but because of his own continued
underestimation of human deceit. James felt like the
proverbial babe in the woods. He had no choice but to cut
his losses and join the conniving group of senators and
representatives so that something truly good might come of
it.

"I have to hand it to you, Reggie; I believe that you
could convince Satan that honesty is the best policy."

"Ah, yes, you will fit right in. Now, rewrite your bill, but
this time create a general bill of equal rights. Don't waste
time trying to do this thing piece meal."

The man was positively unflappable, thought James.
You could tell him in no uncertain terms how disgusting he
was and he would thank you for it.

"How do I get by Attorney Sharp?" James asked.

"Oh yes, our Negro-hater, Mr. Sharp," Reggie said with
a wink. "He isn't the only attorney we have. Take your bill
to Attorney Bernard Cullen. He is from California; he'll file
it for you. In the meantime we will all bring our staff
personnel up to date and have them start working on the
best way to get our constituents to take the bait. Once we
have them hooked we can bask in the glow of job security."

"The next legislative day is one month from tomorrow.
The bill will be ready by then."

"Excellent, James; that will give us time to plan
strategy and then we can put it to use while we wait for the
bill to go through."

"I still have doubts, Reggie. I know a little bit about
Governor Colquitt and I am sure he will fight this bill tooth
and nail."

"Don't let old Alfred H. bother you too much, James. He also has a little dirt that I am aware of. I think it's enough to keep him in line."

James had heard enough. He could not wait for Reggie Marston to pack up his cloak and dagger and leave. When the ill wind that blew no good was finally gone, James relinquished a huge sigh of relief. Then he packed his bag and locked up the house. He was grateful for the break before the senate and the house reconvened. Perhaps a few weeks at home would strengthen his resolve and return him to fighting shape. Another battle was shaping up and, once again, identifying the enemy would pose a problem. Even his chosen camp would be full of treachery.

Arriving at the plantation was like a breath of fresh air for James. When he saw Polly sitting on the veranda swing his mood went from worn out to wonderful. Home was the best place on earth and the most wonderful wife any man ever had was always there to greet him. They exchanged a warm embrace and then made their way into the parlor to sit and compare their recent experiences.

"Everything has been quiet here, James; a bit lonely in fact. Ashton has been coming by often to keep me company, and sometimes Jeremy is with her. Of course I spend most of my time keeping the house in order; the mending, cleaning, and sewing keep my hands busy. And in the evenings I have school lessons to prepare for the sharecroppers' children. But before I go to sleep at night I am always thinking about you and wondering what you have been doing."

"I suppose you might say that I have been getting an education."

"An education, James?"

"Yes, it seems that I never learn. I always give people the benefit of the doubt and more often than not I wind up thinking myself to be gullible and naïve."

"I prefer to think of you as honest and trusting."

"Thank you, Polly, but I might save a lot of time and embarrassment if I would just open my eyes a little wider."

As Polly listened, James told her all about his first weeks in the senate.

When he was finished she said, "Our elected officials do not set a very good example do they?"

"No, but fortunately the citizens don't see them as they really are."

"So what will you do, James?"

"I will see if enough support can be gathered to get an equal rights bill pushed through the senate. As long as I don't break any rules or do anything dishonest I guess I can live with myself for getting involved with men like Reggie Marston. Actually, he has left the way clear for me to remain truthful. Reggie and his comrades have a different motive than I but our goal is the same. We are going to try to pass legislation for equal rights and we are going to tell the white voters that it would be in their best interest. The only difference is that I believe that it is and they do not. I am being candid with the people; Reggie and his friends are trying to flimflam them in order to secure their jobs. They have no sincerity about the problems facing black people but they will invest in them for a good return on their investment."

"I see your predicament, James, but you are not doing anything for which you should be ashamed. If your fellow members are willing to support your worthy cause I don't think the reasons are important."

"I agree, Polly. When I return to Atlanta I will take my revised bill back to the Office of Legislative Council."

James spent a week without a break writing the new bill that he hoped would give blacks the kind of freedom they deserved. When it was complete he laid it aside and made up his mind that he would do something to enjoy the rest of the time before he had to leave for Atlanta. He spent as much time as he could with Polly, taking long walks and carriage rides and visiting with Ashton and Jeremy. It was so necessary for him to unwind and avoid any stressful intrusions. At just thirty-eight years of age, life had asked a great deal of him and it was not as easy as it once was to accept the next challenge.

Four days before he was to leave home again, Polly asked James to drive her to Macon to do some shopping. The idea appealed to him; another day for them to do something together. They decided to leave early in the morning and have breakfast at one of the cafes in town. After they'd eaten, they were strolling down the boardwalk looking in store front windows when a black man with a terribly scarred face and a missing left eye came up to them. He was obviously timid and very nervous about interrupting the couple. Removing his hat and bowing he said, "Is you Mr. Langdon?"

"I am," James replied. "Can I help you?"

"Yes, suh, I would be mighty grateful if I could talk to you, suh."

James sensed that the man was interested in a private conversation so he turned to Polly and said, "Polly, dear, would you mind giving me a few minutes with this gentleman?"

"Not at all, James. You can find me at Mrs. Carson's dress shop."

"Thank you, dear, I'll be along." When Polly was a short distance up the boardwalk James turned to the man and said, "Is this better?"

"Yes, suh. Thank you, suh, I wasn't wantin to upset your misses none but I needs to tell you somethin."

"Please continue Mr ..."

"My name is Jobe. No more name, jes Jobe, but I was hopin you might not ever tell nobody that I talked to you."

"It will be our secret, Jobe. Now, what can I do for you?"

Jobe glanced around to be sure no one else was within earshot and said, "Marcus Poe told me who killed Hiram Jones."

# TWENTY-TWO

## Much Ado about Murder

It was not that everything was going very smoothly for James, although he *was* enjoying a lovely time with Polly, but when Jobe told him that he knew who killed Hiram Jones, it completely turned his day upside down.

"Marcus Poe told Sheriff Strickler that he didn't recognize the two men who were involved."

"Yes, suh, he sho nuff did, but it's cuz he's scared Mr. Langdon, he's bad scared. But he told it to me who done it and he say if I wanna tell somebody I can but he say jes keep mum bout his name. I knows bout you, Mr. Langdon, and I knows it be all right to trus you, suh."

"Who killed him, Jobe?"

"It wuz dem two white trash Glacken boys, Ned and Junior. They runs a still near Johnson's Creek and they drinks more than they be sellin."

"Thank you for your confidence and thank you for telling me. You probably know that Hiram was a good friend of mine."

"Yes, suh, I knows, that be why I figger I oughts to tell you."

"Yes ... and if you don't mind me asking, how did you lose your eye?"

"My old massa done dat when I wuz jes small. By accident I sees him doin something bad to my sister in da barn and massa beat me wit da broom stick."

"I am terribly sorry, Jobe."

"Thank ya, suh. I bes git."

"Certainly, and thank you again."

The poor wretch cautiously made his way across the street and James hurried down to Mrs. Carson's dress shop. When he stuck his head in the door, Polly was discussing a dress pattern with Louise Carson. "Polly, I have a little business to attend to. Will you be all right here for a short while?"

"Certainly," she said, but James knew she was wondering if the business had anything to do with the scarred man that had wanted to speak to him. James went down the street to the sheriff's office. He knew that Simon Strickler was gone but he had no idea who had replaced him. When he walked into the office he soon discovered who had taken Simon's place and immediately two words came into his mind: "bad news."

The new sheriff was a man whom James had known since childhood; a man whose reputation even as a boy described him as nothing but trouble. His name was Colt Jeffers, nephew of Harland Jeffers—the man James had helped hang for the murder of Chet Rawlins. James knew that Colt would remember him even without the circumstances involving his uncle. Considering the vindictive nature of the Jeffers family, Colt would never forget him now. He nearly spun on his heel and left the office when he saw who was in charge but it was too late.

"Well, if it isn't my old friend, James Langdon. I haven't seen you since my uncle's trial in Atlanta. I hear you're a senator now. What in the hell can I do for you?"

James decided not to waste time with fake pleasantries.

"I came in with a report about a crime but I see that one has been committed right here."

"What is that supposed to mean?" said Colt, his eyes narrowing.

"How on earth did you become the sheriff?"

"The people of Macon finally came to their senses, that's all. Things got out of hand when you were running this town ... the niggers were starting to act like they were as good as the white folks around here. The voters decided it was time they had a sheriff who would keep those black sons a bitches in line, and make no mistake, I intend to do just that."

"Like your uncle did?" Colt got up from his chair, came from behind the desk, and walked over to stand within two feet of James.

"If you weren't a state senator I'd work you over for a while and then throw you in one of those cells back there."

"If I weren't a state senator I would oblige you to try. I have no more time to waste here."

James turned and walked out with the words, "Nigger lovin Yankee," echoing in his ears.

What a depressing turn of events, he thought as he headed back to the dress shop. He knew there was little chance that the sheriff's office would get involved in Hiram's death even if James could name the killers. But to find Colt Jeffers as the new sheriff destroyed any hope he had left. He was also upset at himself for antagonizing Colt. It was not like him to do so but it was just so ridiculous, a man like him working for the law.

When he got to Louise Carson's shop, Polly was ready to leave. James escorted her out to the carriage and said, "We must get home."

"Is there trouble, James?"

"Yes, and I feel like my hands are tied … I need some time to think."

On the way home, James explained in detail the conversation with Jobe and the useless trip to the sheriff's office.

"I see your dilemma, James."

"A very big one it is, too. I don't see how I can let this go, knowing who is responsible for Hiram's death and doing nothing. But I have to be back in Atlanta in four days—no need to stress how important that is."

It seemed to take forever to make the trip home from Macon. All the while James was working himself into a state of frenzy. He was not very familiar with the Glacken family, although what he did know would not qualify them as model citizens. Certainly they had no grievance with Hiram; the man was simply not the kind of person to look for trouble or cause any. James was convinced that it was just another senseless killing, which had become almost a sport in the South.

At home, he paced the floor in the parlor and tried to think of a way to handle the situation. Every idea he could come up with seemed to have a flaw or two in it. His irritation was growing roots. Murder was the most heinous crime known to man and yet it was tolerated as if it were the right thing to do. Then James's thinking stopped in its tracks. He was completely around the circle and ended up where he began; it hit him harder than ever before. It was that incredible realization—the truth of the matter. Killing a black man *was* the thing to do and it was not considered murder. It was a good deed; a service performed in order to make the world a better place to live.

Would the killings ever stop? Would he ever get used to it? Could a lifetime that lasted a thousand years be long enough for James to give up his fight to make people understand that we all came from the same God who gave mankind dominion over the animals and the earth but not over each other?

When Polly came into the parlor, James was sitting with his head down and his face in his hands. She sat down beside him, placed a comforting hand on the back of his neck, and began to rub the tension away.

"It hurts me to see what this is doing to you, James," she said. "I remember like it was yesterday this same situation during the war. I remember when you came home with your wounds and we spoke of the price of commitment. We sometimes wondered if we had reached our breaking point. Now your wounds are on the inside but they are just as visible. I guess we will never be anything other than what God wants us to be; you will always put the struggle of others ahead of your own comfort and I will always be here to support you because I know that what you're doing is right. The one constant that we could always lean on besides each other when we thought we might not make it is the power of the Lord. He was there during the war and He is with us now."

James looked up at his loving wife with tears in his eyes. It was uncanny the way they knew each other and before she even made her point, James knew what Polly was going to say.

"James, I know how close you were to Hiram and there is no one on this plantation who didn't feel the same way. We are all friends here and when we lose someone we all feel a terrible loss. Not knowing who is responsible for his death would be difficult; knowing who is responsible for his death and having no way to bring the guilty party to justice is impossible. But this time, I believe, we will have to let it go."

"I know, Polly," James said quietly. "I guess I knew it by the time we got home from Macon ... I just didn't want to accept it. We have a witness who can positively identify the killers—a witness who will never testify because he is terrified of reprisals. Even if he wanted to, his testimony would be worthless because it is against the law for a black man to testify against a white man. But the biggest reason to let it go is because all that happened is that two white men hung a nigger, so why have much ado about nothing? I am sorry Polly, please forgive my sarcasm; I need to work this out for myself. I am going to saddle a horse and go out for a while."

"I understand, James ... we can talk when you get back," she said with a strange look on her face.

"Of course we can. Thank you for your indulgence."

James went to the barn, saddled his favorite mare, and headed out to the main road. He rode aimlessly for perhaps an hour, and when he finally stopped to get his bearings he was surprised to find that he was not too far from Johnson's Creek. He wondered what he was doing there. Was it purely accidental or was he being drawn to that area by some subconscious notion? Then he did something that completely astounded him; he reached back to his saddle bag to purposely determine whether or not his .45 caliber revolver was inside. The revolver was there, but he wondered why he cared. He was not afraid of anything nor did he plan to use the weapon.

After sitting still for five or ten minutes, James wanted to turn for home. He felt somewhat relieved and he knew that going home was the best thing to do. Somehow he had the feeling that Polly was worried about him and it troubled him to leave her that way. Then he nudged his horse forward, but in spite of his thoughts, he continued on a course for Johnson's Creek.

A half hour later James's mare was taking a cool drink of water as she stood mid-stream. It was quiet, too quiet; a foreboding silence to accompany his unexpected presence there. There were a few houses along the creek but James didn't know many people who lived in that area. He rode a little farther and then he stopped suddenly when the roof of a house with two chimneys came into view.

Fear immediately swept over him and for a moment he shivered uncontrollably. James knew that the name of the people living in that house was Glacken. My God, he thought, is this why I've come here? Out of complete despair; because of no alternative have I come here looking for a confrontation?

James was, perhaps, for the first time ever, shaking uncontrollably with fear; but he was not afraid for his person. However, for no reason that he would allow himself to dwell on, he moved closer to the house. At first he saw no activity save for an old hound dog lying on the front porch. As he slowly advanced to the picket fence surrounding the home, an old woman came out of the front door carrying a fry pan, which she sat down in front of the dog. When she straightened up she noticed James sitting on his horse just outside the picket fence. Slowly and with obvious difficulty, she descended the three steps from the porch and walked toward him. Reaching the fence, she looked up at the visitor and her expression revealed an attempt to recognize James. Failing that, she stared into his glazed look for a moment and then she said, "Is there sometin you be wantin here, mister?"

James sat in silence as if he were in a trance. His mind was so fixed on a thought that the old woman's voice came to him as in a dream. A tug of war was going on inside him and he struggled to break away from the influence of the dark side of human conduct. Gradually, a bit of light broke through his tortured thoughts and he realized the old woman was trying to gain acknowledgement.

"Is you tetched, mister? What is you wantin here?"

"I want to talk to your sons, Ned and Junior," James replied.

The woman was skeptical and a bit wary. Apparently she did not trust what she saw in his face or in his aloof manner.

"You have business with Ned and Junior, mister?"

"I have," said James.

The old woman turned and took a couple steps toward the house; apparently she was going to retrieve her sons.

235

James reached back to his saddle bag, slid his hand inside, and rested it on the revolver. Before the woman reached the porch steps she suddenly whirled around and said, "You're here to kill'em ain't you?"

Something struck James like a bolt of lightning; it was like being drenched in ice water or like a brisk slap across the face. He was immediately brought back to perfect vision; the trance had been lifted. He withdrew his hand from the saddle bag slowly so as not to further alarm the old woman. Cold sweat trickled down his back and he knew that he had just broken free from the effects of mental shock. He had returned to his old self and he immediately thanked the Lord for raising him back up to the light of day.

"No ma'am," he replied. "I am not here to kill your sons. I am just here to deliver a message."

"Well then hows about ifen I deliver it for you?"

James knew the old woman was afraid and he did not wish to be responsible for thrusting any more anguish upon her.

"Very well. You may tell them if you like. Just say that Hiram Jones sends his kindest regards and that he has completely forgiven them."

The old woman looked at him, totally bewildered, but as she started to ask for the meaning of his message James turned his horse away from that place and headed for home at a trot.

It was getting dark when James reached the plantation. Polly came out onto the veranda when she heard him coming up the driveway. She met him halfway to the barn, took his hand, and said, "Are you all right, James?"

"I am just fine now, my darling. I just had to deliver a message."

"I'm glad. You know, James, Hiram would be the first one to forgive the Glacken boys for what they've done."

"Yes, Polly, that is the message I just delivered."

# TWENTY-THREE

# The Definition of Freedom

The day after James returned to Atlanta he took his revised bill to the Office of Legislative Council to meet with Attorney Bernard Cullen as Reggie Marston had suggested. Reggie was right, of course; Attorney Cullen filed the bill without a single complaint or racial slur. Later that day, James met with Reggie and a few of the other backers. Introductions were made and then the group discussed what they had been doing and what needed to be done to gain support from the voters. When the discussion broke up, the members went their separate ways except for James and Reggie.

"You realize, James, that you are on the front lines of this thing should there be any consequences."

"What does that mean?" said James.

"It means that we are all involved to a point, but if too many feathers are ruffled, you will be the one to take most of the heat because you wrote and introduced the bill." James was unimpressed with Reggie's disloyalty but he wasn't surprised either. It was that one for all and every man for himself motto by which the senators and house members lived. But James didn't care; the dirt was rubbing off again and he knew that, to an extent, he was using the other members to get what he wanted the same as they were using him.

"I am totally committed to this venture, Reggie, and I intend to ride it to the end of the line regardless of the outcome or the consequences."

"Splendid, splendid. There is nothing less quarrelsome than a willing scapegoat."

There was that language again, thought James; no false pretenses, no battering of the truth. The members of the

237

General Assembly wallowed in one of the highest placed mud holes of society and they were comfortable there.

"I merely believe in sleeping in the bed one makes for himself, Reggie."

"Yes, well, let's hope you can sleep peacefully. Now, we've discussed what needs to be done, obviously not all of the members who support us were at our little meeting but the rest will spread the word. In the meantime, you and I will work on the constituents in our respective districts; aside from that, we wait. I hope you are as well stocked with patience as you are with nerve, my good fellow—you will have need of it. These things take time and a bill as controversial as this one will surely exhaust eternity. But it could be well worth the wait, am I right?"

"Yes, Reggie, let's hope we both get what we want."

James knew that Reggie was entirely correct about one thing: it would take a lot of time for the bill to work its way through the legislative process and there would be much debate along the way. It was also disconcerting to know that the bill could be shot down at any step of the procedure. It would be up to the supporting members to keep it alive. Now it was time for James to get very busy gathering interest in the bill anywhere and everywhere he could. He would have to take a break soon, however, as Jim and Elizabeth would be graduating and he would be going home for that. The graduation was a much anticipated event for James not only because his son and future daughter-in-law's educations would be complete but also because he desperately needed their help with the campaign. He had hired no staff, keeping his promise to Jim. It would also be nice to have family with him during the sessions in Atlanta.

The first of April was a lovely day, a day to inspire hope, James thought. He had spent a tireless day in session taking part in a debate over a bill that would make it compulsory for all children to attend school. It was a restoration of faith in his fellow man to see that the lawmakers were concerned with such worthwhile issues.

As he was leaving the capitol building, that lovely April day took a turn for the worse. Descending the steps he noticed a white haired man standing on the sidewalk watching him come down. When he reached the bottom he was somewhat taken aback to see Governor Albert H. Colquitt standing there.

"Mr. Langdon—excuse me, Senator Langdon, how nice to see you again."

"Good afternoon, Governor," said James.

"Somehow I always knew our paths would cross again, but I have to admit, I never thought it would be on this level."

"I'm a little surprised myself, sir, but we all must do our duty."

"I'm extremely glad to hear you say that, Senator, because disappointment comes a lot easier when you understand the reasons behind it."

"I think I follow you, Governor, but to be certain, why don't you be more specific."

"With pleasure. I heard all about your equal rights bill and I want you to know that you'd have a better chance of the wheat rising again after a hail storm. I have no intention of letting such a bill pass through the senate and I have the power to see to it."

"With all due respect, sir, you have power but you don't have absolute power. If enough members of the General Assembly vote for the bill, your veto can be overridden ... of course I'm not telling you anything you don't already know."

"You may recall I tried to reason with you before. Now, off the record, I'm warning you. If you push this issue you are heading for more trouble than you realize. Do I make myself clear or are you just naturally obtuse?"

"I'll keep the warning in mind, Governor Colquitt. While I have the opportunity, sir, I would like to ask you a question. You don't believe that black people are equal to whites. I am white and you would stand in the way of *my* freedom to vote for a bill that sees them treated as equals. What, exactly, sir, *is* the definition of freedom?"

Realizing he had gotten nowhere, Colquitt turned in a huff and hurried over to a beautiful barouche drawn by two high quality horses.

The brief meeting with the governor certainly served to ruin James's day. Worst of all it was April 1st, but he knew that Colquitt wasn't fooling. Hatred for the blacks was in his blood and thousands of men just like him had fought a war to prove that they were not fooling. When he next saw Reggie, James reported the meeting with Colquitt. If Reggie had any secrets to controlling the governor, it would behoove him to keep them where they would be handy.

Two weeks later, James went home to prepare for graduation day. He was always glad to be with family and the trip to New York with Polly proved to be especially delightful. He tried to put the governor and the trouble he represented out of his mind. The warning, on the other hand, was more difficult to forget. He had no idea how far Colquitt would go to protect his interests but surely a man in his position had an arsenal at his disposal.

Not more than five minutes after James and Polly were met by the young people at the train station Jim was asking his father about things in Atlanta. His enthusiasm had not tapered off in the least, and James was happy to have his strength and support.

The family spent an extra two days in New York, seeing the sights and enjoying the city's fine hotels and world class cuisine. During the train ride home, the ladies napped, being tuckered out by the big city, so James filled his son in on all the details about his experiences in Atlanta.

"I never imagined what goes on behind the scenes, Father. It sounds exciting and a little bit dangerous. We will have to keep a close eye on Elizabeth."

"We will do that, Jim, but I believe the bark will be worse than the bite."

"What about the warning from the governor?"

"I don't know ... a man in his position has to be pretty careful. His reputation is important to him. Don't worry, Jim." James was not as confident as he sounded but he wanted to appear positive to his son.

After a few more days at home, everyone left for Atlanta, including Polly. She wanted to help get Jim and Elizabeth settled. Jim would share James's quarters in an old brownstone on Washington Street. Elizabeth would also live there, occupying the third floor but taking her meals with Jim and James. The couple had picked a date in July to be married, at which time they would begin cohabitating as husband and wife.

James spent a week educating his new staff on exactly what their duties were. He told them that soon they would be going on a speaking tour all over the state, where James would dazzle the people with his oratory in an attempt to raise favoritism of his equal rights bill. They would stop at all of the major cities and a few of the larger towns. Three days before they were to leave, James was called into the office of the Secretary of the Senate. The secretary, Mr. Cavanaugh told James that another member, a Mr. Brandon Creech, had brought a charge of disorderly misconduct against him.

"What, may I ask, is the nature of the charge, Mr. Cavanaugh?"

"Did you have a conversation with Governor Colquitt recently?" James immediately understood the reason for the charge.

"Yes, sir, I did, a few weeks ago."

"What was the mood of the conversation, Senator?"

"It was something less than congenial," James replied.

"I see ... did you raise your voice, become angry, use profanity perhaps?"

"No, sir, none of the above. Due to the governor's personal beliefs he is vehemently opposed to an equal rights bill that I just introduced. We didn't speak long and I said nothing to him that could be construed as disrespectful."

"Very well, Senator. Consider yourself censured; I won't waste any more time on this. With a little more information I would have just met you downtown for a cup of coffee instead of officially here at the office. It is my job to investigate these complaints and especially any charges that are brought but I know the governor and his personal beliefs pretty well and I can put two and two together. Off the record, this is more harassment than anything. If I were you, in the future I would avoid the governor as much as possible. If you ever give him the chance to make a bona

241

fide charge against you, the next step is a fine or imprisonment. You may leave."

"Thank you, sir."

James left the building under a moderate head of steam. He felt that it was a cowardly trick to use one's position to malign another person's character; not to mention involving this Mr. Creech, whoever he was. He mentioned the censure to Polly and she agreed that the governor bore watching.

When the speaking tour began, James scheduled the first stop in Macon so that he could see Polly safely home. As always, he felt she would be out of harm's way with so many friends and family close by. He hoped that Macon would get the tour off to a good start; he knew many of the people and he knew that at least some of them would listen to him with an open mind. Jim wrote the speech that he would deliver and James was impressed with every word of it. His son had become a very good writer; just one more reason he was indispensable to his staff.

Still, it was a bit unnerving to speak to a crowd while staring at some of the signs people were waving; signs that expressed their disapproval in many crude, ugly ways. Some of them left before the speech was over but some who stayed until the end actually spoke to him afterwards—a few even shook his hand.

On they went from place to place. James improved his delivery, each time putting more and more feeling into it, but he couldn't be sure that he was achieving a great deal of success anywhere. The crowd was usually predominately black but they always seemed subdued; perhaps they feared reprisals and kept their shows of enthusiasm to a minimum. It seemed that the minor triumphs peaked and then things went downhill from there. When the death threats started coming in, James hired security to travel with them. Sometimes their schedule crossed the paths of other senators campaigning for the same purpose.

One night in Augusta, Reggie Marston showed up at James's hotel room. Reggie was in town to speak to a group of people at one of the Baptist churches. In spite of their strictly symbiotic relationship, James was glad to see him.

"Good evening, Senator," said Reggie. "I see you are out spreading the good word."

"It is a tough road, Reggie, but I have traveled it before. Is there any subject on earth more unpopular than equal rights?"

"Liquor prohibition maybe," Reggie said with a laugh. "I told you it would take time, James. Just stay the course. We'll wear them down eventually."

"I do admire your tenacity, Reggie, even if it is extremely self-serving."

"You are the only man I know who can say something like that and not offend me. I guess it's because you've been honest and open from the start. I can't say that about anyone else that I know. Well, I should be going; my engagement is in an hour."

"Thanks for stopping by, Reggie, and be careful."

"Don't worry about me." Then he laughed again and said, "Look at the bright side, James, we aren't up for reelection for another year."

The next morning James, Jim, and Elizabeth were having breakfast before leaving the city. After they'd eaten, James sipped a second cup of coffee while Jim read the morning edition of the *Augusta Chronicle*. After scanning the front page Jim looked up from the paper with a look of disbelief on his face. "The first martyr to our cause," he said. Without another word he handed the paper to his father. At the top of the page, far right column, the headline read, "Senator Killed by Unknown Assassin."

James began to read the article out loud becoming more despondent with each word.

"Senator Reginald Marston was shot to death last evening, May 17, 1881 at about nine PM as he spoke to a crowd at the Augusta First Baptist Church at 802 Greene Street. The unknown assailant was reported to have shouted, 'Death to niggers and their white allies!' just before shots rang out. The senator was taken to University Hospital where he died without regaining consciousness."

He laid the paper on the table and looked at Jim and Elizabeth. "What have I done?" he asked.

"What do you mean, Father?" Jim replied. "You are not responsible for Reggie's death."

"You know, Jim, when the late war broke out I left home and helped slaves escape and led them north to freedom. When I started out I thought that I was doing an absolute good; that no harm could come of it. Although it *was* the right thing to do, I didn't realize how much trouble I would cause simply because many people believed that what I was doing was a criminal act; an act of treason. It made them angry and hostile. I soon saw that, due to my actions, others were being killed. An overseer at Live Oak Plantation; a man by the name of Sam Gilmore who ran an Underground Railroad station; Raymond Wilkes, the former sheriff of Dry Branch—they all died because of my activity. They are just a few who were killed; there were others. Even your mother was in serious danger for a time because she was associated with me."

"But, Father, that still doesn't put the blame on you."

"But don't you see, Jim, that it is starting again? If I hadn't begun the legislation proceedings for equal rights, Reggie wouldn't have followed me into the fray and he would still be alive."

"And what about the death threats that *you* have been receiving?"

"You know about them?"

"Yes, Father, I do, and I don't see you quitting because of them. We know that thousands of black people just like Hiram Jones have been killed because the law refuses to prosecute their murderers. Even if they are brought to trial there is no conviction. The only reason Harland Jeffers was convicted was because he hanged a white man. Murder will continue as long as people walk the earth but it will slow down considerably if the threat of prosecution looms over them. You explained it to me yourself; we make laws sometimes to force people to do the right thing."

Elizabeth, who had kept her silence during the conversation, now spoke her mind.

"Jim is right, Father Langdon, and so are you in what you have done and what you are doing. Freedom is the most precious thing we have in this world. Sometimes it takes all that we have to preserve it—even our lives. Many people have died for what they believe, people like my cousin Robert. I don't believe that a single one of them would do anything differently if they had a second chance. We fear death for ourselves and more importantly for our loved ones. But you did what you believed was right during the war and you are doing the same now because God is guiding you. How can you take blame for performing God's work?"

James was deeply moved by the words of his son and his future daughter-in-law. He was inspired by their spirit and rejuvenated by their youth. He would mourn for Reggie and pray for his soul but he would also pick up the fallen flag and carry it deeper into the fight.

"I want to thank you both for your encouraging words. Your perceptions are ahead of your years. Let's get out of here; we have a schedule to keep."

It seemed a bit inexplicable to James but for some reason the rest of their tour went much better after Augusta. The crowds were larger, the welcomes seemed warmer, and his speeches garnered more applause than they had before. By the time they returned to Atlanta, James was very hopeful if not confident that the bill had a chance.

However, by the end of the year the bill had passed the house but failed to make it through the senate.

The second happiest occasion for 1881 was Jim and Elizabeth's wedding; the happiest occasion came four days after Christmas when Jim announced that Elizabeth was pregnant. The announcement brought much joy to the Langdon family and with new life came new hope for the following year; James would begin again by reintroducing his equal rights bill.

# TWENTY-FOUR

# New Generation

When the new legislative session commenced on the 14th of January, James was prepared to work harder than ever to sway the voters of Georgia to support his bill. James knew that mills grind slowly and so do certain changes; especially unpopular ones. But there was something on the distant horizon that foretold of a new world ahead if there were those willing to move away the old obstacles. It would also call for a new generation, one that might evolve and do away with narrow-minded, antiquated thinking.

James also took quick notice that there were many others who were fighting their own isolated battles in the struggle for equal rights. He remembered reading with keen interest a story in the *Atlanta Constitution,* the previous year, about a man named John Burke who police attempted to arrest for physically abusing a white woman. A number of irate black men and women had formed a protective barrier around the man to thwart the arrest. In a frantic move to aid her son, Burke's mother Gertrude secured a gun and attempted to discharge the weapon at one of the policemen.

The gun failed to fire; a group of more than two hundred followed the officers as they took Burke to the police station. The story explained that black Atlantans had protested against false arrest and mistreatment by white officers and had even pleaded for the hiring of black police officers for years, but it had gained them nothing.

As a defense against police brutality, the black working class, people like Gertrude Burke, would often become involved in "collective self-defense."

The paper printed another interesting story in early August, which happened the month before, about a labor organization called the Washing Society, set up by a group of black washer women at a church in an Atlanta neighborhood. Within a few weeks, 3000 women, some of them white, decided to strike for more independence in their work and better pay. In an effort to support the women's cause, black churches, communal organizations, and mutual aid societies all over the city donated money and moral sustenance.

James remembered what Reggie Marston had told him about equal rights for blacks and how it was inevitable that it would one day happen. That was why Reggie supported the bill; he thought being a groundbreaker on the issue would secure him a place in history, not to mention, secure his job as state senator.

The stories in the paper were, in a sense, proof that Reggie's prediction would come true. Black people with their own power in numbers would further educate themselves in the ways of the world and the ways of getting things done by working the system. Throwing off the yoke of slavery was only the first step. Now it was time to join the pursuit of happiness along with their fellow Americans. James also hoped that other people would see all of this the same way and thus ease up on the resistance to his equal rights bill.

But the year was passing quickly and the bill seemed to be stalling out. There were more members of the General Assembly who had taken up the cause—some of them were even calling it the Reggie Marston Bill—but there was still no real progress.

In late August, Elizabeth gave birth to an eight and a half pound baby boy. The Langdon family had begun a new generation. Jim was beside himself, as was the boy's grandfather. That evening, while Elizabeth rested, the new father sat out on the veranda half choking on his traditional cigar and James was basking in the glow of becoming a grandfather.

"I think I'd better throw the rest of this away if I want to live long enough to see him grow up," said Jim.

"I think you've smoked enough to fulfill your duty," James replied with a laugh.

"I'm glad we have this time alone, Father. There is something of importance that I want to tell you. I remember the story you told me about deciding to stay in Georgia after the war. You decided to rebuild grandfather's plantation as a way to honor him."

"That is exactly right, son."

"Well, I wanted to honor grandfather, too, so I insisted that we name the baby John. Elizabeth wanted to call him Robert after her cousin, which I admit is a wonderful thought. But she gave in and settled for naming him John Robert Langdon."

"I am very pleased with that, Jim, and your grandfather would be pleased, too."

"Of course you and I will have to go without Elizabeth for a while in Atlanta," said Jim.

"She can take all the time she needs, son. It is possible that she may never need to go back to Atlanta—not for business reasons at least."

"What do you think our chances are for getting the bill passed this year, Father?"

"If you were a child I would tell you that the chances are excellent, but as you are a grown man I will treat you like one and tell you that I don't think the outcome looks very promising. Maybe I was a fool to ever think we had a chance in the first place. Maybe there are years of upheaval yet to come before the matter is settled. Perhaps even your son John will be needed to join the movement."

"Could it really go on that long, Father?"

"I wouldn't be surprised. It isn't just the last generation … the Old South still stands in the way. Racism is taught, passed on to future generations so that they have no chance of making up their own minds. Maybe without the harmful influence, they wind up living next to a black family and become the best of friends. *With* the harmful influence they wind up making sure that the same black family is not allowed to live in their neighborhood."

"I see what you mean," said Jim. "It really is sad, isn't it?"

"You bet it is, son—very sad. People shortchange themselves in life through their own narrow-minded ignorance. This world is made up of hundreds of different countries with different cultures, different histories, and different beliefs. Imagine what we could all learn if the world pooled its resources and every nation passed parts of itself around until we all had something from every place on earth. Instead, we choose to be blinded by the differences and use them as reasons to hate ... sometimes I despair the species."

"Do you imagine that it is the same in other countries, Father? I mean do you think people in other countries shun us just because we are different from them?"

"I think that is probably the case, Jim. I think the abundance of ignorance is enough to supply the world."

"But we will keep trying," said Jim.

"Yes, because if we don't try then we don't do, and if we don't do, then why were we put on this earth? I believe that God frowns on complacency."

Suddenly from inside the house there was the sound of commotion. James could hear Polly's voice and the voice of a man—it was Jeremy. The front door opened and Jeremy came out to the veranda with Polly right behind him.

"I'm sorry to interrupt, James. I came to the back door —thought you might be inside."

"What is it, Jeremy? You look like a man in a panic."

"Maybe I am, just a little. I have news. I just got back from Macon. I went in to get a few things for Ashton. The Glacken boys, Ned and Junior, they've been arrested for the murder of Hiram." James couldn't believe what he was hearing. How could they have been arrested when no one had accused them?

"Tell us what you heard, Jeremy ... I can't imagine Colt Jeffers arresting two white men for murdering Hiram."

"Colt didn't arrest them. It was a U.S. Marshal from Atlanta. Ned and Junior were running a still in the woods behind their place. Internal revenue agents went up there looking for them because they were violating the whiskey tax laws. When those agents go after somebody they need a U.S. Marshal to go along because they don't have the power to make an arrest. When the law got up to Johnson's Creek they caught those two red handed at their still. The marshal took them into custody."

"How did they come to charge them with Hiram's murder?" James asked.

"Well that's the strange thing: when the marshal took them to the house to get their horses, their ma told the marshal they had murdered a black man named Hiram Jones. Nobody can figure out how she knew about it but she knew."

James kept silent about his ride to the Glacken place. He knew it must have been his message that resulted in the Glackens being charged with murder but it wasn't important or of any consequence to speak of it now.

"There's more," said Jeremy. "The agents and the marshal took the Glackens to Macon and told Colt to lock them up. Colt didn't want to do it; he tried to get them turned loose but the marshal ordered him to. They told Colt the Glackens would be picked up after a trial date was set and until then it was his responsibility to keep them in custody."

"How did you find out about all of this, Jeremy?"

"Do you know Ben Hicks?"

"Only by name," said James.

"Ben is one of Colt's deputies. He was in Watkins's dry goods store telling old man Watkins the story and I overheard every word."

"Well, the Lord works in mysterious ways. I guess the Glackens may be punished for what they've done," said James.

"Maybe, and then again maybe not," Jeremy replied.

"What do you mean?"

"They broke out of jail!"

"Broke out?" said Jim.

"That's right, either they broke out or Colt let them out but when I was leavin town Ben Hicks comes running out of the sheriff's office and I saw him take a couple of shots at somebody riding fast out of town. Then he came running over to me and said that I should warn everybody I saw because the Glackens were armed and there's no telling what they might do. I hurried on back here because those boys could be headed this way and I wanted to get home to Ashton. I wanted to warn you all, too."

"We appreciate the warning, Jeremy. We'll need to warn the others to keep a lookout tonight."

"I'll do that on my way up to the house," he replied.

"All right," said James.

Jeremy hurried out back to warn the other men to keep a watch and guard their families closely.

# TWENTY-FIVE

## Rest in Peace

Two hours later James said, "I hear horses on the road, Jim, and I see some light. Go in the house and get two revolvers." Jim did as he was told. The light appeared at the end of the driveway and then a group of riders came toward the house. Jim reappeared quickly, handing a revolver to his father. The riders stopped at the hitching rail and one of the men dismounted. It was Colt Jeffers.

"Evenin, Langdon," he said. He was not any more cordial than the last time James saw him but he did appear to be a lot less cocky.

"I understand you had some trouble, Sheriff."

"That's right. I lost two prisoners."

"What are you doing here?"

"I think they might be nearby and I wondered if you seen anything"

"I have not. I'm a little surprised you're out looking for them," James told him.

"Why the hell wouldn't I be?"

"I heard that they've been charged with the murder of Hiram Jones. I can't believe that is any concern of yours."

"Now that you mention it, it ain't. But they're also charged with makin illegal liquor and besides that a marshal ordered me to lock em up. If I don't get em back it will be my ass. It beats me how their ma found out they killed that nigger. I hear she's religion crazy in the head. I think she's a damn witch but if she knew them boys killed somebody, she'd turn em in."

"How did they get loose?" James asked him.

"Ned had a hold out that the marshal didn't find; some lawman. Ned forced me to open the cell and that's all there is to it."

"Do you need anything else from me?"

Colt hesitated for a moment; apparently he needed James's help and found it very difficult to ask him.

"I was wonderin if you would help me and my men look for em. You know this area better than anybody. Maybe you know some places they might be holed up. It means as much to you as it does to me to catch em. I know you want them to hang for killin your nigger friend."

"You have a way of making it difficult to grant a favor, but you're right—I do want them to answer for the murder of Hiram Jones. I will go with you."

"James, must you go?" said Polly.

"Don't worry, dear. They might not even be anywhere around here. I'd feel better if I knew for sure."

"I want to go with you, Father," Jim told him.

"No, Jim, I need a man in the house. Stay with your mother and Elizabeth."

"Give me a few minutes to saddle a horse, Colt, and I'll be ready to go."

"Meet us down on the main road," the sheriff replied.

When James joined the posse, the six of them investigated a few ideas that James had without any success. Finally they headed for a deserted cabin in the woods; Buford Bell's old cabin. With James in the lead, the men rode hard until they were about half a mile from their destination. Then he slowed them down, bringing the posse to a stop within a few hundred yards of the cabin.

"I'm going to ask you to wait here with your men, Colt. I'll travel on foot through the woods and try to get close enough to find out if the cabin is occupied. If it is, then I'll try to find out if it's the Glackens."

"All right, but don't spook em. If it's Ned and Junior you come and git us so we can surround the place before they know we're out here. If they get away in the dark we'll never catch em."

"Don't worry, if it's them I'll get back as fast as I can."

James dismounted and tied the reins to a tree branch. Then he started off through the woods as quickly but as quietly as he could. Suddenly he remembered that he had put his revolver in the saddle bag—it was still there. Hopefully the oversight wouldn't come back to haunt him.

He had misjudged the distance by a hundred yards or
so, and consequently it seemed to take forever to find the
cabin. When he spotted it he could see a very dim light
through the only window. Someone was inside all right,
but the question was, who? He couldn't go near the
window; surely if it was the Glackens they would be
keeping watch. Fortunately, the dilapidated structure had
a few wide gaps between some of the wall boards, but
seeing the occupants wouldn't help much because James
wasn't sure what the brothers looked like. Still, if he could
get close enough it would help him to hear any
conversation between the two. Slowly, he inched his way
forward until he was close enough to the cabin to touch it.

After listening for a few minutes, James determined
that there were, in fact, two men inside. They were
speaking very quietly and he could only make out a word
here and there. Squatting next to the cabin soon became a
bit uncomfortable and then a cramp in his right leg caused
him to reposition himself. As he shifted his weight he
suddenly lost his balance, falling backwards and snapping
a dead tree branch. The noise sounded like a gunshot in
the still night air and from inside James heard a voice say,
"What the hell was that, Ned?"

Boots hit the floor and pounded quickly across it to the
door, which was flung open hard enough to pull it from its
hinges. The two men ran to the side of the cabin just as
James was scrambling to his feet. The first man stuck a
rifle under James's chin and said. "Who the hell are you?"

"Shoot him, Ned," said his younger brother. "Shoot him
while you can."

"Shut up, Junior," said Ned without taking his eyes off
of James.

James quickly concocted a story, hoping to bluff his
way past the Glackens.

"I'm not looking for any trouble, fellas. I'm just looking
for a place to spend the night."

"If that's all you want then why you sneakin around
outside? Why didn't you just come to the door?"

"Well," said James, "I'm wanted by the law for stealing a
horse and I didn't know if maybe you boys were lawmen."

"Where's your horse?

"He's tied up back yonder a piece. I'll go get him."

"Not so fast, mister," said Ned. "You just come on in the cabin so we can get a good look at ya."

"I don't trust him, Ned," said Junior. "Shoot him now, Ned."

"Shut up, Junior."

Ned waved his rifle at James, indicating that he was to go inside. James led the way to the door as Ned's rifle barrel poked him in the back.

"Search him for a weapon, Junior." Junior did as he was told and then he looked at his brother and said, "He ain't got no gun Ned. What kind a outlaw ain't got no gun?"

"That's a good question, mister," said Ned. "How come you ain't got no gun?"

"It's in my saddle bag," James replied.

"Ain't gonna do you no good there," said Junior.

You've got a good point there, thought James. The two brothers were as nervous as a weak cup of coffee. They were not buying his story and he was not selling it too well either. Their faces clearly advertised the suspicion in their minds. Ned was pointing his rifle at James's stomach and Junior stood directly behind Ned as if using him as a shield, a revolver filled his left hand.

"I reckon I'll give you one last chance to tell me who you are and what you want here," said Ned.

"Shoot him now, Ned," repeated Junior. James was beginning to think that the youngest Glacken might be a bit simpleminded. Perhaps it served a useful purpose because the irritation of the repeated request and the difficult situation made Ned careless. He turned his attention to his brother and said, "I'm not gonna tell you again to shut up, Junior!"

The distraction was just long enough for James to put his hands against Ned's rifle barrel and shove him hard into Junior. Junior's revolver went off and the bullet hit Ned in the right foot.

"Dang you, Junior, you shot my foot!" Ned yelled.

As Ned was yelling, Junior was apologizing to his brother and James was racing out the door. After about a hundred yards, James stopped to catch his breath. The gunshot had alerted the posse; he could hear them coming through the woods and the light of their torches preceded them. When they got close enough James called out, "Over here, Colt!"

The sheriff led the others to where James was waiting. "What in the hell happened?" he said in an angry tone of voice.

"It's the Glackens. They caught me spying on them but the details aren't important. We'd better get up there fast."

"Damn you, Langdon. They're probably a mile away by now."

"No they're not. Junior accidentally shot Ned in the foot. I'm sure that they are forting up inside the cabin. Now, do you want to argue or do you want to get your prisoners back?"

"Let's go," said Colt.

One of the other men had brought James's horse up with him. He tossed the reins to James and James climbed into the saddle. They moved up to the cabin and then the sheriff stopped about twenty yards away. "Pete," he said to one of his deputies. "You, George, and Jacob get around the back and don't let em get by you. Nathan, you come with me and Langdon. Dismount and tie your horses."

The men dispersed and James, Colt, and Nathan found cover near the front of the cabin and then waited a moment while the other three took their places in the back. When Colt was satisfied with the situation he shouted, "Ned! Ned, this here is Colt Jeffers. You and Junior come on outta there before you get yourselves into any more trouble."

"How the hell can we get into more trouble, Colt?" said Ned in a voice that revealed the pain he was in. "We're wanted by the law, we're surrounded by a posse, and my damn brother shot me in the foot."

"I'm sorry, Ned," they heard Junior say.

"You're resistin arrest, Ned. That's more trouble. And if you shoot one of us you'll hang for sure."

"We're gonna hang anyway, and for a damn nigger, too."

"You know better than that, Ned. The law ain't gonna hang you boys for killin a nigger."

"Don't try to shit me Colt. Maybe if only the local law wanted us you might be right but it was a U.S. Marshal that arrested us and you know how them Feds are; they'll just keep comin like they done during the war. They'll take us to trial and then hang us and we ain't getting hanged for no goddamn nigger." With that, Ned took a shot out the window. The bullet sailed high but it still made everybody duck his head.

"What do ya think, Langdon?" the sheriff said to James.

"I think they're smarter than I would have given them credit for being. You know how much it pains me to admit it, but Ned is right. Local law would never prosecute them for murder but now that the federal marshal is a part of this they stand a real good chance of hanging."

"Then what the hell do we do? I want them boys alive. I wouldn't have arrested them to begin with and anyway, if we have to shoot em then that marshal is gonna find out that they got away from me."

"I see your point, Colt. Then I guess you'd better try to keep Ned talking while I think of some way to get them out of there alive. I don't want to shoot them either; I want the law to punish them."

"All right, you think, I'll talk."

"Right," said James.

"It takes a lot of proof to convict a man of murder, Ned. They might not even have a case against you and Junior."

"We ain't gonna trust you Colt, you're just trying to save your own ass. Once you get us back in that jail we're dead."

"You know you can trust me, Ned. I'll prove it to you. I'll stand up so you can see that I trust you. Then we can talk face to face. I'm gonna stand up now, so don't you or Junior shoot."

"Are you crazy?" James said to Colt. "If you stand up they'll blow your head off."

"I'm runnin this show, Langdon. Ned won't shoot me; I've known him a long time."

"Suit yourself," James replied.

Colt stood up and James watched the window of the cabin intently. Even in the dim light he could see Ned put his rifle to his shoulder and take a fine bead on the stubborn sheriff. Instantly, James reached up and grabbed Colt's right arm and pulled him down just as Ned's rifle went off. The sudden jerk caused Colt's left arm to go up in the air and the bullet took the tip of his middle finger off. The sheriff hit the ground screaming in pain.

"Damn you, Ned! You shot my finger off!"

"Hurts don't it? Now you know how my foot feels."

"I didn't shoot your foot. Junior done that. You had no cause to shoot off my finger, you son of a bitch!"

"Go away and leave me and Junior alone or I'll shoot something else off."

Colt was writhing in pain and now he was ready to take the Glackens dead or alive. The situation was more than out of hand and James knew he'd better think of something quickly.

"Listen, Colt, I think I have an idea."

"I wished you'd a got it before I got my damn finger shot off."

"I told you not to stand up."

"What's your damn idea?"

"Come here, Nathan," James said to the deputy. Nathan crawled over to James and the wounded sheriff. "I want you to sneak around to the back of the cabin. Take your boots off and have the other three men do the same. Then two of you sneak up one side to the edge of the porch and the other two sneak up the other side. Then go up on the porch and get as close to the opposite sides of the door as you can without being seen. I think I can stir Ned up so bad that he and Junior will come charging out of the cabin. When they do, it will be up to the four of you to take them from behind. But be perfectly quiet, step slow and easy or all will be lost. Do you understand?"

"I got it," Nathan replied.

"All right, I'll give you five minutes to get into position. I'll try to keep Ned's attention until you men get up on the porch, now go."

Nathan crawled out into the darkness.

"How in the hell are you gonna get Ned to come a chargin outta that cabin?" said Colt.

"Just wait and see." Then James started talking to Ned.

"My name is James Langdon, Ned, have you ever heard of me?"

"No I ain't and I wouldn't care if I did."

"Well I've heard of you, Ned. That is, I've heard things about you and Junior."

James could see the deputies, two on each side of the cabin, getting ready to move into position on the porch. He kept talking.

"For one thing I've heard that you aren't too fond of black people."

"No self respectin white man likes niggers."

"Oh, I don't know, Ned. I have self-respect and I like black people."

"Then you should be in here with a hole in your foot and I should be out there tryin to take you to jail."

The deputies were on the porch by now and ready to pounce on the Glackens.

"Well, Ned, I not only like black people but as it happens, Hiram Jones was a good friend of mine. In addition to that, I know you killed Hiram and I know who saw you do it."

The information agitated Ned just as James expected.

"And you think you're gonna help get me hanged for killin your nigger friend, is that it?"

"I am sure of it, Ned. An eyewitness will put your head in the noose. You were right not to trust the sheriff. But at least when you hang it will serve as a warning to others like you who think they can commit murder and walk away from it."

"You son of a bitch I wish I'd get hanged for killin you."

"I'm right here, Ned, if you want to try."

"You keep runnin your big mouth and me and Junior are just liable to."

James had Ned right where he wanted him. He was pretty sure that one more push would bring him and his brother out of the cabin.

"Get ready," James told Colt.

"I'll tell you something else Ned," said James. "It was me who told your mother that you and Junior killed Hiram."

"You son of a bitch! Let's kill em, Junior!"

The cabin door flew open and Ned and Junior ran out onto the porch, firing their guns as they came. James and Colt dropped flat on the ground but the attack ended as quickly as it began. The deputies converged on the outlaws and knocked them face down on the porch. They were immediately disarmed and hauled to their feet. Manacles were slapped onto their wrists and they were back in the custody of the law.

James and Colt joined the deputies on the porch.

"Look at my finger, Ned," said Colt, sticking the damaged digit in his face.

"Well, look at my foot," Ned replied.

"I told you, Junior done that, not me. Nathan, Pete, you men get these boys on their horses and let's get em back to town." To James he said, "I guess we'll part company, Langdon. Is that true about you telling their ma they done the killin?"

"Does it really matter?" James asked.

"I reckon it doesn't. You know, Langdon, if you hadn't a dragged me to the ground that fool Ned would have blown my head off."

"I believe he would have, Colt."

"But I still won't ever like you," Colt replied. Then he got on his horse and the posse headed through the woods with their prisoners. Ned was still hollering about his foot and Colt was still whining about his finger. James enjoyed a laugh, mounted his horse, and started for home. "Rest in peace, Hiram," he said.

Jim and Polly were waiting in the parlor when he returned. He could see how relieved they were when he walked through the door. He told them the entire story of the capture and then everyone went to bed; their excitement had turned to exhaustion.

# TWENTY-SIX

# The Final Word

A week later, Elizabeth and new baby John were doing fine and James and Jim left for Atlanta. The final debate on the equal rights bill was coming up and James had to prepare for what might be his last chance to argue on its behalf. For three days he worked on his notes; Jim helped him to be sure that nothing pertinent was missed and the notes were in the proper order.

When the session was called to order, the pro-equal rights members presented their opening statement. As the spokesman for the group, James was called upon to speak first.

"Good morning, gentlemen. We are here today to discuss an issue of epic importance. It is incumbent upon us to make the laws in this state; laws for the betterment of the people, for their way of life, and for the great state of Georgia. The issue today is a bill that would grant equal rights to a race of people who have for many years known only depravation and degradation. It is not only our duty as legislators but as Christians to recognize that we are all equal under God and that God created all of us. How then do we have the right to restrict another's ability to enjoy the same freedoms that we, the white people of this state enjoy? The issue of slavery has been settled. It is now a crime by law to enslave another person.

"I could cite many good, sound reasons why this bill should be passed; for instance, a country is stronger and more productive when all the people work together toward common goals, for the good of one another. But I will instead appeal to the better angels of your nature and ask you to be the first state to set an example for the rest of the South to follow. Allow all people equal rights, fair treatment, and let us show the world the best that America can be."

261

When James was finished, Senator Davis from the Wilcox district made an opening statement for those opposed to the bill.

"Good Morning. I will be brief in the interest of saving rather than wasting time. The reason for the state of affairs which exists in Georgia today is twofold: first of all blacks simply are not equal to whites intellectually, socially, academically, etc. The blacks are an inferior race that could not function or survive without the guidance and guardianship of whites. Secondly, as Senator Langdon said, it is our duty to serve the people of this state and that is why we are a segregated society. We must not mix the two races, thereby upsetting the delicate balance and turning us into a weakened, exploitable nation. In plain language, we are doing what is best for both cultures and by each of us, black or white, accepting our places and remaining in them we can realize that strong, productive, and harmonious country. Finally, we work for the people, i.e. the voters, and today's status quo is the way the people who pay our salaries want it. Thank you."

After the opening statements had been made, the debate continued. The gap between the two sides widened, evolving into a heated argument. The pro-equal rights side did an admirable job driving home, point after point, but the opposition would not climb down from the high horse that had carried the South to destruction by the end of the Civil War. They served to prove that you could drive old Dixie down but you could never expect them to conform.

After about two hours, James got another opportunity to speak. He believed that his side was fighting a losing battle but if he had to go down, he would handle it as did Nathan Hale: regretting that he had but one life to give for his fellow man.

"I have sat here for the last two hours listening to the same decaying reasons for refusing to conform to equal rights for blacks, and most of what I am hearing is in reference to their alleged ignorance, their inability to hold the same positions or contribute the same ideas as whites. The implications give me cause to wonder about *your* intelligence levels. How can you hold illiteracy against a race of people when for more than two hundred years it was a crime for anyone to teach them to read and write? According to the 1847 Virginia Criminal Code, 'any white person who shall assemble with slaves or free Negroes for the purpose of instructing them to read or write shall be punished by confinement in jail and/or by fine.' This is just one case in point of recorded treatment of the slaves since the 17$^{th}$ century. Is it not understandable that these people would be far behind whites in the academic world, kept away from education while at the same time, the whites have been expanding their own opportunities to learn? And we all know why it was illegal to teach the blacks: because if they were educated, they might have been able to devise a way to destroy slavery on their own. But keeping them ignorant was just another way of keeping them down, of keeping them dependent upon those who would bury their freedom and their wellbeing in the same shallow grave. This is not just a plea for equality —this is a debate over right and wrong and I would like to think that after years of the latter, the people we work for, i.e. the voters, would see fit to do what is right."

James sat down amidst a thundering applause from the pro-equality senators and representatives. He was satisfied that he'd had a chance to be heard and all that remained was to wait for the vote. By one PM James heard that the bill had been approved in the House of Representatives; he was beside himself. Later that afternoon the majority approved the bill in the senate. Both votes were decided by very narrow margins but the result was still the same. James wanted to celebrate, set off fireworks, and buy a round of drinks for the General Assembly, but he couldn't. As much as it pained him to think about it, the bill would now be sent to the governor and that was cause for anxiety. But he knew that he had to remain hopeful; after all, was it not a miracle that the bill had made it this far? Yes, he would take Jim out for a nice dinner that evening and they would allow themselves to be happy and to ruminate on the future. It would do them so much good after all of the work and the disappointments they'd endured.

"Do you really expect a veto from the governor father? I know what you've told me about him but since the bill was

approved in the house and senate; will the governor not
take that into serious consideration?"

"You would certainly think so, Jim, but I believe that
Colquitt is not a man to resort to bluffing. I think he means
what he says and I'm sure that he would not be timid
about using the power of his office."

"But he would in essence, be using the proximity of his
office for his own personal use."

"That is true but it could never be proven. If he shoots
it down, we have only one recourse and that is the override
vote. I understand that the bill made it through the houses
by slim margins. We would need two thirds of both houses
to override."

"We'll pray, Father; we will put it in God's hands."

"I like your suggestion, son. I like it a lot."

When James reached the capitol the following morning
he was met by a contingent of unhappy faces belonging to
members of the pro-equality faction.

"The governor didn't waste any time, James; we found
out just a few minutes ago, he vetoed it," said Senator
Joshua Britt from the Sumpter District.

"I'm sure he just couldn't wait. He waited for it like a
child waits for Christmas when they know they are getting
exactly what they want," said James.

"We are all very sorry; we know how much this meant
to you. You wanted it more than we did. We can still hope
that we do better with the final vote but we think the line
has been drawn and what we have is all we'll get."

"Yes," said James. "I expect that you are right about
that; but we'll see," he said with an optimistic smile.
"Could I ask a favor, Joshua?"

"Sure James, what is it?"

"I do not wish to be present for the vote; I would prefer
to do it by proxy. Would you handle that for me?"

"Sure James, I can do that. I will send word when we
get a final answer."

"I appreciate that. I will be at home."

Ordinarily James would hire transportation to and from
the capitol but that morning he decided to walk. He was
full of a mixture of dejection and desperate hope which
made him poor company. Perhaps, he thought, a long walk

might help to restore a modicum of peace. He thought about the past two years and before. Putting together everything that had happened certainly made it seem longer than it really was. But even though he had lost most of his anticipation he could, if necessary, say out loud that he was not ready to quit. He was still willing to pick up his cross and carry it to wherever the last stop might be.

When James got home, Jim was out. He was grateful for his absence because he hoped he might know the final verdict before breaking any news, good or bad, to his son. James decided that, until word came, he would do nothing. All he wanted was a comfortable chair to sit in while he relaxed and reflected. The ticking of the clock on the mantel was the only sound; the usual noises of the city had faded away. He could imagine the thoughts of a condemned man as he awaited his execution. James mused: What could be more important to that man than the clock and the fear of its perpetual motion; unstoppable? Time is the one thing in life which moves all other things forward. Time is the master, the dictator, the authoritarian; taking us through our lives, directing the where and the when. If only we had the ability to stop time and have the opportunity to gather ourselves, to reorganize and prepare before going on; but we never do; perhaps that is why so many bad decisions are made.

Before James was aware of it, the day was nearly gone; it was 4 PM. He had not fallen asleep; it only felt that way. His mind had gone into such deep thought that he had become oblivious to the world around him. It was the sound of someone at the front door that had caught his attention; bringing him out of his chair.

"Father, were you asleep?" asked Jim.

"No, I was just waiting for you."

"I have something for you, Father. I met a messenger at the door as I was coming in." James could see a piece of paper in Jim's hand. It was the final result; the life or death status of the equal rights bill. He reached out and accepted the message. It was the moment of truth; the culmination of two years of work, hope, and prayer. The fate of an entire race of people rested in his hand. He did not know if he should read it quickly or put it on the table and enjoy the bliss of ignorance for a little while longer. He could see the look of anxiety in Jim's eyes; he did not want to harry his father but curiosity was tearing at him. Waiting would not change the contents; once again, time was demanding attention. James opened the communication and read in silence. When he had absorbed the words and taken just a second to let his initial reaction pass, he laid the message on the mantel next to the clock and sat down again. Jim understood immediately and he went to his father's side and rested a reassuring hand on his shoulder.

"I remember what you have always told me father; if it is supposed to happen it will."

"That is very true Jim; still it leaves us wondering as it so often does about God's plan. Surely logic would suggest that the Almighty should be behind us in this endeavor but we must not forget that God gave man free will; something with which he will never tamper. I'm sure He had hoped that his people would do the right thing and I know that he is as disappointed as we are."

"Can we placate ourselves by saying that we will try again?"

"Perhaps Jim, but not from the political arena; I will not seek reelection. Sadly, the people of this country and this state are not yet ready to concede the fact that all men *are* created equal. They can say it in their constitution but the meaning is lost to them. We will go home, son, home to Mother and Elizabeth, and then look to heaven for the inspiration for another way to make them understand."

# TWENTY-SEVEN

# Disenfranchisement and Reminiscence

Any ground gained for the fair treatment of the blacks since the end of the Civil War had been lost by 1883 when the U.S. Supreme Court declared the Civil Rights Act unconstitutional. James saw his efforts to effect integration of the former slaves come to a bitter end. When the war ended slavery, the favored idea was to send the blacks back to Africa—an idea preferred by Abraham Lincoln. However, by then the black population totaled some four million people making it an impractical notion. James would not have supported the idea but now he believed that it might have been the lesser of two evils. With the Supreme Court seemingly in the South's corner and the southern whites' restoration of power, it appeared as though the same two-tiered system of justice that had existed in the slave era had been restored as well. Apparently the Supreme Court had no respect or gratitude for the thousands of black men who fought and died for this "whites only" nation.

By 1890, all of the former Confederate states had written new constitutions; Jim Crow was now fully established and the disenfranchisement of blacks was going full force. James quickly understood that with its 1883 ruling, what the Supreme Court did by making the guarantees of the Civil Rights Act unenforceable was to provide the South with a roadmap showing them how to legally disenfranchise the blacks.

The rout was on now and it appeared as though the situation as such was here to stay. Every time James was in Macon or any other town or city the reminders were ever present. The country lived together but at the same time separated by whites or colored only. Not a day passed without James asking himself what he could have done to make a difference. The newspaper almost always carried a

267

story of a lynching, a riot, or some other brand of trouble brought about through the trials and tribulations of segregation. Without a compromise, surely the country would one day be facing a race war. Regardless of man's actions or the consequences thereto, the clock keeps ticking; time marches on.

For James, an obedient servant to God, was left something that was good and wonderful—something that could never be taken from him, which was the personal world he had created on the plantation. The purest aspect of his world was the fact that he created it not by design but simply from the way he thought, and many times wished, that life should be. It was a place where people both black and white lived in perfect harmony; working, playing, laughing, and crying together as circumstances dictated.

Although his means would have allowed, James had no desire to see distant country or foreign lands; he had complete happiness on the plantation and could not reason why he should want to be anywhere else. He understood and accepted the fact that the changes he prayed for would not come about in his lifetime and that his generation had gained the end of slavery; it was for the next to gain equality for all.

When the turn of the century came, James and his entire family prayed for the future and celebrated the past: remembering those they loved and lost and hoping for the best for those whose lives lay ahead of them. Although the spirit of the plantation remained the same, mandatory changes took place as they always will. Eventually the old mules gave way to newfangled farm machinery and new farming methods replaced outdated ones, but not one sharecropper lost his home or his employment on Langdon Plantation. The black families prospered and sons grew up to take their fathers' places; the elders retired and lived in peace, finding rest in the plantation cemetery when the Lord called them home.

In 1917, the United States became involved in a world war in spite of President Woodrow Wilson's promise of neutrality. James and Polly were sitting on the veranda when Jim walked over from his house to tell them the news. When Jim had gone home, James told his wife of fifty-six years that he wished to reminisce for a while.

"It is hard to say where the world is going, but I do know where the world has been and I want you to know that through it all I thank God that he saw fit to put us together. The world is at war, the Ku Klux Klan has come back stronger than ever, but here on this veranda at this minute I have more contentment than any man deserves. The old days are long gone now and we have seen many changes. We have grown up nieces by Ashton and Jeremy; we have grown up nephews by Kate and Bradford. Our son Jim has a good wife in Elizabeth and our grandson John is married with a family of his own. My only regret is my occasional questioning of the Lord's intentions when I always knew that whatever was going on was right and just, even if I couldn't understand it. I realize now that everything will come out all right at the end of time because there will always be good people in the world and they will never stop doing the Lord's work. Our black friends will be equally treated when the work is done; I only hope that it will be soon and I only wish I might have seen it in my lifetime. I guess what I am really trying to say is that I love you, Polly, and the bond between us will last throughout eternity."

"I love you as much or more, James, and I knew all along what you were trying to say."

# TWENTY-EIGHT

## Passing the Torch

Morning had broken on what promised to be a lovely day in November. James was in the office with Jim when, for the first time ever, an automobile came up the driveway. It was a noisy contraption that backfired a lot, but James was in awe of the invention. He had considered buying one of his own but decided that the horse and carriage was more reliable and self-sufficient. The visitor turned out to be Tucker Finch, a cattle farmer whose property was adjacent to the Langdon Plantation.

"Good morning, James, Jim" said Tucker.

"Good morning to you, Tucker," they replied in unison.

"What brings you over?" James asked him.

"Just came from town, big news, thought you might like to know. The war is over. The armistice was signed three days ago."

"Well," said James, "there is nothing like good news on a beautiful morning. So the Kaiser decided to call it quits, huh?"

"Yep, I knew it spelled doom to the Germans when the good old U.S. got into it."

"Indeed," James replied.

"Well, I gotta be goin. Just thought you might like to know."

"Thank you for stopping. You'll have to give me a ride in that horseless carriage of yours sometime."

"Any time you say, James. So long."

Jim turned the crank on Tucker's auto to get it started for him and away he went down the driveway.

"Quite a machine, don't you think, Jim?"

"It is, Father; maybe you should reconsider buying one."

"I don't think so, Jim. They are nice but too noisy."

Just then Polly came out on the veranda to see what Tucker had to say. She knew it was him because he was the only one around who had an automobile. When James saw her he shouted happily, "Polly! Tucker said the war just ..." Suddenly James clutched his chest and went down to his knees. Jim rushed over, put his arm around his father, and said, "What's wrong, Father? Can you get up?"

"Get me in the house, son," James replied, struggling to get the words out. Polly came running out to help; together they managed to get James into the house and to his bed.

"I'm going for the doctor," Jim told his mother.

"Go over and ask Tucker to go, Jim. It might be faster."

"OK," Jim called back as he ran for the front door.

Even with the help of Tucker's automobile it took nearly two and a half hours before the doctor arrived. Jim hurried Dr. Bartholomew upstairs and then waited in the hallway, comforting his mother until the doctor came out.

"What happened, Doctor? How is my husband?"

"I'm afraid he's had a heart attack, Mrs. Langdon, a bad one. I suggest that if you have family to notify, do it right away. I'm sorry."

After the doctor left, Polly went to the parlor and cried as Jim did his best to give her a strong shoulder to lean on.

"I'm sorry, son," she said. "I don't want to cry in front of your father. I want his last memory of me to be a smile. I will go up and sit with him. Please do as the doctor said; let everyone know and send word to Kate and Bradford; tell them to come as quickly as they can."

"I will, Mother," said Jim through a veil of tears.

Polly sat with her husband all day and throughout the entire night. For short periods James regained consciousness and then he would drift off again. After two days his breathing became shallower and Polly prayed with all of her heart.

By the morning of the third day, all of the family was present, as was the Lord, who granted Polly's wish that James would regain consciousness in order that he might see his beloved family one more time.

One by one they went to his bedside for a final word; first Ashton, then Kate, then John, and finally ... Polly and

271

Jim. James's voice was raspy and weak but his mind was clear; he spoke in a slow, steady manner, first to Jim.

"I'm proud of you, son," he said. "You're a good man and I know that you will take good care of everything. The plantation is yours now; someday you'll pass it along to John. We must keep the memory of your grandfather alive."

"I will do as you have always done, Father, and I am very proud of you, too. If I am a good man it is owing to all you've taught me. I will keep grandfather's memory alive and yours as well. I will not let your dream of equal rights languish. I will continue the struggle until your dream comes true. I love you, Father, goodbye."

Jim got up, left the room, and Polly could hear him crying his heart out in the hallway. James reached out and took Polly's hand. He squeezed it gently and said, "As a wise man once said, parting is such sweet sorrow. I know that if we say not another word to each other, our hearts will communicate for us."

"They do, my dear James, and they will keep us close until we are together again. I love you, James ..." In an instant Polly realized her husband was gone. "My heart will tell you the rest," she said.

# TWENTY-NINE

# Goodbye

The funeral for James Langdon was quite possibly the largest ever seen in Bibb County. Those in attendance not only included family, sharecropper friends, and acquaintances from Macon, but black men and their families for many miles around. Even though they had never worked on Langdon Plantation they all knew of James and his humanitarian beliefs. As James himself had requested, Aaron Parmalee, an old friend and a man of God, performed the service. Many had requested to deliver their own personal eulogies, and Polly gratefully allowed anyone who wished, to speak. It took perhaps two hours for the line of mourners one by one to say a few words about a man for whom they had so much respect. Jeremy Todd was the first in the line that ended with Buford Bell, the black man whose family James spared no effort to save.

After the funeral was over a wake was held behind the house near the sharecroppers' quarters where many a meal had been shared with James after a hard day's work. Polly did her best to find the strength to accept her husband's passing the way she knew James would want her to. But when no one at the gathering was looking too closely she could not help but let the pain show through. Polly believed that the sorrow would one day pass but she did not care to look to that day. She did not want to contemplate life without James; it is the will of a human being that keeps them alive and the lack of it can do just the opposite.

It has been said that in some marital relationships, one simply cannot live without the other. Whether it is subject to the will of God or simply a perfect union between two people, no one knows. In any event, the following morning when Jim went upstairs to see if his mother was awake, he found to his deepest sorrow that she had passed away in her sleep. She was buried in the family cemetery beside her devoted husband and there can be no doubt that they no longer have to rely on their hearts to communicate for them.

www.ingramcontent.com/pod-product-compliance
Lightning Source LLC
Chambersburg PA
CBHW051249260626
47162CB00002B/678